PANDORA'S
DAUGHTER

ALSO BY IRIS JOHANSEN

PANDORA'S DAUGHTER

IRIS JOHANSEN

St. Martin's Paperbacks

This is a work of fiction. All of the characters, organizations, and events portrayed in this novel are either products of the author's imagination or are used fictitiously.

PANDORA'S DAUGHTER

Copyright © 2007 by Johansen Publishing LLP.
Excerpt from Quicksand copyright © 2008 by Johansen Publishing LLP.

For information address St. Martin's Press, 175 Fifth Avenue, New York, NY 10010.

Library of Congress Catalog Card Number: 2007020317

ISBN: 0-312-36805-4
EAN: 978-0-312-36805-0

Printed in the United States of America

St. Martin's hardcover edition / October 2007
St. Martin's Paperbacks edition / May 2008

St. Martin's Paperbacks are published by St. Martin's Press, 175 Fifth Avenue, New York, NY 10010.

10   9   8   7   6   5   4   3   2

PROLOGUE

VOICES.

Megan could feel the muscles of her stomach knot and she tried to block the fear. Don't let Mama know. She had been so happy and relaxed this afternoon. She didn't need Megan spoiling it for her.

"Why so quiet?" Her mother started packing up the picnic basket. "What are you thinking about?"

Voices.

Megan searched wildly for an answer. "I was just wishing that Neal could have come along. Did you invite him?"

"Heck, no. I wanted a mother-daughter time together. Neal tends to dominate the scene when he's around." She smiled teasingly. "He gets all your attention. Not that I blame you. The first time I saw him he reminded me of the portrait of a Renaissance prince I saw once in a museum in Florence. Very elegant and slightly intimidating."

Close out the voices. Lord, how she wished she could make them go away. "There's nothing intimidating about Neal. How can you say that?"

"Hey, I'm not attacking him. It's just an idle comparison."

Voices.

What had they been talking about? Megan wondered.

Concentrate. That's right, Neal. "I like having Neal around. He's fun."

"When he wants to be. Though I'm glad that you like him. I do too. He's been a good friend to me." Her smile faded as she studied Megan. "You're not listening. What's wrong, baby?"

"Nothing."

"Megan."

"Voices," Megan whispered. "I don't like it here, Mama. I hear the voices."

"Nonsense." Her mother quickly looked away from her. "I've told you that's your imagination." She tossed the plastic cups back in the basket. "And there's no reason for you not to like it here." She knelt back on her heels and gazed at the setting sun casting its red-gold glow on the waters of the quarry below them. "It's beautiful. We've had picnics up here on the hill a dozen times and you never mentioned those silly voices. Have you heard them on this spot before?"

She nodded. "But you don't like me to talk about them."

"Because they don't exist." She reached out and gently cupped Megan's cheeks in her two hands. "And you mustn't talk about things that don't exist. When you were younger, it wasn't as bad. But you're fifteen now and people pay more attention. We have to keep this between ourselves, baby."

"Or they'll think I'm nuts." Megan tried to smile. "And this can't be normal. Maybe I am nuts. Am I, Mama?"

"Of course not." She leaned forward and brushed a kiss on Megan's nose. "Who sets the rules? Who can really say what's normal? I've heard that some composers hear the music in their minds and everyone calls them a genius. You'll probably grow out of this."

"You said that when I was seven."

"And you don't hear them near as often now. Right?"

"Right."

"And you said they don't scream, they whisper?"

Megan nodded.

"See?" Her eyes were twinkling. "Progress. And by the time you reach your twenty-first birthday, they'll be gone entirely."

Megan frowned and said tentatively, "Maybe . . . I should see someone."

"No," her mother said sharply. "No doctors. We keep this just between us. Understand?"

Megan nodded but she didn't understand. She had never understood anything except that it made her mother unhappy for Megan to talk about the voices. Maybe she didn't want to admit even to herself that Megan wasn't . . . normal. Okay, let it go. It could be her mother's simple solution to her problem was correct. The last thing she wanted to do was make her mother unhappy.

"Stop frowning." Her mother's finger traced the two creases on Megan's forehead. "You'll get wrinkles like me."

"You don't have wrinkles. You're beautiful." It was true. Sarah Nathan was not conventionally beautiful, but her brown hair shone in the sunset glow and her face was brimming with character and sparkled with warmth and vivacity.

"I have plenty of wrinkles. But if you laugh enough, they blend in with the laugh lines and get lost." She made a face. "That's what you should do, my solemn little mouse. You don't smile enough. You make me feel like a bad mother."

Megan shook her head. "You know better than that. No one is a better mother than you. And I'm not solemn."

"Okay, you're intense." She got to her feet and pulled

Megan to her feet. "Come on, it's getting dark. It's time to get back to the cottage. You have school and I have work tomorrow." She handed Megan the picnic blanket. "Not that you need to worry about school. You're acing your classes. You know, I'd rather you concentrated a little less on your grade point average and a little more on having a good time."

"I have a good time."

"Well, work at it a little harder. The only time I see you light up and bubble over these days is when you're with Neal. You're young. Life has a way of passing so quickly you leave the good times behind before you know it." She smiled. "And you're going to have so many good times. Proms and good friendships and first love and all that other stuff touted on the Hallmark cards."

"Yuck."

Her mother ruffled her hair. "Brat. Show a little sentiment." Her smile faded as she started down the path. "Are the voices gone?"

"Yes," Megan lied. Well, it wasn't quite a lie. They weren't gone but they'd become a dull roar like the sea in the distance. There was no use making her mother upset when she wanted so desperately for Megan not to hear them.

"I told you that you were getting better." She linked her arm with Megan's. "Since I seem to be on a winning streak, remember what I told you about going for the gusto."

"Mama, I'm not—" She broke off as she felt her mother's body stiffen. "What's wrong?"

"Nothing."

It wasn't the truth. Something was wrong. She could see her mother's expression and it couldn't be more clear.

Fear.

Her gaze followed her mother's to the line of pines at the bottom of the hill.

A man was standing there, watching them.

"Who is he? Do you know him?"

"Perhaps." She took a deep breath. "I'd better go and talk to him. Go back to the quarry, Megan."

Megan shook her head.

"Do as I tell you," her mother said sharply. "This is my business. You know the cave on the other side of the hill? Go inside and stay there until I come for you."

"I'm going with you."

"You're not going with me. Get up the hill to that cave. *Now.*"

Megan still hesitated.

"Listen, Megan, it's going to be fine. I just have to talk to him and I don't want an audience." She started down the hill. Her voice lashed like a whip. "Get going!"

"Okay, but if you don't come in twenty minutes, I'm coming after you." Megan turned and started back up the hill at a run.

It wasn't right.

No matter what her mother said, something was very wrong.

KILL THE BASTARD.

Neal Grady's knife sliced across the man's throat and the blood spurted. He pushed him away and let him drop to the ground.

He didn't give him another glance as he tore across the road and through the stand of trees.

He was too late.

Grady cursed as he half slid, half ran down the shale

incline toward the woman lying crumpled at the bottom of the slope.

Dead?

Not yet, but close. Very close.

He knelt down beside her and could feel his eyes sting. "Sarah, dammit."

Sarah slowly opened her eyes. "Hello, Neal. I'm glad . . . you're here. But you . . . shouldn't curse a dying woman."

"Shut up. Save your strength. Maybe there's something I can do."

She shook her head. "Not for me. You know better. But Megan . . . I tried to run and keep him away from her. But he saw her. He . . . saw her. He'll go after her."

"No, he won't," he said grimly. "I was too late for you but not for him. I cut the son of a bitch's throat."

"Good. Megan will . . . I'm getting cold, Neal. I can't die yet. I have to tell you—"

"God, you're such a fool, Sarah," he said unsteadily. "I told you to leave here six months ago. You should have run. You should have hidden Megan away."

"I felt safe. I thought you were wrong. I didn't want to pull Megan away again. I've tried so hard to let her have a normal life. Not like mine. Not like yours." She inhaled sharply. "Everything is getting . . . hazy. I didn't expect it to be like this. I'm . . . frightened. You can help me, can't you?"

He nodded. "I can help you."

"I thought you could. Could I . . . touch you?"

"Yes." He lay down beside her and gathered her close. "Just relax, Sarah."

"I can't relax. Not yet. Megan. You have to help Megan."

"For God's sake, you didn't even prepare her. You lied to her. I don't know if I can do anything for her."

"Try."

"I can't promise you. You know what's going to happen once you leave her."

"Try," she repeated. "Please, Neal."

"No promises." He gently stroked her cheek. "I'll see what I can do."

"I know you will. She's strong, Neal. Much stronger than I am. She has a chance . . . . You'll take care of her. You . . . like her. You like . . . my Megan."

"Yes. Now be quiet and rest."

She was silent for only a moment. "Neal, I'm . . . not a Pandora."

"You are," he whispered. "But it doesn't matter now. Hold on to me. I'll help you through it."

"I was hoping you would." She nestled closer. "Yes, help me . . ."

She let him take control. Warmth replacing coldness, light floods the darkness, glittering sanity instead of a world of madness.

"Thank you, Neal," she whispered.

"Shh, just let go . . ."

MEGAN SCREAMED.

Neal stiffened as the agonized sound tore through him.

Dammit, Sarah had just drifted away from him and Megan was already feeling the release.

Pain.

He gently pushed Sarah away from him and sat up.

Another jolt of agony.

He had to get to her before she tore herself apart.

Before she tore him apart.

Find her.

Where are you, Megan?

More pain.

Mindless panic and agony.
Find her.
Help her.
Find her.

MAMA!

Megan huddled against the wall of the cave as pain tore through her.

Not Pandora. Not Pandora. Not Pandora.

Voices. Babble. Screams.

Not Mama's voice. Where are you, Mama?

Gone.

But the voices weren't gone. They assaulted her, beat her, stabbed her.

Go away. Go away. Go away.

Help me, Mama.

No Mama.

Gone.

Panic seared through her. She was alone with the voices that were tearing at her, killing her.

She screamed again. Help me.

"There's only one way I can help you, Megan."

A man was standing in the entrance of the cave. Dark, slim, tall. Was it the same man whom her mother had gone down to see?

Mama had gone and not come back.

Gone.

No, it wasn't that stranger. It was Neal Grady. Relief surged through her. Neal would help her.

Neal standing behind someone. The gleam of steel as his knife sliced across a throat. Blood spurting . . .

Murder.

Mama? Mama's throat?

No!

She instinctively launched herself at his knees and brought him down.

Another wave of voices struck her and she crumpled in agony.

"Stop fighting me," he said hoarsely. "I'm not going to hurt you."

She bit his wrist.

"My God, Sarah was right. You're much stronger than she ever was."

She could barely hear him, the voices were roaring now, ripping at her.

Fight them.

Fight him.

She tried to crawl toward the cave opening.

"No." He grabbed her by the waist. "It's over, Megan."

Mama.

"Stop it." His face contorted with pain. "She can't help you any longer. And I'm not sure I can do it either."

Mama.

"Don't do this. I told her I wouldn't promise to—"

Mama!

"Dammit, Megan, you have to stay with me." He backhanded her across the face.

Darkness.

But the voices were still there, gnawing at her sinews, devouring her.

"Okay, I can't take it anymore," he whispered. "You win, Megan. Or maybe Sarah wins." His hands grasped her arms, holding her still. "I'm going to shut you down. Don't fight me. I'm not going to hurt you. You're just going to go to sleep and I'll take the voices away."

She opened her eyes to look dazedly up at him. "What . . ."

"Shh." He gently brushed her hair back from her forehead. "You wanted help. I'm going to give it to you. You won't remember the voices, the pain, any of this." His lips tightened. "I wish to God I was that lucky."

ONE

"HE'S DEAD, MEGAN. CALL IT," Scott Rogan said as he looked at her over the body of the fourteen-year-old boy. "Give it up."

"Tell that to his mother." She hit the paddles again to try to jump-start the boy's heart. Come on, Manuel. Come back to us. "I'm not going to do it without a fight."

"We've been working on him for the last twenty minutes."

"Then another few won't make a difference." She counted to three and then hit him again. "Live, Manuel," she whispered. "You have so much to do, so much to see. Don't let it end like this."

But it had ended, she realized in helpless frustration after another two minutes. Dammit to hell. Poor kid.

She ripped her gloves off as she turned away. "Document that the patient died at eleven-oh-five P.M.," she said jerkily to the nurse. She strode out of the ER to wash and change her bloodstained scrubs. She couldn't face the boy's mother like this. The woman was going to have a bad enough memory to carry for the rest of her life.

Damn. She closed her eyes and leaned her head

against the jamb of the door for a minute. It shouldn't be like this. She should be able to do more.

"Are you okay, Megan?"

She opened her eyes to see Scott standing beside her. "No." She straightened. "I wanted a miracle. I didn't get it."

"You did your best. We're just doctors. We can't walk on water."

"I can try. Every day I can try a little harder and maybe someday I'll be good enough to—" She rubbed her stinging eyes on the back of her hand and turned away. "I can't stand here talking. I have to talk to Manuel's mother."

"Wait." He was hurrying after her. "I'll tell her, Megan."

She shook her head. "My job. He was my patient." But, dammit, she didn't want to do this. It was always a painful responsibility but especially traumatic when it concerned the young. "Thanks anyway, Scott."

He shrugged. "It's bad for me too. But it doesn't tear me up like it does you. Sometimes I wonder why you decided to become a doctor. You're too damn emotional. All that psychological training we were given in med school didn't get through to you."

"I'll get used to it." Her gaze was fixed on the small Latina woman sitting in a chair across the waiting room. A deep pang of sadness surged through her. Dear God, the woman's hopeful expression as she saw Megan . . .

No, she'd never get used to it. Not in a million years. Then take it on the chin and go tell that mother her boy is dead.

The woman was tensing, her eyes anxious. Megan could feel her pain and desperation as if it were her own. It was surrounding her, deluging her, drowning her. She braced herself, fighting to pull away from it.

"Megan," Scott murmured.

She shook her head to clear it. "It's okay." She moistened

her lips and forced herself to start across the room. Get it over with and try to offer the woman what comfort she could.

"Mrs. Rivera, I'm Dr. Megan Blair." She drew a deep breath. "I'm sorry to tell you that . . ."

HE COULDN'T TELL WHO WAS suffering more, Scott Rogan thought, as he watched Megan take the woman in her arms. Megan should have let him do it.

"Stop worrying about her. You can't protect your little buddy for the rest of her life."

Scott turned to see Hal Trudeau standing a few feet away. He hadn't been in the operating room, but by now the story of Megan's frantic efforts at reviving the kid was probably all over the ward. He wished to hell Hal had not been on duty tonight. Hal was highly competitive and he considered Megan a threat in his climb at the hospital. The first couple years out of medical school could sometimes be a make-or-break period for a doctor. Hal would like nothing better than to make Megan look unprofessional.

"I'm not worried," Scott said. "She's handling everything fine."

"I hear she almost fell apart when the kid died."

"She was upset. She didn't fall apart. She'd never risk a patient's life by losing her composure." He turned on his heel. "And everyone in that room will tell you the same thing. Don't try to stir up trouble over this. The only mistake she made tonight was caring too much and she didn't let it interfere."

"That's open to argument. I've heard the chief administrator thinks she gives the impression of being unstable." Hal smiled maliciously. "But then, you probably enjoy that emotional side of her. How is she in bed, Scott?"

"I wouldn't know."

"Sure. That's why you trail behind her like a stud around a mare in heat. I bet she's one hot number when she needs to release some of that stored-up energy. I don't blame you for jumping her." Hal's gaze returned to Megan. "She's not bad-looking. I wouldn't mind screwing her myself. If she wasn't such a stuck-up bitch." He turned and walked away.

Bastard.

Scott smothered the surge of irritation that moved through him. He felt like decking the son of a bitch. Yeah, that's all Megan needed was to have the two of them brawling in the halls over her. Hal was right, the administration was keeping a close eye on Megan. They liked their hospital rolling on greased wheels and even a hint of instability in their personnel scared the hell out of them.

And Megan was *not* unstable. No one worked harder. St. Andrews was lucky to have her. She'd been offered a job in a number of more prestigious hospitals in the Northeast before she'd graduated. The only reason she'd stayed in Atlanta was that she hadn't wanted to leave her Uncle Phillip, who had cared for her since her mother had died.

Hell, Hal would probably have made a case against family feeling as well. Anything to bring her down.

Including accusing her of sleeping around with a married man.

The idea was oddly intriguing.

What was he thinking? He and Jana had been married for only two years and they had been good years. Megan had been a good friend to him since med school. He would never have passed chemistry if she hadn't drilled him for almost a complete semester. After he'd married

Jana, Megan had been there for both of them. Jana's young son, Davy, was crazy about her.

She's not bad-looking, Hal had said.

Understatement. She was damn good-looking with her slim, graceful body, glossy dark-brown hair, and those enormous hazel eyes. But none of those features were what drew men to her. Hal had hit the target when he'd mentioned that stored-up emotional energy that never left her. Even when she was relaxed Scott could sense the emotional turmoil that seemed to electrify her. It was . . . interesting.

And arousing.

And he had better stop analyzing his responses to Megan. It wasn't fair to Jana. He would never be unfaithful but he was beginning to feel guilty.

Yes, perhaps it would be better if he made an effort to keep Megan at a distance.

MEGAN'S HAND WAS SHAKING AS she unlocked the door of her SUV. She took a deep breath before she got into the vehicle and started the ignition. She should probably wait until she recovered a little before she left the parking lot but she wasn't going to do it. She wanted to get home to Phillip. She needed her uncle's quiet steadiness and gentleness. She was raw and hurting from those hours she had spent with Delores Rivera.

It would be better once she got home. After a few hours, she would regain the balance she had lost in that waiting room. The pain that was rising, roaring, inside her would fade the longer she was away from that grieving woman.

Now that was really adult and responsible, she thought

with self-disgust. She was planning on running home and dumping all of this depressing angst in Phillip's lap. God knows she had been doing enough of that in the past few years. Get a grip and give the man a break.

She rested her head on the steering wheel, blinking back the stinging tears. So many wild emotions had been hurled at her during those hours. Delores Rivera's blame and agony and guilt mixed with a dozen other incomprehensible feelings that had mounted until she had been overwhelmed.

Don't think about it. Call Phillip and the sound of his voice would help to make everything all right.

No, don't do that to him again. Live with it. Get through it on your own.

She drove out of the parking lot and turned left at the light.

PHILLIP CALLED HER WHEN she was getting on the freeway. She pressed Connect on her cell phone earpiece for hands-free operation. "Everything all right? I don't want to be a worrywart but I knew you got off duty a couple hours ago. If you're out having a drink with Scott and Jana, just tell me to buzz off."

Lord, she was glad to hear his voice. From the moment he had walked toward her at her mother's funeral, she had felt this warm sense of belonging whenever she was around him. "No, it was just a rough night. I had a few problems. I'll tell you about it when I get home. I'm on my way. What are you doing awake anyway? It's after two in the morning."

"I was only dozing. The football game didn't end until midnight. We won in the last four seconds. I was too wired to relax."

"Hoorah Falcons."

"Damn right." He paused. "What kind of problems?"

"A fourteen-year-old boy died on the table. I couldn't save him."

"Shit."

"Yeah. How about having a cup of hot chocolate with me and you can tell me about the game?"

"Sounds good. I'll have it ready. How close are you?"

"I'm on the freeway. Twenty minutes." She frowned as blinding lights glared in her rearview mirror. "Cripes, I've got a tailgater. It's a truck, I think. He must be drunk. At this time of night you'd think he'd realize that he's got plenty of room to pass me." The lights were suddenly gone. "Okay, he's passing in the left lane now. Good riddance. I hope he gets a tick— What the hell!"

The truck had slammed into the side of her 4Runner! She fought the wheel as she was pushed toward the side of the highway.

"What's happening, Megan?" Phillip's worried voice in her ear.

No time to answer him.

The truck slammed her again.

Crazy bastard. He'd rammed her against the low bridge over the river. One more hit like that and her SUV might roll over and go into the water.

She barely managed to straighten before the truck slammed into her from behind, sending her wheeling wildly in a circle.

Straighten out. Get off the bridge. She had a better chance going down the embankment.

She straightened back in her lane and pressed the accelerator.

"Megan!" Phillip's voice.

The truck was next to her again.

Get off the bridge.

She stomped on the accelerator and momentarily left the truck behind her.

Twenty yards and she'd be across the water.

The truck was gaining on her.

He hit her rear door as she reached the end of the bridge.

The 4Runner went off the highway and began bouncing down the embankment.

She had to stop it before she reached the river.

She stomped on the brakes and skittered sideways, slid fifteen yards before she was stopped by a pine tree.

Her air bag went off, pinning her to the seat.

Helpless.

She could see the truck stopped on the road above her and a silhouette moving toward the embankment. He was tall, thin, wearing jeans and a cowboy hat.

Her OnStar program was telling her that her air bags had gone off and that they'd notified 911.

But the man on the bank was already starting down the ridge.

Then she heard the sirens.

Hurry. Dammit, hurry.

The man hesitated and then turned and started climbing back up the embankment. A moment later he was in his truck and driving away.

She felt limp with relief.

Thank God.

PHILLIP ARRIVED AT THE SCENE twenty minutes later. By that time Megan had been helped out of the wrecked SUV and was sitting on the riverbank with a blanket wrapped around her.

He handed her a thermal cup. "Hot coffee. I figured you could use the caffeine."

She nodded and took a sip. "Actually, I could use a stiff drink."

"I'd never offer you alcohol at the scene of an accident. You can never tell when the police might try to breathalyze you." He sat down beside her and tucked the blanket closer around her. "Okay, Megan?"

"No, I'm mad as hell." She grimaced. "I couldn't even get the license number. I think it was a blue Ford pickup but I'm not sure. The only thing I'm certain about is that he's nutty as a fruitcake and should be taken off the road. He scared me, dammit. When I was sitting pinned in that SUV and he was coming down the embankment, I felt like I was being stalked by Freddy from Elm Street." She shrugged. "I don't know. Maybe he'd regained his senses and was coming down to help me. But I was glad when he turned and took off in his truck."

"Me too." Phillip glanced at the policemen measuring and marking the tire tracks. "Do they want you to check in at a hospital?"

"Yes, but I'm not going to do it. There's nothing wrong with me but a sore chest and ribs from the air bag. I want to go home." She shook her head wearily. "It's been a hell of a night."

He nodded and rose to his feet. "Let me see what I can do. Drink your coffee and leave it to me." He moved toward the sergeant giving orders on the embankment.

Megan felt a surge of affection as she watched him. It was always safe to leave anything and everything to Phillip. He didn't give the impression of brilliance and ultra-efficiency, but she had never run across a situation that he couldn't handle. Even now, dwarfed by those husky policemen, he quietly dominated the scene. In his early sixties, thin, small-boned, with a high forehead and large blue eyes, he was calm and reassuring. People instinctively responded to that gentle demeanor as she did. Her mother had never even told her she had an uncle, perhaps because he was only Sarah's half brother and he had moved away when her mother was only a teenager. But from the time Phillip had come to Myrtle Beach to assume guardianship after her mother had died of a heart attack, Megan had known that nothing bad could ever happen to her as long as she had Phillip Blair beside her.

And Phillip's gentle charisma was working its magic once again. She saw the police sergeant hesitate and then shrug and turn away.

"Thank you, Sergeant." Phillip winked at her as he started back. "The kind officer is willing to believe that the physician can heal herself. Now, you mustn't let me down by having a sudden relapse." He helped her to her feet. "He asked you to drop in at the precinct to fill out the reports tomorrow or the next day. He's hoping you'll remember something more about the hit-and-run."

"So do I." She leaned on Phillip as she climbed the hill toward his car. Lord, she was tired. She could barely put one foot in front of another. "But I don't think it's going to happen."

"A shower and bed," Phillip said. "I'll take care of everything. Trust me."

Yes, she could trust Phillip. She was trying desperately not to be a burden to him these days. She wasn't that bereaved teenage kid any longer. But tonight maybe it would be okay to accept that comfort and strength that was always there for her . . .

TWO

"I THOUGHT YOU COULD USE A little of that hot chocolate we talked about to relax you." Phillip stood in her bedroom doorway with two steaming mugs in his hands. "Since I dosed you with enough caffeine at that river to keep an elephant awake."

"I doubt if it will keep me awake." She smiled as he walked toward her bed and dropped down in the easy chair beside it. "I feel drained."

"Good." He handed her the chocolate. "You're usually so charged after a bad night that being empty is practically therapy."

"Therapy?" She made a face. "Don't use that word. I have enough trouble with people at the hospital thinking I'm a little off-kilter." She wearily shook her head. "Maybe they're right. I don't get it. I don't see why they don't feel what I'm feeling. So much pain. . . . How can they just cruise the surface? Even Scott doesn't seem to get close enough to them and he's a good man, Phillip."

"I know." He looked down into the chocolate in his cup. "You're a very sensitive young woman. I warned you that being a doctor might not be a good choice for you."

"You make me sound like some idiotic swooning Southern belle. It *was* a good choice. I've never wanted to do anything else with my life." Her lips tightened. "And

I'm good at it, Phillip. I'll just have to get over this bump in the road. I can do it."

"I don't have the slightest doubt you can do anything you set out to do. I'm just hoping you can be objective enough to walk away if the going gets too rough for you."

She tilted her head. "As cool and objective as you are when your football team is losing?"

He chuckled. "Lord, I hope you do better that that, you scamp." He got to his feet. "Now I'll let you get to sleep." He moved toward the door. "And don't dream about that redneck nut who tried to run you off the bridge. He doesn't deserve another thought from you."

"He's going to get quite a few thoughts," she said grimly. "Drunks like that shouldn't be on the road. I hope to hell the police can track him down."

"Me too," Phillip said. "Just don't fret, okay?"

She smiled. " 'Fret' is a Southern belle word too. Watch it, Phillip."

"I guess I've been in Atlanta too long." He winked as he closed the door.

She felt a warm surge of love as she put down her cup and turned out the bedside light. Phillip had stayed in Atlanta because he had not wanted to uproot Megan from the South after her mother's death. He had only been her mother's half brother and he didn't really have any responsibility toward Megan. But he had taken the responsibility anyway. He had chosen to uproot himself from his comfortable life in Seattle and settle down with her. He had told her that as a freelance engineer, he could work anywhere and he had always liked Atlanta's ambience. He had made it sound like an adventure instead of a sacrifice.

Bless him.

"Go to sleep." Phillip had poked his head in again. "Everything is going to be fine. All we have to do is work at it."

"*I* have to work at it," she corrected. "You've done enough for me. Now stop hovering and get some sleep yourself."

"Yes, ma'am." He softly closed the door again.

Her smile vanished and she tried to relax. As she had told Phillip, it was her job to take care of her own problems. And one of the problems was that she always had trouble sleeping after a traumatic evening. When she did sleep, she dreamed. Strange, disjointed, terrifying dreams . . .

She hoped to hell she wouldn't have them tonight.

PHILLIP WAITED UNTIL HE WAS sure Megan's sleep was sound before he went into the living room and pulled out his cell phone.

It was near dawn but Neal Grady's voice was wide-awake and alert when he picked up. The bastard had probably been expecting him to call, Phillip thought. "We may have a problem."

"That's no surprise. Since you haven't called me in the past three years." He paused. "Is she becoming volatile or erratic?"

"No, dammit, she's fine."

"Are you protesting too much, Phillip?"

"No, she's handling it, I tell you."

Silence.

"Okay, maybe she's a little volatile on occasion when she's faced with some of the things she deals with at the hospital."

"Mood swings?"

"I haven't noticed any."

"What about her personal life? I understand all that emotion could translate into high sensuality."

"I don't think so. Hell, don't you know?"

"I try not to know."

"Well, it's not the kind of thing she'd discuss with me."

"Maybe you should have persuaded her to discuss it. You should have discussed every possible sign of change. You know you have to be on the alert. Any nightmares?"

"Not many. A few after deaths of her patients. Nothing abnormal."

"I told you to steer her away from medicine."

"I tried. Megan's not easy to steer when her mind is made up. I was hoping she wouldn't make it through medical school. There's enough stress to discourage most people, much less anyone as empathetic as Megan."

"You should have found a way. At least, you could have talked her out of choosing ER. Talk about high stress. I told you that you'd have to be careful when I turned her over to you."

"She thought she could make more of a difference in ER. Back off, Grady. You did turn her over to me and I've done a damn good job all these years. I don't need you sitting on your duff and criticizing me. Walk in my shoes for a while before you tell me what to do. Now shut up and listen. I didn't call to have you give me the third degree."

"Point taken. You're right. You've done an exceptional job." Grady paused. "Then if she's not showing signs that a change is coming, why are you calling me?"

"Molino may have found her."

"What?"

"I'm not sure. Someone driving a beat-up pickup truck tried to run her off the bridge tonight. The police think it was some local yahoo on a binge."

"Description?"

"She couldn't get a good look at him. He was just a silhouette against the freeway lights. Tall, thin, jeans, cowboy hat."

"Could the police be right?"

"Yes. But he kept hitting her, going after her. It sounds . . . determined."

"What's her reaction?"

"Anger. Indignation. She believes the cops are right. Just a drunk who deserves to be kept off the road." He tried to keep the anger from his voice. "You promised this wouldn't happen, Grady. You said they wouldn't find her."

"They shouldn't have found her. I buried every record on her and Sarah before I came to see you."

"Well, let's hope you didn't screw up. I'd say a mistake like that makes me not being able to talk her out of medical school look minor. What are you going to do about it?"

"Check it out. I'm in Paris right now. I'll take a flight as soon as I can tie things up here."

"Hurry. I'm not going to chance having them kill her." Phillip added deliberately, "It's time you took responsibility for her."

"You have no idea of the responsibility I've devoted to her over the years. Talk about a monkey on my back."

"I don't care about you. I care about Megan."

"That's why I chose you to look after her. You're all black and white, Phillip. Right is right. Wrong is wrong. I see too many shades of gray." He said wearily, "You've done a good job with her. I may not have stayed in touch, but I read every report you sent me. I wanted to hear good things about her. Believe me, I needed to see myself justified." He went on quickly, "And if it's Molino, he'll try again and again. You'd better tighten security just in case your redneck is bogus."

"You don't have to tell me that. I'll keep her alive and do what I can, but you'd better be prepared to step in if Molino does something to trigger Megan. That's one area where I can't help her." He hung up the phone and leaned back in his chair. He had done his job and told Grady of the threat but he wasn't sure if he felt any better about it.

Grady had always been something of an enigma to him. Yes, Phillip was grateful, but that didn't rule out resentment. He trusted his effectiveness but he had never been confident about which way he'd jump in a given circumstance. Maybe he had an instinctive rejection of the power he sensed in Grady. God knows, it wasn't as if he hadn't lived with some aspect of that power for most of his adult life. Grady's was just more intense and on a larger scope. He'd seen him do some pretty incredible things in the time he'd known him.

But Phillip couldn't worry now about what Grady might do. He was the one who had to be prepared to do whatever was necessary to protect Megan.

He got up from the chair, moved toward the desk across the room, and opened the top drawer. He pulled out the automatic pistol and checked it. Then he sat back down at the desk and leaned back in the chair. As he'd promised Grady, he would sit up tonight and keep watch over Megan. He had a bad feeling about what had happened tonight. He had no psychic talents like Grady or the others like him, but instinct counted for something. He had a hunch that there was a nasty storm brewing.

Sleep well, Megan. You may need it.

Gadsden, Alabama

THE TRUCK WOULD BLOW ANY MINUTE.

Tim Darnell backed away from the gasoline-soaked blue vehicle and watched the flame travel from the front seat toward the gas tank.

Too bad. Damn fine truck. But it had been damaged by contact with Megan Blair's SUV and probably had her paint on it. He'd made sure the registration was in a bogus name but he still couldn't risk keeping it. Could he get Molino to replace it?

Not likely. Molino didn't like failures and he'd be lucky to keep the assignment, much less get him to pay him a bonus for it. Get it over with. Bite the bullet. He took out his cell phone and dialed Peter Sienna at Molino's office.

"I hope you're calling me to tell me that you've completed the job," Sienna said when he picked up the phone. "I expected you to phone hours ago."

"I had to drive the truck across the Alabama border to destroy it." He hesitated. "Things didn't go well. I'm going to need a little more time."

Sienna didn't speak for a moment. "Are you telling me she's still alive?"

"Right now." He added quickly, "But I'll take care of it. I tried to make it look like an accident. I expected her to lose her head but she didn't. She drove that SUV as if she was racing at Daytona. I'll have to try something else. Another day or two. That's all, I promise."

"Mr. Molino doesn't give a damn about your promises. He wanted the matter taken care of immediately."

Hard ass, Darnell thought sourly. If he didn't need the money, he'd tell him to go screw himself. "I've had her under surveillance for the last week. It won't take me long to work out another way to do the job. I'll make sure Mr. Molino won't be disappointed."

"He's already going to be disappointed," Sienna said. "Two days. After that, we'll have to replace you." He hung up.

That bastard was treating him like the scum of the earth. He and Molino thought because they had money and power, they could do anything they wanted to do. Well, he was smarter than both of them. Everyone made mistakes. How was he to know that the Blair woman would be that cool? She was only a woman and he had seen her fall apart only this evening in that waiting room when he'd been on watch at the hospital.

It's not as if he hadn't been prepared for a worst-case scenario. But he had covered his tracks and hidden his other truck in the brush in the woods here outside Gadsden. In moments the truck would be destroyed.

And the homeless guy he'd picked up on Highway 20 had been a stroke of genius. Even if they found the truck they would think that the driver who had tried to run Megan Blair off the road had died in the wreckage.

The vagrant was slumped across the steering wheel and Darnell had made sure that the blow to the head could have occurred in the crash.

Darnell frowned as he saw the man stir, move, in the driver's seat. No, dammit, if he managed to get out of the truck he was going to spoil everything. Should he try to—

The truck exploded as the flame reached the gas tank! *Yes.*

He watched with satisfaction for a moment as the flames licked, devoured, swallowed the truck. How is that for a cover-up, Sienna? Could you and Molino have tied up things so neatly? He moved toward the truck parked down the road.

And he'd be just as efficient eliminating Megan Blair. He hadn't really tipped his hand. There was still a chance at staging an accident. He always preferred to do it that way. He wasn't one of Molino's dumb thugs who was going to risk his neck by using a gun or knife if he could avoid it. He had a future and someday he'd be more powerful than Molino ever dreamed.

He would stay away from her for twenty-four hours to let her regain her composure and the memory fade a little. He would go to his classes at Georgia State, make sure the alibi he'd set up for tonight was still firmly in place, maybe spend a few hours with his lover.

Then, the next day, he would go after Megan Blair again.

SIENNA TURNED TO MOLINO. "He botched the job. He's making excuses and promises, but the bottom line is that she's still alive. Shall I send someone else?"

Molino thought about it. "Not yet. He's not usually inefficient. He killed that child in Orlando last year with no problems for us." He added jeeringly, "I'm surprised you'd even suggest we send the boy packing. He's going to some fancy college just like you did. That must make him smarter than an ignorant wop like me."

Sienna's expression didn't change. "Education is valuable, but it can't replace experience. If he can't do the job then we should make an adjustment."

Sienna sounded like a damned lawyer, Molino thought with annoyance. He used to be able to ruffle that sleek, slightly patronizing surface, but these days, Sienna was able to ignore the jabs. He probably thought any opinion but his own wasn't important. He turned and moved toward the French doors. "There's no urgency. We know where she is now." After twelve long years, they'd tracked the bitch down. Grady had laid a dozen false trails in those years and the frustration had almost driven him berserk. "And, besides, I'd almost like to do the job myself." He could feel the hatred sear through him. *Fucking freak. We almost have her, Steven. Just as I promised you.* "Any report on Grady?"

"We were close in Rome. We didn't get him. But we know he hasn't found the Ledger either or he wouldn't still be on the hunt. We think he's in Paris."

Grady was always close on his heels, Molino thought bitterly. But for how much longer could he keep him from leaping ahead of him and taking the prize?

Forget about Grady. They would get him eventually. Right now they had to concentrate on the enemy at their gates.

Megan Blair.

Paris

HE DIDN'T *NEED* THIS, DAMMIT.

Grady hung up the phone after talking to Phillip and went to the window to stare out at the rooftops around St. Germain. It was too tempting. How could he resist the lure when he was being met with frustration on every front? He'd been trying to ignore Megan Blair for the last twelve years and now she was storming back into his life. He had tucked her neatly away and had hoped she would stay closeted in that little house in Atlanta.

It wasn't happening.

He'd known for the last year that she was stirring, changing, growing. He hadn't had to rely on Phillip's reports after he'd linked with Megan on that night of her mother's death. Monitoring was the only way he could maintain control and keep her steady. She'd grown to love and trust Phillip after her first year with him, and her life had become more serene. He'd been able to distance himself, compartmentalize, and keep that link ember-low.

Not lately. There had been moments so intense it had been like riding a bucking bronco. Her mother had reached her zenith when she was in her mid-twenties and Megan was now twenty-seven. If she was as strong as he believed, then he wasn't going to be able to stall that zenith much longer. Even if there had been no Molino threat, he would have had to do something about her soon.

But there was a Molino threat and time had run out.

He dialed Jed Harley in Miami, Florida. "I'm leaving Paris tonight. I want you to head for Atlanta right away."

"And leave these sunny beaches and half-naked women lusting after my sexy body? There had better be a good reason, Grady."

"Molino may have found Megan Blair."

"Shit. That's bad."

"Very bad. I thought she was off his radar."

"Wait a minute. It's been twelve years. She hasn't done anything that would tip him off, has she?"

"Not according to Phillip. She's been the typical wholesome American girl, smart, hardworking, affectionate with animals, kind to the sick. In short, she's a bloody miracle."

"And you're not believing him?"

"I believe him. But Phillip cares about her and he may be turning a blind eye. He doesn't want her to be a Pandora." Grady's lips twisted. "Hell, I've never tried to persuade him otherwise because I wanted him to be her guardian. Phillip was perfect, everything I wasn't. There was a chance that he might even have been right."

"You're talking past tense."

"Was I?"

"What are you planning, Grady?"

"I let Megan Blair have twelve years, Harley."

"And that means?"

"If she's ready to explode, then why shouldn't I use her to find the Ledger and blow Molino to hell?"

"Are you asking me? I'd already left the unit before you had to yank Megan's mother away from Molino and set her up in North Carolina. I don't know the stakes and if I did, I probably wouldn't understand them. I'm not like you. I'm as normal as apple pie and I like it that way. I wouldn't have your baggage for all the tea in China." He chuckled. "Well, maybe I could handle it if I was emperor of all I survey. But the compensation would have to be substantial."

"You could handle it." He hadn't run across much that Harley couldn't handle in the years he'd known him. He'd been one of the most valuable soldiers in the Special Forces unit where Grady had acted as "consultant." After he had drifted away from the unit and gone on to other things, they'd still kept in touch. He was smart as a whip, experienced, and tough. Very tough. "But there's not enough compensation on the planet, Harley. Trust me."

"Oh, I do trust you. I wouldn't allow myself to be at your beck and call if I didn't. Actually, I find all that psychic mumbo jumbo rather fascinating . . . at a distance. So what am I supposed to do in Atlanta?"

"Surveillance on Megan Blair until I can get there." He rattled off her home address.

"Boring."

"It may not be dull if Molino's man tries to chop her again. You may be able to cut someone's throat."

"That's true. You do know how to brighten my day. I'm on my way." He hung up.

Grady pressed the disconnect. He hadn't been certain what action he was going to take until he'd put it into words with Harley. The hell he didn't know, he thought impatiently. He'd just needed to make it clear to himself what he had to do. During these last years they'd been linked he had grown to know Megan more intimately than he had ever known anyone. It hadn't been an easy decision.

Okay, the choice was made. Let out the tiger.

Get used to me, Megan. We're going to become very, very close.

Don't just stand here. Get packed and go to the airport. She was sleeping now and it would offer him an opportunity to ease her gently into a frame to accept him. While he was on the plane, he'd concentrate on slowly trying to let Megan become aware of him on a subconscious level and cause the link to strengthen.

And God help both of them.

LORD, SHE FELT GOOD, MEGAN thought as she stepped beneath the shower. Her mind was clear and she felt brimming with energy. Perhaps it was the extra sleep she had gotten. She had slept for ten hours and that was uncommon for her. Maybe that accident last night had upset her more than she'd thought. All she'd been aware of at the time had been anger and later a sense of helplessness that had been even more infuriating.

Stop analyzing and forget about it. That creep who'd tried to run her off the road wasn't worth worrying about.

Let the police take care of him. She had a life to lead and it would be a good life, dammit.

Phillip looked up with a smile as she came into the kitchen. "You look full of vim and vigor." He studied her. "And optimism?"

"Why not?" She poured a bowl of cornflakes. "Everything seemed pretty gloomy last night, but I can't go around practicing medicine the way everyone else wants me to do it. I'm doing what's right for me and what I believe is right for my patients. If the hospital kicks me out because I don't fit their mold, I'll go volunteer to work with AIDS patients in Africa. Screw what anyone else thinks."

"I'll second that." He handed her the milk. "You just seemed a little depressed last night. I didn't expect you to bounce back so soon. You're not prone to mood swings. At least, I didn't notice if you are. You're not, are you?"

She shook her head.

"No nightmares?"

"No." She shrugged. "And they say sleep brings counsel. I certainly slept enough last night." She started to eat. "If I don't hurry, I'm going to be late picking up Davy. I have the day off and I promised to take him to the zoo this afternoon after preschool. Could I borrow your Camry until I can arrange to pick up a rental car?"

"Sure." He handed her the car keys. "But you could use a little more rest. You've been burning the candle at both ends for the last couple weeks. You could beg off."

"I don't want to beg off. Davy doesn't get that much attention from Scott or Jana these days. They're too involved in making their marriage work." She shook her head. "Scott tries to ignore the fact that Davy is another man's son but it gets in the way. And Jana is a good mother, but she wants to enjoy being a wife right now."

"So you're mothering the little boy."

"No, he has a mother. I wouldn't try to replace Jana. But love doesn't have to have a name or a title. Davy's a sweet kid and four-year-olds don't have a problem with accepting affection wherever they can get it."

"You should have a child of your own."

"That would be nice." She looked down at her cereal. "Maybe in a decade or so. Providing I can find the right guy."

"And what do you call 'right'? Whatever happened to that young man you were dating in school?" He frowned. "What was his name . . . ?"

"Julio Medera."

"Ah, yes. Very intense and smoldering. He couldn't seem to keep his hands off you. The passionate Latin lover type. Is that what appeals to you?"

"Passion appeals to most women." Her curious gaze lifted to his face. "I can't remember you ever asking me about my love life before. Are you trying to get rid of me?"

"No way."

"I'm out of school now and I could get an apartment near the hospital. I should probably think about it."

"Don't you dare. You wouldn't want to leave an old crock like me alone. I'd probably just fade away into the sunset." He smiled gently. "We're family, Megan. If there comes a time when you want to go, then I'll help you. But don't be in a hurry. These years have been too good for both of us."

She nodded. "I just wondered why you were talking about love and marriage and babies. It's not like you."

"Perhaps I decided we should talk more about what we think, how we're feeling."

She made a face. "Phillip, I talk entirely too much about how I feel about things. Ad nauseam. I'm not going to put you through any more whining."

"You never whine."

"You say that because you love me." Her smile faded. "Thank God. Have I ever told you how much that means to me? That's what we should be talking about." She pushed back her chair. "And your personal life. If I remember correctly, you haven't had a date since I started my internship."

He grinned. "But I have the excuse of my advancing age."

"Bull."

He chuckled. "I certainly hope you're right." His smile faded. "What did happen to your Julio?"

"Too intense." She turned toward the door but glanced back over her shoulder. "What are all these questions about? Nightmares. Mood swings. My nonexistent love life. You haven't been so curious about my doings since the first few years we began to live together. Why are you being so nosy?"

"You shook me up last night," he said quietly. "I almost lost you. I guess it occurred to me that I should take more interest in the little things." He smiled. "I figured maybe I was neglecting my duty."

She felt a warm surge of affection. "Duty doesn't mean anything. You give me love and that's a hundred times more important." She waved at him as she went out the door. Her smile faded as she crossed the driveway to the Camry.

She hadn't meant to be evasive but she still had a problem talking about Julio. She had hurt him and the guilt had never left her. He had mistaken passion for love and she should have been more careful. The remorse had been so intense it had kept her from plunging into any other relationship. She had been tempted any number of times because she'd discovered sex was an outlet that took away the pain and tension when emotion ran too high. But it wasn't fair to take when it hurt the giver.

First, do no harm.

The first rule of the Hippocratic oath she had taken such a short time ago. A smile curved her lips as she began to back out of the driveway. Not exactly the loftiest application to that creed, but honor was honor.

But now she had to forget about Phillip's unexpected fixation on her love life. Young Davy was waiting for her and that was the only thing that was important today.

THREE

LORD, SHE WAS WONDERFUL, Grady thought.

Standing there before the elephant enclosure, bending down to talk to the small boy, Megan was everything he'd known she could be. She was smiling and she seemed to draw all the light to her on this cloudy day. At fifteen she'd been slight and straight as a board, but she'd still had that smile that was part mischief and part breathless anticipation. Now there was maturity in her body and warmth and loving understanding in that smile.

He could see how the little boy responded, laughing, and drawing closer to her. Who could blame him?

Stop standing here staring at her, remembering what Megan had been and what she was right now.

Think about what she could be.

Do what you have to do.

"MAY I RIDE THE ELEPHANT?" Davy asked. "I bet he'd like me."

"I'm sure he would." Megan offered him her popcorn. "But I don't think they let little boys ride the animals. Maybe we could go to the petting zoo instead."

"I want the elephant. All they have there are boring goats and stuff." Davy's endearingly hoarse voice was filled with disgust. "Not even a gorilla."

"How terrible." She tried to think of an alternative. Davy was not a whiner but he could be stubborn once he got an idea in his head. "I don't know why they didn't recruit King Kong for you. What about riding the train?"

"I guess that would be okay." He looked longingly at the elephant. "If you're sure they won't let me ride—"

"I'm sure." She pushed him gently toward the train. "But we'll talk to your mom and see if we can't do—"

Swirling darkness.

Voices. Voices. Voices.

"Megan?"

Davy was tugging at her sweater and looking up at her with a frown. "Aren't we going to get on the train?"

She shook her head to clear it. The voices were gone now. Strange. No, somehow . . . not strange. Frighteningly familiar. "You bet we are." She settled him on the seat and sat down beside him. Her heart was beating hard, fast. What the devil was wrong with her?

Mama.

"Look at the seals, Megan." Davy was leaning eagerly forward as they passed an outdoor pool. "I saw a movie about a seal. It was funny."

"Animals can be funny. But then, so can people, Davy. The only difference is that sometimes we don't realize we're—"

Voices!

Stronger. Louder. Screaming.

Indistinguishable roaring, echoing.

Voices. Voices. Echoing. Echoing.

No!

She crumpled in the seat as the pain hit her.

Davy screamed.

She had to get up. Davy was scared. Had to take care of—

The voices faded and then vanished.

She was vaguely aware of the uniformed conductor beside her, his face concerned, saying something . . .

She slowly sat up in the seat.

Davy was crying.

She instinctively put her arm around him and drew him close. "It's okay . . ." Her voice was slurred. She tried to steady it. "Everything's okay, Davy."

"Would you like me to take you to the first aid station, miss?" the conductor said. "Do you have someone you'd like me to call?"

"No, I'm fine." But she wasn't fine, she thought in panic. Dear heaven, the voices . . . What if it happened again? Davy. She had to protect Davy. "Maybe I am a little unwell. Perhaps you could have someone stay with me for a little while until I can get Davy's mom here to pick him up?" She reached for her phone. "I'm going to call your mom, Davy. I must be coming down with flu or something." She gently stroked his hair as she hugged him close. "You remember a few months ago when you got sick? You were great after a few days but you felt a little wonky for a while."

"Wonky," he repeated, burying his head against her. "I don't want you to be sick."

"I'm only a little sick. I'm a doctor so I know things like that. By tomorrow I'll be okay." She brushed her lips against his forehead. "So will you help me by just being quiet and holding my hand? Sometimes that helps to make people feel better . . ."

"YOU'RE BACK EARLY." PHILLIP looked up as she came in the door. "I wasn't expecting you for another couple hours. Didn't Davy like—" He broke off as he saw her face. "What's wrong?"

"Nothing." She moistened her lips. "Just a bad headache.

I had Jana pick up Davy at the zoo. There wasn't any use ruining his day."

"You never have headaches."

"Well, I do now." She headed for her bedroom. "I'm going to try to sleep it off. I'll see you in a couple hours."

She leaned against the door after she closed it behind her. She hated lying to Phillip. Since that first day they'd met at her mother's funeral, they'd always been honest with each other.

It couldn't be helped. She couldn't face anyone right now. She wanted to crawl into her bed like a wounded animal into its cave.

Cave.

Quarry.

Mama.

A man. . . . Dark eyes holding her own. Fear flaring. Fear dying.

Was she going mad?

No, Mama had said . . .

She couldn't remember what she had said. It was blurred, like the voices, like the pain . . .

Sleep. Take a nap. Let everything drift away. After she woke she'd be able to think and plan how to handle this weirdness.

She crawled under the covers and curled up in a ball. It was going to be okay. She could handle whatever was happening to her. She just needed a little time to clear her head and decide what action to take.

And pray that the voices stayed away.

"I WANT TO SEE HER," GRADY said when Phillip opened the door two hours later. "And I don't want any arguments or protective crap, Phillip."

Phillip stiffened. "Why should I argue? I'm the one who phoned you. Remember?"

"But by this time I'm sure you've been mentally cursing me and considering the possibility that you'd be better off without my interference."

"Maybe."

"May I come in?"

Phillip didn't want to let him in, he realized. Grady had changed in the years that had passed. He had been only a young man of twenty-five when he'd approached Phillip about taking on the care of Megan. Now he must be in his mid-thirties and although still lean, still darkly handsome, beneath that glittering exterior he seemed weathered and scarred by experiences Phillip could only imagine. Even when he was younger he'd had an aura of power and confidence that was a little intimidating. Now that power was refined, more subtle, but infinitely stronger.

He shrugged and stepped aside. "I couldn't stop you, could I?"

"Yes. You could shoot me." He came into the house and closed the door. "But that wouldn't be smart. I may not be what you want for Megan, but you don't like burning your bridges." He glanced around the living room. "Nice. Cozy."

"We like it," Phillip said. "Megan and I picked out the furniture when we moved into the house after her mother's funeral. It was a new start for both of us and I wanted her to feel perfectly comfortable."

"I'm sure she does. You did a good job in cocooning her. When you're a youngster, you need security."

Phillip stiffened as he caught the implication. "You mean she doesn't need that security, now that she's an adult. You're wrong. Everyone needs to feel safe."

"But sometimes we don't get what we want or need. Where is she?"

"She's lying down. She's not feeling well." He stared at him accusingly. "Did you have something to do with that?"

"Yes." He glanced at his watch. "I can give her another thirty minutes to rest. I could go in and help, but she'd be better off if she came out of it herself. Why don't you give me a cup of coffee while I'm waiting?"

"I'm not feeling hospitable." He gestured to the kitchen. "Get it yourself."

"Whatever." He headed for the kitchen. "I'll even make one for you."

Phillip followed him and stood in the doorway watching him while he rummaged through the cabinets until he found the coffee. "What did you do to her?"

"I did a little experimenting." He scooped coffee into the coffeemaker and started it. "I had to see how much she could take."

Phillip stiffened. "What do you mean?"

"I lifted control." He gave Phillip a level glance. "I let her voices attack her. I thought the zoo was a good place since it's generally a happy escape for most people and there was a good chance the impact wouldn't be too heavy. I didn't want to make her face her particular demons, but I made sure she'd know they were there."

"Damn you."

"I thought that would be your reaction." He shrugged. "I thought it necessary. I had to see if she was still as strong as she was when she was a girl."

"By hurting her?"

He nodded. "By hurting her."

"And what did you find out?"

"That she's a thousand times stronger. Molino would

feel that he'd made a tremendous coup if he managed to kill her. She's not only her mother's daughter, but she's a powerhouse in her own right." He added impatiently, "I know you don't want to hear that. Too bad. Face it, Molino is either on her trail now or will find her eventually. It will be better if she's prepared. If *we're* prepared." He poured a cup of coffee. "And she can help herself. She has a talent. I'm going to use it."

"Screw you. I won't let you near her."

"Phillip." Grady's voice was soft. "You have no option. You're not her uncle. She's mine. I only lent her to you. Now I'm taking her back."

"That's crap. She's a human being and she doesn't belong to anyone."

"She belongs to me until I find the Ledger. After that, she can walk away. The two of you can disappear into the sunset." He paused. "We have to find it, Phillip. You know we do. Risking one life is a small price to pay."

"It's not a risk I'm willing to take. Not if it's Megan's life."

"I told you that it might come to this when you agreed to take her on."

"I didn't think—it was all abstract. She's my family now."

"Then I'm sorry for you," Grady said wearily as he sat down at the table. "But there are other people out there who are going to die if we don't risk Megan."

"It's not fair. Molino's a crazy son of a bitch. She's probably only a Listener. Not a Pandora."

"I hope she's not. But if she's a Listener, then she's one of the strongest talents I've ever run across. She can still help us if I can channel it. All I need is a clue, a path to take. I'm running into blank walls and out of time."

"She has her own life."

"And she can go back to living it after she gives me what I want."

Phillip shook his head. "I can't believe you're that hard."

"Not hard enough. If I was, I'd have let your Megan kill herself or go crazy in that cave instead of carrying her on my back for twelve years." He looked down in his cup. "And I believe you're wrong. I think she's a Pandora."

"That doesn't mean she should be shot like a rabid dog."

"Tell that to Molino."

"She deserves a chance."

"She's had her chance. I gave it to her. It wasn't easy." He raised his cup to his lips. "Now it's time for her to pay the piper."

"Like her mother," Phillip said bitterly.

"Possibly. No promises." He finished his coffee and stood up. "I'm going in to see Megan now. If you're going to stop me, you'd better go get that gun you keep in the top left drawer of your desk. You've been thinking wistfully about it for the last ten minutes."

Shit.

"Sorry. I didn't eavesdrop purposely. I respect you and I can understand your concern," Grady said. "Actually, I'm no Mind Reader. Sometimes it just seeps around the edges."

"I hate all this psychic crap," he said through his teeth.

"Yet you took it when you needed it." He waved his hand as Phillip started to speak. "I didn't mean to try to give you a guilt trip. I never wanted your gratitude. And you're not alone. Most of the world is uneasy with the thought of psychics. So is Molino. It's not only hatred and revenge that goads him on. He's afraid of us and he's jealous. He sees talent as a weapon of power and he doesn't want anyone to possess it if he can't." His lips twisted. "Molino is definitely into power."

"We're not certain that man in the truck was really one of Molino's men. I checked with the police and they haven't located him yet."

"If they haven't caught him, there's a good chance he wasn't just a stupid drunk playing demolition derby. I've had Jed Harley in town keeping an eye on Megan and trying to scout around and see if he can come up with any information. But so far he's come up with zilch." He added, "Therefore, I'd suggest you keep that gun more readily at hand for the foreseeable future." He headed for Megan's bedroom. "I'm going to need at least an hour alone with her. It will be better for her if you don't interfere. She's going to have enough to deal with."

Phillip was afraid that was true and the knowledge filled him with frustration. Dealing with Grady was going to be a nightmare for Megan. He wouldn't pull his punches and she was terribly vulnerable right now. "Dammit, don't hurt her."

Grady didn't look back and his reply was absent, his mind already on Megan. "Not if I can help it."

CAVE.

Quarry.

Voices. Voices. Voices.

Hands holding her down. Dark eyes looking into her own, shutting out the voices.

Mama!

"Easy, Megan. That's all gone. It's in the past."

No, the voices were there. They were always there.

"Open your eyes. Look at me and they'll go away."

Yes, make them go away.

"No, you have to help. Open your eyes."

She slowly opened her eyes to see Neal Grady sitting beside the bed.

He reminds me of a Renaissance prince . . .

Prince? Grady? She must still be half-asleep. She didn't know any Grady. No, this was a stranger lounging in her chair, in her room. She scrambled upright in bed. "Who the hell are you?"

"No threat to you."

"Don't tell me that. Get out of my room."

"Presently. Why don't I get you a glass of water?"

"I don't want a glass of water. I want you out of here. Where's Phillip?"

"He's waiting outside until I tell him that it's all right for him to come in."

"He knows you're here?" She had a sudden memory of Phillip's concerned expression before she'd gone to her room. "Are you a doctor? For God's sake, I'm fine. I don't need a doctor."

"You're not fine." He leaned back in the chair. "And unfortunately you'll be a lot worse before you're better. And, no, I'm not a doctor. My name is Neal Grady." He nodded as he caught her change of expression. "Oh, yes, we've met before. You're beginning to remember on your own. That's very promising . . . and a little scary. You shouldn't be able to break through like this."

"What on earth are you talking about?" She threw the cover aside. "I'm going to go and see Phillip."

"I'm sorry. You can't do that. You have to listen first."

"I can do anything that I—"

Voices. Screaming. Voices. Pain.

"No!" She buried her head in the pillow, but she couldn't shut them out.

Voices. Agony. Screams.

Mama, help. Mama, help.

"She can't help you. You know that. But I'm taking them away," Grady said roughly. "Do you think I like doing this to you? But you have to let me talk to you. Will you stay and listen?"

"Take . . . them . . . away."

"They'll be gone in a few seconds. Relax. You're too tense."

Relax? He had to be crazy. How could she relax when the pain—

The voices were gone.

Relief so intense it made her limp poured through her. She drew a deep breath. She had to stop shaking. "Get out of here," she said unsteadily. "I don't know what you did to me, but I want you—"

"You know what I did to you," Grady said. "You just don't want to admit it to yourself." He grimaced. "Or maybe it's my fault. It's hard to only partially lift control when you've been with me for so long. It's usually all or nothing."

"I don't know what you're talking about." She glared at him. "And I don't want to know. I just want you to leave."

"But you're not risking running to Phillip. Because you know that the voices will come back. Suppose I just get it over quickly and let you absorb it. Let's start with bringing back your memories of me. You were fifteen. You lived with your mother in a cottage on the North Carolina coast. The two of you were very close. I rented a cottage down the beach from you that summer and you and your mother were very kind to me. We became good friends. We went horseback riding on the beach. We played cards in the evening."

Neal laughing at Megan as she tried to bluff at poker.

Her mother shaking her head with amusement as she went past them on the way to the kitchen.

Memories were flowing back to her, surrounding her, flooding her.

Neal helping Megan with her homework in that Latin correspondence course.

"You never really needed help," Neal Grady said quietly. "You just liked the company. You were always a very affectionate girl and you sometimes got lonely living by yourselves on the beach."

"I was not lonely," she said fiercely. "Mama and I had each other. We liked it that way."

"You were lonely. But she did what she thought best for you. She was torn between wanting you to have a normal life and trying to protect you." He paused. "Because neither one of you was quite normal. You both were a little . . . different."

Megan could feel her every muscle stiffening, locking. "No, that's a lie."

"That's what Sarah told you to say. You were to deny it to anyone who asked. It was the only way she could guard you. She even lied to you and told you that the voices you heard were caused by a mental problem, didn't she?"

"I'm not listening to you."

"Yes, you are. Sarah had a powerful psychic gift and she passed it on to you. But she never regarded it as a gift but a curse. She didn't want it tainting your life so she ignored it existed."

Panic was soaring through her. "It's a lie."

"You don't have to protect yourself from me." He shook his head. "Or maybe you do. But not from this particular truth. No one is more aware of that gift than I am."

She shook her head. "I don't know anything about any psychic bullshit."

"Then it's good that I know a good deal about it, isn't it? There are all kinds of psychic talents out there. Mind reading, healing, precognition."

"Charlatans."

"Some of them. Others are quite genuine."

She moistened her lips. "Not me. I'm none of those things."

"No. So far you've only exhibited one talent. You're a Listener."

"What?"

"You hear echoes. Put you in a place or situation where something highly stressful or tragic occurred and you can hear the scene play out." He added quietly, "Only there are too many tragedies, too many human beings in pain or distress. The echoes bombard you, push against each other until they're one long scream."

He was wrong, she thought. Each scream was individual and defined, and the pain was incredibly personal.

"And your mother never taught you how to suppress them. Maybe she didn't know how to teach it. She had to learn how to manage her own gift, but she wasn't around any other psychics. She was pure, raw talent when I first met her. A huge talent that was like none I'd ever run across. It was all trial and error and terribly traumatic for her. I tried to help her but I was too damn young and still struggling with my own problems."

"This is crazy," Megan said unsteadily. "There was nothing wrong with my mother. I was the only one with—"

"She heard the voices too. She just pretended she didn't."

"She wouldn't lie to me."

"She wasn't a strong Listener and there may have been times when she didn't hear what you heard. But she knew what they were. When she found out that you had the same gift, she was able to control your mind enough to keep the echoes at bay. She never tried to go that extra step and help you to take charge. She desperately wanted you to have an ordinary life. She was probably going to do it later."

We'll just forget about it, baby. Come to me if you have that trouble again.

"She loved you, Megan," he said quietly. "She was confused and made huge mistakes, but she always loved you."

"You don't have to tell me that," she said jerkily. "You were with us for one summer. You don't know anything about us."

"I know that when she gave up and let you go, I had to step in and clamp a control on you. Otherwise you would have gone with her." He paused. "But the only way I could keep you on an even keel was to change a few of your memories."

"What memories?" She ran her hand through her hair. "Lord, I can't believe I asked that. It gives credence to all this nonsense."

"Because deep within, you know the truth. I could only put on a Band-Aid but self-preservation did the rest. Are you sure you want to know what those Band-Aids covered? I can wait."

She was silent a moment, fighting to resist the temptation. Why not? She wouldn't permit herself to believe it, but she might as well see how far he'd go with this story. "What memories?"

"It was best that you didn't remember me or that last night with your mother. If you were going to have a normal life, it was better that you didn't remember your voices or your mother's interpretation of them. It would have only made you doubt your sanity."

"Like I'm doubting your sanity right now."

He smiled. "Self-preservation again. You're beginning to remember . . . and believe."

"Bull. I'm a doctor. I believe that I should go to a reputable psychiatrist and discuss buried and suppressed memories. There are logical and scientific reasons that don't have anything to do with psychics and . . . echoes." It had been hard to say that last word. Echoes and screams and voices. Just the thought was causing the panic to start. She tried to make her tone mocking. "And I gather from what you've said that you're supposed to be one of these voodoo psychics too?"

"I wouldn't have been able to help you if I hadn't possessed a talent of my own. But you probably have the potential for being much stronger and multifaceted. That's why I'm going to need your help."

"Then you're knocking on the wrong door." She hesitated before she had to ask the question, "Why didn't you want me to remember what happened that night?"

His gaze narrowed on her face. "Suppose we leave that for another time."

Fear sleeted through her. "No, why, dammit?"

He didn't answer for a moment. "Because you would have had to deal with your mother's murder."

"Murder?" She tried to laugh but her throat was tight and closed. "Now I know you're nuts. My mother tumbled down an incline and broke her neck. It was an accident."

"Her neck was broken by the man you saw at the bottom of the hill that night. And when she died you knew she'd been murdered. I could sense it in you as if it were written in neon."

"No, it didn't happen. No one would have wanted to

kill my mother." The tears were trickling down her cheeks. "Dear God, how ugly can you get?"

"Pretty damn ugly." He stood up. "I think I'd better go away and give you a chance to absorb all of this. You're in denial and it will take a while for you to adjust your thinking. One thing you should know is that you don't have to be afraid of me relaxing control again. No more voices. I had to make you listen to me and that was the quickest way to illustrate the point."

"Quickest and most brutal," she said unsteadily.

"Yes, I'll send in Phillip and let him comfort you and hold your hand. He's very good at that."

"Don't you make fun of Phillip," she said fiercely. "He's a finer man than you'll ever be."

"I wouldn't think of it. You're probably right. I wouldn't have chosen him if I hadn't the utmost respect for him."

She frowned. "Chosen?"

"You had to have someone to give you stability, and Lord knows I can't give anyone that. I sent Phillip to do the job."

Her eyes widened in shock. "That can't be true. He's my mother's half brother. He's my uncle."

"No, Phillip Blair never met your mother. He wasn't her half brother. That was a necessary falsehood I was forced to fabricate." He turned to the door. "I paid him for the job, but he would have done it for nothing. Phillip's an idealist and he has a very warm heart. I told him of the need and he volunteered to fill it."

"That can't be true," she whispered again. "He wouldn't lie to me."

"Ask him."

The door closed behind him.

Mama. Phillip. Of all the shocking and painful words he'd uttered, those last sentences had been the hardest to bear.

She closed her eyes. She felt as if she'd been beaten. Crazy. It was all crazy.

People won't understand, Megan. They'd say you're crazy. We both know that's not true, baby. We'll just keep it between ourselves.

Her mother had never said anything about psychics or talents or any of that crap. She had let Megan think those voices were caused by an illness that shouldn't be talked about. From the time she was seven she had heard the voices, but then they had been faint and far away. It was only after she had reached puberty that they had attacked like sharks. But Mama had been there to comfort and soon the voices were silent.

She managed to keep the echoes at bay.

I had to step in and take over or you would have died with her.

What was truth? What were lies?

If she believed Grady, her entire life had been based on lies.

Oh, God, and she had the terrible feeling that she was beginning to believe him.

FOUR

DAMMIT, HE HADN'T LEFT her with anything, Grady thought bitterly, as he moved toward the living room. That's right, strip her down, and then apply the whip.

No, that wasn't right. He hadn't told her everything. He had merely prepared the way to the path of thorns ahead.

"Well?" Phillip looked up when he walked into the living room. "How did she take it?"

"Exactly how you'd expect her to take it." He went to the window and looked out at the garden. "She accused me of being a nutcase. She's fighting tooth and nail to crawl into a hole and bury her head."

"I'm not surprised." He paused. "Did you tell her she could be a Pandora?"

"No, I told her she was a Listener. That was heavy enough for her to handle."

"It could be true that's all she is."

Grady hoped he was right. He had been able to keep objectivity until he'd gone into that bedroom today. Through all the punishment he'd handed Megan, she had displayed a courage and stamina that had touched him in a way that had nothing to do with pity. He had hurt her but not brought her down. He had wanted to ease her pain, but it was pain that was going to goad her to do what he wanted her to do. "And I didn't tell her about Molino or the Ledger. She's having enough trouble accepting the truth about her mother." He glanced at Phillip. "And you."

"You told her about me? Thanks a lot, Grady. Couldn't it have waited? Dammit, I'm her best friend."

"No more lies. It's time to clear the slate."

"Even if it leaves her out there alone."

Grady nodded. "I put her in a cocoon and wrapped her in a tangle of lies for twelve years. She has to come out and face the truth." He headed for the door. "Now get in there and help her. She's hurting."

"Thanks to you."

"Do you expect me to deny it?" he asked roughly. "Of course, I did it. I'd do it again." He slammed the door behind him and ran down the porch steps. He needed to get away from Megan Blair and Phillip and all the pain he'd visited on both of them. It didn't matter that he thought it necessary. Sometimes doing what was necessary sucked big-time. He wanted to be the one to go back in that bedroom and give Megan comfort and hope. He wanted to hold her hand and tell her that he'd keep all her personal demons at bay.

He couldn't do it. A threat was also a goad and he might have to use it. Let Phillip save the princess in distress.

Grady was used to being the Black Knight.

"MAY I COME IN?" PHILLIP asked quietly. "If you like, I'll come back later."

"Why?" Megan sat up in bed. "Would it make what you're going to say any more palatable?"

"No." He closed the door. "Lies are always dirty and this one has been sticking in my throat for years. I'm glad it's out in the open." He sat down in the chair beside her bed. "You look like hell. Can I get you something?"

Her lips twisted. "Maybe another cozy hot chocolate? Don't bother. You don't have to play that game any longer."

"It was no game," he said gently. "It was my pleasure. I treasured those times together."

She felt a melting inside her. No, she couldn't let herself soften toward him. He'd betrayed her. "He said he paid you. Is it true?"

"Yes, I had to live until I could get myself established here. But that wasn't why I did it. I wanted to help you, Megan."

"Yeah, sure."

"Look at me. I know you're feeling confused and hurt and alone." His hand closed on hers. "You're not alone. I'm here for you. I care for you. If I had a daughter, I couldn't love her more. I wish you were my daughter." He paused. "I know how much you're hurting. I'm hurting too."

He was telling the truth. She could *feel* his sorrow and pain. She tried to ignore it.

It was impossible. This was *Phillip*. She couldn't let him remain unhappy. But she also couldn't let what he had done slide. "It was wrong, Phillip. You shouldn't have done it."

"If I hadn't gone along with Grady, he would have gotten someone else. He gave me a chance to back out. He told me to go to the funeral and meet you. If I didn't feel I could help you, I could just walk away." He smiled. "But he knew he'd have me as soon as I saw you. You were standing there at the grave, bewildered and hurt and trying to be brave. It wasn't a question of whether I wanted to help you, but how I could do it. But it turned out that was so easy. We meshed and became a family. So I let Grady do his sleight of hand with forging documents and making me seem legitimate." His smile faded. "Don't back away. Don't take my family away from me, Megan."

She felt the tears well. "How do I know that you're not just doing what Grady would want you to do? He seems to be—I don't know what he seems to be. He told me— He said I'm some kind of freak."

"I'm sure he never used that word. That would be the pot calling the kettle black."

She stiffened. "But you're not arguing with the concept, are you? For heaven's sake, Phillip. I'm not—I've never done anything weird in my life. You know that's true."

"Not as long as I've known you." He paused. "And it's not what you've done, but what you are. Just being a Listener has made you a victim. Sometimes it happens that way."

She stared at him incredulously. "You actually believe that hogwash?"

"I have to believe it. My wife, Nora, was a Listener."

"Your wife?"

"She died a few years before I came to you. That's why Grady knew I'd help you." He shook his head. "Though you've had it easy compared to Nora. Grady has been helping you. I couldn't help my wife. I didn't even know there were people who could ease her." His face lit with a luminous smile. "I wish you could have known my Nora. You're a lot alike. She always moved at the speed of light and was into everything. And loving . . . Lord, she was loving. She was the gentlest, sweetest woman on the face of the earth. We'd been married ten years before she started hearing the voices and then it was very seldom. We could ignore it." His smile vanished. "Then the night-mares started and the voices surrounded her all the time. She thought she was going crazy. Therapy didn't help. She begged me to put her away someplace and leave her. I fought her for another three years before she made her first suicide attempt."

"Suicide," Megan repeated numbly.

He nodded. "She won. I committed her and she spent five years in a psychiatric hospital before Grady appeared on my doorstep. We took her out of the asylum and she was happy and normal for the last years of her life. I owe him."

"Asylum," she whispered. "I'm not crazy, Phillip."

"No, you're not. But you're terrified because that's what your mother hinted to you all your life."

"My mother loved me. She was my friend. She was wonderful, dammit."

"I'm not arguing. I didn't know her. Grady said she was . . . exceptional."

"What is that supposed to mean?"

"Don't be defensive with me. Take it up with Grady."

"I don't want to take it up with Grady. I'm not even sure he'd tell me the truth if I asked him." Her hand involuntarily clenched on Phillip's. "He was—I don't like what he did to me. Who the hell is he?"

"He didn't lie to you. His name is Neal Grady. He said you spent an entire summer with him so you probably know him better than I do."

Neal throwing back his dark head and laughing at something Sarah had said.

Neal sitting still on a dune, his arms linked around his knees, watching Megan as she waded in the surf.

"Good Lord, you can't keep your eyes off him, can you?" Her mother's voice teasing her. "I believe you have a crush on our Neal. Oh, don't worry, I won't tell him." Her smile faded. "Don't like him too much, baby. I know he's been a wonderful playmate this summer but he's not really young like you. He's been through too much. When I first met him, I was feeling very maternal toward him. Then, as we became friends, I felt as if he was like Merlin and aging backwards."

"That's silly, Mama."

"I guess so." She smiled. "But it's rude of you to point it out when I'm trying to be deep and profound."

Yes, she had thought she knew Neal Grady, Megan thought. But she had seen him through a lonely adolescent's eyes and she had been blind to everything but what she wanted to see. "I didn't really know anything about him. When he showed up that summer, my mother said she'd met him before, but she didn't mention where. He didn't seem . . . he was like anyone else." She repeated, "Who is he? Stop dodging, Phillip."

"I'm not dodging. I'm gathering my thoughts. I'll tell you what I know about him. He was born and raised in the ghettos of New Orleans. He was recruited by the military when he was sixteen and eventually sent to work with a Special Forces unit." He grimaced. "When he wasn't slaughtering off the supposed bad guys, he was acting as consultant."

"Consultant?"

"Our government has had psychic programs in place for decades. So have the Russians and several European countries. They're not talked about but they definitely exist. The CIA has been been using them more and more frequently in recent years. In some Delta units, they sometimes have someone with special sensitivity; mind reading, precognition, controllers. Any talent that can give them an edge. A talent like Grady must have seemed like a gift sent from heaven to them."

"Why? What talent is he supposed to have?"

He shrugged. "I don't know everything he can do. I think with some people he can blur reality, cause memory loss, control the thought process. I do know he acted as buffer for my wife and kept her sane. After your mother died he cut his ties with the military and started working with a Psychic Investigative Group at a think tank in Virginia, headed by Michael Travis."

She shook her head in disbelief. "More crackpots."

"No, genuine psychics. I made Grady take me there to check it out before I trusted him enough to let him help Nora. I'm not gullible and I was very impressed. I expected a bunch of crooks and charlatans. I found something that opened my eyes to a new world." He made a face. "And it scared the hell out of me. It took me a week to get over it and decide to let Grady help my wife."

"You're saying he's some kind of psychic do-gooder going around and turning water into wine?"

"No, I'm saying Grady occasionally helps out in special cases. His main focus is in another direction."

"What direction?"

He shrugged. "I believe he's searching for something. Ask him about it."

"Would he tell me?"

"Yes." His lips tightened. "I'm quite sure he'll tell you all about it."

She was silent a moment. "You don't trust him."

"I trusted him with Nora. I don't know if I'd trust him with you. The situation is different."

"You don't have to trust me with him. I'm not a child. I'm the one to make the decision." She wearily shook her head. "And I don't know what to think. It's all crazy. If I believe you, then I have to believe what Grady told me." She whispered, "I don't want to do that, Phillip."

"I know." He squeezed her hand and then released it. "But you've always faced up to even the hardest facts. This is just another one." He smiled. "Well, I suppose that's an understatement."

"I suppose," she repeated ironically. She looked away from him. "It's not bullshit, Phillip?"

"I can't blame you for doubting. No one was a bigger doubter than me." He paused. "I don't understand it, but it's not bullshit. I swear to you, Megan."

"I don't *want* it," she said fiercely. "I'd almost rather be nuts than a freak. How do I get rid of it?"

"You don't. You learn to live with it." He released her hand and stood up. "It's the only way to survive."

"You don't know that. You're not a freak. You probably only know what Grady told you."

"I did research on my own too. Nora was too important to me to trust anyone's word without checking."

She had hurt him again. She was filled with anger and frustration, but she shouldn't take it out on Phillip. "I'm sorry. I'm just—" She reached out and took his hand and put it against her cheek. "It's not you. I just want to wake up tomorrow and have this be a nightmare."

"I know," he said gently. "I want that for you too. But I can't make it happen. The only thing I can tell you is that I'll be here for you. I won't let Grady have it all his own way."

"Why did he come back? I was getting along just fine. I don't want him in my life."

"You were getting along just fine because he was running interference for you . . . just as he did with Nora."

"I *won't* be dependent on him. God, I felt helpless. He was able to hurt me, bend me. It was like being a cripple. I've got to do something."

"I can't help you there, Megan. I'm afraid you're on your own." He patted her cheek before stepping back. "But you've never been shy about taking the initiative. I'll enjoy watching you work it out."

She suddenly remembered something else that had been lost in the shock and confusion. "Grady said he needed me to help him. Help him do what?"

"I'm sure we'll find out soon enough. Grady can be patient but not in these circumstances."

She watched Phillip move toward the door. When he had come into the room, she had been filled with hurt and anger and a feeling of isolation. Yet it had only taken a short time for her to come to terms with this new place Phillip was occupying in her life. It was a strange and bizarre role, but Phillip himself had not changed. He was still her friend. She still loved him with all her heart. As long as he stood by her, she was not alone.

He would stand with her against Grady.

She suddenly stiffened as she realized what she was thinking. She was relying on Phillip as she had all these years. Grady had given him that role and she had nestled close to Phillip like a child in the dark.

Well, she was no longer a child. She was an adult who had fought her way to become a doctor. Grady had said her mother had lied to her and perhaps she had. She didn't know about that any longer. And Phillip had said that she was as dependent on Grady as his wife to keep the voices away, to keep her sanity intact. But she would never know that until she stood alone without Phillip or Grady to help her.

If Grady would let her stand alone. She had a hideous memory of him letting those voices bombard her.

Letting. Not *making* them attack her. If what he'd told her was true, then he could only leash those voices, not set them to ravage her. She was the only one who could stop or control them. If her mother had been able to do it, then Megan should also have that ability.

Maybe.

She closed her eyes as panic jolted through her at the thought of trying to harness that horror. She wanted to curl back up in a ball as she'd done when she'd come into this bedroom this afternoon.

Stop being a coward, she thought with disgust. You don't even know if all this psychic bullshit is true, yet you're already cringing. Find out what's truth and what's manipulation. Grady had said he was only releasing partial control of the voices and that might also mean her memories were being filtered by him. She had to take that power back from him.

She couldn't live like this. She had to know if her mother had been murdered as Grady claimed. She couldn't bear the thought of never really knowing whether she was a mental case or not. She couldn't stand the thought of being under Grady's thumb.

And she couldn't let those damn voices rule her life.

She threw the cover aside and jumped out of bed. Get dressed. Stop shaking. You know what you have to do.

You know where you have to go.

PANIC!

Grady jerked upright in the chair at his computer as he felt Megan's jarring terror.

What the hell . . .

His cell phone rang. Phillip.

He picked up the phone. "Dammit, what's happening, Phillip?"

"You tell me," he said curtly. "She's gone."

"Where?"

"I don't know. I heard a car starting and I ran down to check it out. My Camry was gone and so was Megan. Molino?"

"Possibly." No, the fear Megan was feeling wasn't fo-

cused on a person. "I don't think so. But she's scared almost witless about something."

"You? She said she felt helpless and didn't like the
idea of you being able to call the shots."

"She was angry with me, not afraid."

"Then why did she run? She was okay with me when I
left her. Dammit, all that psychic crap you're supposed to
have and you can't even use it when you need it?"

"I told you I wasn't a mind reader. Occasionally, I get a
drifting ribbon of thought but I can't—"

"Then how can we find her?"

"I don't need to be a mind reader to be in contact with
Megan. Her every emotion is screaming and I may be
able to get a fix on her. We've been together mentally for
twelve years and she's broadcasting loud and clear."

"Then where is she going?"

"It's not that easy. I can feel her, so I may be able to
track her, but otherwise I'm as blind as you are." He got up
from his chair. "And I don't have time to argue with you.
I'll pick you up in fifteen minutes. We have to go after her.
I may need you along to act as buffer when I find her. If
she's not afraid of Molino yet, she may be soon. I'd bet
your house was being watched tonight at the time she left."

Phillip muttered a curse. "I'll be waiting." He hung up.

Grady grabbed his jacket and headed for the door. The
terror Megan was feeling was increasing every minute.
He could feel the tension, the cold chill that was attacking
her every limb.

DEAR GOD, SHE WAS COLD, Megan thought.

She clenched her hands on the steering wheel to keep
them from shaking. She told herself to take deep breaths

and not think of what she was going to do when she reached her destination.

Think of something pleasant, something happy.

She hadn't realized until this minute how difficult it was to zero in on something carefree and pleasant in her life. Since her mother had died everything had been all work and duty.

Davy.

Davy running, Davy begging her to ride the elephant, Davy smiling at her.

Yes, she could hold the fear at bay if she could just keep thinking of Davy.

"WHERE IS SHE?" PHILLIP ASKED through set teeth. "You've been driving around for the last hour."

"Shut up, Phillip." Grady was just as on edge. "If I knew, I'd be— She's calmer. She's not as frightened. I can't locate her, blast it."

"And what if Molino finds her first? You said he probably had a tail on—"

Oh, God, I don't want to do this.

"East." Grady interrupted, stomping on the accelerator. "Somewhere near the Carolina border. She doesn't like where she is. It's scaring her."

"Carolina?" Phillip turned to look at Grady. "Why should she—" He broke off. "The place where her mother died?"

"No," he said grimly. "That wouldn't scare her. She's going to the cave."

"Why?"

"Why do you think? It's where her mother sent her that last day. Maybe she believes that it's safer for her."

"Safer?"

Grady was cursing softly. "The damn woman is going to issue an invitation."

It's not safer, Megan. Don't do it. Let me help you.

He couldn't reach her. She was too focused on what she was doing.

"Invitation?"

"She's going to let in the voices."

"No," Phillip whispered. "It'll be like Nora. She'll go crazy. Stop her."

"I can't stop her. She's too damn strong. She's fighting me as much as she's fighting the voices. I can't help her. Maybe once I reach her I can do something."

"If it's not too late," Phillip said dully. "Nora tried to commit suicide three times before I finally had her committed, and she'd lived with her voices for years. Facing that kind of trauma with no preparation is—"

"Stop talking about it," Grady said roughly. "I know what could happen. But Megan's mother survived without anyone to help her. Maybe Megan will be able to—" He shook his head. "I don't know what she's able to do. We have to get to her."

HE'D LOST HER, DARNELL THOUGHT with annoyance, as he saw Megan Blair's Camry parked on the beach. She wasn't in the car and was nowhere in sight. He'd been afraid to get too close while he was following her. She'd proved to be a little too sharp when he'd tried to run her off the highway. He'd seen her pull off the road a few minutes ago and drive toward the beach. He'd parked his truck behind a deserted hot dog stand near the road and walked down.

Had she gone into one of the beach cottages? There were no lights on in any of them. He couldn't barge in and search for her.

He glanced at the surf rushing against the shore several yards away. Drowning could be accidental or suicidal. Either way it would be a convenient method of disposal.

Why try to stalk her? She would come back for her car. And he would be waiting.

TWELVE YEARS.

She didn't want to walk into that cave.

Stop shaking. Do it.

So many times she had come here with her mother during those years they'd lived on the beach, but she could only remember running up the hill that last time.

She sank to her knees and huddled against the cold stone.

I'm here, Mama.

But Mama wasn't here. No one was here but Megan.

And perhaps the voices.

Did you lie to me, Mama?

Okay, let's see if I can find out. How do I do it?

Relax. Open your mind. Let's see what happens.

Voices. Shrieks. Pain.

She flinched and tried to back away.

No. Face it. See what's there. Force yourself.

Her teeth bit into her lower lip until she tasted blood.

Babble.

It seemed to go on forever.

I can't understand. I can't understand. I can't understand.

Voices. Pain. Indistinguishable echoes.

She whimpered and buried her head in her arm.

No, not completely indistinguishable. One voice stronger than the others, a man's angry voice.

"Slut. Whore. My own brother."

"No, Hiram. Stay away from me. Don't push me. We didn't—"

A woman's long, drawn out scream . . .

And the babble returned.

"My baby. My little John. Don't leave me."

Babble.

"It's your child, you bastard. Don't you walk away from me because you're one of the high and mighty Pearsalls. I'll tell everyone that you . . ."

Gone again.

Babble.

She could feel the tears run down her cheeks.

Go away. I don't want to hear your pain. There's nothing I can do about it, dammit.

Voices. Pushing, stabbing, suffocating her.

Anger flared through her. "Go *away*. I'm not going to let you do this to me. I won't *have* it."

The voices vanished.

She gasped in shock. Is that all it took? Anger channeled, aimed, to ward off that bombardment?

Dammit, she was wrong; she could still hear them.

No, it wasn't a voice.

Mama, don't go away. Don't leave me.

Not . . . Pandora.

Neal standing in the doorway.

Blood spurting from that throat as his knife slit across it.

Mama.

Death.

"No!" She jumped to her feet and ran out of the cave.

"Megan!"

Grady.

Panic tore through her. She pushed past him and darted down the path.

"Megan, I'm not going to hurt you. God, I didn't think

you'd get that far on your own or I would have told you everything myself. You shouldn't have been able to do it." He started after her. "I wouldn't have left you alone if I'd thought—"

"Stay away." Her voice was shaking. "Stay away from me."

"No way." He was beside her, reaching for her arm.

She drove her fist into his stomach, whirled, and kept running.

He was behind her, gaining on her. "Megan, I'm not trying to hurt—"

"Blood. Death. I could see it. You killed her."

"Not your mother. Dammit, okay, I killed someone that night, but it wasn't your mother. It was the son of a bitch who murdered her. Let me talk to you. Oh, to hell with it." He tackled her and brought her to the ground.

She fought frantically but he was on top of her, holding her down. She glared up at him. "You killed her."

"No, I told you the truth."

"You killed her and you were going to kill me."

"That's what you were thinking that night, but that doesn't make it the truth. You were out of your head." His voice vibrated with intensity. "I didn't do it. The man who you saw down by the pines killed her. She tried to lead him away from you. He caught her and he killed her."

"No." She tried to free her arms. "I don't want to—" She closed her eyes. "I shouldn't have let her go. I knew something was wrong. I should have stayed with her."

"You couldn't have saved her and you would have robbed her of her chance to save you."

"From you."

"No, you're not believing that any longer." He swung off her and stood up. "It's not good to be out in the open like this. Let's get back to your car. Phillip is waiting for us."

She opened her eyes and glared up at him. "I'm not going anywhere with you."

"Yes, you are. Even if I have to carry you."

He would do it. She slowly got to her feet.

"Good. Let's go."

She shook her head. "Leave me alone."

"I can't do that. From now on we're joined at the hip." His lips tightened grimly. "I almost lost you the other night when you were forced down that embankment. I've invested too much in you to let you get blown away. Let's get back to Phillip."

Anger and frustration seared through her. He was right. She didn't know what to believe any longer. She wanted to hit out at something, someone. It would be an exercise in futility to strike out at Grady. She'd already found out how strong he could be. Better to save her own strength until she could make it count.

She turned on her heel and strode down the path that led to the beach.

FIVE

"MEGAN." PHILLIP HURRIED EAGERLY toward her as he saw her coming down the hill. "Are you all right? I was worried about you."

"I'm fine." She wasn't fine. She was angry and frightened and she wanted to get away from here, away from Grady. She could feel Grady's eyes on the center of her spine as she moved toward Phillip. "There was something I had to do."

Phillip's gaze was searching her face. "And did you do it?"

"Hell, yes," Grady answered for her as he reached them. "She was fighting off those echoes while I was running up the hill toward the cave. I couldn't believe she could do it." His lips tightened grimly. "And then she came up with an unexpected tidbit or two that surprised me."

"If you can call murder a tidbit," Megan said coldly. She turned to Phillip. "Did you know about what happened there twelve years ago?"

"Of course, he did," Grady said roughly. "Though I admit I filled him in with broad strokes that wouldn't offend his conscience. There was no use making him worry." He glanced uneasily around the deserted beach and then nodded at the Camry parked a few yards away. "Phillip, you drive her back to your house. I'll follow. I want to scout around and make sure that—"

"I don't need anyone with me," Megan said. "And I may not go back to the house. I have some thinking to do." That was an understatement, she thought bitterly. Her mind was whirling and she couldn't process anything in that chaos.

"You'll go back to the house," Grady said. "Or I'll trail behind you until you settle down and let me talk to you. Take your choice."

"I don't have to make a choice, you bastard." She glared at him. "I don't need you. Go ahead. Try to hurt me. Let loose your damn echoes. I'll handle them without your help."

"They're not my echoes," he said quietly. "They're yours, and I've never wanted to hurt you."

"Bullshit."

She started toward the Camry.

"Let me go with you, Megan." Phillip hurried after her. "When you calm down, you'll realize you can use a friend in—"

"Down!"

Megan was knocked off her feet as Grady pushed her and Phillip to the sand.

A bullet splintered the glass of the windshield of the Camry!

"Shit." Phillip was crawling toward her. "Get her in the car, Grady."

"You get her in the car." Grady was covering her body with his own. "The gunfire is coming from around the side of the house over there. I saw a glint on metal. We can't risk exposing her to that—"

Another bullet plowed into the sand next to her.

Another bullet followed.

Grady was cursing. "Damn him to hell." He rolled them both over behind the car. "Stay here. I'm going after him."

"Who is—"

But Grady was gone.

Don't just lie here. Get inside the car. She'd left her purse underneath the front seat. She had to reach her cell phone and call 911. She started crawling toward the passenger door.

Another bullet hit the side-view mirror.

Where the hell was Grady?

And where was Phillip?

And then she saw him.

SHE WAS KNEELING IN THE sand beside Phillip when Grady came back to the car ten minutes later.

"I've been waiting for you," she said jerkily. "He's been shot. We have to get him to a hospital. I called 911, but I don't know when they'll get here."

"Any minute." Grady fell to his knees beside Phillip. "The sirens scared away the shooter. We were playing cat and mouse, but he jumped into his truck and took off. How is he?"

"I don't know. The bullet plowed across his skull. He's unconscious." Her teeth bit hard into her lower lip. Hold on. Don't let go. She had to help Phillip. "Head wounds can go either way. Any trauma to the cerebral hemisphere is chancy. He could be okay tomorrow. Or he could be a vegetable. I slowed the bleeding. That's all I can do." Her hands clenched into fists. "I feel so damn helpless. I want to *help* him, Grady."

"We'll get him the best help, Megan," Grady said. "At the best hospital. I promise you."

"Why would anyone shoot Phillip?" she whispered. "He was *good,* Grady. Even you couldn't make him into something he wasn't."

"Then obviously he must have been guarded by the

angels," Grady got to his feet as he saw the flashing lights of the ambulance spearing the darkness. "They've come for him. It's a bullet wound and there will be questions. I'll take care of them. You go with Phillip to the hospital."

She nodded, her gaze never leaving Phillip's face. She felt as if she were splintering inside. She wanted to scream and pound her fists into the sand. "I won't leave him. I'll never leave him."

PHILLIP DID NOT REGAIN consciousness in the next ten hours.

The next day he was transported by helicopter from the local Myrtle Beach Hospital to the ICU at Emory Hospital in Atlanta.

"No change?" Grady asked the next morning as he came into the waiting room where Megan was sitting. He handed her a cup of coffee. "Test results?"

She shook her head. "They think there may be brain damage, but they're not sure. He just won't wake up. They say he may never wake up." She had to wait a moment to steady her voice. "He's in a coma. They have him hooked up to those machines to keep him alive." She swallowed. "I don't know how many times I've ordered patients put on life support. But this is different. This is Phillip."

"I'm sorry," Grady said gently. "He's a fine man. He didn't deserve this."

"No, but he got it, didn't he? It doesn't matter if he deserved it or not." She looked away from him. "I've been thinking a lot about Phillip while I've been sitting here. I never had anyone but my mother who cared about me until he came into my life. That's why it hurt so much when I thought he'd betrayed me. I felt . . . fooled. I thought he'd just been pretending."

"He did care about you, Megan."

"I know that. I could *feel* it. And it wasn't any of that psychic business. He was . . . We were a team." She shook her head. "He said he wished I could have been his daughter. I wished that too. My father died before I was born and I never knew him. But no one could have been more loving than Phillip. You can't imagine how good he was to me."

"I can imagine."

"Of course, you brought us together. But you know, that doesn't even bother me any longer. The important thing is that we had those years together." She drew a deep breath. "I have questions but I don't want to think about anything but Phillip right now." She had to talk to Dr. Pretkay, the specialist they'd brought down from Johns Hopkins. Not that they'd given her much hope. It was only one more avenue to explore. "I just have to know one thing. That bullet wasn't meant for Phillip, was it? He was shooting at me."

Grady nodded. "You were the prime target. Though I'm not saying that the shooter might not have wanted to eliminate all witnesses."

"And that night I was run off the highway?"

"Deliberate. Probably the same man."

"Why?"

"Nothing you did. The man who killed your mother wanted to eliminate every member of her family."

"What? That sounds like some Mafia vendetta."

"Molino would appreciate that comparison. He grew up in Sicily in the shadow of the Mafia."

"Molino? He's the one who killed my mother?"

"He gave the order. The man who actually killed her was one of his men, Ted Dagnos."

"Why would Molino want my mother dead?"

"Revenge."

"Revenge for what?"

"It's a long story and you said you didn't want to think about it now. I'll be here to answer questions when you're ready." He studied her. "You've accepted the fact that I wasn't her killer, haven't you?"

"As I said, I've had a lot of time to think sitting here. It was hard for me to accept that she was murdered." She added unsteadily, "But I have to do that. Whatever other madness and mental chaos I went through in that cave two nights ago, I do believe that my mother's death was not an accident. Everything else is still suspect. I have to prove it to myself." She immediately shook her head. "No, you're right. Not now. But I'm going to want all the answers, Grady. You'd better be prepared to give them."

"Any day. Anytime." He added soberly, "Let me know when you hear something more about Phillip."

She nodded jerkily. "It should be soon."

"Would you like me to stay?"

She gave him a level glance. "No, I can't say I like the idea of leaning on a man who's been as deceptive and manipulative as you've been with me."

He smiled. "You have a point. And I don't think you're afraid of me manipulating you anymore."

"I'm not." But it was true she no longer felt the danger from him was immediate. In the past days he had been with her constantly, fast, efficient, arranging everything for Phillip. He never intruded but was always a quiet presence in the background. "And you weren't the one shooting at me at the beach. You may have saved my life. I'm sure it was probably for purely selfish reasons, but you clearly don't want me dead."

"Very clearly." He turned toward the door. "You have my cell number. Call me if you need me."

"Where are you going?"

He shrugged. "You don't want me here, but I have to keep an eye on you. I'll be around. Give me five minutes' notice and I'll be here. I should tell you that I've asked Jed Harley to stop by and check on you occasionally. I don't want you to think he's one of Molino's pet vipers."

"Who's Jed Harley?"

"I've hired him to keep an eye on you. He's a good man."

"How good? In what way?"

"In all kinds of ways. Guns, knives, karate, tai chi. If you don't need him to put down someone, he's very good at keeping you entertained."

"I don't believe I'm in need of a court jester."

"Harley doesn't care what you need. He is what he is. Since you're having trouble enduring my presence I have to make sure you're safe. Nothing's going to happen to you, Megan." He walked out of the waiting room.

She felt a surge of comfort at those last words. She was feeling very much alone at this moment and was filled with confusion and sadness. Grady was not motivated by love or kindness but he wanted her protected. She would need that protection if she was to work her way through this bewildering maze.

"HI. BAD SCENE, HUH? Anything I can do?"

She opened her eyes to see a tall, loose-limbed man in a red Hawaiian shirt standing in the doorway. She straightened in her chair. "No, thank you."

"Sure?" He came into the waiting room. "I'm not just a busybody poking my nose into your business. That would piss me off too. My name is Jed Harley and I've been paid to stick my nose in your business." He dropped down in the chair beside her. "That should make you feel better. Protect and soothe. That's my job."

She stared at him. He was in his mid-thirties, tanned, with sandy hair and bright blue eyes. In that Hawaiian shirt he looked more like a beachcomber than the man Grady had described. "Your bedside manner is very unusual, Mr. Harley."

"Harley." He grinned. "And you're not in bed. Actually, my bedside manner is pretty damn good. I once had a job as an EMT driver and I was comforting as hell. The patients loved me. I just fit the manner to the situation. You're not a lady who would appreciate someone patting her on the back and soothing her. You're very independent."

"How do you— Oh, for Pete's sake, are you some kind of freak like Grady?"

"Lord, no." He shuddered. "Perish the thought. I relish the simple, uncomplicated life. I'm just a decent judge of character. I've been keeping my eye on you and you're not difficult to read. I feel as if I know you already."

"How nice," she said dryly. "Lately, I've been wondering if I know myself."

He grinned. "Talk to me. I'll set you straight." He leaned back in his chair. "Now, I'll shut up and let you relax. No, there's no way you'll relax. But you won't have to put up with my bullshit. Under other circumstances I'm sure you'd find it fascinating but not now. Just lean back in your chair, know I'm here for you and I'll do whatever I can."

To her amazement she found herself doing as he told her and leaning back in her chair. There was something curiously soothing and gentle beneath that brash exterior. "You don't have to be here for me. I'm sure Grady didn't mean for you to sit here and hold my hand."

"So I'm an overachiever. I believe that life should be

all parties and fireworks and it brings me down when I see someone who's been left out of the party. I have to try to do something about it." He crossed his arms across his chest and stretched his legs out before him. "Now ignore me until you need me."

Bizarre. He was totally bizarre.

But oddly comforting.

She closed her eyes again, her hands tightening on the arms of the chair, waiting.

Ten minutes passed.

Fifteen.

Twenty.

"Megan." Suddenly Harley's hand was covering her own. Warmth, strength, comfort. "I think that's your doctor coming."

Her lids flew open.

"Dr. Blair?" Dr. Pretkay, the specialist from Johns Hopkins, was standing in the doorway. Her grip tightened on Harley's. Pretkay's expression was sympathetic, compassionate and . . . regretful.

Damn. Damn. Damn.

PHILLIP WAS A SMALL MAN BUT he looked even slighter in the white hospital bed.

"Hi, Phillip," Megan said unsteadily as she moved toward the bed. "I'm not sure if you can understand me. All those specialists can't agree on what coma patients are able to process." She took his hand. It was cool and unresponsive, completely unlike the warm, affectionate grasp to which she was accustomed. "I thought I'd give it a try. If you can understand what's going on here, you may feel helpless and that sucks." Don't start crying again. "They say they can't do anything to help you right now. So we're moving you to a private nursing home and you'll have wonderful care. I may not be able to visit you right away, but I'll never stop looking for a way to get you well." She swallowed and whispered, "I love you. Thank you for all the years, Phillip." No, that sounded like good-bye and she would *not* give up on Phillip no matter what Pretkay said. "But we'll have more years together. Just give me a little time to work it out." She bent and brushed a kiss on his forehead. "See you."

She moved quickly for the door but she was blinded by tears by the time she reached the hall.

"Hey, easy." Grady was pulling her into his arms, cradling her. "Don't fight me. You need a shoulder to lean on and I want to be the one to help, dammit."

She didn't fight him. He felt warm and strong and alive. She needed that life after facing the half death that Phillip was experiencing. "Pretkay said he probably wouldn't ever wake up. He wanted to know if I wanted to take him off any life support." She buried her face in his shoulder. "Screw him. No way. Phillip hasn't even had a chance to fight his way out of this. I haven't had a chance to fight for him."

"Shh." Grady was stroking her hair. "You're right. We'll take care of him. And we'll find a way to help him."

"Damn right." She pushed away from him and wiped her eyes. "And the first thing we'll do is find that son of a bitch who shot him. I don't want that bastard prancing around when Phillip is lying there like a zombie."

"I've been working on it." His lips tightened. "Don't look so surprised. I'm the one who sent Phillip to you. There wasn't any question that I wouldn't go after that shooter. What do you think I was doing while you were sitting in that waiting room?"

"Who is it?"

He shook his head. "I'll know soon."

Her lips twisted. "Crystal ball?"

"No, Atlanta Police lab. There were tire tracks in the sand from his truck and fiber on the porch where he was kneeling."

"That's not much."

"It's a beginning. I have contacts with the CIA and they'll put pressure to hurry up the investigation. And I called Michael Travis and he said that he knew someone who might be able to help."

She remembered that name. "Phillip said there was a Michael Travis who headed a Psychic Investigative Group in Virginia. I thought you said no crystal ball."

"It's the truth. Michael was talking about Atlanta City Hall. His contacts aren't limited to—"

"Freaks."

"Call it what you like." He looked her in the eyes. "No one has a better right."

He meant because she was one of them, she thought wearily. "I won't admit that yet."

"What? Not even after what you went through in that cave?"

"It could still be a mental problem. I'm a very pragmatic person and I have no evidence that would prove otherwise."

"The hell you haven't," he said roughly. "Accept it, Megan."

"When I can prove it to myself. I don't believe I'm schizophrenic. But do I trust what my instincts tell me and go against my logic? Do I go against what my mother told me? But what you did to me at the zoo has no logical explanation. Phillip believes what you told me and he'd never steer me wrong. I just don't know." Her hands clenched into fists. "You said that the voices are usually connected to the scene of a particular emotional disturbance. Is that right?"

"Yes."

"This hospital must be overflowing with those echoes. Why aren't I hearing them?"

"I'm helping a little."

"A little?"

He nodded. "You're doing a lot of blocking yourself. That's pretty incredible. It's got to be instinctive. I didn't have a chance to teach you."

"Why would you want to teach me? It would have taken away any threat you might be able to wield over me."

"True. I considered that possibility. However, eventually you would come into your own and it's better if you help me willingly."

"Come into my own?" she repeated bitterly. "Oh, yes. This great gift that could send me around the bend like it did Phillip's wife."

"She wasn't anywhere near as strong as—"

"I don't want to hear it." She cut him off. "Not now. I have to go home and check on something. Afterward I have to pack up Phillip's belongings." She shuddered. "They do that after someone dies. He's *not* going to die, Grady. And he's not going to go on living in that silent hell." She moved down the hall. "I have to find a way . . ."

THE COMPUTER SCREEN GLOWED blue in the light of Megan's desk lamp on the desk in the library.

Do it. Don't just stare at a blank screen. Tap the World Wide Web of information. You could find anything on a computer if you looked long enough. Or at least it would tell you where to go to find what you wanted.

But she didn't really want to know if her mother had lied to her.

Bite the bullet.

Concentrate. Remember the only echoes that had come clear.

Hiram.

A long scream, fading . . .

A woman falling?

John, my baby . . .

What baby?

Pearsall. A woman done wrong by a man named Pearsall.

She didn't even know during what time period those episodes happened. It was pitifully sparse information to go on, she thought in frustration. Of course she could go back to the cave and try to let the voices return.

Yeah, sure. She was going to put herself through that again? No way.

She typed "Myrtle Beach" in to the search engine.

She would dip into the local newspaper files and see if that babble was the echoes that Grady claimed them to be. Considering those references were so scanty as to be close to nonexistent, Lord knows how much time it was going to take her.

It didn't matter. She'd stay with it for as long as it took.

GRADY LEANED BACK IN THE driver's seat, his gaze fixed on the light streaming out of the library window. She had been up all night and he had an idea what she was doing.

Go ahead, Megan. Work it out for yourself.

I'll be here protecting your back.

SIX

IT WAS CLOSE TO NOON BEFORE Megan finally shut off the computer and leaned back in her chair.

Done.

She should be exhausted, but she was too wired to feel anything but excitement, tension . . . and fear.

Get over it. She hadn't spent all this time and effort to let herself be blocked by an outpouring of emotion. Go take a shower and make a fresh pot of coffee. Think clearly and logically, go over the notes, and then come to a conclusion.

No matter how unclear and illogical the conclusion might prove to be.

"YOU PHONED?" GRADY SAID when she opened the front door to his ring two hours later.

"Ten minutes ago." She frowned. "You must have been practically on the doorstep."

"Close enough." He came into the foyer and shut the door. "I told you I'd come when you called."

"But that was at the hospital."

He smiled. "That doesn't make any difference. I don't believe in short-term commitments. If you phoned, then you must have had a good reason. I'm not one of your favorite people at the moment."

"That's true." She turned on her heel. "Come into the kitchen and sit down. I need to talk to you. I'll even give you a cup of coffee."

"You're feeding me under your roof? Isn't that a medieval gesture of truce?"

"I'm not feeding you. I'm giving you a cup of coffee." She pulled out a chair at the kitchen table where she'd already set out cups and a carafe of coffee. "And the truce depends entirely on what you tell me."

"Then I'll start telling you about Phillip. I called the hospital and they have him comfortably settled in Bellehaven Nursing Home. I had Harley arrange for a guard to keep an eye on him."

She stiffened. "Wait a minute. You had no right to choose a nursing home without my input. Do you have any idea how many substandard nursing homes there are? A coma patient is totally helpless."

"I wouldn't put Phillip in a place where he'd not be well cared for. I checked it out. It's a fine place. Bellehaven has a special Coma Rehabilitation Unit in the annex run by Dr. Jason Gardner. It's small but high quality. They don't just let a patient lie there and vegetate. They try experimental medication, physical therapy, even study past psychological evaluations. I talked to Gardner and he's passionate about what he does. You should appreciate that."

"I do." Phillip needed all the passion they could give him in that dark world. "Has he evaluated Phillip yet?"

"No, he'll do that tomorrow. Right now there's no change in his condition. They're to contact both of us if there's any alteration, good or bad, tonight. Tomorrow you can talk directly to Gardner. He gave me his number and told me he's available to the families of his patients at any time."

"He sounds like a good doctor, a good man." She paused. "Thank you." It was clever of Grady to soften her attitude by appealing to her affection for the one person that they could discuss without conflict. "I just didn't think they were going to move him until tomorrow."

"I wanted him more comfortably settled."

"So that you could check him off your priority list?"

"No." He stared her in the eye. "So you could check him off yours. Yes, I wanted him to have the best possible care, but I also wanted your mind and focus clear. If that makes me a bastard, then so be it." He poured coffee into her cup. "But I don't believe my selfishness is that important to you at the moment or I wouldn't be here. Your move, Megan. Why did you want to talk to me?"

"Because you're the one with the answers." Her hands clenched around her cup. "I need to know more."

"More than what?"

She took a folded page of paper from her pocket and handed it to him. "When I was in the cave, these were the only conversations that I could distinguish out of that hideous cacophony. They were the strongest echoes."

"And?"

"I had to *know* that what you told me was true." She shook her head. "No, there's no way I can know, but I had to believe." She drew a deep breath. "That's why I spent the last sixteen hours at the computer searching through newspaper morgues trying to find some rock of reason to cling to."

"And did you find it?"

She didn't answer directly. "It wasn't easy. I had no date factor to enter into the equations. I had to go through every reference to the quarry since 1913, when the newspaper was established. I wasn't even sure what happened there would be mentioned. If there were crimes, they might not be known. If the emotional trauma was personal, there was no reason for it to be in the newspapers."

"No reason at all." His gaze narrowed on her face. "But you did find something. You're . . . pumped." He tapped the first name on the paper she had given him. "Hiram?"

"In 1922, Hiram Ludlow, a worker at the quarry, was tried for the murder of his wife, Joanna. He pushed her from the cliff only a few yards from the cave. Then he went after his brother, Caleb, and shot him. He died in prison in 1935."

Grady pointed at the second name on the paper, "Pearsall."

"In 1944, Kitty Brandell sued Donald Pearsall for child support for her illegitimate daughter. She worked in the Pearsall Carpet Factory near town and when Donald came back from serving in the Army in World War Two, he evidently swept her off her feet. They had several clandestine meetings in the cave that summer and her daughter, Gail, was conceived there. He denied being the father and she was fired from her job and practically run out of town. But she fought back, saved up money for a lawyer, and filed the suit when her daughter was seven years old."

"Did she win?"

"No. His family had the power and the money. She ended up with nothing but court costs and a bad reputation, which was pretty terrible in those days. I wanted to find what happened to her later, but I didn't have time to investigate anything that wasn't pertinent to what happened in that cave."

He glanced down at the third name. "What about baby John?"

She shook her head. "I couldn't find anything in the newspapers. Maybe nothing violent happened to him at the cave. Maybe his mother just ran up there like a wounded animal when her baby, John, died or was hurt. There's nothing more wrenching than a mother who's lost her child."

Grady put a question mark beside baby John. "Two out of three. Not bad."

"Not bad? It's terrible. It's all terrible." She held up her hand as he opened his lips to speak. "Yes, I know you were talking about my so-called success ratio. But I just can't separate the voices and what they went through to cause that agony. I can't stop my own pain. It's as if I absorb it and can't let it go. Did Phillip's wife ever succeed in doing that?"

He nodded. "But she never felt the intensity of emotion that you do. Nora was never able to separate the voices. They were just one tidal wave of sound to her, like the howling of the inmates in Bedlam. I think it's like that with most Listeners."

"Then how did I get so lucky?" she asked bitterly.

He looked down into his cup. "Your particular talent may have other facets." He changed the subject. "You didn't answer my question. You were looking for a rock to cling to, some proof that could convince you. Did you find it?"

"It could all be pure guesswork, coincidence."

He repeated. "Did you find it, Megan? Do you believe me? Do you believe in what you are?"

She didn't answer for a moment. She didn't want to say the words. To make that final admission would be to change everything; her past, her present, her future. She would never be able to look at herself in the same way again.

"Pretty scary? If it will help, you won't have to face it alone. I'll be here for you."

"I don't want your help." It wasn't the truth. She wanted

all the help she could get, but she couldn't take it. "I am what I am. I'm the one who has to handle any problems."

"And exactly what are you, Megan?" he asked softly. "Say it."

"I'm a fairly intelligent woman and a doctor."

"And?"

She hesitated and then haltingly said the words, "I'm a Listener, dammit."

He smiled. "At last."

"But I'm not Nora and I will *not* be dependent on you as she was."

"That thought did occur to me after I had to chase you down when you decided you had to face your demons instead of being traumatized as most people would have been. I don't believe 'dependent' could ever be included in your, character description."

She had stopped listening after that first sentence. "Demons," she repeated. "You said that before. But I can't think of the voices as demons if I have to live with them. They have to be people. Bad people, good people, selfish, generous, helpless, powerful, but human. Always human. If I have to deal with demons, then my life would truly be hell."

"My God."

"What?"

"You're already molding, defining, fashioning the situation to suit yourself."

"I'm trying to survive. I *will* survive."

"I'm sure you will." He took another drink of his coffee. "But you didn't invite me here to watch you struggle with your gift. You said you needed answers."

"I have an orderly mind. I had to take one problem at a time."

"You've obviously leapfrogged over the first one. Give me the questions."

Leapfrogged? She was still moving as sluggish as a turtle in accepting that damn Listener concept. Yet she had accepted it and now had to move on. "You said my mother was killed by a man named Molino. A revenge killing. Why?"

"He blamed her for killing his son, Steven. Molino is the slime of the earth, but he did love his son. He was proud of him and considered him a chip off the old block, and he was probably right. From what I could gather, the boy was a liar, a sadist, and a rapist. All qualities that Molino shared."

"And he thought my mother killed his son?" She shook her head. "He was wrong."

"It depends on how you look at it."

"No, it doesn't. She was kind and gentle."

"Yes, but kind and gentle people do kill in self-defense."

"Why would she have to defend herself? Who the hell is Molino?"

"Scum. He dips his hands in quite a few cesspools. He's a drug dealer, owns a chain of whorehouses in Africa and South America, and he dabbles in child slavery."

"What?"

"He pays bandits to steal children from the villages in Africa and handles the kidnappings in the U.S. and Europe himself. He sells them to clients all over the world. It's a very lucrative trade. Many tribal men in Africa believe breaking a virgin will rid them of AIDS."

She couldn't believe that horror. "No," she whispered.

"I wouldn't have given you ugly details but you had to realize just what a son of a bitch Molino really is." He paused. "And why your mother would have left you when she was approached to help stop him."

"And who approached her?"

"The CIA. They were getting flak from the government about the drugs that Molino was using to pay off the bandits flooding the market." He shrugged. "Not that it was more than a drop in the bucket. Molino's network was so extensive that they didn't think they could stop him, but they decided to make the attempt."

"Why involve my mother?"

"They had to locate him and then scoop him up when he was in a position where they could gather evidence with him. At that time he was moving around Africa with the speed of light and the usual informants weren't proving effective. So they borrowed me from my unit and set me loose on trying to track him." He shook his head. "But it wasn't my area of expertise. I can control, not locate. I called Michael Travis, head of a Psychic Investigation Group in Virginia, and asked him to send someone who could do the job. He gave me the name of a woman whom he'd run across about three years before. She had come to him because her daughter was exhibiting signs of being a Listener. She wanted to know how to block the echoes. She could block her own but she needed help in stopping the child's. She'd been able to do it when the voices had started when the little girl was seven, but after puberty the problem became too hard for her to handle alone."

"Me?" she whispered.

He nodded. "Michael Travis helped her as much as he could, but he said she was already stronger than he was. He tested her extensively and found out that she was amazingly multitalented. She was not only a Listener, she was also a Finder. Give her a glove, a scarf, a half-smoked cigarette and she could not only sense the person within a mile's distance but distinguish him in a crowd. He thought she'd be just what we needed if we could get her to cooperate. She didn't want to be involved with anything to do with psychic phenomena. She just wanted the tools to survive it and build a normal life for the two of you. Michael was very disappointed because he kept seeing hints of possible talents he'd rarely run across and wanted to do still more tests. She told him thank you, but no thanks."

"She walked out on him?"

"He never saw her again. But he kept tabs on her because he felt it would have been irresponsible for him to ignore that potential."

"That sounds so . . . clinical." She shivered. "She wasn't 'potential,' she was my mother. She had a right to ignore your damn potential and live a normal life. You should have left her alone."

"We didn't force her. We told her the situation and left it up to her." His lips twisted. "I'm not saying that the CIA didn't persuade her with a few photos of the children that they'd managed to free from their owners. Two of them were already AIDS victims."

"Dear God."

"It was enough to make her agree to one job and one job only. She had to make arrangements for your care while she was gone and sent you to summer camp for six weeks. You were thirteen then. Do you remember?"

"Of course, I do. I didn't want to go to the blasted camp. I wanted to stay with her. She said I needed to be around people my own age." But she had never dreamed what her mother had been planning. Her mother was always urging her to be more outgoing, and sending her to camp had seemed perfectly natural. "Where did she go?"

"Central Africa. Molino was to rendezvous with one of his bandit cohorts, Kofi Badu, for a payoff. That's where I met her. We became . . . close."

"How close?" She paused. "Lovers?"

"No. She was scared and I tried to help her. I was used to being a freak in everyone's eyes, but it was the first time she was exposed to it. She'd always hidden her gift." He met her gaze. "Is that what you thought when I showed up at the beach that summer when you were fifteen? That we were lovers?"

"Not at first. Yet sometimes you seemed to read each other's thoughts." And she had been jealous, she remembered suddenly. Her mother had been right. Megan had had a king-sized crush on Grady. From the moment she'd seen him, he'd caught and held her. He'd been her friend and teacher, yet she couldn't deny that he'd drawn her sexually. There had been moments when she'd only had to look at him to have her heart start pounding crazily.

For God's sake, she'd been only fifteen. It was an entirely natural response for a young girl when brought into contact with a man as physically attractive as Neal Grady.

"I assure you that if we read each other's thoughts it wasn't psychic-related," Grady said. "We lived in each other's pockets when we were in the jungle and that's bound to draw anyone close."

"And did my mother find Molino?"

"Yes." His lips twisted. "We furnished her with a red shirt Molino had left at one of his whorehouses in Madagascar and it was enough for her. We flew into the jungle where we thought the bandit, Kofi Badu, had a hideout, and spent three days there. She located Molino and went with the team to keep them on target."

"And that's where she killed Molino's son?"

"No, that was later. The raid proved a bust. They were waiting for us. We lost seven men . . . and your mother was captured."

She went rigid. "What?"

"We got her back two days later. But by that time the damage was done. She'd already killed Molino's son, Steven."

"I don't care about his son," she said fiercely. "What about my mother? Did they hurt her?"

"Yes. But she survived it and came out on top."

"What did they do to her?"

"Are you sure you want to know?"

"Hell, yes."

"Molino's son raped her."

She felt sick. "Then I'm glad he's dead." Dear God, what her mother had gone through. "She never let me know. She didn't let it change her. When she came home, she was the same as the day she left."

"I told you, she came out on top. Sarah was strong enough not to let that filth make her any less than she was." He paused. "But when she came back home we decided to take precautions and have her disappear for a while. That's why we whisked the two of you away from Richmond the minute she came back."

"She said she had a better job."

"We wanted to give her new credit cards and documents in a new name, but she said that it wasn't necessary since Molino was on the run from the CIA. She said Molino might be caught any day. Sometimes Sarah believed what she wanted to believe. She didn't want you to know anything about him or the talent she'd been trying to hide from you all your life. I tried to talk her out of it."

"Why?"

"Molino is relentless. He digs until he reaches pay dirt. He went underground for a long time and Sarah was feeling safer and safer every week. All the time he was working, searching, bribing everyone to find out everything he could about her and where we'd found her. After her death we discovered that the day before, Molino's men had raided Michael Travis's library at the think tank and stolen all the records pertaining to her." He shook his head. "Dammit, I knew he'd find her. He was raised to believe in the vendetta and he wouldn't quit until he'd killed Sarah and her entire family. As the years passed, Sarah was getting more confident and I was getting more uneasy. That was why I rented that cottage and stayed close to you both all that summer."

"Not that last day."

"No, Sarah wouldn't let me come. She was beginning to be impatient with having me near all the time. She wanted to forget what happened with Molino and I wouldn't let her."

"So she died."

"Yes."

"Shit." Tears were streaming down her cheeks. "Because of me. Right? She wanted everything to be safe and normal for me and they found both of us."

"It was her choice, Megan. None of this was your fault. You were the one person she loved in the world and she didn't want you to feel hounded because she'd decided to go after Molino."

"But she didn't stop him, did she? He's still out there selling drugs and children. He killed my mother and all she tried to do was for nothing. How can that be?"

"He's clever. He's rich. He has contacts in the governments of several countries. Corruption. Bribery. Fear." He shrugged. "His main headquarters is in Madagascar and it's as secure as a fort. And when he moves around to other locations he has the money to stay virtually invisible. The CIA has been trying to get their hands on him for years and they can never find the bastard. I almost had him twice but he slipped away."

"Had him?"

"Sarah was my friend. You don't think I'd let him kill her and live?"

"I don't know what to think about you, Grady."

"You knew what to think about me at one time."

Summer Sun. Gentle Surf. Grady smiling at her.

"You were pretending even then."

"Perhaps." He added wearily, "Perhaps not. Those were good days for me. I felt as if I had a family again. I had no business feeling like that. I was there to protect both of you and emotion always gets in the way. I should have ignored Sarah when she told me to stay away from both of you for a while. But I cared too much about what she thought and felt. I won't make that mistake again. Not with you, Megan. That's why I told Phillip to tell you that he was Sarah's half brother so that he could talk you into taking his name, changing your name from Nathan to Blair. I had to find a way to cover your tracks after Sarah's death."

"Phillip said that we should make a new start together and that would be part of it. We'd be a family again." She was shaking. She didn't want to believe Grady. She didn't want to feel this softening. "You don't have to worry about what I'm feeling. You have to worry about how to make sure I get my chance at Molino."

"To kill him?"

Kill. The word was ugly and foreign to her. She had spent years training to save lives and now she intended to kill.

He shook his head. "You see? It's not an easy choice for someone like you."

"He killed my mother. Phillip may never wake up again. The choice isn't that difficult. You can help me, can't you?"

"Yes, but there's always a price to pay. If you help me, I'll help you. I promise we'll get Molino."

A price. He'd mentioned before that he wanted her help. "What do you want me to do?"

"I'm searching for a certain object. I believe you can help me find it."

She frowned. "I'm not like my mother. I can't find people or things."

"Actually, Finding is fairly common. It often accompanies more significant gifts. You can never tell what talent is going to pop up." He shrugged. "But I'm not counting on you inheriting that particular one. All I need is a Listener. That will be harrowing enough."

She shivered as she remembered just how harrowing that episode in the cave had been. Now he wanted her to expose herself to that trauma again?

"And it will probably be worse than what you went through before." He was watching her expression. "Is it worth it to you?"

Dear God, of course it was worth it to her. She could bear anything if it meant that Molino would be destroyed. His grotesque presence was casting a shadow over her entire life. "I won't be your puppet. I won't do anything I regard as immoral."

"Then I'll have to make sure that I either keep your part of the project above reproach or lure you to the dark side." He continued briskly, "We'll have to leave here right away. Molino is having you watched and I want you off his scope so that we can move freely. I'm surprised he hasn't made another move since Phillip was shot. We're not going to give him another chance at you."

"Where are we going?"

"France. Do you speak French?"

"High school French. I've forgotten a lot. Will I need it?"

"I don't know."

"And I don't have a passport."

"No problem. I already have one for you."

She remembered what Phillip had said about Grady furnishing him with documents to prove he was her uncle. "How convenient. You must have been very sure of me."

"No, but I always like to be prepared. Like the Boy Scouts."

As he sat there, relaxed, dark, his posture gracefully indolent, she was reminded of the comment her mother had made about him looking like a Renaissance prince with all the lethal radiance of that age. "You're definitely no Boy Scout." She pushed back her chair. "I'm going to go pack a bag and call the hospital and tell them I'm taking an extended leave. I'll be ready to leave in an hour."

He nodded. "I have a few arrangements to make too."

She headed for the door. "Not entirely prepared then." She stopped at the door to look back at him. "Have you told me the truth, Grady?"

"Absolutely."

Her gaze searched his face. "But you haven't told me everything, have you?"

He was silent a moment. "I should have realized you'd sense that. No, not everything."

"Why not?"

"It's not to my advantage. And ignorance won't put you in any more danger than you will be anyway."

He wasn't going to tell her any more. "I'm going to find out, Grady."

"I don't doubt it. But not now, and not from me."

"I could make it part of the deal."

"Go ahead, call my bluff." He said quietly but firmly, "Not now, Megan."

She hesitated. She had no desire to do battle with him

at the moment. She believed what he had told her was the truth. The rest could wait until she was more in control of herself and the situation. "I *will* find out, Grady. You'd better be prepared for that, Boy Scout." She strode down the hall and slammed her bedroom door behind her.

SEVEN

SHE PROBABLY WOULD FIND out everything more quickly than was comfortable for him, Grady thought with amusement, as he watched the door close behind Megan. He was just lucky that she had too much on her plate to concentrate on anything but Molino. It was going to be an interesting dance trying to keep her spinning fast enough so that she wouldn't have time to stop and think. He wasn't sure how much she had sensed in that cave as her mother had died and how much she had been able to understand through the haze of pain. It was incredible that she was willing to undergo that kind of pain again.

No, not incredible. He had been counting on that strength and determination when he had decided he had to have her help. No one knew Megan the way he knew her. From the moment he had met her at Sarah's beach cottage he had felt a bond that had developed and strengthened over that summer. He had tried to keep that bond safe and fraternal but he'd never been able to feel like a brother to Megan. She had always been mature for her age and so damn alive and glowing that it was hard as hell not to reach out and touch her. He remembered one morning he had been watching her lift her face to the sun, her throat arching as if the breeze was caressing it. Lord, she had a beautiful throat and shoulders. He was young but no inexperienced boy, and he was so hot for her he'd nearly had a meltdown. He'd had to turn on his heel and walk away from her.

How many times had he had to walk away from Megan that summer? It had been a sensual, tender, bittersweet experience being with Megan those months. And after the link, in a weird way, he had felt as if she had become part of him.

Yeah, sure. If she was part of him, then he must be a masochist to plan on putting her through what was waiting for her in Paris. He was just along for the ride. She was the one who was going to suffer.

Then accept it and get the show on the road. He reached for his telephone and quickly punched in the number he had for Venable with the CIA.

"I may need some help," he said as soon as Venable picked up. "Megan Blair is being targeted by Molino and I don't know what's going to be coming down. I want you to be ready."

"In Atlanta?"

"Not right now. Probably Paris. We're going after the Ledger."

"Shit. Can't you keep her out of it?"

"No, I need the Ledger. Guilt feelings, Venable?"

"Hell, yes. I've always wondered if I could have prevented that nightmare with Sarah at that camp in the jungle. Maybe I could have done something different. I was so damn young and eager and I went by the book."

"We were both young and I've had a few second thoughts myself over the years."

"But not enough not to use her daughter."

"You've been after Molino for as long as I have. We have a chance to get him and the Ledger. I need Megan to do it." He paused. "I didn't call you to discuss this, Venable. Will you help me when I need it?"

"Dammit, of course, I will." He hung up.

It was strange that it was Grady who'd had to be the one to take the hard line about Megan Blair, instead of Venable, who'd had years of working with the CIA. No, not really. That episode with Sarah had affected all of them. Venable was a fine agent and there was probably nothing that he could have done differently on the night of the raid. Grady had thought he'd done his best and yet it hadn't been good enough either.

But it mustn't happen this time. No mistakes, dammit.

He quickly dialed another number.

MEGAN STOPPED IN SURPRISE in the kitchen doorway. "What on earth are you doing here, Harley?"

"Waiting for you." Jed Harley grinned as he rose to his feet. "And catching my breath. Grady didn't give me much time to get over here." His glance went to the small suitcase she was carrying. "You're traveling light."

"My computer is in the suitcase and my medical bag is in the hall. I don't intend to make this an extended trip. Where's Grady?"

"He went ahead to prepare the way. He asked me to make sure you got safely to Paris." He gave a half bow. "I'm to deliver you physically intact and emotionally serene. What do you think my chances are?"

"How do I know? Probably not very good. Maybe fifty-fifty. Serene isn't how anyone can describe my mood these days."

"Then I'll have to rely on keeping you alive." He took her suitcase. "Let's go. I don't think you're too pleased about me substituting for Grady and being on the move may keep you from venting. I have very tender feelings."

He was right. She had felt disappointed when she had come into the room and seen Harley sitting in the chair Grady had occupied. She supposed she should have been relieved. The time she had spent with Harley in the waiting room had been comforting. She had found him very sympathetic in his slightly off-kilter way. On the other hand, there was nothing comforting about Grady. She was wary all the time she was with him. She was always on edge and walking a fine line between suspicion and tentative trust. Lord, it had better be tentative. He had already admitted that he had not told her the entire truth. Yet the disappointment still existed. Perhaps it was because every moment with Grady was a challenge, the challenge he issued and the challenge his presence made her confront in herself.

Harley sighed. "You're not rushing to pat my head and swamp me with sympathy. Usually that tender-feelings line gets a more enthusiastic response."

"Bull." She smiled. "You don't need anyone to pat your head. You wouldn't know what to do with that kind of hogwash."

"I could learn. You're not buying it? I guess I'll have to try another tack. Let me think about it." He took her arm. "On the way to Stockholm."

"Stockholm? I thought we were going to Paris."

"We are. By way of Stockholm. Grady needs a little time to pave the way."

"And you don't want Molino to know where we're going if he's following us?"

"Oh, he's following us. But he won't be for long. Once we're in Stockholm, we'll vanish in the mist. Come on, we'll miss our British Air flight if we don't step on it." He smiled as he took her elbow. "I promise I'll make the flight interesting for you. I didn't get the chance to display my wit in that waiting room. I was too busy being kindly and consoling."

"You did a good job." And he was doing a good job right now. She realized she hadn't been nearly as nervous and apprehensive since he had appeared. Harley was not only distracting her, but his gentle touch nudging her toward the door was giving her the same sense of comfort and ease as it had in that hospital waiting room. "But you should stick to what you're good at. Admiring someone's wit is too exhausting for me at the moment."

"What a relief. The pressure is off."

And the pressure was off her too, she realized. She had a long flight to think about all the elements that had turned her life upside down.

And many, many hours to prepare herself for the next encounter with Grady.

Was that Grady's purpose in arranging for Harley to take her to Paris? Possibly.

"Let's go." She went ahead of Harley through the door. "The sooner we start, the sooner we get this over."

"SHE'S ON A FLIGHT TO STOCKHOLM," Peter Sienna said as he turned to Molino. "Darnell said the plane took off forty minutes ago."

"Was she with Grady?"

"No, Grady left her house almost two hours before she headed for the airport. Darnell thought you'd prefer that he stay and watch the Blair woman. She boarded the flight with Jed Harley, the man who was with her at the hospital."

Molino muttered a curse. "Which is the same as her being with Grady. Harley has been working for him for the past four years. Who do we have in Stockholm?"

"No one. But Max Wieder is in Berlin. Should I call him and tell him to go to Stockholm?"

Molino nodded. "I want him at the airport when that flight arrives. They may board another flight from there and I want to know where they're heading." He grimaced. "Besides directly toward Grady. This has to be his work."

"He's trying to protect her?"

"Maybe. But he wouldn't have to send her out of the country to do that. I'd bet he has her working on the Ledger."

"Working?"

"If she's a freak like her mother, she may be able to help him find it."

"Oh, I see."

Sienna's expression was bland but Molino could sense his skepticism and even perhaps a touch of scorn. He knew Sienna didn't believe in all this psychic mumbo jumbo. He wished to hell he didn't. Even when Steven had died, Sienna had thought it had been caused by normal means. What did he know? He had been in Miami when Steven had been killed. But Molino had known it was that bitch. He had watched it happen.

The remembered pain washed over him again. Bitch. Bitch. Bitch. He had seen to it that she rotted in hell, but her daughter was still alive. And so were all the other ugly freaks who were like her.

But not for long.

He would ignore Sienna's scarcely hidden contempt as he had all these years. He could resent but not blame him for not believing that Steven had been a victim of that witch. Sometimes when Molino woke in the middle of the night he didn't believe it either.

But it was true until he could make it a lie. Until he could wipe out those freaks.

Until he could destroy Megan Blair and find the Ledger.

"WE'RE BEING FOLLOWED." Harley's gaze was fastened on the rearview mirror of the rental car they'd picked up at the Stockholm airport. "Black Volvo. One man, I think. That probably means surveillance, not murder."

"How comforting," Megan murmured. "May I point out that there was just one man in the car that ran me off the highway?"

"Yes, but I wasn't with you." He grinned. "My reputation would be much more intimidating. I'd strike terror in their hearts."

"I don't find you intimidating."

"Because I've made an effort to tone down my aggressive nature for you." He glanced again at the rearview mirror. "I'm going to have to lose him. I don't want him on our tail when we reach the dock."

"Dock?"

"We're taking a speedboat to a private airport up the coast. We'll be flying to Paris from there." He pressed his foot on the accelerator. "Hold on. Here we go."

Hold on was right, she thought as Harley made an abrupt right down a narrow street and then screeched a left down the second boulevard.

"He's still with us," Harley murmured. "He's pretty good. It's going to take a little skill. What a pleasure . . ."

Pleasure? The next fifteen minutes were like riding a roller coaster, Megan thought desperately. By the time Harley was satisfied that they had lost the Volvo and they had arrived at the dock, Megan was dizzy and completely disoriented.

"Don't they have traffic police in Stockholm?" she asked as she got out of the car. "I'm surprised we didn't get stopped."

"Actually, Stockholm is very law-abiding and the traffic control is very strict here. Which is why we should jump in that speedboat and get out of town. I'm sure we've been reported a dozen times." He helped her into the boat. "I don't think Grady would like us to be detained."

"You should have thought of that before you started driving as if you were at the Indianapolis speedway."

"No, those drivers are skilled, but they have no spontaneity. I'm much better at street driving than they are. Did I mention I was once a stunt driver in Hollywood?"

"No, you didn't. You said you were once an EMT driver. What else?"

"Oh, all kinds of things," he said vaguely as he started the boat. "I like change." He shot her a glance. "And I'm not like Grady or you, who are shackled by that psychic stuff. I do what I like and let other people tote the heavy burdens."

"How nice for you. But I have no intention of being shackled by anything but my own will. I chose medicine and that's what I intend to do."

"Good for you." He gunned the boat. "Then I only have to feel sorry for Grady."

GRADY WAS WAITING FOR THEM when their chartered flight landed at a small airport in Chantilly, a short distance outside Paris.

Megan felt the familiar tension tighten her muscles as she watched him cross the tarmac toward their plane. The wind was blowing his jeans and navy blue sweater against his lean body and there was something . . . different about him. Before he had given the impression of contained power, but now his stride was purposeful and charged with energy. The power was present but it was no longer contained. It was channeled, flowing, ready to ignite. She instinctively braced herself as if to combat that energy.

"It's okay," Harley murmured, studying her expression. "You can handle him."

Of course, she could. And that change in Grady's demeanor could be her imagination. She nodded, rose to her feet, and headed for the exit. "No doubt about it. He just looks primed."

"He's in action mode. He usually does." Harley followed her down the aisle. "But maybe not this much . . ."

"Any problems?" Grady asked Harley as he helped Megan from the plane.

"A tail in Stockholm. I got rid of him."

"By driving like someone from an old Steve McQueen movie," Megan said dryly.

"I'm better than that," Harley protested. "That stunt driver would never have managed to shake that tail. He was pretty good." He glanced at Grady. "What next?"

"I've made reservations at an inn nearby. I've arranged for one of the cottages on the grounds. We'll stay there while you go check everything out."

Harley nodded. "I'm on my way. I'll rent a car and start tonight." He headed for the tiny terminal at the end of the runway. "Get her something to eat. She wouldn't have anything but peanuts on that flight from Atlanta." He grinned back over his shoulder at Megan. "I wouldn't want anyone to think I hadn't delivered you in tip-top shape. I take pride in my work."

"Whatever it is?" She made a face. "Now you're acting like a mother hen. I don't believe that was one of your previous occupations."

"God, no. Now that's scary. Much too much responsibility."

She found herself smiling as she watched him disappear into the terminal. Harley was odd and quirky and not like anyone she had ever met but she felt more at ease with him than she did with people she had known for years.

"You like him." Grady's gaze was fastened on her face. "It doesn't surprise me. Most people gravitate toward Harley."

"Gravitate? That's a strange word to use."

He shrugged. "It fits. He draws people to him like a sun does a planet."

"I think he'd laugh at that simile." She smiled. "Or maybe not. He'd probably be flattered and take it as his due."

"You did manage to get to know Harley well on the way here." He took her elbow and nudged her toward the waiting car. "I believe I'm a little jealous."

She shot him a skeptical glance. "And I believe you're lying to me. Why?"

"Because I'm detecting a hint of intimacy. For the past twelve years I've been the one living intimately with you." He stared directly into her eyes. "I don't like anyone else coming that close."

She felt a surge of heat move through her. His words had come out of nowhere, surprising her. So had her response to those words. "You may have been living intimately with me but it was completely one-sided. And do you think I haven't had genuine intimate relations with other men during those years?"

"Oh, yes. One of them was a lukewarm affair during your sophomore year in college. It didn't bother me at all.

The other was with that young Latin boy. What was his name? Julio something." His lips thinned. "Now your going to bed with him bothered the hell out of me. You were feeling too much. It was a cross between screwing you myself and erotic voyeurism. It was disturbing as the devil. After that I had to find a way to close myself off from you during intimate moments."

Her cheeks were stinging as the color flooded them. "Are you trying to embarrass me? Stop talking like this. You're almost a stranger to me."

"Almost." He opened the door of the car for her. "But that's the key word. You knew me very well that summer on the beach."

"I thought I did." She got into the car. "What are you doing, Grady? What are you up to?"

"My, how suspicious you are. You said you wanted me to be honest and aboveboard with you. I'm merely obliging."

And exerting that charisma and sexuality that had drawn her to him all those years ago. "Why now?"

"Because we're going to be very close in the next few weeks. I want to get everything out in the open so that you can focus. I don't intend for anything to get in the way. There's only one element that could cause immediate trouble." He got in the car and started the engine. "And there can't be any distracting subtle undercurrents. Sometimes they can be worse than—" He broke off as he backed out of the parking space. "You don't want to hear this, so I'll cut it short. I want to go to bed with you. I'd like to do everything that Medera kid did to you and more. From the moment I caught sight of you at the zoo, I wanted it to happen. Hell, maybe before."

She couldn't speak for a moment. "You're right," she finally said unsteadily. "I don't want to hear this."

"I'm almost through. If you see me looking at you as if I want to jump you, it's because I do. You're not going to have to wonder or worry about what I want or what move I'll make if you give me a chance. That part of me is purely basic and entirely selfish." He drove out of the parking lot into the street. "On the other hand, your primary value to me isn't between your legs. I'm not going to jeopardize having your help just to drag you into bed."

She tried to keep her voice level. "Are you done?"

"Yes. Is that aboveboard enough for you?"

If you could call being in the middle of a red-hot oven aboveboard, she thought. The rawness of his words could have offended her. Instead, they had aroused her. She was tingling, short of breath, and her body was readying. Memories of the Grady she had known that summer and this other Grady, darker, more dangerous, more experienced, seemed to blend and become one.

"Frank enough." His dark eyes were glittering in his lean face, holding her own. Her mother had compared him to a Renaissance prince and she could see it at this moment. The sensual curve of his lips, the hollowed cheeks, the expression that was as knowing as it was passionately intense. She quickly looked away from him. "It doesn't bother me that you want to go to bed with me as long as you don't try to rape me. If you did, I'd knock your socks off. Now may we talk about something else?"

"By all means." He made a face as he glanced down at his lower body. "This conversation is making me very uncomfortable. But I thought it necessary to clear the air before we moved forward. You're too sensitive not to have become aware of what I was feeling."

Clear the air? The air between them was so charged with electricity that she could scarcely breathe. "For God's sake, can we stop talking about how horny you are and get down to why I'm here? I believe that's a little more important."

He stared at her in surprise and then threw back his head and laughed. "Sorry." His eyes were twinkling. "The state of our horniness is of utmost importance to men. It tends to dominate our world." He turned onto the highway. "I'll try not to bore you with the subject from now on. There's a restaurant up ahead. Suppose we stop and get dinner? Harley was very concerned about your lack of food intake. I'm sure he'll ask me about it when he reports in."

He had changed, turned down that sexuality as if it were a lamp that had burned too bright. It was still there, but she could ignore it now. "I could eat something. I was a little edgy flying to Stockholm."

"I know." He pulled off the road and parked in front of Le Petit Chat, a long, low-timbered building with diamond-shaped, beveled glass windows. "That's why I sent you with Harley instead of forcing you to cope with me."

"I guessed that was your reasoning." She suddenly turned to him. "It was reasoning, wasn't it? Just how much is normal and how much isn't?"

"Can I read your mind? No. Am I extraordinarily sensitive to what you're feeling? Absolutely. You've instinctively learned to block me from controlling you, but that sensitivity remains." He got out of the car and came around to open the passenger door for her. "But even if the link wasn't there, I would have known that you needed an escape from me. It's just good sense."

"You're telling me the truth?"

"I'm telling you the truth. I might omit telling you something, but it would be stupid of me to lie to you." He smiled. "Because you're extraordinarily sensitive to me too. It works both ways."

"Because of the link? I don't need you any longer to block the voices. Can't you just break the link?"

"I don't know. I don't know how it works. I've never linked with anyone before. That's why I didn't want to do it that night in the cave. I didn't have any choice." He helped her out of the car. "So we may be stuck with each other."

"I won't accept that."

"Why not? You weren't even aware of me for the past twelve years."

But she was acutely aware of him now. She couldn't separate the mental and physical, past and present, but there was definitely a disturbing bond. "I don't like Peeping Toms. Even if you can't read my mind, I don't appreciate having anyone able to tell what I'm feeling. My emotions are just as private as my thoughts, dammit."

"I'll try to keep that in mind." He opened the door of the restaurant. "In the meantime, you can practice your French by reading a menu and listening to the waiter extol the catch of the day."

THE CATCH OF THE DAY WAS salmon and it was prepared with typical Gallic excellence.

"Dessert?" Grady asked as she finished the last bite and leaned back in her chair. "I'm sure Harley would endorse it." He grinned. "Though you probably don't need it. You ate like a truck driver."

"It was good. And I was hungry." She shook her head. "But no dessert. Coffee, maybe."

He motioned for the waiter. "Café, s'il vous plaît."

"And I did manage to understand the waiter," Megan said as the server hurried away. "But why should I have to understand French? You're very fluent. You rattled off our dinner order as if you were Gallic born and bred."

"Because I don't know exactly how being a Listener works."

"What?" Her brows lifted. "There's something you don't know about all this psychic business?"

"Don't be sarcastic. Listeners are very rare. Even Michael Travis's group doesn't know much about them." He added, "And there's a hell of a lot I don't know about a hell of a lot of things."

"For instance?"

"If the voices are issuing from a French or German or Italian, will the echoes the Listener hears be in that language? Or are the echoes an emotional transmittal that are translated in the language and understanding of the Listener?"

"Oh, for heaven's sake." She frowned. "Am I to understand I'm supposed to not only listen to these damn voices but have to translate them?"

"We'll only know that when you try to access them." He was silent while the waiter poured their coffee and then discreetly vanished. "Regardless, you'll have to try."

"I don't *have* to do anything. It's my choice." She lifted her cup to her lips. "We made a deal. If this will help me get Molino, I'll try to do it."

"It will help you get Molino."

"Who am I supposed to hear?"

"Edmund Gillem."

She moistened her lips. "Is he . . . dead?"

"Yes, he was supposed to have killed himself six weeks ago."

"Supposed?"

"He's dead. He probably did commit suicide. But I need to know the circumstances."

"Why?"

"I'm searching for a Ledger. I believe he knew where it was."

"And you think I'll be able to find out?"

"There's a strong possibility." He paused. "Or I wouldn't make you go through this. It's going to be ugly."

"You're warning me."

"Yes. Just because I want you to do this is no sign I want you to go in blind. Be prepared, Megan."

She gazed down into the coffee in her cup. "That Ledger must be very important to you."

"It's important to quite a few people. Do you want me to tell you about it?"

She thought about it. Then she shook her head emphatically. "I don't want to know anything about it. I don't want to be involved in what you're doing. I want to find out what you want me to find out and then go after Molino."

"Ah, I see. You want to stand apart until you can go in for the kill?"

She flinched. "If that's the way you want to put it."

"It's the way it is." He shrugged. "And I can't blame you. You're still teetering on the bank of the quicksand and trying not to fall. It's perfectly natural to try to protect yourself as much as possible." He gestured to the waiter. "Are you ready to leave? The inn is about twenty miles from here and it seems pretty comfortable. At any rate, we'll only be there for one night. Providing Harley does his job and we get you in safely."

"Why shouldn't it be safe?"

"I just like to be certain. There's a possibility Molino might have staked the place out or hired someone to watch or report."

"I can't believe he's expecting a Listener. That's too weird."

"No, he was expecting me. But I managed to slip in and out in Rome without him knowing I was on the grounds."

"What grounds? Where are we going?"

He threw down cash on the waiter's tray and rose to his feet. "The circus."

EIGHT

"WHAT DO YOU MEAN, CIRCUS?" Megan asked as soon as she got into the car.

"Exactly what I said. Edmund Gillem died in his trailer at Carmegue Circus. He was outside Rome at the time. The circus travels all over Europe, and Chantilly is the second stop since Rome."

"And I'm supposed to go and sit in his trailer and wait and see what happens?"

"That's right."

"If he died in Rome, how do you know that the trailer is still with the circus?"

"It's owned by them. They only rent the trailers to the performers."

"Was Edmund Gillem a performer?"

"Yes."

Her lips twisted. "A fortune-teller?"

"No, he wouldn't take the chance of being that obvious. He was a horse trainer. He had a powerful empathy with animals and had six beautiful horses that did some pretty neat tricks. Nothing fancy. Nothing that would get him a contract in Las Vegas. But that's the way he liked it. He didn't want to attract too much attention and the job allowed him to constantly travel around the continent."

"He sounds like a gypsy."

"He enjoyed the vagabond factor but he regarded the travel as part of his job."

"Was he married?"

"Not at the time of his death. He was married several years ago to a German shopkeeper, but they were divorced after five years."

"You know a good deal about Gillem."

"I researched him extensively before I decided he was the man I was looking for and zeroed in on him. He was a good man. I think I would have liked him."

"He must have been unstable if he committed suicide."

"Maybe."

"You said that the voices were only centered and heard in places that had known extreme high stress or tragedy."

"As far as we know."

"Then you think that trailer was the site of one of those factors. Suicide is certainly a tragedy, but it doesn't have to always be high stress. Sometimes it's only sad and resigned."

"I don't believe Gillem's death was either quiet or resigned. He died violently. He cut his throat with a jagged piece of mirror."

Horror sleeted through her. "Why?"

"He left no note. You'll have to tell me."

"If I can." She shook her head. "I don't know anything about this. I don't know if I'm even capable of hearing anything but a meaningless jumble."

"You were able to distinguish conversation in that cave."

"But can I do it again?" And did she want to do it again? Of course, she didn't. She was already dreading going to that trailer. "You said yourself you didn't know what to expect from a Listener. And I have to be the most inexperienced Listener on the face of the planet."

"Are you backing out?"

Yes.

"No." She wouldn't run away at this first challenge. It wasn't only her deal with Grady, but the fact that if she didn't face the voices again, she would fear them all her life. "I won't back out." She looked out the window of the car. "But I want your promise."

"That I'll help you?"

"No, that you'll stay out of it. I want to be alone in that trailer. I don't know if you're able to make things easy for me. You said you weren't able to do it that night at the cave. If you can, I don't want that to happen."

"I couldn't do much unless you let me. You're too strong now." His hands tightened on the steering wheel. "Let me, Megan. Don't close me out again."

"I don't want you. I have to handle this by myself. I *won't* be a cripple. Promise me."

He was silent before he reluctantly nodded his head. "Okay, you have my word." He added bitterly, "Happy now?"

"No." She tried to steady her voice. "I'm scared. But it doesn't make any difference. It's the way it has to be."

"You mean it's the way you want it."

It wasn't the way she wanted it. She wanted to lean on his strength. She wanted to be cocooned and protected against sharp winds and the voices that never stopped. She repeated, "It's the way it has to be." She changed the subject. "Are we almost at the inn?"

"A few miles ahead. I booked a cottage with adjoining rooms. I want to keep an eye on you."

"Good idea. I've no objection to being kept safe. I have enough on my plate. As far as I'm concerned, that's your job."

"And I'll do it. I wish you'd—" His cell phone rang

and he glanced at the ID. "Harley." He picked up the call. "What's the word?" He listened for a moment and then looked at Megan. "He's scouted out the circus and he sees no sign of Molino or his men. We can't be absolutely sure and he's still checking. He can arrange for you to have the trailer either tomorrow night—" He paused. "Or tonight. Your choice."

She tensed. She hadn't expected to have to make that decision. She had thought she'd have time to mentally prepare herself.

"No pressure," Grady said quietly. "Tomorrow night is fine."

But that would mean she would have all those hours to dread and imagine what waited for her in that trailer. And how could she mentally prepare herself anyway? She didn't have any idea what was going to happen. "Tonight."

He hesitated and she thought he was going to argue with her. Then he said curtly into the phone, "Tonight." He hung up the phone. "It's only nine now. We'll have to wait until about three A.M. before we move. We'll go on to the inn and get settled."

"Fine." Don't shake. Don't let him see how frightened she was. "I'll take a shower and try to call Dr. Gardner and introduce myself and ask about Phillip. Then I'll e-mail my friend Scott and his wife, Jana, and tell them I'm fine and not to worry. I didn't get a chance before I left Atlanta. I'm going to ask Scott to keep tabs on three of my patients. I can trust him to make sure they'll be okay."

"And that's all you'll tell them."

"Of course, that's all. They wouldn't understand any of this. It would worry them. Hell, I don't understand."

But what she did understand was that in only a few hours she was going to be on her way to Carmegue Circus and that the fear was growing by the moment.

• • •

MEGAN FOUND DR. JASON GARDNER as warm and direct as Grady had said.

"I've read your uncle's report and I can't promise you anything but that I'll do my best to bring him back," he said gently. "I'll never lie to you, Dr. Blair. You've been told how serious his condition is and many people have a tendency to regard coma patients with very little hope."

"Of course, they do. Most patients remain in a deep coma no more than four weeks. After that they either die or they go into a vegetative state. Now what can we do to keep both those results at bay?"

"I believe your Mr. Grady has told you the procedures I use to treat my patients."

"Do they work?"

"Not as often as I'd like. I wish I could bring them all back," he said wearily. "It's a constant fight to keep the nursing home from shutting my annex down because the results don't warrant the cash outlay. I can't make them see that saving just one human being is worth all their fund-raisers. But I always have hope. And I work my butt off trying everything I can to bring them back. You can be sure that Phillip Blair will be given every chance, every effort by me and my staff."

"How can I help? Should I be there?"

"Not until the coma shows some sign of lessening." He paused. "Some of the patients respond. Some don't. And in the end, I don't know if my successes are due to what I'm doing or what God decides to do. How is that for a scientific approach?"

"It's an honest approach. May I call you tomorrow?"

"Anytime."

She felt a mixture of emotions as she hung up the phone. Gardner had not been optimistic but she hadn't expected optimism. But it was good to know that Phillip was being taken care of by a man who believed that a coma could be broken. As Grady said, Gardner had passion and that kind of drive could move mountains . . . or perhaps pull Phillip from his darkness.

"Was that Gardner?" Grady was standing in the doorway of their adjoining rooms.

"Yes. Do you always listen at doors?"

"I was standing by to tell you to keep the call short. Any phone calls from now on should be limited to less than three minutes. Phones are wonderful technical gadgets but they can be traced."

"I'll remember." She looked at her watch. It was only a few minutes after midnight. Three hours before it would be time to leave for the circus. Great heavens, she was nervous. She wanted it over. She wanted to leave *now*.

"Do you want a cup of coffee?" Grady asked.

She shook her head.

"How about a walk?"

She frowned. "At midnight? What are you trying to do?"

"Waiting is always hard."

And, as usual, Grady could sense what she was feeling. "I'll be fine." She sat down at her computer. "I can keep myself busy."

She could feel Grady's gaze on her back and a moment later the door closed behind him.

Distraction was the name of the game. It's only three hours . . .

CARMEGUE CIRCUS.

The banner over the fairgrounds was a bit faded, but the red script was bold and joyous. The same shade of red in the stripes on the big top tent in the center of the fairgrounds.

It was after three in the morning and the fairways were deserted and the booths closed.

"Edmund Gillem's trailer is on the far side of the grounds," Grady murmured. "It's being used by one of the roustabouts, Pierre Jacminot, but Harley bribed him to go into town for the night. He should have left the door unlocked."

"I'm relieved we're not going to be arrested for breaking and entering." She followed him down the fairway. It was tense and a little eerie walking down this aisle that was usually crowded with busy, happy people and that was now dark and without life.

And the trailer where she was headed was also without life. It was the place where a man had killed himself in that terrible way.

"I wouldn't be that inefficient," Grady said. "You have enough to face without dealing with the local gendarmes."

"Maybe." She could see the small silver trailer gleaming in the distance. Her palms were cold and sweating. "What if Edmund doesn't come to the party?"

"Then you'll be relieved and I'll have to find another path to follow." His gaze was also fastened on the trailer. "You could put it off until tomorrow."

"I've always hated procrastinators. I won't be one, Grady." They had arrived at the door of the trailer. "Let's just get me in there."

"Right away." He opened the door and stepped aside. He handed her a small flashlight. "Don't turn on the lights. You're sure you don't want me with you?"

"At the moment I'd welcome anyone, even Dracula, with me in this trailer." She stepped up into the darkness of the trailer and was immediately assaulted with the smell of lemon polish and sweat. "I'm okay." She slammed the door behind her.

Darkness.

Isolation.

She couldn't get rid of the isolation, but she could do something about the darkness. She turned on the flashlight.

She was standing in a tiny room with a comfortable-looking Hide-A-Bed couch and a TV on a stand. An even tinier kitchenette led off the room. A black sweatshirt was tossed on the back of the couch.

Edmund's sweatshirt?

No, what was she thinking? It had to belong to the roustabout, Pierre . . . what's his name, who had taken over this trailer after Edmund's death. It just seemed that everything that concerned her was connected and focused on Edmund Gillem. She could *feel* him here.

Imagination.

Or not.

What did she do now? She didn't want to sit on that couch. She didn't want to touch anything that had belonged to Edmund. She sank down on the floor beside the door and played the beam of her flashlight around the room. A landscape print of a poppy field hung above the TV. The furniture was cheap and well used, but the carpet was gray and looked brand-new. She lifted the beam to the walls. They were wood-paneled and the surface also appeared old and discolored.

Except for a lighter, two-foot square beside the curtains. The square was an entirely different color from the rest of the walls. A photo or picture must have once occupied that spot.

Or a mirror.

He cut his throat with a jagged piece of mirror.

New carpet.

Because the bloodstains would not come out of the old one?

Lord, she felt sick.

Poor man.

He was a good man. I think I would have liked him.

Were you a good man, Edmund?

What made you take your life?

An overwhelming sadness enveloped her. Life was precious and Edmund's mental agony must have been exceptional to lead him to want to leave it.

Well, it was time to stop wondering and see if this so-called gift she possessed was only a fluke or if she could really find out the answers to those questions.

She drew a deep breath and turned off her flashlight. It was pitch-dark but in her mind's eye she could still see the bareness of the wall where the mirror had once hung.

Edmund . . .

She braced herself and slowly, tentatively, opened herself to the voices.

Nothing. No whisper. No roar. Nothing.

Relief poured through her. She had tried. She had done what she had promised. It wasn't her fault that she couldn't hear anything. Perhaps it was a fluke after all.

And then they came.

A scream of agony so intense that it hurt Megan to the bone.

"Tell us. Don't be a fool, Gillem. Where's the Ledger?"

"No," a broken gasp. *"I'll never tell you, Molino. You'd only kill me anyway."*

"Perhaps not. Try me."

"No."

"Sienna, continue to persuade him."

Another long drawn-out cry of pain.

"We know you don't have it here. Where have you hidden it?"

"I never . . . had the Ledger."

"But you know who does. Who has it now, Gillem?"

"I don't . . . know."

"Start on his testicles, Sienna."

Another shriek that made Megan press back against the wall as if the pain were being inflicted on her body, not Edmund's. *Make it stop, Edmund. Tell them. Don't let them hurt you anymore.*

"Why protect them, Gillem? They're only freaks. They wouldn't help you. Not those Finders or Listeners or Mind Readers. Probably most of them are phonies anyway."

"Then why do you want to find them?" Edmund gasped.

Molino didn't answer. *"Tell me about the Pandoras."*

"I don't know what you're talking about."

"Who are they? How many?"

"I don't know—"

"I'm getting impatient. The Ledger. Sienna, do it."

Edmund screamed again.

But he didn't tell them.

The pain went on, the screams echoed on and on.

"No," she whispered. She curled up in a ball on the floor. "They're hurting us, Edmund. It's not worth it. Tell them . . ." What could be so important that it would keep him silent while enduring punishment like this? But it had been important enough to him. He could barely mutter his refusals now, but he wouldn't give them what they wanted.

Brave, she thought dimly, and good. Good men should not be tormented like this.

God, she wanted to close them all out. She felt as if she were joined to Edmund and the pain was unbearable.

She couldn't do it. She wouldn't do it. She could feel his terrible loneliness. "It's okay, Edmund. I won't leave you alone." She reached jerkily up and locked the door before burying her head in the crook of her arm. "Play it out. You're not by yourself this time. I'll stay with you . . . until the end."

HE HAD TO GET IN THERE. To hell with his promise.

Grady's nails bit into his palms as his hands clenched. Pain was swirling around Megan with tornado force.

"What's happening?" Harley was coming toward him. "You look as if you're about to tear the trailer apart."

"If I can, I will. She locked the damn door."

"And you're not trusting her to come out on her own?"

"She's *hurting*. I'm going to go back to the car and get a crowbar."

"That would take time. Let me see what I can do." He bent to examine the lock. "Did I tell you I was once a locksmith?"

"No."

"Good, it would have been a lie. But during my misspent youth I did dabble in safecracking."

"Hurry," Grady said harshly.

Harley's smile faded. "A few more seconds."

The lock sprang open.

Grady jerked open the door and was into the trailer.

Megan was curled into a tight ball on the floor. She was unconscious.

Or dead?

No, she was opening her eyes. "I had to stay until it was done. It's . . . over now, isn't . . . it?"

"Yes."

"I'm . . . glad." Her eyes closed again. "He was hurting so . . ."

He didn't know if she was unconscious again but he wasn't going to wait to find out. He picked her up and carried her out of the trailer. "I'm taking her back to the inn, Harley. Close up the trailer and meet us there."

Harley nodded. "I'll be ten minutes behind you."

GRADY WAS SITTING BESIDE HER bed when Megan opened her eyes again.

"You . . . didn't tell me they tortured him," she whispered.

"I wasn't sure they did."

"But you suspected it."

"I thought there was a good possibility. Molino wants the Ledger."

"Yes, he does." She moistened her lips. "He did unspeakable things to Edmund. Molino and a man named Sienna."

"Sienna is Molino's second in command."

"I think Molino enjoyed it. It went on for a long time. He kept calling him a freak and telling him how he was going to hurt him next. He wanted him to be afraid, to anticipate." She shuddered. "He's a terrible man."

"You knew that before we went into this."

"I knew about him, but I didn't *know* him. Edmund and I were lost in that filth and we couldn't get away."

"Edmund and you?"

"That's what it seemed like. It was different than before. I wanted to leave him, but I couldn't do it. He was all alone when he died and I didn't want to desert him. I knew I couldn't do anything, but it didn't matter." She shook her head. "It's hard to explain."

"You shouldn't have locked the door."

"I didn't want you to interrupt us. I thought you might know we were hurting."

"It wasn't Gillem hurting, it was you, dammit."

"It was both of us." She raised her hand and rubbed her aching temple. "You were right, Edmund was a good man. He deserved better than to die like that. He should have lived a long, long life."

"What do you mean, it was both of you?"

"I found out some answers about Listeners you can pass on to your friend, Michael Travis. One, Edmund could have been speaking Zulu and I would still have understood him. It's emotional transmission. Two, they didn't even have to speak. I knew what they were feeling, thinking." She closed her eyes as the emotions of the night bombarded her again. "I particularly know what Edmund was going through. He didn't want to die."

He was silent a moment. "Dammit, I feel helpless. I want to help you. How can I do it? Does your head hurt? Would you like an aspirin? Hell, that sounds lame."

She opened her eyes. "I ache all over. I don't think an aspirin would help." She glanced at the strong morning sunlight streaming in the window. "What time is it?"

"Nearly eleven. You were out for almost seven hours. You scared the hell out of me."

"Good. You should get a little of your own back." She sat up in bed. "You're the one who sent me into that trailer. I was pretty scared myself." She swung her legs to the floor. "And now I'm going to shower and brush my teeth and dress. All the common routine things that make up our lives. I need to get away from Edmund and Molino and what happened in that trailer."

"May I ask one question?"

"No, you may not." She headed for the bathroom.

"We'll speak again later. Order us dinner in your room. I need to think and absorb before I talk to you again."

He asked the question anyway. "Were you with him at the end?"

She stopped but didn't turn around. "You mean that moment when he knew he wasn't going to be able to hold out any longer and had to make sure they didn't get the Ledger?"

"Yes."

"You're damn right I was there," she said unevenly. "They thought he was unconscious and left him alone in the room. The mirror was the only weapon he had. He used it." She shut the door behind her and leaned back on it as sadness surged through her. *Don't fall apart now*. She had gotten through the night and the memory would be with her always but she mustn't let it weaken her. Edmund had not been weak. He had suffered and died and never let that scumbag have what he wanted.

She straightened and moved toward the shower.

"We'll get through this, Edmund," she murmured. "Molino isn't going to hurt anyone else. I promise you that he's not going to win."

GRADY'S PHONE RANG A MOMENT after the bathroom door had shut behind Megan.

"Is she conscious yet?" Harley asked when he picked up.

"About fifteen minutes ago."

"Is she okay?"

"No, she's walking wounded. What do you expect? She went through hell tonight."

"Easy. Don't bark at me. Remember, I have no basis for expecting anything. On the surface all I or any normal Joe can tell is that she just spent an hour or so in the dark."

"Sorry."

"No problem. Is she going to be all right?"

"Maybe. She's . . . different."

"How?"

Grady wasn't sure. He hadn't known what to expect when Megan woke. He'd only prayed she wouldn't be permanently damaged. And she might in fact be damaged, but if so, he couldn't see in what manner. When she had gone into that trailer, he had sensed confusion and fear. When she woke, Megan had given off an aura of being deeper, stronger . . . formed.

And he had been aware of pure steel beneath that strength. "We'll have to see. I think she's working it out for herself right now. Have you located Molino's man at the circus grounds?"

"Woman," Harley corrected. "It's Marie Ledoute, a trapeze artist. She's a heavy gambler and she's recently been tossing around more money than she could have obtained from her salary. This morning she was very curious and asking questions of where Pierre, our roustabout, had been for the night."

"Did he tell her?"

"No, but he will and everything else she wants to know. She's in bed with him now."

"Keep an eye on her. She probably won't contact Molino until she leaves Pierre Jacminot. That will give us a little time."

"Right." Harley hung up.

Not much time, Grady thought. As soon as Molino knew where they were, he'd send someone on their trail. He should really bundle Megan up and whisk her away from here.

Not yet. He had a weird idea it would be like disturbing a butterfly when it was emerging from a cocoon. She appeared not to have been damaged last night and he wouldn't risk doing it now. She needed time and he would give it to her.

NINE

MEGAN OPENED THE ADJOINING door to Grady's knock at six fifteen that evening. He gave a mocking bow. "Dinner is served. I hope it's not too early for you. I want to be at the airport by eight tonight."

"Why? Is there a problem?"

"No, but you can never tell. It's better that we head out." He turned and preceded her to the white damask-covered table and held her chair for her. "You have more color. Did you get some rest?"

"A little." She sat down and spread her napkin on her lap. "But I didn't sleep."

"I didn't think you would." He sat down opposite her. "I ordered chicken and I found mushroom soup on the menu. You love it, don't you? I remember Sarah used to make it for you all the time."

"Yes, I do like it." Her brows lifted. "But it's such a little thing that I wouldn't have thought you'd remember it."

"Little likes and dislikes reveal character." He picked up his fork. "You love running in the surf, puppies, people who are honest and caring, and watching the sun come up. You hate food with mushy textures, ranting politicians, cruelty in any form, feeling helpless."

"Some of those things aren't so little."

"No. And they only give indications of the total Megan Blair. Try the salad. It's excellent."

She started to eat. "You remember all those things from that summer with Mama and me?"

"I always try to remember the good things. It always helps during the bad times. That was a very good summer for me." He smiled. "And you were a big part of what made it good. Sarah kept telling me how solemn you were but I never saw it. You were eager and funny and brimming with life. God, I'd never known anyone with that much energy and joie de vivre."

"And it didn't hurt your ego to know that I had a crush on you," she said calmly. "You did know that, didn't you? I was pretty transparent. Even Mama could see it."

"Oh, yes. I knew. I was . . . honored." He grimaced. "When I wasn't trying to fight off the dark side. I had to keep telling myself that you were no Lolita and I'd be sorry as hell if I seduced you." He shrugged. "Sometimes I even believed it. But if I'd stayed with you for a few more months, I would have been in trouble. I was only twenty-five myself, headstrong as the devil, and used to having my own way."

She could feel that now-familiar wave of heat moving over her as she looked at him. Everything tonight seemed clearer, simpler, every emotion keener and resounding to every word, every nuance. "I would have had something to say about being seduced. A crush doesn't necessarily guarantee that I'd jump into bed with you."

"It would have been a start." He got up and replaced her salad with the soup. "After that, I'd just have to work on giving you everything you want from me."

She raised her brows. "Like mushroom soup?"

"Ah, you've found me out." He leaned back in his chair. "I'm plying you with mushroom soup instead of champagne or strong drugs."

Mushroom soup, memories, and hints of sexuality that

were more potent than any drug. She took a taste of the soup. "It's good. You chose well." She looked up when she was half finished with the soup to find him studying her. "What?"

"I was just wondering why you told me you had a crush on me all those years ago. You've been hiding your head in the sand about what happened that summer since I came back into your life."

"That's not true."

"You're right, only the parts that concern me."

"Maybe I decided that I didn't like burying my head in the sand. There was no reason for it. Why should I be ashamed of how I felt then or now? As long as I act according to my own code, there's no reason to hide anything. Do you have a problem with that?"

"Oh, no problem at all. I admire clear thinking. I was just wondering why it was manifesting itself at this particular moment."

She didn't speak for a moment. "Perhaps because I've recently had a lesson about clarity and weighing what's important and not important." She stared down into her bowl. "Life is important, keeping faith is important, all the rest is pretty far down on the scale."

"According to Edmund Gillem."

"And according to Megan Blair." She raised her eyes. "He died to keep Molino from getting his hands on that Ledger. But he was protecting more than the Ledger, wasn't he? He was protecting lives. Molino called them freaks. That means they were like me . . . and you. Right?"

He nodded.

"I want to know about the Ledger. I want to know why he was willing to die for it."

"I told you that I'd tell you if you wanted to know. You

didn't want to become any more involved than you had to be."

Her lips twisted. "I couldn't be any more involved than I am right now. Tell me about the Ledger. What is it?"

"It's a sort of elaborate, detailed family tree."

"What family?"

"Don José Devanez was the patriarch but over the centuries the name has almost died out."

"Centuries?"

"The Ledger was started in 1485 at the time of the Spanish Inquisition. The Devanez family were landholders in southern Spain and they were very prosperous. They invested in overseas ventures and success followed success. It was rumored at the time that they'd gained their riches from using devilish powers to draw ducats to them. The family was very private and stayed in the country away from the cities and royal court. It was only when the Inquisition reached fever pitch that they felt in danger. The local priests had heard tales that members of the family practiced everything from shape changing to predicting the future. Some of the stories were pretty wild."

"And some of it was true?"

"There was no doubt the family had strong psychic abilities." He made a face. "And it didn't take a crystal ball for them to see the writing on the wall. Torture and death. The priests accepted hearsay about witchcraft and there was plenty of talk about the Devanez family in the area. Fray Tomás de Torquemada had recently become the Grand Inquisitor and the burnings were becoming almost commonplace. The family knew their only chance was to leave Spain and go where they couldn't be found. José Devanez prepared several havens for his family and gave the word to take off when he heard the priests were preparing their case against the family."

"Where?"

"England, Scotland, Ireland, Denmark, Germany. He scattered his family over most of the civilized countries of the world. He thought it safer for them. They were supposed to lose themselves in the culture of the country until they could go back home."

"The Ledger," she prompted.

"José knew that it was possible that the family members might lose touch with each other. He didn't want that to happen. He believed in the strength of unity. So he created a Ledger that listed names, addresses, relationships, even talents. It would have been disastrous for it to fall into the hands of the Inquisition, so he sent the Ledger out of the country in the hands of his brother, Miguel. Miguel was the only family member to know the exact locations of all the havens. His job was to maintain the Ledger and every five or six years, visit the different branches of family and get new information about births, deaths, et cetera. In that day and age anyone with a psychic gift was in constant danger of extermination. Most people think the Inquisition was short-lived, but it lasted over three hundred years in one form or another. If there were problems, he was to help the branch of the family in jeopardy to resettle in a safe area. He grew to look upon it as a sacred trust."

"Like Edmund."

"These days it's usually a volunteer who accepts the responsibility of maintaining the Ledger. The descendants are so widespread and so much time has passed that most of them don't know about each other or their history. The story has been passed down only through the core family descended from the first Miguel Devanez. Though from what I can gather that branch is large enough. Evidently it's a very fertile family."

"And how do you know all this? Are you one of the Devanez family?"

He shook his head. "I didn't know they existed before about fifteen years ago. Michael Travis has a library he's been gathering for years about everything to do with psychic phenomena. He came upon a document written by the priests who were given the task of investigating the Devanez family during the Inquisition. It was a report on the heathen activities of the family and mentioned the Ledger in some detail."

"How did they know about it?"

"Not all members of the family escaped Spain. Another of José's brothers, Ricardo, was captured at the border. He was tortured and eventually revealed everything he knew about the exodus, including the existence of the Ledger." He grimaced. "The holy priests were as good at torture as Molino. It was lucky that Ricardo wasn't in José's confidence regarding the location of the havens set up for the family. He knew about the Ledger but nothing else of value to the Tribunal. Of course, they didn't believe him and he died on the rack."

"What about José Devanez?"

"He stayed at the estate until the last family member was safely away."

"And then?"

"He heard the priests were on the way to arrest him. He killed himself before they could question him."

"Just as Edmund did . . ."

"José became a martyr in the eyes of the family. He'd saved them, given them new lives, and then protected them by taking his life. The job of being Keeper of the Ledger became not only an honor but the stuff of myths.

Galahad and Lancelot had nothing on them in the regard of the family. But myths tend to fade and become forgotten with the march of progress."

"Edmund didn't forget."

"No, he had a gentle soul and was full of ideals."

"How did Molino find out about the Ledger?"

"I told you that he raided Michael Travis's headquarters to try to find information about your mother." He paused. "He found her records in the same file with a transcript of the report from the Tribunal on the Devanez family."

She stiffened. "What?"

"Michael was fairly certain that Sarah was a descendent of the Devanez clan."

"Why?"

"She had certain potential talents that were . . . unusual. He'd only heard of them in connection with the Inquisition report. He'd already sent investigators to try to track down the core family and there were preliminary reports in the file."

"On Edmund?"

He shook his head. "It's taken me years to locate a logical candidate for a Keeper of the Ledger. I can't tell you how many false leads I've followed. The family protects itself. Finally, I got a break by following news reports of supposed psychic phenomena. If it hit the press, then there was a chance that it might be a family member who didn't know they were Devanez and just discovering their talent. And who would be there but a member of the core family to help and find a way to suppress the story or make it seem phony?"

"Edmund?"

"No. It was a different individual every time. But I watched and made notes and I gradually compiled a list of possible family members. Most of them appeared not to associate with each other but I found one man who was different. He seemed to know everyone and was constantly on the move."

"And that's how Molino found Edmund too?"

"I don't know. He might have started that way. But I suspect his men found one of the core family and made them talk." His lips twisted. "It was quicker. Molino located Edmund Gillem two days before I did." He muttered a curse. "I was just two damn days too late."

"Molino has to be crazy, you know. I've never seen anyone that vicious."

"Ugly. Very ugly. And obsessed with finding the Ledger. So far Peter Sienna has gone along with Molino, but I think it's because of the bank accounts."

"Bank accounts?"

"There are rumors that the Ledger also contains a list of numbers of Swiss and offshore bank accounts of the Devanez family. I told you that the Devanez family did very well with investments. Over the centuries you can imagine how much wealth they were able to accumulate. That amount of money is dangerous. It attracts attention and that's the last thing the family wanted. They siphoned it off and buried it in anonymous accounts in case it was needed."

"And anyone who has the Ledger would have access to those accounts," Megan said. "It would be like tapping a gold mine."

"And I'd bet Sienna would love to do that," Grady said grimly. "I've heard reports he's working toward snatching enough cash to set up his own network. He doesn't have a gang background like Molino and he's something of a snob. He thinks he's too smart to work for anyone but himself. But Molino doesn't give a damn about the accounts."

"You said he believes in vendettas?" She shook her head in disbelief. "He'd want to destroy any member of the family he can find listed in that Ledger?"

"He hated your mother. He hates you. Yes, and I think he'd kill anyone connected to you. He'd enjoy it. As I said, it's become an obsession with him. His son, Steven, was the only person he loved and Sarah took him away from him."

"He did enjoy hurting Edmund," she said in a low voice. "I couldn't understand it. That kind of emotion is . . . alien to me. It was so different than what Edmund was feeling. He was just trying to hold on and not betray his duty."

"Is that how he looked at the Ledger?"

"Yes, he kept thinking that he couldn't break. He had to protect them all." She could feel the tears sting her eyes. "He was like José. He gave his life for them."

"And you're hurting like hell because he did," he said roughly. "For God's sake, you didn't even know him."

"I knew him. After last night there's no one I know better." Her throat was dry, parched. She reached for her water goblet. "And he knew me. At least, he knew of me. Toward the end he was talking to Molino about me, trying to convince him I was no threat to him. I didn't understand what he was talking about. I didn't know why he would think Edmund knew anything about me."

"The Ledger. He probably thought information about you would be in the Ledger."

"I don't know. By that time he was practically incoherent. But I believe he was trying to protect me." Her hand was shaking and she had to put the goblet back down on the table. "I was a stranger to him, but he was still trying to keep me from being hurt. And all the while Molino was hurting him horribly."

Grady's gaze was narrowed on her face. "Tell me what he and Molino said."

She shook her head. "I can't remember. There's too much. It was all a horrible blur. I need to think about it." She drew a deep breath and sat up straighter in her chair. "But not now. There's nothing I need to do more than find that Ledger. I'm not going to let Molino get his hands on it. I'll see him in hell first." Her lips tightened. "That should please you. Isn't that why you brought me here?"

"If the voices were cooperative, I hoped you might be able to point me in the right direction."

"Oh, they were very cooperative. What a clever man you are, Grady."

"You have a right to be bitter," he said wearily. "I don't blame you. I made a choice. I did what I thought was best, but it wasn't best for you."

She opened her lips to agree with him and then closed them again. It was evident he hadn't wanted to subject her to that punishment. What decision would she have made if she had known Molino might be able to find and try to destroy so many innocent people? "I know why the Ledger was important to Edmund, but why are you obsessing about it? You said you weren't a Devanez."

"Self-preservation. If there's one thing I've learned, it's that the majority of people fear what they don't understand and their instinct is to strike out and crush it. The Inquisition was a lesson we should heed. It's much safer for us to move in and out of the shadows than be in a spotlight. Molino isn't rational and there's no telling what he'll do if he gets his hands on the Ledger." He paused. "Or what the family will do in retaliation."

"Retaliation?"

"Don't get me wrong. I'm not talking about a bunch of X-Men. I'd bet most of them are bewildered victims of their talent like your mother. It's just that I don't want those victims pushed into a corner by Molino." His lips tightened. "I know what I'd do."

Fight back. And Megan would do the same thing. "You could have warned me what to expect in that trailer."

"I didn't know what to expect. I told you that our knowledge of Listener capabilities is limited. I only knew it would be nasty. I tried to tell you that much."

Yes, he had. "Well, now you know more than—"

Grady's cell phone rang.

He glanced down at the ID. "Harley." He accessed the call and listened for a moment. "Okay, we're on our way. We'll meet you at the airport." He hung up and pushed back his chair. "Sorry, no time for dessert. We have to get out of here. Molino's informant at the circus made a phone call ten minutes ago. Molino will have someone on their way here by now."

She stood up and headed for her bedroom. "I'll go get my suitcases. It will only take me a few minutes. But it's not going to give you much time to get us entry documents."

He frowned. "We can use the same ones to get back into the U.S. that we used leaving."

"But we're not going to go back to the U.S. Not yet."

His gaze narrowed on her face. "And where are going?"

"Munich, Germany."

"Why?"

"Because that's where the Ledger is." She stopped at the door. "At least, I hope it's still there. Edmund didn't get a chance to warn her."

"Who?"

"Renata Wilger. He gave the Ledger to her for safekeeping on his last trip with the circus through Munich. He was uneasy and he'd learned to obey his instincts."

"You're certain?"

"Oh, yes." She smiled mirthlessly. "I couldn't be mistaken. He didn't tell Molino anything, but all his emotion was focused on her before he cut his throat. He was praying for her."

"Do you know anything else about where—"

"Nothing," she interrupted. "Over to you, Grady."

"Right." He was already dialing a number on his cell phone as she closed the bedroom door.

HARLEY MET THEM WHEN THEY dropped off the rental car. "You made good time. I just finished arranging for the charter." He made a face. "It wasn't easy to do since I wouldn't give them the destination. I think they suspect me of being a terrorist or something. It's only because I'm loaded with boyish appeal that I was able to pull it off." He turned to Megan. "You look a lot better than the last time I saw you. Did it ever occur to you that it would be a lot healthier if you stayed away from Grady?"

She smiled. "It occurred to me."

"Where's the plane?" Grady asked. "And did you call your contact, Biel, and arrange for him to meet us in Munich with the documents?"

"Hangar fourteen." He started toward the tarmac. "And Biel will be there waiting when we get off the plane. Megan's now Ella Steinberg. I'm Henry Higworth." He smiled. "I was that close to changing it to Higgins but I was afraid that someone would catch the Pygmalion connection and might cause us a headache or two."

"This is no game, Harley."

"Sad. I always try to lighten the burden." He gestured to a Learjet parked outside the hangar. "There she is. Nice, huh?"

"Beautiful," Megan murmured. "Do you have him working on tracking down Renata Wilger?"

"Yes, but he probably won't have anything but preliminary findings when we get there." He stepped aside for Megan to precede him up the steps to the plane. "You didn't give us much notice, Megan."

"I wasn't sure that I'd give you any notice at all. I was wondering if it wouldn't be safer for both me and Renata if I tried to find her by myself."

"Independence raises its pesky head again," Grady said. "Don't wonder any longer. It wouldn't be safer."

"How can you be certain? You and Molino have been playing cat and mouse for years. He probably knows your methods and patterns as well as you know his."

"Good point. But I've tried to periodically alter my movements so that they didn't form a pattern." He followed her up the steps and settled her in a seat and fastened her seat belt. "And evidently you did decide that we could be of some slight service to you or you wouldn't be here."

"You seem to be able to hop over borders with no trouble and you still know things that I don't."

"And once you have no use for me and you've wrung me of all needed information, then you'll cast me aside?"

"Why not?" she asked lightly. Then her smile faded. She wasn't being entirely honest and she was done with deception. "I would never leave you if you needed me. I'm too close to you. I don't like it but it's there. But that doesn't mean that I won't walk my own path."

"That goes without question." He sat down beside her. "But it's reassuring that you don't regard me as totally discardable."

"I couldn't." She tried to smile. "What if Molino killed you? If Edmund had that great an effect on me, I think you'd probably haunt me."

He shook his head. "I'd do my best not to do that. I'd want you to go on with your life and not look back. If there's any way to prevent it, you're not going to hear my voice after I bow out."

She felt a wrenching pang as she thought of Grady dead, Grady gone. The intensity of it took her by surprise. She didn't want to feel this close to Grady. It was as if that adolescent summer madness and the sexual attraction she was feeling now were blending, becoming stronger. She tried to edge away from that whirlpool of emotion. "I wonder if it's possible to control any of this. Ever since I found out about how all this psychic stuff has been surrounding me all my life I've been feeling resentful. I don't like not being in control."

"Welcome to the club. I've been trying to find answers since I was ten years old."

"You knew you had a gift that young?"

"Yes, but it didn't bother me. I was exhilarated at the thought of controlling situations. Children are instinctive savages and most savages want to be leader of the pack. It was only later that I realized that I wasn't regarded as a leader but a kind of Frankenstein."

"When?"

He shrugged. "When my father kicked me out. I was sixteen and he said I could take care of myself. He wasn't putting up with having a weirdo in his house."

"What about your mother?"

"She took off a few years before my dad decided that I wasn't welcome." He made a face. "Maybe he thought she wouldn't have left him if she hadn't had to contend with a problem child. I was a big headache to both of them. First, they took me to social workers and a couple psychiatrists paid by the state. Later they gave up and told everyone that I was a little peculiar and to just leave me alone."

"Alone? That's a terrible thing to do to a child."

"Are you bleeding for that poor kid? Don't waste your pity. I was a tough little bastard. Feel sorry for my parents. They never wanted a child anyway and then they got me."

"I don't feel sorry for them. They should have worked harder with you." She added fiercely, "And your father should never have kicked you out of the house."

"I can see I'm not going to be able to convince you that you're rooting for the wrong team." His lips lifted in a half smile. "I won't bother. I kind of like it."

She didn't like it at all. Now a protective thread had been added to the mixture of emotions she was feeling for Grady. Just the fact that he had not tried to defend or justify himself made her all the more defensive on his behalf. "Is that when you joined the service?"

He nodded. "It seemed a good way to get fed, trained, and kept out of jail. Of course, I managed to get myself in the stockade quite a few times before I started to grow up a little. Then I found my niche and I was on my way."

"I was surprised when Phillip told me that the services used psychics. It was like something from a sci-fi movie. I always think of the military as being clear and sharp and no-nonsense."

"They also believe in weapons, hi-tech or otherwise. They can swallow almost anything if it means winning a battle." He leaned back in his seat and gazed out the window as they started to taxi. "And according to Michael Travis's research almost everyone believes in some form of psychic or paranormal experience. In fact, a great percentage believes they've had a psychic episode in their lives."

She shook her head skeptically. "A great percentage?"

"Sit down at a dinner table and lead the conversation in

that direction. You'll be surprised how many fascinating stories you come up with."

"*Stories* being the key word?"

"There's an interesting theory regarding psychic abilities. Suppose that we all have varying degrees of psychic gifts but they stay safely tucked away in ninety-eight percent of the population. Michael has had MRIs and chemical tests made on the brains of psychic volunteers and the fluid balance appears to be higher and closer to the brain center. What if the fluid in that area contains a DNA factor that opens and enables the brain to function on a different level? If that chemical makeup is hereditary, it would account for talents being passed down through families."

"Like the Devanez family."

He nodded. "Your mother's tests showed an unusually high percentage of that fluid."

"What about your tests?"

"Not as high as Sarah's. Her results were practically off the charts." He met her gaze. "I'd bet your tests would be astonishing. Sarah said you were stronger than she was."

"We're not going to find out. I don't want to be a guinea pig for your Michael Travis."

"You may change your mind. I wasn't enthusiastic either, but you can't control a problem without knowledge. I'm all for control." He smiled. "I thought you'd embrace this particular hypothesis. It's much more scientific than voodoo, witchcraft, and black magic."

"Do you believe it?"

"I believe it's entirely possible. First, you have to accept that the universe is not necessarily laid out in nice, logical patterns for us. Then you only have to accept that we're not all capable of seeing, hearing, and experiencing to the same degree the universe around us. Dogs and cats see and smell things differently than we do. Birds see more brilliant colors and nuances of shades than we could ever dream." He smiled. "I don't hear what you hear. I'm deaf to it. You can't do what I do. You don't understand it. Maybe every now and then someone who ordinarily has no psychic ability has a rush of adrenaline or a chemical shift that surges the pertinent DNA to the brain. For a second, a moment, five minutes, whatever psychic gift being suppressed breaks free."

"Maybe."

He chuckled. "But you do like that explanation. I knew you would. Your practical soul has felt violated since you were plunged into all this."

"You're right. I'm reaching for whatever sanity I can find." She made a face. "And maybe I like the idea of everyone having some degree of psychic ability. It makes me feel less alone."

He reached out and covered her hand on the chair arm. "You're not alone."

Her hand was warm, tingling, beneath his grasp, and the pulse in her wrist was pounding erratically. He might have meant to touch her in comfort but it wasn't comfort she was feeling. Did he know? Dammit, of course he knew. He'd said he was sensitive to her emotions and she was being bombarded with emotion right now.

"Don't . . . touch me."

"Why not? You like it. You want it."

Lord, that was no lie. The tingling that had started in her hand was now suffusing her entire body. She was acutely aware of him. The tension of his muscles, the faint scent of spicy aftershave and musk, the heat he was emitting. Don't look at him. She knew what she'd see and it would only add fuel to the fire. Her hand clenched on the arm of the chair. "I don't always take what I want."

"Neither do I." He muttered a curse. "And this is a hell of a time. I didn't intend to start this now. It just happened."

And how had it happened? A mainly cerebral discussion and then this explosive sexual tension. "Then take your hand away."

"I'd better do more than that." He unbuckled his seat belt and stood up. "I'm going up to the cockpit to talk to the pilot and Harley." He looked down at her and she caught her breath as she saw his expression. "But you'd better get used to the idea. I could control it when I wasn't sure you wanted it too, but that's not the case anymore. Is it?"

He didn't wait for an answer.

She watched him stride away from her down the aisle and smothered a ripple of disappointment. For God's sake, what was wrong with her? Had she wanted him to jerk her onto his lap and screw her?

She closed her eyes as the answer came to her. Yes, primitive, raw, any way he wanted. She still wanted it.

It would be a mistake. Right now she was on an emotional roller coaster and she didn't need to have sex thrown into the mix. She drew a deep breath and unfastened her seat belt. She'd go wash her face and give herself time to calm. By the time she saw Grady again she must be cool and composed.

Not likely.

TEN

"JED HARLEY?" MOLINO REPEATED. "That circus bitch was sure that Harley did the payoff to that roustabout?"

"The description Pierre Jacminot gave her fit him like a glove," Sienna said. "But that means Grady."

"And I'd bet the Blair woman."

"Why would they want inside the trailer? Grady has to know we wouldn't leave evidence."

Ordinary evidence, Molino thought bitterly. Who knew what information one of those freaks might come up with? "I don't care why they wanted inside the trailer. If they found any lead to the Ledger, I want to know about it. Did you send someone to Chantilly?"

"Five minutes after I got the call. Falbon should be there in a few hours." He paused. "What are his instructions? If he sees an opportunity, should he kill the woman?"

Molino thought about it. Two attempts at downing Megan Blair and no success. It was totally ridiculous. If Falbon could do the job, he should let him kill her.

The Ledger.

Lists of names of all those other monsters like the one who had killed his son.

"No, we can wait. Just tell him to find her and then watch every move she makes."

And let the bitch lead him to the Ledger.

◆ ◆ ◆

"RENATA WILGER." HARLEY SHOOK his head as he glanced over the list he'd been handed at the airport. "Seven names. It's not going to be easy. What do I do? Just go up to them and ask if they'll please give me the Ledger? She'll probably know what happened to Edmund Gillem."

"Maybe not," Grady said. "Gillem wouldn't have entrusted the Ledger to anyone who was known to be close to him. Molino's probably paid a visit to everyone who might fall in that category."

"What about his ex-wife?" Megan asked. "Even though they were divorced, would Molino—"

"She drowned in a boating accident a week after Edmund died."

"Molino?" Megan whispered.

He shrugged. "She was a good sailor and the weather was fine. There were bruises on her body when it was found."

"You didn't tell me."

"What good would it have done? It was declared an unfortunate accident and you were facing enough ugliness."

"I don't want you keeping things from me."

He shrugged. "She probably didn't know anything about the Ledger. From what I found about the divorce, it was a complete break. Edmund wouldn't have confided in her."

"I still want to make up my own mind." She turned to Harley. "I'll help you go through the list."

"No, you won't," Harley said. "It's my job. I'll narrow it down and then I'll let you and Grady sift through what's left." He glanced out the window. "The Sheraton's right ahead. Nice hotel. I spent a few days there last year. Luscious feather mattresses and steaming hot chocolate in silver pots. A little *Sound of Music* ambiance, but that's not bad. I like schmaltz."

"What were you doing here?" Megan asked.

"Attending a pastry school. Everyone thinks that Paris has the finest schools for cuisine, but I learned how to make the most—why are you laughing?"

"Another career, Harley?"

"Not a career. I only took an internship for a month or two. There was a chef here who had the secret of how to make incredible Baumkuchen. He created twenty-eight layers of batter and each one was magnificent."

A smile was still tugging at her lips. "And you can never tell when you're going to need to know something as valuable as that."

He beamed. "It's wonderful to be understood." Grady had pulled up at the front entrance and Harley jumped out. "I'll check in for you. One glance at Megan and the desk clerk would be able to describe her. She's got that kind of face. Wait in the bar."

"Adjoining rooms," Grady told him.

"Right." He disappeared into the hotel.

"You tensed up when I said that," Grady said tightly. "A door between us isn't going to make any difference. It's a matter of choice."

"That's why I didn't say anything." But the intimacy of the thought had had an effect on her. Dammit, everything about him was having a physical effect on her. She opened the door and got out of the car. "This isn't an old fifties B movie. I'm worried about staying alive, not about preserving my honor." She smiled without mirth. "Do you know I've always thought that phrase was ridiculous when you consider keeping their women pure and intact was historically to preserve a man's honor. Actually, they thought women were livestock and had no honor."

"They'd be wrong about you. You have honor," Grady

said as he got out of the car. "But it's not between your legs."

Her eyes widened. "My God, how rude." Then she chuckled. "I don't believe I've ever felt flattered by such a crude compliment. It was a compliment, wasn't it?"

He took her elbow and moved toward the entrance. "Hell, yes."

"How long do you think it will it take him to find Renata Wilger?"

"Harley is good and he has excellent contacts."

"Are you being evasive?"

"Yes. One day if he's lucky. Three if he strikes out."

"What do you mean?"

"He has to find her, establish a connection with Gillem, and convince her that we're not going to kill her. It may take time. I know you don't want to hear that."

"You're damn right I don't." She didn't want to wait around and cool her heels in a hotel room. Particularly a room with Grady near enough to be within calling distance. "What if Molino finds Renata Wilger before we do?" What a stupid question. He'd just told her that Edmund's ex-wife had been killed and she had been ignorant of anything to do with the Ledger.

"The chances are we're ahead of the game. Providing Edmund didn't give Molino anything to work on."

"He didn't." She frowned. "But you said that he'd been tracking down family members. Wouldn't Renata Wilger be a family member? Edmund wouldn't have entrusted the Ledger to someone outside the family."

He nodded. "You're right. It would have been smarter, but he wouldn't have wanted to put anyone at risk that had nothing to gain."

"Then Molino could be searching now for Renata Wilger."

"Do you realize how large and far-flung the Devanez family is? And the core descendents don't want to be found. It took twelve years for me to track down Edmund Gillem."

"And Molino was ahead of you. He could be ahead of us now." She made a motion with her hand as he started to speak. "Sorry. I know worrying isn't productive." She headed for the bar. "I just have to keep busy until Harley finds her."

"How?"

"I want to read a copy of that ancient Tribunal Inquisition report about the Devanez family that Michael Travis managed to unearth. Can you get him to fax it to me?"

He didn't speak for a moment. "Yes."

But he was reluctant to do it, she realized. His face was without expression, but that hesitancy had spoken for itself. "Is there a problem?" She paused and then stared him in the eye. "Did you lie to me?"

"No." He moved toward the bar in the lobby. "I didn't lie. But there may be a problem. You'll have to decide that for yourself when you read it. I do have to warn you the description of the torture they inflicted on Ricardo Devanez is graphic."

"After what I went through with Edmund, reading about a torture session isn't going to send me around the bend. I won't like it but it's not going to stop me from sifting through it to get the entire picture. When can I expect the fax?"

"I'll call Michael tonight. He'll send it right away." He held her chair for her and motioned for the waiter. "There's a line at the reception desk. We may be here awhile. What do you want to drink?"

"Just coffee."

"I need something a bit stronger." He ordered her coffee

and bourbon for himself. "Have you heard anything more from Dr. Gardner about Phillip?"

She shook her head. "Not yet. It seems as if a long time has passed since I talked to him. But it hasn't really. I can't expect any treatment to work overnight." She smiled. "But on the positive side, Scott e-mailed me that one of my patients suffering with staph has taken a turn for the better. Maybe they don't need me as much as I thought they did."

"They need you," Grady said. "And you need them, don't you? You told me you've always wanted to be a doctor. When did you realize it?"

"When I was just a little kid in grade school. I had a friend, Antonia, who was in an automobile accident. Everyone thought she was going to die. She didn't die. They saved her." She paused. "I thought it was a miracle. I wanted to be able to be part of that miracle. It didn't take me any time at all to find out that miracles seldom happened, but I could still help ease the pain. There's so much pain in the world, Grady."

"And so much joy," he said. "There's always a balance."

She nodded. "I know. Every time I forget that, I go pick up Davy for an outing and he brings it all back. Children know all about joy."

"Davy's the little boy you were with at the zoo?"

"Yes." A smile lit her face. "Scott e-mailed me a new picture of Davy with his report. He has his first bike. It has training wheels, but you should see how proud he looks. It's wonderful."

"I can see it must be." His gaze was fastened on her face. "You're obviously crazy about the kid. I'm surprised you don't go into pediatrics."

"I have to get stronger. I have to build myself up to it." She made a face. "I get enough criticism because I don't have enough objectivity with my patients. A sick child tears me to pieces."

"Then, dammit, give yourself a break," he said roughly. "Why be so hard on yourself?"

"Because the joy is worth the pain." She sat back in her chair as the waiter put her coffee before her. "I'm no martyr. You can't imagine how I feel when everything goes right and a patient goes home well and happy."

"Yes, I can." He lifted his bourbon. "You forget that no imagination is required when it comes to knowing how you feel. Sometimes I wish to hell it did."

She was abruptly jerked back from the intimacy that had been growing between them. "That's right, I did forget." She looked quickly at the line at the reception. "Harley's at the front of the line. Maybe we'd better join him."

"In a few minutes. Drink your coffee." His lips twisted. "I promise I won't bring up any more subjects that make you feel uneasy."

SIENNA PUT THE NOTE IN FRONT of Molino. "Falbon managed to track them to Biestrop Airport, outside Chantilly. They have no regularly scheduled flights so they must have arranged a charter."

"To where?"

"Falbon's still working on it. It may take a while. Grady's an expert at covering his tracks."

"Don't tell me that. I need to know now." He reached in the file drawer in his desk and drew out a thick folder. "Is this the most up-to-date information we gathered about possible Devanez family members?"

Sienna nodded. "But we stopped when you decided that Gillem was the one who had the Ledger. And then when we located Megan Blair, we—"

"You shouldn't have stopped. When we located Megan Blair, I had to take care of her, but that didn't mean that I was no longer interested in that damn Ledger."

Sienna shook his head. "I had no intention of not continuing. As far as I'm concerned, the Ledger should be the prime target. But there are too many names and they're spread over a dozen countries. It will take time to—"

"Edmund Gillem visited five countries in the six months before we scooped him up. Denmark, Sweden, Russia, Germany, and Italy. He must have given the Ledger to someone in one of those countries. All we need is a clue and Megan Blair may give it to us." He started to go through the file. "If Falbon does his job."

LUSCIOUS FEATHER BEDS AND silver pots of hot chocolate.

Megan smiled as she came out of the bathroom after taking her shower. The tray with the hot chocolate was sitting on the ottoman in front of the couch and the bed had been turned down to reveal the plump feather mattress and comforter.

"Nice." Grady was leaning against the doorjamb. "I ordered the chocolate and let the maid in. Harley would approve of you sampling on his recommendations." His gaze ran over her. "You look cozy."

Megan tightened the tie on the terrycloth robe. "Harley slipped up. He didn't mention the complimentary robes." She moved toward the ottoman and poured a cup of chocolate. "Would you like one?"

"No, thanks. I just wanted to make sure you were comfortable. I should be receiving the fax from Michael any minute and I'll bring it in to you."

"Good. I called Dr. Gardner and he said there's nothing

really to report yet. Phillip is physically the same. But Gardner has a hunch that there's something going on with him."

"What?"

She frowned. "I don't think he knows. I couldn't pin him down. But he says he's developed an instinct with patients like Phillip. He thinks there's something . . . stirring. He says as soon as he has something concrete, he'll phone me."

"I believe in hunches." He straightened. "I've ordered you soup and a sandwich for later. That's probably all I'll get down you after you start reading the transcript."

She nodded. "This chocolate is pretty rich. I won't be hungry." She wished he would leave. She was too aware of him and was feeling very vulnerable at the moment. The soft rub of the terry against her body as she moved was sensuous and provocative. It was crazy. In this bulky robe she felt more exposed than if she were naked.

Shit, face it. Any touch, any texture would have been arousing right now. She was acting like an animal in heat. She lowered her eyes to the liquid in her cup. "I don't want to be a bother. Suppose I call room service when I'm ready?"

He smiled sardonically. "Why do I feel you're dismissing me?" He shook his head as she started to speak. "It's okay. I'll be a good boy and run along." He started to turn away and then whirled back to her. "The devil I will." He had reached her in three strides. His hands closed on her throat. "Don't freeze on me." His dark eyes were glittering recklessly in his taut face. "I'm not taking much. I just want my hands on you for a minute." His fingers were moving caressingly up and down the sides of her throat. "Then I'll let you send me on my way."

"But I don't want . . . your hands on me." It was a lie

and he had to know it. The flesh of her throat was tingling and every brush of his fingers felt hot, probing. She moistened her lips. "At first, I thought you were going to strangle me."

"I've always thought you have the most beautiful throat on the face of the earth. Long and soft, and your skin is so thin in the hollow that I can see the pulse pounding when you get excited."

"It's a little bizarre having a fetish about necks," she said unevenly. "Are you sure you don't have any relations in Transylvania?"

"Not that I know about. I'm glad you're not struggling very hard," he said thickly. His face was flushed and she could feel the heat his body was emitting. "Thank God. I need this. It's not enough but it's something."

He was now resting his hands on her collarbone encircling her neck and his thumbs rubbing slowly in the hollow. She wanted his hands to go lower, to slip beneath the robe, and touch her.

Her body was readying, her breasts swelling. She instinctively moved closer.

"Damn." His hands tightened around her throat for an instant and then dropped away from her. He stepped back. "No. Later."

She stared at him in shock. "What?"

"You're reading that damn report tonight. You're not going to accuse me later of trying to distract you and establish a beachhead before everything is clear and out in the open."

First, bewilderment and then anger surged through her. "Then why the hell did you touch me, you bastard? Was it a game? Some kind of control move? Who asked you?" She backed away from him. "Get out of here."

"Control move? If I was in control, I'd have had you in

bed five minutes ago. That's probably what I should have done," he said through his teeth. "And you would have loved it. You're probably the most sensual woman I've ever met. I should know. I've been linked to you all your adult years. You couldn't help but enjoy it. I just didn't want you looking back later and thinking I'd— Oh, screw it."

The door slammed behind him.

She was shaking, Megan realized. She was hot, yet shivering as if she had a fever.

It had to be with anger.

No, she wouldn't lie to herself. She was aching with frustration. Her body was primed, ready . . . empty.

Damn him.

She curled up in the easy chair and tucked her legs beneath her. Don't shake. Don't think how much she wanted it, how much she wanted him. It would go away soon.

And would she ever be able to look at him without remembering his hands on her? She hadn't even gone to bed with him. He'd only petted her, stroked her.

Yet her heart was pounding so hard she was having trouble breathing.

Damn him.

A SOFT KNOCK SOUNDED ON the adjoining door an hour later.

She didn't answer.

"Megan. Open the door. I come bearing gifts."

Harley's voice.

She got up and opened the door.

He smiled and handed her a folder with a sheaf of papers. "The faxes of the Tribunal Reports you asked Grady for. He asked me to pass them on to you. He said there are a couple more pages, but he'll give them to you after you've read the report."

"Thank you. I didn't expect to see you tonight. You said you'd be too busy."

"I tracked down the first two Renata Wilgers and came up with zilch. However, I have a promising lead that I'm going to follow up on tonight."

"Tonight?"

"This Renata Wilger works for an international brokerage company and from what I've discovered, she's amazing at predicting stock and real estate trends. Wouldn't you say that could reflect one of those so-called talents?"

"Possibly. But would this company be open at night?"

"Her apartment manager said that she's a workaholic and seldom gets home before midnight. So I'll be off in an hour or two to contact her. But first Grady asked me to come and have dinner with him and play errand boy." His brows lifted. "I take it you're not joining us for dinner?"

She shook her head. "I need to read these Tribunal Reports."

"From what Grady said, some of the content will give you nightmares. Ring my cell phone if you need a sandwich later. Grady doesn't want you calling room service." He gave her a mock salute and closed the door behind him.

Megan looked down at the folder. She didn't care if the reports were going to be gory and upsetting. At least it would give her something worthwhile on which to focus. She needed that distraction right now. She sat down, opened the folder, and took out the first fax page.

I write this on the twelfth day of June in the year of our Lord Fourteen hundred and eighty-five by command of

Tomás de Torquemada, Inquisidor General, regarding the just and holy investigation of the heretic Devanez family.

"AT LEAST, SHE DIDN'T THROW the folder back in my face," Harley said as he strolled across the room to where Grady was standing at the minibar. "But she did appear a little tense. What on earth did you do to her?"

"Not nearly enough." He poured himself a drink. "And it's none of your business."

"Of course it is, when I have to delay my own business and rush in and run interference. Am I supposed to stick around to hand her those last pages you told her you'd give her later?"

"No, she'll want to talk to me about them."

"That's a relief." He picked up the phone. "What do you want to order for dinner?"

"Anything." He carried his bourbon to the window and looked down at the street below. There hadn't been any doubt in his mind that she'd take the report. He just hadn't wanted to add fuel to the tinderbox he'd already set in place. He'd been supremely clumsy. Why couldn't he have just either not made any move, or gone for broke and gotten her into bed?

Because he'd waited too long to touch her. Because when she finished reading that report she was going to be questioning everything he'd ever said or done to her. "Just make sure you order plenty of coffee. It's going to be a long night."

ELEVEN

ANOTHER DAY OF TORTURE for Ricardo Devanez.

Megan wanted desperately to skip over the brutal details, but the reports had interwoven the questions and answers into the torment inflicted on that poor man.

She drew a deep breath and closed her eyes. She'd give herself a break for a few minutes. The first part of the report had not been too bad, the preliminary heresy investigation into the Devanez family. Painstakng reports from the local priests who'd been ordered to spy on José Devanez and all his close and distant relations were repeated. Both the immense wealth the clan had acquired and the stories the peasants told of their strange powers were carefully documented as the Tribunal prepared to act.

Strange powers, indeed, Megan thought. A good many of the stories had to be fabricated. A shape changer who turned into a beast at the full moon, healers, mind readers, a woman whose touch made an old woman go mad, a child who could find water on barren land. With such outrageous stories circulating the countryside, it was no wonder that the family had been put at risk. They had been charitable, peaceful, and tending to keep to themselves, yet even their kindness aroused suspicion. They were accused of deception and secret devil worshiping.

It was when the priests had captured Ricardo Devanez that the report became almost unbearable to read. He had held out for three hideous days of extreme torture before he broke and told them of the exodus of his family from Spain. At the point where she had stopped they were making him talk about the family members and their demonic powers. José, who could see the future and tell if a venture would be successful, Isabelle, his daughter, who could grow flowers where there was no sunlight or rain, his brother Diego, who could make fire by wishing it to flare.

Was it truth as Ricardo saw it, or telling his torturers what they wished to hear? It didn't matter. Megan had to finish the report. But she'd try to scan the rest and see if there was anything to which she could relate. So far Ricardo had not mentioned any Listeners among the family members.

She opened her eyes and started to read again. Skim, don't absorb that horror.

Ricardo must have been babbling at this point, pouring out his soul. The list of psychic talents was astonishing and Ricardo gave names and examples. If any of these people were captured by Torquemada's agents, there would have been no doubt they would have been burned at the stake.

It was almost at the end of the report, the last page, that Ricardo started to talk about his sister, Rosa, who was a Listener.

Megan stiffened, her gaze flying over the paragraph. *Clearly the most heinous and wicked of all the demons,* the priest wrote.

Not only did the woman hear voices from hell but she was a demon incarnate herself. It's fortunate that the subject, Ricardo Devanez, states that only with great rarity was a woman with that power born. Because each Listener almost always is also possessed of the darker curse they are generally known as a Pandora.

Megan froze, memories rushing back to her.

The night at the cave when her mother died.

Not Pandora. Not Pandora. Not Pandora.

Molina questioning Edmund.

"Tell me about the Pandoras."

Darker curse? What on earth could be the nature of the curse the priest had written about?

And this report wasn't complete, dammit. There were the last two pages that Grady had withheld from her.

She jumped to her feet, strode to the adjoining door, and pounded on it. When he opened the door, she said, "I want those last two pages. And I want to know about these Pandoras."

"You'll get the pages. But I wanted to be here to answer questions. The Tribunal's description of Pandoras is colorful but hardly unbiased." He stepped aside. "Come in. I'll give you a cup of coffee and we'll talk about it."

"I don't want to talk— Yes, I do." She moved past him and sat down in the easy chair by the window. "Give me that coffee."

He poured a cup from the carafe on the end table and handed it to her. "I'm at your service. Start your questions."

"The priest is talking about a dual 'curse' that's inflicted on women who are Listeners. I know I'm not listening to demons, so that's bullshit. What other hat am I supposed to be wearing? What else is a Listener supposed to be able to do?"

"Not all Listeners."

"Don't quibble. Ricardo says most Listeners are also this . . . Pandora thing. What do they do?"

He was silent a moment, choosing his words. "According to the Tribunal's interpretation of Ricardo's confession, a Pandora is a demon who kills or drives mad."

She stiffened. "And that's obviously bullshit too."

"Not entirely." He added, "But the priest also quoted Ricardo's exact words as well as his own interpretation. Ricardo said that a Pandora was no demon, that she just opened doors."

"What?"

"Pandoras are facilitators. They have the power to release dormant psychic powers in those around them. If a person has even the smallest psychic ability, a Pandora is supposed to be able to trigger that talent."

She stared at him incredulously. "How?"

He shrugged. "Ricardo didn't know. Believe me, the priests spent a long time trying to make him talk about it. They thought they'd found an archdemon in Rosa Devanez. All they could get out of him was that he thought she had to touch them." He paused. "And sometimes it went wrong. Sometimes the person she tried to help break through the barriers went mad. One man was later found dead after she visited him."

Megan frowned. "But why would that happen?"

"Michael and I have discussed it and we think there's a possibility that some minds just can't handle it. There's no picking and choosing which psychic ability. You only get what's inherently there. And even if the subject thinks he wants the power, when it comes, it sometimes completely blows them away. It's too much, too soon. It's like giving a massive dose of heroin to someone who's never had it before."

She shivered. "And why would Rosa want to prance merrily along tossing out psychic powers like Johnny Appleseed did his seeds?"

"Evidently the subjects volunteered and there were some successes. Ricardo said that Rosa was able to help her cousin, Maria, become a great Finder. And her uncle, Franco, suddenly acquired the same gift of prediction José possessed after he spent a few days with her."

"Then if there's good and bad, why did they call her a Pandora? According to mythology, wasn't Pandora supposed to have opened a box and released all the troubles into the world?"

"It depends on how deeply you probe into the myth," Grady said. "According to the writings of Hesiod, Pandora was given gifts from all the gods and that's why her name was Pandora, which means all gifts. Hermes gave her cunning, boldness, and charm, Aphrodite gave her beauty, Apollo gave her musical ability and the power of healing, Hera gave her curiosity. Then Zeus threw in mischief and foolishness." He smiled. "But there are feminist scholars who argue that according to earlier myths Pandora was the great goddess who made life and culture possible. They say that accusing Pandora of being responsible for letting loose all the wickedness that made men miserable was just another ploy to make women shoulder the blame for everything that went wrong. There are several comparisons to Eve in the Garden of Eden." He paused. "But everyone agrees that there was hope in that box she opened. If hope was present, then why wouldn't there have been other good spirits as well as evil?"

"Because it's a myth and written by a man." Her lips tightened. "And it was easy to compare that poor Rosa Devanez to Pandora and her release of evil powers into the world, even though Rosa was asked to try to help those people."

"Good point. But Rosa wasn't the first Pandora in the

family. According to Ricardo, at the time of the Inquisition the talent had already been passed down through the family for at least three hundred years. A facilitator didn't appear in every generation; it sometimes skipped three, even four. But it was always a woman and she was often a Listener."

"Ricardo told the priests all of those details?"

"I told you, the priests thought they had discovered an archfoe in Rosa Devanez. They wanted to know how to fight the demon when they hunted her down. They spent a long time questioning Ricardo about all the characteristics common to a Pandora."

"And what were they?"

"High energy, extreme empathy, intelligence, deep emotional responses." He paused. "Very strong sensuality. The last characteristic clenched her condemnation in Torquemada's eyes. Ricardo said the family forgave Pandoras for that fault since deep emotion would generate it, but it wasn't acceptable to the Tribunal."

"Is that all? Was there anything else in the report?"

"Only a final condemnation of the Devanez family and a resolution to search out and destroy the demons and heretics among them."

"Then why didn't you give those pages to me with the rest of the transcript? Why did you want to tell me about it yourself?"

"I think you know." He repeated softly, "High energy, extreme empathy, intelligence, deep emotional responses, sensuality. Sound familiar?"

Of course, it sounded familiar. "You're saying that I'm one of those Pandoras." She shook her head. "Even if I believed in this Pandora concept, that doesn't mean I'm one. Don't Listeners have similar characteristics?"

"Yes. On a lesser scale."

"And who knows if that part of Ricardo's confession isn't fabrication? Facilitation is even less believable than other psychic abilities."

"And frightening. The responsibility could be awesome. Touch someone and you create a Frankenstein." He smiled. "Or a Mother Teresa."

"I'm a doctor. I've handled a lot of people in my life and not one has turned into a monster or angel. So I think this so-called gift has passed me by."

"Perhaps. Even the family wasn't entirely sure how the talent worked. Ricardo did say it didn't manifest itself until a woman was in her mid-twenties. It could be that you haven't reached the right stage of development yet. Or maybe certain circumstances have to be present to trigger it."

She shook her head. "You're reaching. It's enough for me to accept being a Listener. I'm not going to let you throw this at me when there's no evidence. I'm *not* a Pandora."

"That's what your mother said," he said quietly. "It was the last thing she said to me. She was fighting admitting it until the end."

Not Pandora. Not Pandora. Not Pandora.

"And you knew it." His gaze was narrowed on her face. "I thought you did. That's why I didn't want you to read this part of the report when you were alone."

"She was dying. Why would she—"

"Because she was a Pandora, but she didn't want to admit it. If she accepted that she was a Pandora, then she'd have to accept that you'd probably become one. A Listener was bad enough, but a Pandora was big trouble. It had already destroyed her life."

"How?"

"Molino. She killed his son."

Megan shook her head. "No."

"She did it, Megan. She didn't stab him or shoot him, but she did kill him." He held her gaze. "No one deserved it more. I told you she was raped when she was held captive. It was Molino's son who did it, many, many times and with great brutality. That last night he brought her out by the campfire and started to rape her in full view of Molino and the rest of his men."

"You've already told me this," she said shakily. "I don't want to hear the details. It . . . hurts me."

"And I don't want to tell them to you. But I have to do it. It's time, Megan."

"I won't listen. I can't stand thinking about—" It didn't matter what she wanted or her own pain. This was her mother he was talking about. She had to listen. She braced herself. "Go on. Do it."

"There's not much more. It must have been like being surrounded by a pack of wolves for her. There was shouting and laughing, humiliation, and pain. She'd been raped by him before, but this was even more hideous. I don't know if it was an accumulation of the horror or if she just couldn't take it any longer. Something must have snapped in Sarah. She screamed. Then she grabbed hold of Molino's son's hand to stop him from touching her and screamed again. Everyone was laughing at her. It was a big joke." He stopped. "And then Steven Molino started screaming. He got off Sarah and backed away from her as if she had the plague. He was shrieking and crying and muttering curses. He ran off into the jungle. When they found him an hour later, he was still running, still trying to get away from Sarah. They brought him back to the camp and Molino arranged for a helicopter to pick them up. He was completely out of his head and muttering things that his father was thinking, that the other men in the camp were thinking."

"Mind reading," Megan whispered.

He nodded. "Evidently his latent talent. But it must have exploded in him like a rocket when Sarah grabbed his hand. Molino hustled his son on the helicopter and flew out to Nairobi to get him medical help. When they got off the copter, he was distracted for a moment when he was talking to the doctor who had met the flight." He shrugged. "A moment was all it took. Steven Molino turned and walked back into the rear blades of the helicopter. Not a pretty way to die."

"Good," she said fiercely. "I wish I could have been there to finish the job with a machete."

"So did I when we took Sarah back from them and I heard what happened from one of Molino's men we captured. But it wasn't necessary." He paused. "Sarah had taken care of it herself."

"Just because Molino's son went bonkers? That's pretty flimsy evidence that my mother had some kind of malignant power that sent him over the edge." She was trying to think clearly, logically. "Maybe it was guilt, or it could be he was schizophrenic anyway."

"Perhaps."

"But you don't believe it."

"The second page I was withholding from you was the report that Michael had compiled on your mother before Molino's son's death. Her DNA blood tests confirmed that she was connected to the core DNA family."

"How could you know that?"

"José Devanez was buried at his estate in Spain after

his suicide." His lips twisted. "Not on hallowed ground, but I don't believe he would have cared considering the circumstances. I'm not sure what strings Michael pulled but he managed to get a DNA sample from José's remains."

"Even if she was a Devanez that doesn't mean my mother could destroy someone just by touching them. Rosa's story could be a fairy tale."

"Or it could be truth. The witnesses to that slimeball's death were sure that Sarah had driven him to it."

"And I'm supposed to believe a bunch of sadistic bastards who cheered when my mother was raped?"

"You'll believe what you have to believe. My job was to lay the facts before you. If you're the daughter of a Pandora, then you need to be prepared." He added roughly, "Your mother let you blunder through life ignorant and blind. I'll be damned if I'll let it go on."

Her hands clenched on the cup. "You'd rather I be terrified all my life of killing someone accidentally?"

"Ignorance breeds fear. If there's a chance the danger is there, then you should know about it and how to control it. If it took repeated rape to cause Sarah's gift to explode, then this facilitating can't be that easy. As far as I know, it never happened again with her. She didn't want the gift and she shunted it away from her. She refused to admit she possessed it."

"Perhaps she didn't. Perhaps Pandoras don't exist."

He shook his head. "Lord, you're as stubborn as your mother. Whether you want to believe it or not, realize that Molino believes it. He saw what happened to his son, he saw Sarah turn his son into a madman. And when he stole the copy of those records from Michael's library, he made the connection. Oh, yes, Molino believes Pandoras exist. He regards them as a scourge upon the earth."

"Pot calling the kettle black," she said bitterly. "For God's sake, he's as bad as those priests who thought Rosa was an archdemon sent to destroy the world."

"He's worse. At least the priests thought they had some reason to fear Rosa's gift. Your Johnny Appleseed comparison wasn't far off the mark. Indiscriminate facilitation could be a disaster. What if Hitler had had the power to see the future? Could he have changed it and won the war? What if Saddam Hussein had the ability to read minds? Would he have been able to unite the Arab world against the West? Think about it."

"I don't want to think about it."

"Do it anyway. There may be other people who want to destroy you as much as Molino does if they become convinced you could be a chess piece in the enemy camp." He paused. "Or you could be killed because some idealistic do-gooder thinks they're going to save civilization by ridding it of a threat."

"Me? Ridiculous." But there were a lot of crackpots in the world. Grady's suggestion wasn't all that far-fetched, she thought with a shiver. "You're not being very encouraging."

"If the talent is a two-headed coin as Ricardo said, then it could be either hideous or wonderful. Since we don't have any concrete evidence of the pros and cons, you'll have to define them for yourself. Providing you don't choose to close your eyes and ignore the truth as Sarah did."

"My mother was happy and she made me happy. Maybe that's the way to go."

He smiled. "Don't give me that bull. I can't see you content to drift along, hiding from reality."

What he called reality right now was confusing and frightening. She didn't want to hide but she needed time to absorb and decide how much to believe and what to do next. She stood up and held out her hand. "Give me those last two pages."

"You don't believe me?" He went to the desk and picked up the fax sheets. "By all means, study them carefully."

She did believe what he had told her was the truth. "I have to see it for myself. Interpretation can alter everything. It's the only way it will sink home to me." She took the pages and turned toward the door. "Good night, Grady."

"If you need me, I'll be here," he said quietly.

"Thank you."

If you need me. Those words would have had an entirely different meaning earlier in the evening when she had been lost in a haze of sexuality. She gave him a ghost of a smile over her shoulder. "How quickly things change."

"Nothing's changed," he said curtly. "Not really. Give me any encouragement and I'd have you in bed in a heartbeat. But I'm not fool enough to think I have a chance while you're this upset. I can wait."

She felt a ripple of shock. "Evidently I was giving you too much credit for sensitivity."

"You want sensitive? I'd give you sensitive. Hell, I'd like to comfort you. But you're too defensive to accept it. So I'll take what I can get. You like sex. That's fine with me. My God, it's more than fine."

She had a sudden memory of the description of a Pandora in Ricardo's confession. "Don't believe everything you read. I'm no Pandora and any sensuality I possess is both normal and healthy."

He grimaced. "You see? Defensive. That's what I was afraid would happen when you read the Tribunal's report."

"Dammit, you've just told me I could be some kind of walking time bomb. I have a right to be defensive."

"Yes, you do. But not with me. I'm on your side. Believe

me, other than the possibility of the Pandora talent, I think you're beautifully normal in every way. I don't give a damn what's in that report. You're no carbon copy. But I'm not going to ignore the fact that I know you like sex. I've been linked too closely to you not to realize that. And whatever you want, I'll give you." He added, "And you'd better get out of here before I start elaborating. The line between the sympathetic and the erotic is a little blurred in my mind right now."

Erotic. Grady's fingers caressing her throat. Her body changing, tensing, coming alive.

"Don't worry, I'm leaving. Good night." A few seconds later the door closed behind her. She hadn't needed those last few moments of sexuality thrown into the mix. She was confused and upset enough. Yet, in a way, that raw earthiness had grounded her after all the talk of Pandora and the horror her mother had undergone. Had that been Grady's intention? He was clever and he knew her very well.

Don't analyze, don't try to make excuses for Grady. She had to read these last pages and then think about what they meant to her. Wildly improbable? Yet in the beginning she had thought being a Listener was beyond belief. Was her skepticism based on fear?

Then come to terms with it. Grady had said he was into controlling talents instead of letting them run wild. It made sense. She couldn't let herself be terrorized by her own helplessness to cope. She had conquered her fear of Listening. Well, almost. It was coming.

And it was doubtful that this Pandora thing would ever affect her in any meaningful way. As she had told Grady, as a doctor she had exhibited no signs of being a so-called facilitator. She might be worrying over nothing.

God, she hoped that was true.

• • •

"GET THEM, PAPA. I HATE *them all. Why haven't you killed them yet?"*

Another dream? But his son was standing there, gazing at him accusingly. "I'm trying, Steven."

"It's been too long. You have to kill all those freaks. Look what they did to me."

Steven's mangled face. His son's head flying from his body as the rotors struck him.

"Oh, my God." Molino was sobbing. "I know. I know. Forgive me."

"I'll forgive you when you kill the freaks." Steven smiled at him. "I'll help you. Together we can do it. We'll get all of them. We'll butcher the freaks."

"Yes. Together." Exhilaration flooded him. "We'll do it, Steven."

"YOU ASKED ME TO WAKE YOU if we heard from Falbon."

Molino sluggishly opened his eyes to see Sienna standing in the doorway. For a moment he thought Sienna was the dream figure instead of Steven. "What is it?"

"Falbon says the chartered plane landed in Munich. He's on his way there now."

Molino sat up in bed and shook his head to clear it. "Munich. Who did we have on the suspect list in Munich?"

"Renata Wilger. Edmund Gillem was seen with her on his last visit through Germany."

"Then Grady will be searching for her. Tell Falbon he has to find her first." He lay back down again and closed his eyes. "I want a report when I get up in the morning."

Sienna turned out the light and closed the door.

I'll help you, Papa.

Yes, help me, Steven. Molino was suddenly filled with boundless confidence. Who was to know if his son had not been able to break through the barriers of death to join with him? The freaks shouldn't have a monopoly on power.

Help me, and we'll butcher them all.

TWELVE

RENATA COULD HEAR THE footsteps behind her. They slowed when she slowed, quickened when she speeded up.

Bastard.

Molino? No, probably not. One of his men.

Keep calm. She had prepared for this eventuality and she would meet it with the same strength that Edmund had shown.

The hell she would. Edmund had been a martyr. She wasn't going to let them force her to do anything she didn't want to do. She was only twenty-three and had her whole life before her. She was going to live.

And there was only one man following her. It didn't have to be one of Molino's scumbags. He could be a masher or a thief. It was after midnight and this wasn't the first time she'd had men try to follow her the two blocks from her office to the lot where she parked her car.

But this man wasn't trying to get closer. He was keeping her within view but not attempting to make an approach. She didn't like that. Not at all. Okay, let's bring him out in the open.

She turned left at the next block and ducked into the vestibule of a shop.

He came around the corner a few minutes later, a heavyset man in his forties with thinning brown hair. He stopped cautiously, his eyes searching the street in front of him. His hand reached into his jacket pocket. She caught the gleam of metal.

A gun.

She didn't give him the chance to bring the gun out.

She jumped out of the vestibule and struck his arm with the edge of her hand. The gun dropped from his nerveless hand to the street. Then she followed through with a fist to his stomach.

"Bitch," he gasped. "I'll cut you to pieces, you—"

She gave him a karate chop to the back of his neck. He crumpled, but he had drawn a knife by the time he reached the ground. He lunged upward toward her.

Lord, she hated knives. She'd always had a horror of cold steel going into a body. She dodged to the left and then brought her palm crashing up under his nose. This time he didn't get up.

Dead?

Oh, yes. The splintered bones of his nose had entered his brain. She fell to her knees beside him and started searching through his pockets for ID and found a passport. Raoul Falbon.

"I saw a police car cruising a block behind us. I believe we'd better forget gathering the spoils and get out of here."

She stiffened, her gaze flying to the man who stood watching her a few yards away. She tensed, ready to spring, her hand moving toward the gun Falbon had dropped on the ground.

"Oh, dear." He drew a gun from his jacket. "I'm no threat but I really don't want to be treated to the same punishment as that poor fellow on the ground, Renata. Now shall we go? You don't want to talk to the police, do you? I certainly don't."

"Who are you?"

"Jed Harley. And I have no connection to Molino. To

prove it, I'm graciously ignoring the fact that you're considering going for that gun on the ground. As soon as we
have time to talk, I'll put my gun away. Deal?"

She shrugged. "Sure. I'd be very stupid to—" She dove
forward in a roll and struck him in the knees and brought
him down. The next moment she was on top of him.

"No, ma'am." He backhanded her and then bucked her
off him.

Dizzy. She shook her head to clear it even as she dove
for the gun beside Falbon.

He reached it before she did and threw it skittering
down the street.

She bit his arm and reached for the gun still in his
hand.

"Ouch. You little cannibal." He clipped her on the side
of the head with the gun.

Pain. Ignore it. She came at him again and went for the
jugular.

He grabbed her, spun her around, his arm around her
neck jerking her head back. "Listen. I could break your
neck. I don't want to do it."

"Because then I'd be useless to you," she said fiercely.
"I couldn't tell you what you want to know."

"No, because my orders are to find you and keep you
safe from Molino until you can talk to Neal Grady.
Breaking your neck would be frowned upon." He added
wistfully, "Though it might almost be worth it."

If she kicked backward, she might get him off guard.
His grip had to loosen just a little and then she'd—

He sighed. "You're not going to give up, are you? I
guess I'll have to resort to dire methods." He took her
hand. "Stop struggling. You're getting what you want."
She felt him closing her hand around something hard and

metal. Then he released her and stepped back. "Okay, go for it."

She stared down at the gun he'd placed in her hand. "What are you doing?"

"You obviously have to be on top or you won't listen." He spread out his arms. "I'm at your mercy, Renata Wilger."

She frowned. "Is the gun empty?"

He smiled. "My God, I believe you're disappointed. Is it too easy for you? No, the gun has bullets and they're not blanks. What are you going to do now?"

She wasn't sure. The move had taken her by surprise. He had obviously meant to take her off guard and disarm her mentally if not physically. But she had never known a man who would take a chance like that.

"May I make a suggestion? I interrupted you while you were going through that deceased gentleman's wallet. Why don't you continue?"

"I have his passport and his name is Falbon. That's all I need to trace him."

"Then why not leave the scene of the crime and come with me to the Sheraton to see Grady and Megan Blair?"

"I don't consider killing Molino's men a crime." Her eyes suddenly widened. "Megan Blair? She's here in Munich?"

"At the hotel." His gaze narrowed on her face. "How do you know about Megan? Does that make a difference?"

She didn't answer either question. "Dammit, she shouldn't be anywhere near me. She might have led Molino here."

"Then tell her that yourself. She's not going to listen to me. I'm going to phone her." He slowly took out his phone, making sure that she could see that it was not a weapon. "Okay?"

She hesitated. Then she nodded her head. "But I won't go into the hotel. Tell her to meet us across the street in the park."

"Very smart. Then you can check her out and make sure that I'm not leading you down the garden path." He dialed the number. "Grady, I need you and Megan to meet me at the park across the street from the hotel in about an hour. I'll bring Renata Wilger." He listened for a moment and then smiled. His gaze wandered from Renata, who still aimed the gun at him, to the dead man crumpled on the street. "Oh, yes, I'm sure she's the right Renata Wilger."

HARLEY WAS WAITING UNDERNEATH a street lamp by a park bench when Grady and Megan came through the gates. He was alone.

Disappointment surged through Megan. "Where is she, Harley? Did you lose her?"

"No, and she didn't lose me." He took her arm and pulled her into the light. "Lift up your head."

"What are you doing?" Grady took a step forward.

"I'm not hurting her." He called out into the darkness. "Here she is. Delivered as promised. Come out, come out, wherever you are."

"That sounds like a children's game," Grady said.

"Hide-and-seek." Harley nodded. "But hopefully the seeking is over and she's not exactly hiding. She just doesn't trust us. That's why she has a gun trained on me. My gun."

"*Your* gun?"

"It's a long story." Harley called again, "Renata, you've had time to get a good look at Megan. Is it yes, or no?"

"How would she even recognize me?" Megan asked.

Harley shrugged. "Ask her." He was looking beyond her toward the bushes. "My dear girl, I understand your concern but it's really not polite to point guns at strangers. It makes them nervous."

"I'm not pointing the gun at them," the woman coming toward them said. "I'm just ready. How do I know that Molino isn't staking her out?"

Renata Wilger was younger than Megan had thought she would be. She was perhaps in her early twenties, small, slim, red-haired with a sprinkling of freckles over the bridge of her nose. Her brown eyes were glittering with fierce intensity as she stared at Megan. "And if you're not being used, you're either stupid or criminally negligent for coming here. Get the hell out of Munich and away from me."

What a little tigress. "You wouldn't have decided to come out of the bushes if you'd really thought Molino was using me to trap you. And I'm not going anywhere until I get what I want." She glanced at the gun Renata was holding at her side. "So give Harley back his gun and let's talk."

"Why should I want to talk to you? You've probably already ruined things for me here. I'm going to have to go on the run."

"Maybe not."

"She's right," Harley said. "She had another tail tonight besides me. She'd already disposed of him by the time I made an appearance, but his ID was Raoul Falbon: I sent a picture on my cell phone to Venable, that friend of Grady's at CIA headquarters, and he just got back to me. Falbon is for hire to the highest bidder, but he works extensively for Molino."

"Disposed of him?" Megan asked.

"I killed the bastard," Renata said bluntly. "What do you think? That I'd give him a tap and have him come after me again tomorrow? That wouldn't have been smart."

"No, it wouldn't," Grady agreed. "And now Molino will have to send someone else. It will give us a little time."

"Give me a little time," she corrected. "Thanks to you, I'll need it now."

"We didn't lead Molino to you," Megan said. "There was no way he could know the name of the person we're searching for. I didn't know myself until a few days ago."

"Then he found out from the same source."

Megan shook her head. "No way."

"Don't tell me that. You don't know what he'd do to get what he wants."

"Believe me, I do." She stared her in the eye. "I've been there."

"Bullshit. You've been safely tucked away in Georgia all these years. You don't know anything."

"How do you know that?" She remembered something else. "And how did you know what I looked like?"

"It's in the Ledger."

"What?"

"Photos. Reports. Your mother was found and documented when she was in her teens. After that we were able to keep track of both of you until you slipped away when you were fifteen. It took a long time, but Edmund was finally able to trace you when you were in your second year in medical school."

"Edmund . . ."

"Edmund Gillem." She was silent a moment. "He's not alive any longer."

Renata's voice was steady, but there was such a wealth of pain in those words that it shook Megan. She wanted to reach out in comfort but it would have been like comforting a wolverine. "No, he died in that trailer in Rome. He was very brave."

"He was a fool. I told him to run." She drew a deep, shaky breath. "Like I'm going to do."

"Too many people have run from Molino."

"Do you think I don't want to stay and take my chances to get that son of a bitch? I can't. Not now."

"Because you have the Ledger," Grady said.

"I didn't say that."

"No, that's true," Megan said. "But Edmund said it."

Renata went still. "You're lying. Edmund would never have told anyone. He would have died first."

Megan nodded. "You're right; he did die to keep anyone from knowing you had it." She added quietly, "And as he died, he prayed for you, Renata."

Renata stared at her for a long moment. "Oh, shit." She whirled on her heel. "Come on, let's walk, Megan."

"I take it Grady and I aren't invited?" Harley said. "Stay on the path so that we can keep you in view."

Renata didn't answer and Megan had to hurry to catch up with her.

Renata's hands were jammed into her pockets and she was looking straight ahead. She didn't speak for a few minutes and when she did, her voice was no longer steady. "You're a Listener?"

"Yes."

"In the Ledger it said you probably would become one, but we weren't sure." She was blinking quickly to keep back tears. "Edmund bet me that you'd develop the talent in the next few years." She swallowed. "I told him he was crazy and that if you hadn't shown signs by now it was going to skip a generation."

"I wish it had."

She nodded jerkily. "But then you wouldn't be able to tell me about Edmund, would you? When was it?"

"Three days ago. In his trailer outside Paris."

Renata was silent again. "Was it . . . bad for him?"

She wouldn't lie to her. "Horrible."

"My God." She stopped on the path and closed her eyes. "I knew it. But I had to hear it."

"He was very brave and he was determined that no one else be hurt by Molino."

"He was such a fool. He'd agreed that if there was even a hint of someone coming after him that he'd go on the run. But he didn't do it. When he came to see me three months ago, he said that it was just a feeling and it wasn't as if he could see the future. He laughed about it."

"But he felt uneasy enough to give you the Ledger."

"Yes."

"Will you give it to me? I promise I'll keep it from Molino."

She stared at her in astonishment. "Hell, no. Edmund died for that Ledger and he gave it to me for safekeeping. I'll never give it up." Her voice was vibrating with determination and passion. "Who do you think you are? You don't know anything."

"I'm trying to learn, Renata. Teach me."

"I don't have time. Just stay away from me. You're bad news."

"I can't stay away from you. I have to get Molino and he wants the Ledger. Grady says that Molino always stays in hiding and we have to draw him out. The Ledger may be the only way we can stop him."

"Then you'd better find another way. I won't risk the Ledger."

"It won't be a risk. We'd never let it—"

"No," Renata said curtly. "Back off."

Megan shook her head. "Okay, don't give us the Ledger. But don't run away from us. We'll protect you. God knows, we don't want anything to happen to you too."

Renata's lips twisted. "Because you're afraid then you'll never find the Ledger."

Anger suddenly flared in Megan. "Damn you. Is it too much for you to believe that I don't want you dead? Edmund must have cared about you. He prayed for you. He made me care about you. They tortured him, they did terrible things to him, and then killed him. I won't let anything else be taken from him. He wanted you to live and by God, you're going to live. If you run, I'll follow. If you hide, I'll find you."

Renata was staring at her in surprise. "I didn't mean that— Well, maybe I did." She lifted her chin defiantly. "But I have reason to doubt you. You're a stranger to me."

"Except what you read in the Ledger."

"That was bare bones. Edmund couldn't get a detailed profile on everyone. There are too many."

"Then I'll fill in the blanks. Because you've got to know me. You've got to trust me." She started walking again. "I won't let it be any other way. I don't want you to panic and dart away from me if there's any lingering suspicion. What do you know about Neal Grady?"

"I know he's been trying to find members of the family for a long time. He was CIA and he has a talent. Edmund thought it might be a good idea to approach him before he located any of us. He said that he thought he could talk to Grady. He liked what he'd found out about him."

"But he didn't do it."

She shrugged. "We're careful. We don't do anything on impulse. Edmund was going to give it another six months before he made a move."

What a tragedy, Megan thought. The two men had been

gradually moving toward each other. If Grady had been two days earlier finding him, if Edmund had not been so cautious, that horror in the trailer might not have happened. "But he didn't have six months," Megan said. "How I wish he'd contacted Grady."

"He had to be sure. Grady wasn't the only one after us." Her lips tightened. "And it was through your mother that Molino found out that we even existed. That Tribunal Report on the family would never have meant anything to him if it hadn't been connected to Sarah."

"Do you expect me to apologize?" Megan asked. "Forget it. My mother never even knew about the Devanez family. She was just trying to survive and keep Molino's filthy hands off those helpless kids. And she went through hell doing it. So don't try to give me a guilt trip about your precious Ledger."

Renata was silent for a moment and then said slowly, "It is precious." She smiled faintly. "But so are children. And, you're right, I may have been trying to give you a guilt trip. I'm feeling defensive."

"No one is attacking you. You don't have to defend yourself."

"Yes, I do," she said simply. "It's a way of life with me."

Lately it had become a way of life for Megan too. She was beginning to feel a kinship with Renata Wilger. The woman was impulsive, distrustful, and from what Harley had said, violent, but she had cared about Edmund and she was willing to fight to keep his Ledger from being found. That last statement had possessed a poignancy that had touched Megan. "Then guard yourself from Molino. You're among friends here."

"Am I?" Renata looked away from her. "Do you trust Grady?"

"Yes."

"And Harley?"

"Yes. Though I don't know him as well."

"I don't trust any of you. So you might as well stop pushing me."

Megan shook her head. "That's not going to fly. You *will* trust me. All right, we'll start at step one. You can't trust someone you don't know. You said you know only the bare bones about me? I don't like confiding in strangers. I'm a private person and it hurts me. But you're going to know as much about me as if you were my sister." She drew a deep breath. "And I have to start with my mother. She was kind and funny and she always made me feel safe. That was important to her but I didn't realize why until I . . ."

"GOOD GOD, THEY'VE BEEN talking for over an hour." Grady's gaze was on Megan and Renata, who were now sitting on a park bench several yards ahead of them. "What the devil are they saying?"

"I wouldn't presume to guess," Harley said. "And I'm completely without curiosity." He gave him a sly glance. "But I'm sure it's driving you crazy. You have to be in control and it's very hard when you're shoved out of the picture. However, I'd bet that Renata Wilger is proving to be a hard nut to crack. Megan is probably doing well to keep her from running off. I'm surprised she's being this patient."

Grady wasn't surprised. Megan was volatile in some areas, but she could be completely focused. "She wants the Ledger and Renata is the key. She's not going to let her walk away. What do we know about her background?"

"Father and mother both dead. Her father was German

and her mother was a U.S. citizen. She spent most of her childhood in Boston with her mother. No brothers or sisters. She's been pretty much alone since she was thirteen except for a distant cousin, Mark Altman, who took her in for the holidays when the schools were closed. She's evidently on the genius level and got all the scholarships going. She received her doctorate in finance from Harvard two years ago and took a job with a brokerage firm, with whom she's been interning since she was sixteen. She's totally focused and been on the fast track with them." He paused. "It's going to be rough on her if she has to abandon the job and go on the run."

"It will be worse if Molino gets his hands on her," Grady said. "What about this cousin? Can Molino use him to get to her?"

"He'd have a hard time. Mark Altman was an agent for the Mossad, the Israeli secret service, before he retired." He shook his head ruefully. "And I have an idea he taught our Renata a good many things books couldn't teach her. She's a lethal little scorpion."

"I imagine those lessons could be the most valuable she'll ever learn. Was her father Jewish?"

"Yes. His grandparents were in the concentration camp at Auschwitz and most of the family immigrated to Israel after the war. He stayed in Munich but remained close to the family in Israel."

"Any family connection with Edmund Gillem?"

"Not as far as I know. Give me a break. I haven't had a chance to do any in-depth probes." His gaze went back to the two women. "But Megan may be doing it for me."

"Don't count on it. Megan seems to be doing all the talking right now." But even as he spoke Megan and Renata Wilger stood up and were coming down the path toward them. "At least your scorpion isn't running the other way."

But the expressions on both women's faces were wary, he noticed. Not hostile, not friendly, wary.

"She's not going to let us have the Ledger," Megan said. "But she's kindly consented to let us try to save her neck."

"I can save my own neck," Renata said. "But she said you were after Molino and I can't do that alone." She stared at Grady. "I want Molino dead. He has to die. I'll do everything I can to help make that happen. But if I believe that the Ledger is in any danger, I'm gone."

"Will you stay at the hotel where we can keep an eye on you?" Harley asked.

She shook her head. "But I'll be in touch."

"Do you have friends you can stay with, Renata?"

"Are you joking?" She shook her head again. "If I stayed with them, I wouldn't be a true friend. Edmund told me years ago that he was going to give me the guardianship of the Ledger if things went wrong for him. He'd been watching me since I was a little girl. He'd stayed with us every time he came to Munich and it was like having a big brother. I thought he was just my friend, Mark's friend, but then he told me I was going to be the Keeper. He said I was perfect. I had no family except Mark and he was pretty safe. I was such a bookworm that I didn't have time to make many friends. After he told me that I was going to take over the Ledger, I let those drift away." She turned away. "Don't worry, I've been preparing for this for a long time. I'll call you tomorrow after I'm settled." She didn't wait for a reply but walked down the path toward the park gates.

"What the hell," Megan murmured as Renata disappeared from view. "She gave up any friends she had because she knew she was going to have to shoulder the responsibility for the Ledger? She couldn't have been much more than a kid."

"Gillem must have really brainwashed her," Harley said.

She whirled on him. "He did *not*. He wouldn't do that. He cared about her. I know he did."

"Okay. Okay." He held up his hands defensively. "Just a comment."

"She had to want to protect the Ledger as much as he did. And it had to be hard for him to put her at risk." Megan started toward the park gates. "Evidently their whole world revolved around that damn Ledger."

"And still does," Grady said as he followed her. "And it seems that our world is beginning to be a mirror image. Coming, Harley?"

"Not yet. I'm going to give Renata a few more minutes and then go after her."

"What?"

"I planted a bug in her jacket on the way here." He took out a minuscule receiver from his pocket. "I originally meant to use it at her apartment but I didn't want to take a chance on her walking away from us into the sunset. I don't trust her."

"I spent a long time convincing her that she was safe with us," Megan said. "I'm not going to be pleased with you if she finds that bug and gets pissed."

"You'd like it less if she decided to take off and we didn't know where she was." Harley moved toward the gate. "Trust me. I'll be careful."

RENATA FLIPPED OPEN HER cell phone as soon as she got into her car. Another moment later she had reached Mark in Berlin. "I had to kill a man tonight. Molino knows I have the Ledger. Megan Blair came after me and that tipped him. I'm on the run."

"Megan Blair . . ." Mark repeated thoughtfully. "You said she might be coming after you."

"It was one of three possible scenarios I ran. This result depended if she came together with Grady. She did. She wants to use the Ledger to trap Molino."

Mark chuckled. "Incredible. But, at least, she's got her goals right. Can you find a way to use her?"

"Maybe." She was silent a moment. "She's a Listener, Mark. She was with Edmund at the end. It was . . . bad."

"We suspected as much."

"But I didn't know." She tried to keep her voice steady. "She said . . . he prayed for me."

"He was praying that you'd be strong enough to keep the Ledger safe."

"I don't think so."

"Renata."

"I'm okay. It just came as a shock." She cleared her throat. "And you know I'll always keep the Ledger safe."

"Then find a way to use Megan Blair. Molino's coming too close."

"She's family, Mark."

"And this is Molino, Renata."

He was right, of course. Megan Blair had already jeopardized Renata's safety and the safety of the Ledger by coming here. She had to ignore her instincts to protect family members. Sometimes sacrifices had to be made. "I know we have to get him. I won't fail you."

"It's not me you'd fail, it's the family. I'm sure you'd never do that. Call me if you need any help. I'll come to you through hell and high water." He hung up the phone.

Yes, she knew Mark would always be there to help, she thought as she hung up. But his solutions were sometimes quick and deadly and she was reluctant to turn him loose on Megan Blair.

She'd try to work her way through it herself first.

IT WAS CLOSE TO FOUR A.M. when Megan and Grady got back to the hotel.

"You can only sleep for a couple hours," Grady said as Megan moved across the sitting room toward her bedroom. "Renata bought us some time by ridding us of Falbon, but we don't know how much information he gave Molino. If Molino knows we're in Munich, then we'd better move out of the city."

"Not without Renata Wilger," Megan said. "I won't leave her. We can find another place here in Munich." She opened the door. "You wanted the Ledger. We're going to get it."

"And you want to protect Edmund Gillem's little protégée."

"He prayed for her," she said. "His prayers are going to be answered." The door closed behind her.

Lord, she was tired, she thought as she moved toward the bathroom. Harley's call had woken her from a dead sleep and she was now even more emotionally frayed than she had been before. The Ledger was beginning to take center stage in her mind as it was in the minds of the people around her. It was starting to take on mythical proportions and it was only a book, dammit. People shouldn't be willing to die for a book.

And people shouldn't be willing to kill for a book as Molino was doing.

What was she thinking? No matter how she tried to minimize the Ledger, it clearly had an impact on the lives of thousands of people or Edmund wouldn't have been willing to die for it.

She washed her face and started to undress. Stop thinking about it. Grab a few hours' sleep and then get ready to move on.

No, before she went back to bed she'd call and check on Phillip again. It was probably stupid to keep hoping that there would be a change but she wouldn't give up.

Pandora had left hope in that box when she'd let all the other spirits out.

Well, she wasn't Pandora, she *wouldn't* be a Pandora, but she'd cling to that hope for Phillip with all her strength.

THIRTEEN

"RENATA IS STAYING IN A cottage at the edge of town,"
Harley said when Grady picked up his call the next day.
"As soon as it got light, I started looking for a place for you
to stay nearby. I rented a cottage about a mile from her." He
rattled off the address. "I'll keep an eye on her until you get
here. Then it's up to you while I get a nap." He hung up.

"Where is she?" Megan asked as she came out of her
bedroom.

"On the outskirts of the city. Harley arranged for us to
be near her. Okay?"

She nodded. "I'll go get my suitcases." She frowned as
she stopped at the door. "This Michael Travis keeps track
of all kinds of psychics, right?"

He nodded.

"Does he know any healers?"

"What do you mean?"

"What do you think I mean?" she said curtly. "Phillip.
I'm willing to try anything."

He shook his head. "I've never run across a genuine
healer. I don't believe Michael has either. He told me that
he thought he'd found one in Brasilia about a decade ago,
but it turned out the man was a fake. Evidently it's a very
rare gift."

"Shit." Her lips tightened. "It's the one talent that would
be worthwhile in this mess. I'm a doctor. I'd give my

eyeteeth to have that kind of ability to help people, to help Phillip. Do I have any chance of becoming one? You said my mother had other talents besides being a Listener. She was a Finder. Couldn't I have—" He was shaking his head. "Why not, dammit?"

"The odds are against it. Finders are fairly common. Sarah was just an extremely good one. Healers are almost nonexistent. The chances are slim to none that you could develop into a healer."

"I *am* a healer. I'm a doctor and a good one. I just want an edge to help be a better one." She shrugged. "Maybe you're wrong. It's such a waste to have all this medical training and only be able to Listen to the woes of the world."

"I hope I'm wrong. I don't like disappointing you. If it was in my hands, I'd give you anything you wanted, do anything you asked." He met her eyes and added softly, "Anything, any way, Megan."

She stiffened. "My God, Grady."

"Just thought I'd reestablish the playing field." He smiled. "Since you've read the Tribunal Reports, you know everything I know. That means all this honorable restraint can go down the drain. Thank God. It was completely out of character for me. Let the games begin."

She didn't answer for a moment but heat flushed her cheeks. "You sound like the opening ceremony of the Olympics."

"It could turn out that way. But maybe I used the wrong word. Let the resolution begin. We've both been wanting this to happen for a long, long time. We won't get any peace until it does, until we taste it, until we know each other." He could see the pulse beating in the hollow of her throat. "Good. Feel it. Come toward me. Feel *me*. I'm not going to touch you. You have to be the one to take the first step."

For a minute he thought she was going to take that step.

Then she turned and closed the door behind her.

Dammit. He took a half step toward the door before he could stop himself.

No, it had been close. Don't ruin it because you're so hot you're about to explode, he told himself. Be patient.

Patient? No way.

MEGAN LEANED AGAINST THE door, fighting to keep herself from opening it again and going to him.

There it was again, sexuality, raw, hot, tingling, taking her breath away. An emotional and physical response that had completely blown her away.

Stop shaking. Get over it. Get your suitcases and leave the hotel and go find Renata.

Not yet. Give it time.

If she saw him in the next few minutes, she wasn't sure they would leave the bedroom, much less the hotel.

THE COTTAGE WAS SMALL, WITH a thatched roof and flowers in the window boxes.

"Talk about *Sound of Music* ambiance," Grady murmured as he held the car door open for her. "You expect to see Julie Andrews running back to the abbey."

She shook her head. "No mountains. Just forest. And I'd rather see Renata running toward us." She avoided his hand and got out of the car. "Is Harley supposed to meet us here?"

"Yes. The key is under the rock beside the door. I'll call him when we get inside." He moved toward the cottage. "He said he needed a nap. He's been watching her cottage since she arrived last night. I'll see you settled and then take over watching Renata for him."

"That's fine with me."

"I'm sure it is," he said dryly. "The more distance between us, the more you'll like it. You're treating me as if I have a contagious disease."

It was true. On the trip here she had been very careful not to touch him even casually. Yet sitting beside him had still been too provocative. She had been able to feel the heat of his body, smell the faint scent of him. "Really?" She didn't look at him. "And you're cut to the quick?"

"No, I kind of like it. It encourages me to know that I'm having an impact. The worst response would be no response with a woman with your emotional makeup." He stopped at the door. "Coming?"

She hesitated and then came toward him. "You think you know so much about me. I'm not a Pandora and even if I was, I wouldn't accept being put into a niche. I'm me and that means my character, my attitudes, my soul. Screw you, Grady."

He grinned. "That's exactly what I'm aiming toward." He reached down and retrieved the key from beneath the rock. "And I hope you don't turn out to be a Pandora. I wouldn't wish that headache on anyone." He unlocked the door and turned to face her. "It would hurt you. I won't allow anything to hurt you, Megan. Not even me."

Dammit, she couldn't breathe. She was dizzy, melting.

"Oh, shit," he said unevenly. "You remember when I told you that you had to take the first step?"

She nodded.

"I'm willing to renegotiate. Just say the word. Any word. As long as it's not no."

It should be no. She wasn't able to think clearly and logic should rule in a situation this volatile. She should be prudent and control this physical response that was making her weak. Yet all she could think about was the Neal

Grady who had been her playmate and mentor that summer on the beach. Playmate and mentor . . . and the object of a young girl's first passion. He had said he had wanted her for years. How long had she wanted him? Had desire been smothered with memory or had it merely been kept burning low? It seemed impossible that it could ever have been any less than the need she was feeling now.

To hell with it. Reach out and take it. Take him. "Inside," she said shakily. "Now."

"That'll do." He grasped her arm and opened the door. "Oh, will that do. Come on, let's find a bed."

Her arm was tingling, hot, beneath his touch. "Hurry. I don't care about the bed."

"Good." He turned on the light and pushed her back against the front door. His body rubbed slowly against her as he tilted her head back. His lips pressed against the hollow of her throat. "I don't think I could wait anyway." He was unbuttoning her shirt as his tongue licked delicately at her neck. "Hell, my hands are shaking so badly I'm not sure I can get these clothes off you."

"I'll do it." She backed away from him and stripped quickly. "I don't trust you. If you have time to consider, you might come up with some stupid reason why you won't—" She stopped and inhaled sharply as his hand went between her legs. "Or maybe not."

"Good call." He was pulling her down to the floor. "I can't reason at all right now." He took off his shirt and threw it aside. He was astride her and she felt the roughness of the denim of his jeans against her inner thighs. The sensation was vaguely erotic, she thought dazedly. Everything about him was erotic, his scent, his hands between her thighs, his flushed face above her.

"How do you want it?" he asked hoarsely. "Tell me. Anything you want, Megan."

His hands were driving her crazy. She arched upward as she jerked him down to her. "Just do it, dammit. I don't care . . ."

"I SUPPOSE WE SHOULD FIND the bedroom." Grady's hands cupped her breasts from behind. "Or a shower." He pulled gently on her nipples. "Or a kitchen."

"Why?" Lord, she still wanted him, she realized in surprise. How many times had they come together in the past few hours? They had made love frantically, endlessly, with almost animal ferocity. "I don't want to move."

"I told you that I didn't want you hurt." He was rubbing her bottom. "And I'll bet you have rug burns on your ass."

"Maybe. Battle wounds."

"Now that the edge is off, I think we can get off this floor." He got up and reached down to take her hand and pull her to her feet. "Come on. The shower first, I think."

"You want to take a shower?"

"No, I want to continue doing what we've been doing in a different location." He was leading her across the living room. "I figure by the time I become guilty enough to call Harley and tell him I'm ready to relieve him that we'll have had time to make love in every room in this house. It's good that it's such a small place or Harley would be out of luck."

Make love. Not screw. Not fuck.

They were just words, she told herself. They didn't mean anything. Yet why did she feel this sudden flow of warmth that had nothing to do with passion?

"What's your view on kitchen tables?" Grady asked.

"Interesting. I don't believe I've ever done it on one."

"Good. I'll have to try to make sure the experience is memorable. I wouldn't want you to be disappointed. . . ."

◆ ◆ ◆

"YOU SHOULD CALL HARLEY," she said as she rolled over in bed. "He'll wonder why he hasn't heard from us."

"He'll make an educated guess. Harley is damn perceptive." He pressed her cheek to his shoulder. "In this case he wouldn't have to be. A blind man could have seen how I felt about you."

"Um-hmm. Lust is pretty difficult to hide."

He chuckled. "That's an understatement. Physically it's damn well impossible for a man." He reached for his phone on the bedside table. "You're certain I can't persuade you to forget about Harley for another hour?"

"No."

"Thirty minutes?"

"No."

"Fifteen? I promise I'll make it worth your time."

She was sure he would. The last hours had been almost unbearably passionate. Lord, she'd gone crazy. She'd never had an experience this intense. She was tempted even now to roll back on top of him and start again.

"Fifteen?" he whispered.

She reached out and touched his chest. He felt warm and alive, his heart pounding harder beneath her palm. She could do this to him. She could make his muscles clench, his breath quicken. Power. Yet he could do the same thing to her. Together the power and delight could go on and on and on . . .

Oh, God, she was feeling too much. It was passion and yet not passion. What was happening to her? she thought in panic.

"I don't think so." She sat up and swung her feet to the floor. "Call Harley. He's waited long enough." She jumped up and grabbed the cotton patchwork quilt at the foot of the bed to wrap around her. "I'll jump in the shower."

"Again?" He was smiling. "It's better with company."

"But faster alone." She headed for the bathroom. "I'll see you later."

"Megan." She turned to see him gazing at her with narrowed eyes. "You're running away."

"Perhaps. Or maybe I'm trying to put things in perspective. You said that we needed to resolve the past or it would be with us forever. We've done that, Grady."

"The hell we have. I haven't resolved anything. I just want more." He paused. "And right now forever doesn't sound all that bad."

"Well, it scares the bejesus out of me." She went into the bathroom and closed the door. The next moment she was in the shower stall with the water flowing over her.

Wash away the feel of him, the scent of him. Perhaps then she could think calmly and coolly about what had happened.

Not likely. The moment she thought of Grady, she saw him on the beach with the wind blowing his hair. Or holding her in that hospital waiting room when she'd been told about Phillip's condition. Or naked over her, hard and strong yet shaking with intensity.

It scared her that the sexual memory had come last in order. It should be first after their recent coupling. It was too blasted significant that the gentler, sweeter memories had evidently meant more to her.

Passion was fine. Anything else would weaken her and he had already shown her how ruthless he could be. He was into control and could she keep her physical and mental independence when she felt like melting whenever she was with him? Emotional involvement with Grady could be a disaster.

◆ ◆ ◆

HE WAS WAITING OUTSIDE THE door as naked as when she'd left him when she opened the bathroom door thirty minutes later. "You locked the door."

"I wanted privacy."

"And you're backing away from me."

She stared him in the eye. "Yes. You're a bit overwhelming. I don't need to have an emotional overload right now. According to that damn Tribunal Report, it's also a Listener characteristic to have intense and volatile emotions. But even if I believed that bull, I don't have to give in to them."

"No, you don't." He smiled. "But, on the other hand, you could look upon me as therapy to take the edge off. I'll cheerfully volunteer for the role."

The intensity was gone, but the charisma that had captured her all those years ago was in full force. He was standing there, naked, totally at ease and so damn beautiful that she couldn't stop staring at him. With an effort she pulled her gaze away. "I'm not taking volunteers. I won't be distracted, Grady."

"And I won't stop trying." He passed her and went into the bathroom. "It was too good. A little distraction is good for the soul. I'll be out in thirty minutes. Harley should be here by then." The door closed behind him.

She drew a deep breath. Stepping away from Grady obviously wasn't going to be easy. It didn't surprise her. Nothing about their relationship had been easy from the very beginning.

Keep busy. She opened her suitcase and pulled out an outfit and began to dress. Move forward on Molino and the Ledger and Grady would become too focused to think about "distracting" her. That was what was important to both of them and Grady had been obsessed for years before she had even known it existed. Yes, get things back on a normal, even keel, and she would be able to rid her-self of this confused mixture of emotion and lust.

She would go to the little kitchen adjoining the living room and make coffee. She pushed her feet into loafers and opened the bedroom door. By that time Harley should be here and they would be able to—

"I've already put the coffee on. It should be ready in a few minutes."

Megan stopped short, her eyes widening.

Renata Wilger was lounging in the easy chair by the window, one jean-clad leg thrown over the arm. "Though I was wondering if you'd ever come out of that bedroom. You didn't tell me you and Grady were lovers."

"We're not. It just . . . happened." She frowned. "What are you doing here?" She vaguely remembered Grady locking the door after they left the kitchen for the bed-room. "How did you get in?"

"I picked the lock. It was too easy. You're lucky that it was me and not Molino." She stood up. "Come on. Let's get that coffee. Harley should be here soon and I came to talk to you and not him or Grady."

"Why only me?" She followed her into the kitchen. "Why not Grady?"

"You're family. I trust family." Renata went to the cof-feemaker on the counter and poured the liquid into two cups she'd set in readiness. "Trust Grady if you like. I suppose it's hard not to trust someone you've gone to bed with. If you trust them with your body, I guess it goes along with the territory."

"Not necessarily. But I do trust Grady." She took the cup Renata handed her. "But if you mean I'm part of the Devanez family, I didn't even know they existed until a few days ago. I can't claim to have any family feeling for any of you."

"You have a feeling for Edmund. And the bond is there. We're the same blood." She looked at Megan over the rim of her cup. "And I think you do have a feeling of family. You can't help it. It's been bred in us for centuries."

"Last night you didn't seem to think I was particularly worthy of trust," she said dryly. "You wouldn't even tell us where you were staying."

She smiled faintly. "I knew you'd find out from the bug Harley planted on me."

"You knew he planted it?"

"I'm not unskilled in this sort of thing. My cousin, Mark, has been training me since I was a youngster. The question was, what you would do with the information once he found out where I was holed up. Would I be raided by Molino? Would I be paid a visit by your Grady? He wants the Ledger and he strikes me as being very ruthless."

"He can be." She frowned. "This was some kind of test?"

She shrugged. "I had to be sure. If you just watched and waited, then I would be able to trust you."

"And if we were the bad guys, then you'd have put yourself in danger."

She shook her head. "I was ready for you." She smiled as she took another sip of coffee. "What I wasn't expecting was having to wait here while you and Grady indulged in fun and games." She glanced around the kitchen. "I had to put all the chairs back around the table before I made coffee."

Megan could feel the heat flush her cheeks. She changed the subject. "How did you know where to find us?"

"I used a device to tap Harley's cell phone through the nearest tower. I thought he'd contact you."

"And how did you get out of your cottage without Harley seeing you?"

"There's a root cellar in the cottage that leads to a passage down the hill."

"You could have just told him you were coming here."

"I could." Her eyes were suddenly twinkling. "But I wanted him to have egg on his face. He's too sure of himself for my taste. He thinks that his little bug is going to keep me firmly in view."

"You still haven't told me why you've come." She paused. "Will you let us use the Ledger?"

Renata shook her head. "But I'll let you use me."

"What?"

"The chances are that Molino knows that Edmund gave me the Ledger. He sent Falbon after me. If you back away, pretend you haven't found me, he'll think I still have the Ledger and go after me the way he did Edmund."

"My God, Renata."

"I'll have to send the Ledger to someone safe in case something goes wrong. I've already chosen my replacement. Edmund told me I had to do it when he gave me the Ledger."

"Your cousin, Mark?"

She shook her head. "No, but I wouldn't tell you anyway. It doesn't matter if I trust you. This is the Ledger. But once it's safe, you can use me."

"No," she said flatly. "I won't stake you out and let Molino have his chance at you. I went through that with Edmund."

"And I won't let Molino live after what he did to Edmund. It was only a matter of time anyway. He's been quietly murdering anyone with psychic ability he's been able to track down for years. Two years ago, a young woman in Arizona was a hit-and-run. Last year, a young boy in Orlando was drowned in a lake. I'm not even sure that

Molino knew they were Devanez. They were freaks and that was all he cared about. Lord knows how many deaths can be laid at his door." Her grasp tightened on her cup. "But I know exactly how many deaths he'll be able to cause if he gets his hands on the Ledger."

"Then for God's sake, destroy it," Megan said fiercely. "If he can't find the people listed in the Ledger, he can't hurt them. Don't let one book cause all this misery."

"I can't. Do you think it's some kind of outdated tradition that keeps us maintaining the Ledger? Some of the people in that book don't even realize they're part of the family. We try to leave them alone to live their lives. But some have talents they can't control that bewilder them. Some will develop talents later and we have to have someone there to help them." She paused. "And some will have to be saved from the Molinos of the world. Do you think he's the first monster to go after the Ledger? They've always been hovering on the horizon. That Tribunal Report was public record for centuries. By most people it was considered an example of the wild tales the Inquisitors brought from the mouths of their victims. But there were others . . ." She put her cup down on the counter. "Did you know my great-grandfather was in Auschwitz?"

Megan nodded. "Religious persecution?"

"No, he might have ended up there anyway, but he was sent to Auschwitz to be interrogated. Hitler and the entire Nazi party were founded on the occult. He had his own astrologers and fortune-tellers. Even the Nazi symbols harkened back to esoteric traditions from the Scottish Masons and Knights Templar and other societies; the swastika, the eagle, the red, black, and white color scheme. Hitler himself believed he was the chosen one of the 'Superiors' who endowed him with uncanny hypnotic power." She paused. "But he was also absolutely convinced of the coming of a new race of supermen. He expected them to be a mutation of homo sapiens just by arriving at the higher level of consciousness. That's why he was so obsessed with the so-called purity of the Aryan race."

"I've read about his attempt to form a master race."

"Then you can imagine how overjoyed he was when he came across the copy of the Tribunal Report. It meant that he didn't have to wait for evolution to take place. He could create his own supermen. It fostered his image of himself as being godlike. He was going to find the least offensive members of the Devanez family and breed them with his blue-eyed Aryan favorites. He'd use the talents of others in the family to make his dictatorship invulnerable." She shook her head. "He was even willing to risk the purity of the blood to breed mental supermen. Of course, it meant he had to find them. So he sent Himmler on a witch hunt to track down any stories of anyone with psychic abilities and try to trace their lineage back to the family. Himmler found documents that led him to my great-grandfather Henrich Schneider." Her lips twisted. "Unfortunately, he was no good to Hitler as a stud. He was a Jew and that made him too polluted to risk contamination. But there was a chance that he'd know where other, more acceptable, psychics could be found. He arrested him and most of his family and sent him to Auschwitz. His older son was in Israel and we managed to warn him. The interrogators killed his wife and two children before his eyes because he refused to tell him about the location of the Ledger."

"Dear God."

"He didn't know where it was. He wasn't the Keeper. He underwent years of starvation and torture. When he was released from the camp at the end of the war, he was in such poor condition he died four months later. But during the war years we were able to smuggle most of the

Devanez family out of Germany to safety. Six hundred and twenty-five people crossed the borders and were settled in other countries." She added deliberately, "Because we had their names and where they were located. Because we had the Ledger. There will always be Torquemadas and Molinos and Hitlers in the world. We just have to be ready for them." She lifted her cup. "So that we can crush the bastards like cockroaches."

"It appears you've been running from those cockroaches."

She shrugged. "You're right; I have a problem with that too. I promised Edmund I wouldn't risk the Ledger. I'll keep my promise." She added, "But I won't let Molino live after what he did to Edmund. So use me to trap the son of a bitch."

"No."

"Think about it." She set the cup on the counter. "I'll give you a day or two to change your mind. You know where to find me."

"If you don't decide to scurry out the root cellar again," Harley said from behind Megan. "I let myself in after waiting a discreet amount of time. She obviously wanted to talk to you without an audience." He looked from Renata to Megan. "Are you finished with your discussion? I'll escort her back to her cottage."

Renata tilted her head. "You knew about the root cellar?"

"Most of these cottages have root cellars. I checked with the landlord who rented me this cottage and he told me that your rental was very interesting. That's why I set up shop in a spot where I could watch the front door and the tunnel exit."

"That was very clever of you," she said slowly.

"I have my moments." He glanced at Megan. "You didn't answer me."

"I believe Renata has said all she wants to say."

"Then I'll take her home. I don't think you'll have to ask Grady to watch her cottage. It wouldn't do much good. I went inside the cottage after I saw her come here and she has enough hi-tech equipment and weapons to rival James Bond."

Megan's brows lifted. "Cousin Mark?"

"Of course," Renata said simply. "He believes in being prepared for any eventuality. He's been training me since my parents died."

"Training you to guard the Ledger?"

"And to survive scumbags like Molino." She headed for the front door. "I contacted Mark last night after I reached the cottage and asked him to try to find out who Molino might use now that Falbon is dead." She opened the door. "Molino will probably be eager and moving fast now." She glanced back at Megan. "Speed can cause mistakes. He'd jump at getting his hands on me. We have an opportunity."

Megan shook her head. "I won't risk you."

Renata shook her head in exasperation. "You don't understand. I *want* this."

Megan shook her head again.

"Stubborn." She was silent a moment. "I'd feel . . . touched by your concern if it wasn't getting in the way. No one has tried to protect me for a long time." She crooked her finger at Harley. "If you're coming, let's go. And if you try to go in my cottage again when I'm not there, you'll get an unpleasant surprise. Booby traps are easy to rig. I didn't give you warning before, but you have it now."

"Duly noted." Harley moved after her. "Megan, I'll be back in a few minutes."

Megan watched the door swing shut behind them.

Dammit, Renata was being difficult as the devil. She had called Megan stubborn, but the woman was just as obstinate. She wanted everything her way and she wasn't about to listen to reason.

And Renata's way would put her squarely into Molino's path. Why wouldn't she let Megan and Grady have the Ledger to use as a decoy instead of her? Life was precious.

Yet Megan was beginning to understand the passion that drove her. The story she had told her about her great-grandfather's death at Auschwitz had shone a light on the persecution and need for self-preservation that had driven the Devanez family for centuries. They had saved hundreds of lives because they had kept accurate records in the Ledger. What other stories of sacrifice and salvation existed in the history of the book? Renata probably knew them all. She had lived and breathed the Devanez family from childhood. Edmund had died for the Ledger. It had not been an idealistic abstract concept to him. He had wanted to save lives and the Ledger was the key.

"You're frowning. What's wrong?"

She looked up to see Grady standing in the doorway. His dark hair was wet from the shower and he looked lean and tough in jeans and a dark green shirt. She felt a little jolt of pleasure as she saw him. He hadn't been out of her sight for much more than the thirty minutes he'd told her he'd be and she was feeling this response. "Renata paid us a visit." She turned and got him a cup down from the cabinet. "Sit down and I'll tell you about it."

FOURTEEN

"SHE'S RIGHT." GRADY STARED down into the coffee in his cup. "It could be an opportunity."

Megan stiffened. "What do you mean? We are *not* going to use her, Grady."

"I'd bet she wants to use us. She's no victim."

"Just because it's her idea is no reason we have to help her. And she could be a victim if anything went wrong. She's as obsessed with the Ledger as Edmund. She doesn't believe Molino can beat her, but if it came down to choices, she'd never let him have the Ledger." She shivered. "She'd reach for that jagged piece of mirror just like Edmund did. And the scary thing is that I'm starting to understand why."

"Forget it," he said sharply. "You're beginning to identify with the family. Dammit, this is what I was afraid would happen."

"I'm not identifying. I just understand."

"Keep it that way." He reached across the table and grasped her hand. "Listen. Your emotional response in ordinary situations is extreme. Imagine what it would be if you accepted yourself as one of the Devanez family with all the accompanying baggage. Strangers in pain or jeopardy hurt you. When Phillip was shot, you were in agony. Empathy with this family would send you over the top."

She shook her head. "Family is just a word. I don't know any of these people but Renata."

"But you're already hurting for them." His hand tightened. "Don't be drawn in, Megan."

She smiled faintly. "But you're the one who drew me in. You sent me to get the Ledger. The family has the Ledger and evidently I can't get it without them. It's a Catch-22."

"Distance yourself. That's the only way to—" He stopped and shook his head. "What am I saying? You don't know how to distance yourself. It's against your basic makeup. You're even having trouble convincing yourself to distance yourself from me."

She looked down at their hands. His grasp felt good, safe. He was right, she didn't want to let go of that strength. She deliberately drew her hand away. "But I can do it. You talk as if I'm some kind of emotion-charged junky. I can do anything I have to do. I can walk away whenever I want to do it."

"But it hurts you more than it would other people," he said softly. "And if you're a junky, then I wouldn't have it any other way. You shine, you glow, you burn. I feel warm inside just being with you."

She didn't know what to say. The melting sensation deep within her was like nothing she'd ever felt before. She wanted to reach back across the table and touch him.

And then she'd be back where she'd been when she'd gotten out of his bed only a short time ago. "We were talking about Renata."

"Yes." He leaned back in his chair. "And you want to get back on an impersonal subject. But nothing is impersonal between us. Haven't you found that out? We start out perfectly cool and practical and then it all goes downhill. You're wondering if I'm going to touch you. No, not right now. I can hold off since you're obviously suffering an overload. But it will happen. I can't help it." He smiled. "But we'll try to backtrack and give you some breathing space."

"How kind," she said dryly before she changed the subject. "I won't have Renata risk herself and she won't let us use the Ledger, but there must be some way she can help us."

"I got the impression from what you said that it was going to be her way or nothing."

Megan's lips tightened. "Then she'll have to change her mind."

He chuckled. "Lord, at this moment I can definitely detect a family resemblance. I don't know about the Devanez clan, but you may be sisters under the skin."

"That's ridiculous. We're nothing alike."

"Yet you're fighting with all your strength to protect her. You like her."

Yes, she did like Renata. In spite of her barbed toughness and stubbornness, Megan could sense vulnerability just below the surface that she instinctively wanted to shelter and protect. Since childhood Renata had not really had anyone to take care of her but her cousin, Mark, who had clearly concentrated on keeping her alive and not given her the security of a home and affection. "It's natural that I should want to help her. We both have had to be on our own, but I had Phillip. I don't believe she really had anyone."

"Well, evidently that lack caused the two of you to spin in different directions. You became a doctor and she became Lara Croft–slash–James Bond." He waved his hand as she opened her lips to speak. "I'm not putting her down. There's a lot about her that I respect." He smiled. "But then, I respect Lara Croft and James Bond too. However, you'll have to accept that Renata will never hesitate to pull the trigger if she's cornered. You'd agonize and try desperately to find a way to keep from doing it, but she'd consider her options in a split second and then do what had to be done." He lifted his cup to his lips. "And it's not necessarily the difference in character and upbringing. It could be the talent. Your talent is based on emotional responsiveness and carries over to every part of your life. Renata's gift is more abstract. She can see patterns and connections in situations that lead her to be able to predict the next step, sometimes the final result. It's mental rather than emotional."

She grimaced. "I'd much rather believe in normal personality and environmental traits. Anything else would put entirely too much importance on all this psychic stuff."

"Heaven forbid," he murmured.

She ignored the faint mockery in his tone. "But we might as well take advantage of any edge we have." She frowned. "Though I can't see how a Listener would be of any help in trapping Molino."

"You found Renata," he pointed out.

"Much good that's doing us if we can't persuade her to give us the Ledger." She added slowly, "But you're both right. There's an opportunity to turn the prey into the hunter here. It's just that the prey can't be Renata."

He stiffened. "I don't like the sound of that." He studied her expression. "I don't like it at all."

"Why not? You're all into this opportunity bull." She turned toward the door. "I have to think. I'm going for a walk."

He rose to his feet. "I'll go with you." He shook his head. "I know you don't want company. It doesn't matter. I'm not letting you out of my sight. We don't know how much Molino knows and where he is on the game board.

And I won't trail behind you as I did last night. You'll have to put up with me."

She didn't want him. He would disturb her. Just looking at him disturbed her.

"Get used to it," Grady said softly.

"I will." She turned and headed for the door. "For the time being."

"FALBON IS DEAD," SIENNA SAID. "He was found murdered on Onstadt Street in Munich late last night. A blow that sent splinters into his brain. We received a call from him at nine and he said he was going to have Renata Wilger before the night was over." He shrugged. "It seems he was wrong. Grady?"

"Probably." Molino thought about it. "But that doesn't mean he has to have the Ledger yet. Edmund Gillem was very stubborn and he held out for a long time. Grady may be hesitant to use the same methods we did. If we move fast, we may be able to snatch her away from him." He paused. "And Megan Blair is still with him?"

"Presumably. She was on the plane to Munich."

That was good, he thought with satisfaction. If Renata Wilger, Megan Blair, and Grady were together there was a possibility that he could scoop up all these murdering freaks at one time.

"Was Falbon able to give us anything to use to find Renata Wilger?"

"When he was doing surveillance at the brokerage office, he was able to zero in on her cell phone. There's a chance that we can use a satellite to locate her if she doesn't have it blocked."

"Do it."

"I'm already working on it. We're too close to that Ledger to make mistakes now." Sienna tilted his head. "I thought you'd be more upset that Falbon had bought it."

"No, it won't matter in the long run. I just have to be patient. I'll have them all."

"I'm glad you're so confident." Sienna turned and left the room.

And Sienna wasn't that sure they'd succeed, Molino thought. Let him doubt. He would see that Molino was right.

I'll help you. We'll kill them all, Papa. We'll butcher the freaks.

He could feel the tears sting his eyes. "Yes, Steven," he whispered. "I know . . ."

A SHADOWY FIGURE WAS standing beside her bed!

Renata's hand snaked beneath her pillow. Where was the gun? She gasped and then dove forward and butted her head into the man's stomach.

She heard a grunt as she reached out to dig her hand into the attacker's gonads.

"Shit!" He grasped her shoulders and threw her back on the bed. "I'm not here to hurt you, dammit."

Grady.

She froze as she was ready to launch herself forward again. "You shouldn't be here at all." She reached over and turned on the bedside lamp. "I don't like intruders. You're lucky to be alive." She sat up in bed. "How did you get in here?"

Grady sat down in a chair across the room. "You mean your booby traps? It was like making my way through a maze, but Harley is good at disarming those little toys."

"No, that's not what I mean. I didn't realize you were

here until it was almost too late. You were actually able to get my gun from beneath my pillow before I woke. I'm not usually that vulnerable." She stared him in the eye. "I heard you were supposed to be good, but I've been trained to block Controllers."

"By whom?"

She didn't answer.

"If it's any comfort, I wasn't able to do anything with your mind while you were conscious. You were very, very tough. I had to wait until you were asleep."

"If you wanted to talk to me, you could have phoned."

He grimaced. "It would certainly have been easier on my nuts. However, I needed to find out who you are and how much I could sway you."

She shook her head. "Not at all."

"It was worth a shot." He leaned back in his chair. "And I know you better now."

She swung her feet to the floor. "But not as well as you do Megan. She's probably as strong as I am at blocking you. Tell me, did you find it necessary to screw her to control her?"

The jab didn't faze him. "No, that was pure pleasure. And I get very annoyed at other people trying to control Megan."

She stiffened warily. "Is that supposed to apply to me?"

He nodded. "You've had a very strong effect on Megan every time you've been together."

"I'm no Controller."

"I know. But you're very intelligent, genius level. And your gift has trained you to study cause and effect."

"In situations, not people."

"I don't believe you could separate the two."

"Believe what you like."

"Oh, I will," he said softly. "For instance, I believe that

you recognized that Megan would be very defensive of you if you said you were going to stake yourself out for Molino. You're very clever and you know that since she feels things so deeply that she'd be very protective and search every way she could to avoid that happening." He paused. "Even if it meant staking herself out instead."

She stared at him without expression. "I didn't suggest that."

"Because, as I said, you're very clever."

"What did she say when you told her that you suspected me?"

"I'm not stupid. I would never hint that you would be so conniving. She likes you. You've even got her feeling like a member of the family. She thinks she knows you and that you wouldn't try to manipulate her."

She didn't speak for a moment. "I like her too."

"But that wouldn't stop you from manipulating her."

Her brows lifted. "That's your opinion, on pitifully slim evidence. You haven't been around me long enough to judge."

"I wasn't able to control you, but I could sense enough to do a pretty accurate character judgment. I'm familiar with obsession and you're definitely obsessed. It radiates out of you in waves. I think you'd do anything to protect that Ledger from Molino."

"I've never denied that."

"But you have to destroy Molino to protect the Ledger. That's where the danger lies. If you risk yourself, then you have to give up the custody of the Ledger to someone else. People who are obsessed hate giving up the object of their obsession." He studied her. "And I don't see you as a martyr like Gillem."

"You'd be blind if you did. I'm not Edmund."

"But Megan thinks if it came down to choice you'd make the same decision."

She shook her head.

"Megan usually has excellent instincts. You might surprise yourself."

"You just said she couldn't see through me. You can't have it both ways."

"Of course, I can. You're a complicated woman and she's seeing another dimension than I am." He rose to his feet and put her gun on the nightstand. "I'll let you get back to sleep now. I'll see you in the morning."

"Wait. Why the hell did you come here? Is it some kind of threat?"

He smiled. "Perhaps I wanted you to realize that you're not as invulnerable as you think you are."

He had done that, she thought bitterly. She hadn't felt this uneasy since she'd first started training with Mark. "You proved nothing. I never thought I was invulnerable. But I did break away from you and woke up when you were trying to keep me asleep."

"Did you break away?"

She had a sudden twinge of doubt. Had he let her go? She searched his expression. "You're bluffing. Damn right I did."

He chuckled. "You're right. You slipped out from under in the end."

She hadn't expected him to admit it. "Then you might just as well not have come."

His smile faded. "Except to let you know that I wouldn't be pleased if you do anything to hurt Megan. In fact, I'd be so upset that I believe you'd end up in small, bloody pieces." His words were spoken softly, almost casually, but that didn't alter the deadliness.

Damn, he was an intimidating man. She wasn't used to being frightened but in this moment she was afraid of Neal Grady. Don't let him see it. "Get out of here, Grady."

"I'm on my way." He nodded. "Have a good night."

The next moment the door was closing behind him.

She drew a deep relieved breath. She wished Mark was here to tell her how ridiculous she was being. He'd always said that fear was the most dangerous enemy she'd face. She'd laughed and told him that quote was completely unoriginal. Shades of Franklin Roosevelt. It was idiotic being afraid of Grady when she had no fear of Molino.

Guilt?

Maybe. She didn't feel good about this or what she was going to do. What difference did it make how she felt? Edmund had not felt good when he had cut his own throat. You did what you had to do to protect the Ledger. Grady was right, it was not a sacred responsibility to her as it had been to Edmund, but it was a duty and an obsession.

And she mustn't let Grady stop her from doing what had to be done. She'd been hesitating, waiting until she could smother any lingering regret and function efficiently as she'd been taught. But Grady wasn't hesitating and she had to move fast now.

She reached for her cell phone and dialed the number Mark had given her last night.

WHERE THE HELL WAS HE? Megan thought in frustration. After she and Grady had returned to the cottage, she had gone directly to her bedroom. But an hour later she had heard Grady leave the cottage and he had been gone for hours.

Where?

It didn't matter. Grady could take care of himself. There was no use panicking because the stupid man had not had the consideration to tell her he was going out when Molino was hot on their trail.

She'd tried to ignore the fear, tried to go to sleep, tried to work on her patient records on her laptop. No way.

She ended up sitting in the living room in this damn chair like a wife waiting for a wandering spouse.

It was nearly morning when she heard the key turn in the lock.

Relief poured through her, immediately followed by anger.

His brows rose as he saw her. "Hello. Are you as annoyed as I think you are?"

"You should have told me you were leaving."

"Why? You didn't want to be around me. You ran like a jackrabbit when we got back to the cottage."

"So you left because you knew I'd worry? To punish me?"

His lips tightened. "God, what a stupid thing to say. I'm no kid who'd pull a stunt like that just because I wasn't going to be allowed bed privileges. I knew how you'd respond to a threat to me. You'd panic, you'd hurt. It's your nature. I may not be your favorite person right now but you do care for me. I'd never make you go through that if I could help it."

It had been stupid. If she hadn't been emotionally overwrought, she would never have said those words. Grady was not petty and he was an intelligent, mature male. "Then why didn't you tell me you were leaving?"

"I hoped you were asleep. You've learned to block me so well that I couldn't tell if you were. I waited an hour before I left. I had a few things to do."

"What things?"

"I called and got an update on the police investigation on Phillip's attack. They've traced the tires and found they belonged on a Chevrolet truck manufactured between 1995 and 1998."

"And how many thousand trucks were sold during those years?"

"But they may be able to narrow it down. The tires were new, the tread showed no more than two months' wear. The police are going to go around to tire dealers in Atlanta and ask questions."

"It might take a long time."

He nodded. "Or they might get lucky and come up with an answer on the first day."

"Why didn't you phone from here?" Her gaze narrowed on his face. "A call like that would take minutes, not hours. That's not the only thing that you were doing, is it?"

"No."

"And you're not going to tell me."

"That's right. It wasn't anything that would hurt you or interfere with our common aim." He turned away. "And now I'm going to bed down on this couch unless you've changed your mind. Just invite me and I'll be in your bed in two minutes." He smiled. "I have no pride where sex is concerned."

And neither did she. They had gone far beyond pride last night. She wanted nothing more than to have him touch her. Lord, was that why she had been sitting here waiting for him? Worry, yes. But hunger had been present too. Hunger to see him, to touch him, to feel his hands on her.

"Invite me," he repeated softly, his gaze holding her own. "You won't regret it."

She wouldn't regret it tonight. But only hours before,

he'd closed her out, and he still was refusing to confide in her. Everything he did was beginning to mean too much. She didn't know if she could keep herself from giving everything and she wouldn't be cheated.

She turned on her heel. "Good night, Grady."

"Sleep well, Megan."

There was no mockery in his tone but she wasn't going to sleep well and he probably knew it.

She turned out the bedside light and stared into the darkness. If she couldn't sleep, she could plan.

Think of Molino. Think of the Ledger.

Don't think of Grady lying on that couch only a few yards from the bedroom door.

SHE WAS STILL NOT ASLEEP when the cell phone on her bedside table rang four hours later.

"Get out of there," Renata said when she picked up the phone. Her voice was crackling with urgency. "Now. I don't know how much time you have. Dammit, I don't know how much time I have. Molino wouldn't have only sent one man. Not after Falbon."

Megan jerked upright in bed. "What's happening? Why are—"

"What do you think? Molino. He traced me. If he's found me, he might know you're right on my doorstep. I can't talk to you any longer. I have to get on the move."

"Wait. I'll call Grady and—"

Renata had already hung up.

Megan threw back the covers and jumped to her feet. "Grady!" She grabbed her clothes and started dressing. "Dammit, Grady, where are you?"

"Right here." Grady stood in the doorway. "What's wrong? Who was on the phone?"

"Renata." She sat down and put on her shoes. "Get dressed. She said Molino may be on his way. He's traced her. She wanted to warn us."

"How does she know?"

"I don't know. She hung up. She said something about Molino wouldn't have sent just one man. She was in a hurry." She grabbed her jacket. "We have to get over there and make sure she's okay."

"Wait." He turned and went toward the bathroom. "I'll be dressed in a few minutes. We'll call and tell Harley to go to her place and check it out."

"I'll go on ahead. I'm not going to wait."

"You will unless you want me to trail behind you naked." He was throwing on his clothes. "I don't want you walking out that front door without me. Hell, I don't want you walking out the front door at all. We'll go out the bedroom window in case Molino has men outside waiting for us." He threw her his cell phone. "You call Harley. He's on speed dial."

"How could Molino trace her?" she asked as she scrolled for the name.

"It's a technical world and almost anyone can be tracked if you have the right equipment." He grabbed a jacket and pulled her toward the bedroom window. "Have you got Harley?"

She nodded and handed him the phone. "Tell him to hurry. Renata sounded— Just tell him to hurry."

SHE WAS BLEEDING, Renata realized dimly.

Ignore it. Keep on moving. She could hear them behind her in the forest. At least two men and they weren't woods-savvy. They sounded like elephants moving through the shrubbery.

Deadly elephants. One of them, the taller of the two, had managed to clip her with a bullet from a distance of more than a hundred yards when he had caught sight of her running out of the root cellar into the forest.

And she couldn't ignore that wound for long. She was still bleeding and she couldn't risk fainting or being too weak to function when they caught her. Okay, slow down, find a place to wait for them. Maybe she could find a minute to bind up the shoulder.

Or maybe not. They were closer. No time to do anything but wait and let them pass her. Then pick off the one in the rear as Mark had taught her. It had to be silent and quick so that the first man wouldn't realize what was happening.

And that meant using the knife and, God, she hated knife work.

No choice.

She put on speed as she rounded a turn in the path. Good. There was another curve in the path several yards ahead. The huge oak tree at the side of the trail should give her enough cover.

She darted behind it and tried to catch her breath.

She could hear them.

Closer.

Now she could see them as they rounded the turn.

The smaller man was a good eight yards in the lead, his slight wiry body moving piston-smooth.

Wait until he passed and went around the curve.

The taller man, the one who'd shot her, was coming barreling down the path toward her, passing her.

Move silently, as Mark had shown her. She was wounded and she couldn't rely on physical strength. The man was too tall for her to reach up and cut his throat so she had to rely on one accurate stab to the heart.

Fast. Silent. *Now.*

The knife entered his heart and he made only a low gasp as he staggered and fell to the ground.

Dead.

Blood on her hands.

Lord, she hated knives.

The other man. She took her gun out of her jacket and started to fade into the shrubbery.

"Stay here. Let me do it."

She whirled to see Jed Harley running down the path toward her.

"It's okay," he said quietly as he reached her. "I'll get him. You take care of yourself."

She watched dazedly as he disappeared around the turn. She could feel the adrenaline that had kept her going draining out of her and sank back against the tree. Yes, if Harley said that he would get that other bastard, he would do it. She'd experienced his skill and she could trust it.

She was beginning to feel sluggish and light-headed. She had to stop the blood before she got any weaker. Pressure bandage. She flinched as she shrugged off the jacket and began to unbutton her shirt.

FIFTEEN

"THAT'S A VERY CLUMSY BANDAGE," Harley said.

She looked up as he came back around the curve of the path. "Did you get him?"

He nodded, his gaze still on her shoulder. "Good Lord, did you have to use the whole shirt?"

"Shut up. I did the best I could. I couldn't tear the damn thing." She had been so weak she'd barely managed to get the shirt in a pressure position. "I didn't hear a shot."

"I broke his neck. Much less messy than your knife."

"I didn't have a choice. I had to get rid of them quickly."

"I'm not criticizing you. You did very well considering that it was two against one and you were wounded."

"Don't patronize me. I did well, period."

He smiled. "Yes, you did. More training by Cousin Mark?"

"He took me to a guerilla antiterrorist training camp near Zurich when I was sixteen. He wanted to make sure I could survive in any situation."

"And I'd bet he made sure you had hands-on experience later."

She gave him a level glance. "That's none of your business."

"You're right. Since we're going to have to dispose of these scumbags, would you consider it my business if I asked you if there are any other bodies to add to the count?"

"One man in the cottage." Her lips twisted. "He was much clumsier than you and Grady were at burgling my place. I knew he was inside seconds after he sprang the lock."

"Dead, I assume?"

She nodded. "I led him down to the root cellar. But he wasn't easy like Falbon. He knew exactly what he was doing." She paused. "And he had chloroform. Molino wanted me alive if he could pull it off."

"So you phoned, warned Megan, and then took off. You could have waited for reinforcements. I was at your cottage five minutes after I got the call."

"It would have been too easy for one of them to toss an explosive through a window." She paused. "Five minutes? You were staking me out again. Grady's orders?"

"No, my call. I admit I'm finding your entrance into the situation fascinating and didn't want you to make an abrupt departure. I arrived at the root cellar too late to intercept you. You were already running into the woods with Molino's men at your heels." He knelt beside her and began to unwind the makeshift bandage. "May I? I believe I can do a little better. I was once a driver for an EMT unit. I'm good with wounds."

"I bet you are." She leaned back against the trunk of the tree. "Go ahead. Show me what an expert you are."

"In what area? I'll have to limit your exposure. I wouldn't want to dazzle you." He had finished unwrapping the bandage and he gave a low whistle. "This is pretty ugly. It's going to need some stitches. I'd better get you back to the cottage and let Megan get to work on you."

"You mean you're not capable of doing it yourself?" Her lips twisted. "You're not dazzling me, Harley."

"I could patch you." He tore the shirt in strips and began to rewrap the wound. "But I'm an amateur and you've got beautiful shoulders. I'd hate to be the one to cause a scar."

"I wouldn't worry about it."

"I would." He finished the bandage and sat back on his heels. "You might change your mind and go after me with a machete."

She shuddered. "Not with a machete. I hate knives. Killing is bad enough, but knives . . ."

"Then all I'd have to worry about is a bullet? What a relief." He pulled her to her feet. "We should get you back. Can you walk?"

She nodded and started back down the path.

"You're not exactly steady," Harley said after a few minutes. "Would you be too proud to take a little help? You're a little too slow for me. I want to get back to Megan and Grady in this decade."

"Bastard." She stopped and took a deep breath. "I suppose it's too late to refuse help now. After all, I let you kill a man for me."

"That's true. I guess that did set a precedent." He gently took her arm. "I promise I won't let it go to my head. Lean on me."

His grasp was warm and comforting, she thought wearily. He was not a safe man but he somehow made her feel safe. It had been a long time since she had felt this secure.

She relaxed against him and let him carry more of her weight. "If you let me fall, I'll cut your throat."

"No, you won't." He chuckled. "You don't like knives."

•

"YOU'RE LUCKY IT'S ONLY A flesh wound," Megan said as she finished stitching. "Though it's ugly enough. It was a high-caliber bullet. You'll have a nasty scar."

"Whew," Harley said in mock relief. "I'm glad I left it for a professional to mess up her shoulder."

"I didn't mess it up," Megan said. "I did the best I could, but I can't—"

"He's just joking," Renata said. "He has a peculiar sense of humor."

"At least I have one," Harley murmured. "Cousin Mark should have concentrated on that instead of antiterrorist tactics."

Megan looked from one to the other. Harley and Renata were nothing alike. She was intense and wary, and Megan could almost feel the electric force that energized her. In contrast Harley gave the appearance of being totally laid back and he was much more people-oriented. Yet Megan could sense a bond, an understanding . . . something.

"It was a good battlefield bandage, Harley," Megan said as she finished bandaging Renata's shoulder. "She'll have to be on antibiotics for a while and take care not to damage the stitches but she'll be fine." She frowned as she touched a round, white mark on Renata's upper arm. "This looks like another bullet wound."

Renata nodded. "Syria." She pulled up her shirt to cover the scar. "Aren't you finished? We should get out of here. I don't think there was time for Molino's men to call for help but it wasn't—"

"When Grady gets back," Harley said. "He called some of his CIA buddies and they're sending a cleanup crew out here. He's meeting them in the woods."

"If it would help, I could call Mark."

"I'm tempted to let you do it," Megan said grimly. "I'd like to meet your cousin."

"Oh, my, she's getting all protective and maternal," Harley said. "Perhaps I should have a talk with her, Renata."

"Shut up. You don't know anything. She's a Listener. She can't help it."

He made a face. "Pardon me. I'm not familiar with the nuances of all this psychic business." He headed for the door. "And I think you've had enough of me for a while. I believe I'll take a tour of the perimeter and make sure it's secure. Call me if you need me." He slanted a mocking glance at Renata. "If it wouldn't offend your dignity."

He didn't wait for an answer.

Renata frowned as they heard the front door close behind him. "He's such a fool."

"You don't really think that," Megan said as she helped the other woman button her shirt. "So don't say it."

Renata looked at her in surprise. "Are you telling me what to do?"

"Yes." She leaned back and stared her directly in the eye. "I believe it's time someone did. Just because you seem to be fairly capable at killing and mayhem is no sign that you're not criminally headstrong."

"What?"

"You heard me. We're trying to help you and you won't listen unless everything is your way. I'm tired of it. Yes, I feel sorry for you but I—"

"I don't want you to feel sorry for me." She glared at Megan. "I don't need anyone to—"

"Be quiet. I don't care what you want. Harley is right; somewhere along the way you missed out on a few important experiences that might have made you a hell of a lot more human. You're brilliant and perceptive and driven, but, dammit, there's more to life than that. You defended me because you thought my softness toward you was due to my so-called gift? Bullshit. I don't believe that your Ledger can either dictate or explain my character. What I feel is due to the soul I was born with and the people I've interacted with during my life. My mother, Phillip . . ." She stopped and drew a deep breath. "Even you, Renata. You're so full of defensiveness that it hurts me to think about it. So if I decide to pity you, then you'll just have to accept it. Understand?"

Renata didn't speak for a moment. "I understand." Then a slow smile lit her face. "Not really. I've never met anyone like you before."

Megan shook her head. "Is that all I'm going to get out of you?"

Renata's brows rose. "Did you expect me to fall into your arms and bare my soul?"

Not a tough nut like Renata, Megan thought resignedly. "A few words that were both honest and not convoluted would be nice."

Renata thought about it. "Okay, Harley isn't really a fool. I just don't—I don't know what he's thinking and it bothers me." Her lips twisted. "Is that honest enough for you?"

"It's a start." She paused. "Now, tell me. Are you going to go after Molino with us or are you going to try to use us and the whole world to get him on your own?"

"I'll think about it."

"No, you've already thought about it. I want an answer. It's the best way to go. Admit it."

"Perhaps."

"Renata."

"Okay." She smiled. "I'll make it a joint effort . . . if the Ledger isn't compromised."

"Well, that was like pulling teeth," Megan said.

"No, it wasn't. Someday I'll let Mark tell you how he lost three teeth being interrogated by the Taliban." She got to her feet. "And now I have to pack up my equipment before Grady comes back. We're on borrowed time."

"I can do it for you. You should rest."

"No one touches my equipment but me. I can rest

later." She moved slowly, carefully, toward the living room. Megan could tell that she was making an effort not to sway or totter.

"Now who's the fool?" Megan asked softly. "No one is going to hurt your precious equipment."

"But it may hurt you. Someone like Harley may be able to negotiate the traps I've laid, but anyone else is walking a tightrope." She looked back over her shoulder. "And I don't want to have to pick up the pieces if you take a fall. Stay away from my stuff."

Just how deadly was that "stuff"? Megan wondered. Harley had said that her electronic gadgets would rival James Bond's, but evidently it was also a deadly trove. Let her deal with it herself. Megan hadn't gotten all she needed from Renata; the Ledger was still clearly out of bounds. But she had gotten a promise of cooperation and that would have to be enough.

Would it be enough? Tonight had shown her how close Molino was to them. They seemed always to be only one step ahead of the bastard.

Or less. Renata could have been killed tonight and who knows if they would have gone after Grady and her if they'd gotten Renata.

Borrowed time, Renata had said. Lord, she was tired of scurrying away from the shadow Molino cast over her life.

She closed her medical bag and got to her feet. Come back, Grady. It's time we cast a few shadows ourselves.

GRADY ARRIVED BACK AT Renata's cottage thirty minutes later. "Let's go," he said curtly. "I sent Harley back to our cottage to pack us up and get the car. We're out of here."

"Did the CIA cause any problems?"

"No. Venable made it clear what had to be done. But while Harley was checking out the perimeter he found fresh tire tracks on the ground by the root cellar. Tracks, not a getaway car. That means there were probably four men, not three. The driver saw what was happening and took off when his buddies didn't come back. That means what he knew, Molino knows by now. He'll know we're with Renata and he has a chance of getting us all if he can move fast enough." He looked at Renata. "Are you coming with us?"

She nodded. "It seems like a good idea." She picked up her suitcases and headed for the door. "Right now."

"That's what I like. Total commitment." Grady reached for her bag. "I'll carry this. It will be faster."

"No one touches her 'stuff,'" Megan said. "Evidently it's wired to blow."

"I'd make an exception in his case," Renata said. "But you'd get upset if he ended up blown to smithereens." She headed for the door. "Where are we going?"

"The airport. We're chartering a flight to Atlanta. We managed to trace the last call on the cell phone I took from one of Molino's men. It was an area code in southern Tennessee."

"You think Molino is there?" Megan asked.

"Probably."

"You said his main headquarters was in Madagascar."

"But that's too far from the action now that he has a chance to get what he wants. Molino must be feeling pretty frustrated by now. He has you in his sights and he'll want to be in on the kill."

"Can we locate him?"

"It will probably come out zilch. Molino's phone has probably been routed through a half a dozen other numbers in the state to keep it from being traced. I've asked

Venable to try to zero in on him." He shrugged. "But our best bet may be to wait and watch."

"No, it's not," Renata said flatly. "You have to prod him. You know he's sent his men every time, Grady. He never goes himself. How do you think Molino's lasted this long? Edmund said that he has an excellent sense of self-preservation. The only time he actually showed up himself was when he went after Edmund. I think that was because he was getting desperate about finding you, Megan. At that time he probably didn't want the Ledger as much as the possibility of finding your location listed in it. He must have thought it was safe and he had a chance to inflict some pain on a freak."

Megan's eyes widened. "You're saying I'm responsible for them going after Edmund?"

"No, Molino would still have sent someone else to do his dirty work. He just wouldn't have come himself. And after he found out you were working at St. Andrews and he had no immediate need for the Ledger, he crawled back into his hole." She turned to Megan. "How did he act when he was with Edmund?"

"Excited, vicious, filled with a kind of exultation that he'd caught a 'freak.'"

"Desperate?"

Megan thought about it. "Yes, there was a sort of feverishness."

"There's your answer. We have to excite him, stir the bloodlust, play on that frustration and desperation he's feeling about not getting his hands on you. Make him want to come out in the open."

"I'm sure you're going to tell us how," Grady said.

"Yes." Renata looked at Megan. "Grady thinks that I want to set you up as a decoy for Molino. That I'm trying to manipulate you."

Megan frowned. "But you suggested that you be the decoy."

She shrugged. "Yes, I did."

"Ask her," Grady's eyes were narrowed on Renata's face. "Something's changed. She may tell you the truth."

"She doesn't have to ask me." Renata turned to Megan. "I was playing you."

Her eyes widened. "What?"

"I needed a sure thing. Molino wants you dead more than he wants the Ledger. Your mother killed his son. He wants to kill her daughter. Molino isn't sane where his son's death is concerned. Edmund said that he thought his attitude would be totally fanatical toward you. In comparison, the Ledger is dwarfed in importance. Yes, he wants it, but not the way he wants you. To get you he'd take chances he wouldn't risk to get me or the Ledger. The bait wouldn't be good enough. We have to make him take those risks."

Megan's lips tightened. "Dammit, you could have told me that instead of trying to manipulate me."

"I needed it to happen," Renata said simply. "I could see that all I had to do was set up the scenario and you'd do the rest. But you have a strong will and it had to be your idea. It was very clear to me. I've always been able to work out cause and effect. It was like one of the projects I work on for my company. I wouldn't have let Molino hurt you. I just couldn't be the one to do this."

"Charming," Grady said.

"Don't be smug," Renata said with sudden fierceness. "Do you think I liked doing it? But Molino is too much of a threat. I have to get rid of him." She looked at Megan. "You have to get rid of him."

"And that justifies anything?"

"Yes. And if you have Molino's telephone number, you

may be able to make him come after you himself. Call him. Make him angry. Put him in a rage."

"Shut up, Renata," Grady said.

"You see, he doesn't want you at risk." She paused. "There's something else you should know. I made a call last night and had the block taken off my phone so that it would be easy to trace." She made a face. "Too easy. I didn't think they'd come at me quite this soon. I wasn't ready."

Megan's eyes widened. "You let Molino's men know where you were?"

Grady muttered a curse.

"Grady was trying to put a roadblock in my way. He didn't want you to run any more risks. I thought it would push you over the edge if the threat was closer." She met Megan's eyes. "It did, didn't it?"

"And you got shot."

"I made a small miscalculation. The premise was valid."

"Why are you telling me this?"

"I don't like lies. Mark says they're necessary, but I didn't want to lie to you. You lie to your enemies. You're not my enemy. I just had to nudge you in the right direction. Now it's up to you." She paused. "Do you still want me to go with you?"

Megan gazed at her, filled with a multitude of emotions. Anger, disappointment, and pity. One part of her wanted to shake her. Renata had an almost childlike single-mindedness coupled with her brilliance and that damn gift. Yet hadn't that single-mindedness been bred and taught to her? She was just trying to survive and do her duty in the only way she knew how.

"Well?" There was defensiveness and wariness in Renata's expression.

Oh, what the hell. "Of course you're going with us." Megan moved toward the door. "You may not think you're the card that will draw Molino but every bit helps. You told me you were also a Finder. My mother was able to find Molino once. You may be able to do it too. Besides, you have the Ledger."

"And she'd probably trade you to keep it," Grady said dryly.

"Maybe." She glanced at Renata. So much defiance and fierceness and vulnerability. "Would you?"

Renata was silent. "I don't know." She added wearily, "Probably. So we'd better make sure I don't have to make a choice."

"THEY'RE ON THEIR WAY back to Atlanta," Sienna said. "They boarded a flight two hours ago. They're walking right into our hands."

Molino shook his head. "You're too eager. It won't be that easy. But nothing worthwhile ever is." He smiled. "You'll be glad when this is over, won't you?"

"Yes," Sienna said bluntly. "It's getting in the way of business. I agree that the Ledger is worthwhile. If we can use those Swiss bank account numbers, it would set us up for a lifetime. But you can't think of anything else but Megan Blair." He added, "I've been wondering if you wouldn't like to concentrate fully on finishing your dealings with her and turn the rest of the business over to me for a while."

"Ambitious, Sienna?" Molino asked softly. "And after I kill the bitch, would I find that I'd been permanently eased out of the picture?"

"Just a suggestion," Sienna said without expression. "It's getting more and more difficult to keep that son of a bitch Kofi Badu under control. He has other buyers for the children and you're not giving him the money fast enough to please him. He wants to meet with you and discuss new arrangements."

"More money."

Sienna nodded. "And you don't want to bother. Let me do it."

Molino shook his head. "Tell him I'll meet with him next week. Set it up."

"If you opt out, he'll walk away."

"And you'll say, 'I told you so.'" It would be the last thing Sienna would say, Molino thought. "But I won't opt out. I'll be finished with Megan Blair in the next few days."

"How?"

"I've been thinking about her. She wants to find me? I'll let her. I'll make her come to me on her knees." He bared his teeth in a faint smile. "You've never believed her mother actually was able to drive my boy mad, have you? Would you like to rape Megan Blair? I'll let you have her for a night before I slit her throat. I'll even let you play with her as you did Gillem. Don't you want the chance to prove me a fool?"

"I never said you were a fool."

"Go ahead," Molino said softly. "Do it. I dare you."

Sienna shrugged. "If you insist. I'll enjoy banging the bitch. I've never been afraid of things that go bump in the night. But you have to catch her first and then bring her here alive."

"I'm not worried." Molino reached for his cell phone. "I have a few aces in the hole. I'll start pulling them out one by one."

THE FLIGHT GRADY CHARTERED arrived in Georgia early in the afternoon. Yet they didn't arrive at the international airport, but a small private airport north of the city.

"We have to get a move on," Harley said as he handed Renata her duffel. "I bribed the pilot to change the flight plan at the last minute to Kennesaw, Georgia, but Sienna's not dumb. If he knew our departure point, he'll have traced us this far. He'll be on to our arrival city soon."

"Where are we going?" Megan asked as she followed Harley and Grady down the aisle.

"Dalton, Georgia," Grady said. "It's an hour or so up the highway. Harley arranged to rent a house outside town. We'll settle and wait."

"Wait for what?"

"Developments."

"Watch and wait?" Megan asked. "No, Grady. I think Renata's right. We have to prod him. We'll stir things up a bit and make a call or two ourselves."

"I was afraid that you'd say that."

"Renata said we had to raise the bloodlust. That's hard to do when the only contact with him is when his men come after us."

"Dammit to hell. You're not going to give up until you talk to him, are you?"

"No," she answered immediately and hoped her revulsion at the thought didn't show. The idea of actually talking one-on-one with Molino brought instant shock and rejection. She knew him intimately from the episode with Edmund Gillem and the story Grady had recounted about his treatment of her mother. But it would be entirely different confronting him. "If it will help. What do I say?"

"Play it by ear. You've got good instincts and you're not shy about speaking your mind. It will come to you." He glanced at Renata. "Or maybe our little friend will coach you. She said she's good at cause and effect."

"Back off," Renata said. "If we're going to let loose the dogs, you'd better be prepared to protect her."

"I'm not letting them loose. You are," Grady said as he went down the steps. "And after she makes that call, I'll stash her away somewhere safe until the battle is over."

Renata made a rude sound. "Do you really think she's going to let you do that?"

"Stop talking about me as if I weren't here," Megan said. "I'll do as I please, Grady. I'm not going to be stashed anywhere."

"Told you so," Renata murmured. "Gosh, I never thought I'd love saying that to anyone."

"And you stop acting like a smug child." Megan followed Grady down the steps. "Let's just get on the road." She caught up with Harley, who was heading for a dark blue car parked on the tarmac. "I want away from them. It's like being with two cats fighting over a mouse."

Harley grinned. "Not at all. They'd kill the mouse. Grady and Renata are scratching at each other to try to keep you alive."

"Grady, maybe. But Renata?"

He nodded. "She may feel obligated to use you, but I believe that she'd put her neck on the line to keep Molino from getting you. She's not as hard as she'd like you to think."

"I don't think she's hard." She'd always been aware of that vulnerability in Renata. "Sometimes I feel sorry for her." She got into the passenger seat of the car. "And sometimes I want to shake her."

"Like a bratty younger sister?" he asked softly.

She made a face. "If the sister was Calamity Jane."

SIXTEEN

THE WHITE CLAPBOARD HOUSE Harley had rented was on the outskirts of Dalton, surrounded by hills and hidden from the road by a thatch of pine trees. It was at least seventy years old with a wraparound porch and steps that appeared worn with wear.

"Not very impressive," Harley said. "It's an old country farmhouse but the farmland was sold off and the family moved away. Evidently it was a large family. It has four bedrooms and two baths and a big country kitchen. The realtor said the key would be in the hanging basket of ivy."

"It's fine." Grady reached up and retrieved the key. "Food?"

"I'll run to the grocery store in town." Harley looked at Renata. "Would you care to come with me?"

She shrugged. "If you like." She got in the front seat. "I have something to buy too."

"A missile launcher?"

"How did you guess?"

Megan shook her head as she watched the car pull out of the driveway. "She may not be kidding."

"Well, it won't be a missile launcher." He unlocked the front door. "They're not that easy to come by in a small town. And Harley will keep an eye on any other purchases."

There was no foyer and the furniture in the living room was shabby and none too clean.

She wrinkled her nose. "I hope the bedrooms are better."

"We can make do." He headed for the kitchen. "It won't be for long."

She followed him. "That's good. I'm a little tired of listening to Renata and you jab at each other." There were glasses in the cupboard and she got one down and rinsed it. "And I don't understand it."

"Maybe I resent the fact that she tried to use you." He smiled. "I regard that as my privilege." He held up his hand as she opened her lips to speak. "Just joking." His smile faded. "Somewhat. I know you only allow people to use you at your discretion. But ever since that night you spent in the trailer with Gillem, I've noticed a change. Renata is closely connected to Gillem and that's touching you."

She couldn't deny it. "It's not affecting my judgment." She turned on the kitchen faucet and let it run for a moment until the flow was clear. "Well water." She took a sip. "It's good. Remember we had well water in the beach house that summer? It had too much iron in it and it made my hair limp and flyaway. You used to tease me about it."

"I remember," he said thickly.

She stiffened and her gaze flew to his face. Oh, shit. She glanced quickly away but it was too late. She could still see the sensuality, the earthiness, the familiar readiness. And her own body was mirroring all of those responses. She turned away, finished the glass of water, and set the glass on the counter. "I'd better take a look at those bedrooms. The sheets may need washing and—"

"Shh." He was behind her, his hands sliding around to

cup her breasts. "The sheets can wait." He was rubbing slowly against her. "We can't."

My God. Her entire body was alive, tingling. A shudder went through her. Heat. Overpowering need. She arched back against him. "This shouldn't be happening."

"Yes, it should. I said I'd give you time, but you want this." He was pulling her down on the floor. "Don't you?"

Oh, yes. More than water in the desert, more than fire in winter. His hands reached out to grasp his shoulders. "Harley will . . ."

"He'll let us know when he comes into the house." He was unbuttoning her blouse. "Damn, I've missed you."

"Ridiculous," she said unevenly. "It hasn't been that long." Yet it seemed forever, she thought dazedly. She knew what he meant. The hunger had been there, ignored, but waiting. "This isn't going to make any difference. I won't let it."

"I'll take what I can get. If you think you can walk away from me afterwards, do it." He pulled off his shirt and threw it aside. "Just don't lie to either one of us that it won't make a difference. Every time makes a difference." His palm was rubbing her, caressing her. "Every single touch . . ."

MADNESS.

Her breath was coming in gasps as she forced herself to unclench her fingers that were digging into his shoulders. "I have to go. I need to—" She closed her eyes. She didn't want to go. She wanted to stay here and hold him and then do it again. She pushed him away and sat up. "Harley and Renata will be back soon." She grabbed her clothes and jumped to her feet. "I'm going upstairs and find a bathroom."

He didn't move, watching her as she moved toward the door. "Have I ever told you that you've got a spectacular ass?"

"No."

"Probably too busy with more important observations," he said. "Like the way you squeeze around me until I go berserk when I'm—"

"Be quiet." She glanced at him over her shoulder. "In case you haven't noticed, I'm walking away from you, Grady."

"I noticed." He smiled. "And now you know that you can do it. It's not as if I have some Svengali power over you. So why not enjoy ourselves at every opportunity? Life is short and you never know what's coming around the corner."

He did have power over her, she thought. Just staring at him lying there naked she could feel a stirring. She had never seen a more beautiful male specimen and that male could do things to her that no one else had ever done. She was no Galatea, but the sexuality between them was too strong to ignore and she should be wary. After today nothing was clearer.

"No?" His gaze was narrowed on her face. "I'm having a hell of a time getting you to bypass that control fear. Think about it. There were moments when I wasn't in control, when you made me feel weak and sappy as a high school kid. Maybe I should be wary of you."

She moistened her lips. "Maybe you should."

He smiled. "I'll take my chances. Every time I sense a weakness, I'm going to move in." He made a shooing motion. "Go get dressed. I'll bring your suitcases up and put them in one of the bedrooms. I'll see you at dinner."

"Okay." She flew up the stairs and moved down the hall throwing open doors until she came to a bathroom. A few minutes later she was stepping into a tub shower and pulling the plastic curtain. The cold water was a shock on her warm, relaxed flesh, making it taut and firm. She wished it could also shock her mental faculties that had not been able to prevent that sexual encounter from happening.

Forget it. So she had wanted Grady and took him. He was right, if he had power over her, she had also been aware her touch could weaken and make him shudder. Why shouldn't they enjoy—

That's what Grady had said. Persuasion or control?

It was too dangerous to opt for persuasion with a man who had controlled her memories for all those years.

But sex was sex. It wasn't as if there was anything deeper, that she was in—

No! She wouldn't even go there. She would get Molino and then dive back into the life she had chosen before any of this craziness had revealed itself. Lord, that life seemed far away and alien now.

Alien? It was her present existence that was weird and alien. It was frightening that she hadn't instantly realized that fact. Grady had said she had changed, but she'd still be able to go back once this was over.

Lord, she hoped she'd be able to go back.

WHEN MEGAN LEFT THE BATHROOM, she passed Renata in the hall carrying an armful of bed linens.

"I'm putting these in the washer and then I'm going to hit the shower myself," Renata said. "This place must not have been rented for years. It's kind of sad to think about it. Like a little old lady who's been neglected and forgotten."

"That is sad." And Megan found it curious that Renata would make that comparison. "You like this house?"

"Yes, particularly that wraparound front porch. It reminds me of a house in Boston I lived in with my mother. I was only five or six, but it seemed . . . embracing." She shrugged. "Or maybe I thought so because I didn't see that much of my mother. I was shuttled back and forth between her and my father in Germany and that year was a good year." She headed for the stairs. "I took the second bedroom on the left since I noticed your suitcases were in the first one." She glanced over her shoulder. "Only your cases. You're not sleeping with Grady here?"

"No. Not that it's any of your concern."

"I just wondered if I was going to have to tiptoe around the 'situation.'" She made a face. "Then I guess I wouldn't have had to be tactful and gone shopping with Harley."

"Tactful? You?"

"I can be tactful. I think it's a mistake for you to sleep with Grady. He's a Controller and I don't know how you could trust him. But if he brings you pleasure, then I want you to have it."

"Thank you," she said dryly.

"I probably said that wrong. You'd never guess that I'm considered very well spoken at the office."

"No, I'd never guess."

"But in the office it's as if I'm an actress on a stage. It's easier." She started down the steps. "I'll get these sheets in the washer and then I'll put in a meat loaf before I take my shower. Harley says he's going to make his favorite dessert."

"Baumkuchen."

"That's it. It took forever to find all the ingredients."

"Then I guess you didn't have time to buy your missile launcher," Megan said teasingly. "Grady said you'd have trouble finding it in Dalton, Georgia, anyway."

"If I'd wanted it, I could have gotten it. Mark would have found a source."

"Your cousin must be an amazing man."

"Amazing? You could call him that." She called back, "You make the salad. Okay?"

"Okay." She finished toweling her hair as she headed for her bedroom. The encounter with Renata had done her good. It had brought her back to a form of normalcy that didn't revolve around Grady and her feelings for him. There were other people in the world, other viewpoints, other goals. There were memories of childhood and wraparound porches and Cousin Mark who was an enigma still to be deciphered.

With any luck she'd be able to concentrate on all those peripheral figures tonight and forget about Grady.

IT DIDN'T WORK.

She couldn't have been more acutely conscious of Grady during dinner. She was aware of his every move, every intonation of his voice. Dammit, she hoped it wasn't obvious to Harley and Renata. It was ridiculous to feel like this.

She escaped right after Harley's Baumkuchen. She murmured an excuse and fled to the wraparound porch with which Renata had been so enamored.

The moon was almost full and shining brightly over the woods in the distance. She took several deep breaths. That was better.

"Megan."

She went rigid. She didn't turn around. "I don't want to talk to you right now, Grady."

"I didn't think you did." He came forward to stand beside her. "And that's okay." He pulled out his cell phone. "How do you feel about talking to Molino?"

She stared at him. "Now?"

"You said you were going to speak to him. Now's as good a time as any."

"I just didn't expect it to be so soon." She slowly reached out and took the phone. "Not tonight."

"You're so on edge I don't think Molino could faze you." His lips twisted. "Believe me, I prefer that I be the focus of any disturbance you're feeling, but I want this over. He's going to try to hurt you any way he can. He probably will hurt you."

She shook her head. "I'll handle it. Did you bring up his number?"

"Yes." He reached out and took the phone back from her. "But I'm going to have to set up the call. The first thing Molino will assume is that we're trying to trace him. I'll get it for you and introduce you to the scumbag. It will be safe for you to speak for only a few minutes." He quickly dialed the number and waited for it to ring. "Molino? No? Sienna, this is Neal Grady. I have Megan Blair here. She wants to talk to Molino. No, don't hang up. I knew you'd be afraid the CIA would arrange for a satellite trace so I'm hanging up. If Molino wants to talk to Megan he can call us on whatever phone he considers safe. She's going to be on the phone for three minutes. When her time's up, she's gone." He hung up. "Now we wait."

"Do you think he'll do it?"

"Oh, yes. I hate to admit it but Renata is right about that scumbag's—"

The phone rang and he handed it to Megan. "Talk to him."

"This is an unexpected pleasure, bitch," Molino said. "Though if you're going to plead with me to let you live, it's not going to happen."

"I'm not going to beg you. Why should I? Your men are bunglers. They haven't been able to touch me." Bloodlust, she thought. Renata had said to raise his bloodlust. She added deliberately, "Are you as inadequate as they are?"

He was silent, but Megan could sense the fury. "Your mother didn't think so," he said softly. "Do you know how many men raped her while we held her?"

Shock and disgust seared through her. "Your son, Steven."

"But he was such a generous boy. He liked to share on occasion."

Pain twisted inside her. Smother it. Grady had said he would try to hurt her. Don't let it go on. Attack. Find a weakness. What did Molino fear?

And then she knew what path to take.

"But he was punished for what he did, wasn't he? My mother made him go mad. She held his hand and all the putrid foulness of his mind exploded. It was so easy for her. She should have done it before that night. I hear your son wept like an infant. He was a weakling who never—"

"Shut up," he said harshly.

She was getting to him. "In a minute. I've no desire to talk about a loser like your Steven. I just want to make sure you know that you have no chance of killing me as you did my mother."

"Is that why you called?"

"Yes, and I wanted to hear your voice. It helps me focus."

"Focus?" he repeated slowly.

"I'm tired of you hunting me down. I want you to die, Molino. But first I want you to become a mindless, gibbering idiot like your son." She added with soft venom, "Would you like to hold my hand, Molino? The madness must be hideous if your Steven killed himself to escape it. Would you like to join your son?"

"Freak," he said hoarsely.

"Yes. But you knew that I was my mother's daughter or you wouldn't have tried to kill me. But you've lost your chance. You've driven me to come after you."

"Hang up," Grady said.

She nodded at him but continued, "And my mother found you, didn't she, Molino? It was the middle of the jungle and she still located your camp. I'll be able to do that too. You're helpless just as your son was helpless."

"I'll kill you." Molino's voice was shrill. "Freak. Freak. Steven and I will slice you to pieces. You can't get away from us."

He was still raving as she hung up the phone. She was shaking. "I believe there's no question that Molino will come after me himself. He's not about to hide out in Madagascar and let someone else cut my throat." She handed Grady the phone. "And to put it on the record, Molino has gone around the bend. He was talking about his son, Steven, as if he was still alive."

"I told you that he was obsessed."

She shivered. "And ugly. I've never been that close to such ugliness."

His lips lifted in a mirthless smile. "So you decided to wallow in it."

"We wanted him angry. I had to stab him where it hurt. He believed my mother was responsible for his son's death, so I decided not to argue with him."

"You sounded very convinced yourself."

"I'm still not convinced she was a Pandora. Even if it turns out she was, I don't think I am. I just had to make him believe it. He hates 'freaks' and there's a part of him that's afraid of them. I had to play on that fear. Did I get off the phone before the call could be traced?"

He nodded. "I gave you a little leeway."

"I thought you might." She turned away. "And now I think I'll go to bed."

"Come here," he said softly as he took a step forward. "And don't tense up. I just want to hold you. You're shaking."

"I don't need anyone to—" Her face was buried in his chest as he pulled her into his arms. Lord, he felt good, closing out the horror Molino had brought. "After my switching in the woodshed, you're giving me hot chicken soup?" she murmured. "This isn't necessary, Grady."

"It is to me." His hand was stroking her hair. "I had to watch your face while you were taking Molino's filth. I need a little comfort."

"How selfish," she said unsteadily.

"What's new? I've never been anything else."

"You weren't selfish that night in the cave the day my mother died. You helped me even though you knew it wasn't going to be an easy fix. You could have left me alone with the voices."

"No, I couldn't. I tried, but it was already too late for me." His fingertips gently brushed her temple. "So that was selfish too."

"You're not convincing me."

"Amazing. And you're so wary of my intentions. Are you getting soft, Megan?"

"No." She pushed him away. "I just believe people aren't all black and white." She headed for the door.

"Except for Molino. He's all black to the bottom of his soul. Will you get me a photo of Molino? If he's coming after me, I need to know what he looks like. I wouldn't know him if he walked up to me in the street."

He nodded. "I'll contact Venable and have him send me a photo on my cell phone and print it out."

"Sienna too. He was enjoying torturing Edmund Gillem. He wasn't just obeying orders."

"I'm not surprised. He was a hit man before he joined Molino's group and he's an ice man. He and Molino agree on some things, but he's been known to diverge on others."

"When can I have the photos?"

"Tonight. I'll call right away."

She opened the screen door. "Fine."

"You did a good job tonight, Megan," he said quietly.

"Damn right I did." She left the porch and headed for the steps leading to her bedroom. She wasn't shaking any longer but she was still upset. The ugliness of that conversation seemed to be still swirling around her, touching her with filth.

"Are you okay?" Renata met her at the top of the steps. "You called Molino?"

"Yes, how did you know?"

"I followed Grady out to the porch. I thought he was going to bother you and you were disturbed enough."

Her brows rose. "So you were going to protect me from him?"

Renata didn't speak for a moment. "Maybe."

"I can take care of myself, Renata."

"But you care too much. You let people hurt you."

"Then that's my choice."

"It's all in how you look at it. Life is made up of different scenarios ready to be triggered by a word, an action.

If I'm there to say that word or make that action, then the hurt never happens."

Megan stared at her in amazement and then she started to laugh. "My God, that's the most convoluted explanation for being a busybody I've ever heard."

She tilted her head. "Really? I can get much more convoluted without even trying."

"I'm sure you can." Her smile lingered as she asked, "Why me? Why choose me to protect?"

"I don't know." Her tone was suddenly awkward. "I think . . . I like you." She added quickly, "Of course, it could be that you're family and I've been trained to protect the family."

"Yes, it could be that," she said gently. "But I hope it's not. I don't have many friends, Renata. It would be nice if you turned out to be one."

Renata looked away. "We'll have to see, won't we?" She changed the subject. "What about the Molino call?"

"He was frothing at the mouth when I hung up. I let him think I was a Pandora and a Finder like my mother. He bought it."

"He thinks freaks are freaks and he doesn't know enough about us." She paused. "You could have told him I was the Finder. It would have taken some of the heat off you."

"It was better if he had a primary focus for all that paranoia. That way you could fade into the shadows. Did the CIA manage to get a possession of Molino's for you to use?"

"Not yet. They're trying his house in Madagascar and it's pretty well protected."

"Well, I think we can be sure he won't be going back there until he knows I'm dead," she said dryly.

"Frothing?" Renata repeated with a grin.

"As a mad dog." She headed for her bedroom. "With the emphasis on mad. I think he's slipped a few cogs." She stopped at the door. "I want to know about Finders, Renata, what to expect. Will you come in and tell me about them?"

Renata nodded. "Though there's not much to know." She followed her into the room and dropped down on the window seat. "You said your mother was a Finder."

"But I didn't know that until Grady told me. I didn't know anything about her talents."

"That would feel . . . odd. I've always known about the family and that most of us have one talent or another. I knew I was a Finder by the time I was seven. I didn't develop any other talents until later."

"You weren't frightened?"

"Mark wouldn't let me be frightened. My mother was pretty busy and had no time for training, but she sent me to Mark." She smiled. "I think he was impatient with dealing with me sometimes until Edmund told him that he'd chosen me as the Keeper for the Ledger. After that he never let me know if I was a bother to him. He knew he had to prepare me."

And teaching the Keeper of the Ledger was more important than the needs of a little girl.

Renata was smiling at her and shaking her head. "You're feeling sorry for me. Mark was very good to me. You don't understand."

"No," Megan said. "But I'm trying to do that. Tell me about being a Finder."

"I'm pretty good at it. Mark thought it was a valuable talent and worked with me."

"How do you do it?"

"First, you have to have an object belonging to the person you're trying to find. You already know that. The object is generally called the anchor because it's the only thing that keeps you steady once you're on the trail. Then you concentrate and see if you can make a connection."

"Connection?"

Renata frowned, trying to explain. "It's kind of a . . . touching. But most of the time you have to get close enough for the tether to work before you make the connection. Then you reach out and connect and it's like a rope pulling you, leading you. A tether."

"And that's all?"

She nodded. "Unless the connection is strong enough to give you a viewing. Sometimes after you make the connection you get a picture of the subject. If you're lucky it can give you a clue and you won't have to entirely depend on the tether to find the subject."

"But having something belonging to Molino is the key?"

Renata nodded. "Give me a strong enough object to use as an anchor and I can find anyone."

"Well, hopefully Venable will be able to deliver one to you soon." She was silent a moment. "It really works, Renata?"

"It really does." Renata smiled. "I give you my word. If I can go on the hunt right away, there's a chance we may be able to find Molino without dangling you over the fire." She got to her feet. "Have I reassured you?"

She nodded. "Knowledge always helps. I feel as if I'm walking around in the dark."

"At least you have company." She headed toward the door. "You have the kind of personality that makes people want to share your dark days. Someone will always be there ready to help you, Megan. Grady, Harley, even me."

She closed the bedroom door behind her.

Megan moved toward the window and stood looking out at the moonlit fields.

Molino was out there somewhere, eaten up with hatred, planning, moving.

How close?

THE PHOTO OF SIENNA AND Molino was under her door when she woke the next morning. She experienced a ripple of shock when she saw the picture. She had unconsciously expected a mug shot or passport photo, but this was a shot of the two men together at a bistro table in an outdoor restaurant. They were casually dressed and smiling, two ordinary-looking men in their fifties, relaxing, perhaps on vacation. Grady had arrowed and labeled each man on the fax. Molino was a little heavier, with a hooked nose and a thatch of thick brown hair, sprinkled with gray. He wore an orange-and-brown striped shirt and khakis. Sienna's hazel eyes were slanted and vaguely catlike in his triangular face and his hair was fair and thinning. His shirt and trousers were immaculately tailored and he gave the impression of being ultra-fastidious.

She was still staring at the photo when Grady knocked on the door a few minutes later.

"I wanted to make sure you got it first thing," he said. "It came in late last night. Surprised?"

"Yes. I probably shouldn't have been. I don't believe it was the fact that they look so ordinary but the photo itself. They're sitting there in the sun, drinking wine, having a good time as if they deserved it."

"Yes."

"They *don't* deserve it." She swallowed to ease the tightness of her throat. "They kill, they torture, they sell little children to beasts that destroy them. If there was justice in the world, they'd be writhing in hell."

"Sometimes justice takes a long time coming."

"Then let's hurry it along, dammit. Can't we do something more?"

"Venable is pulling every string he can with the FBI and local law enforcement in Tennessee to try to locate Molino. It takes time."

"Meanwhile Molino and Sienna are sitting in the sun and living the good life," she said bitterly.

"Not at the moment." He smiled. "I think you stirred him up enough last night to make sure he's not sitting on his duff."

"Good."

"And I did hear from ATLPD about the truck belonging to Phillip's attacker. The tires were purchased from National Car Service by credit card."

"You have a name?" she asked eagerly.

"Tim Darnell. He's a student at Georgia State University. Twenty-two years old, bright, good-looking, no police record."

"Then it might not be him," she said, disappointed.

"And it might be. He grew up on a farm in South Georgia and he was crazy about guns and hunting. His parents are dirt poor, but Darnell appears to have plenty of money. The police interviewed one of his ex-girlfriends and he's into dominance and power games. She left him because she was afraid of him."

"Can't they bring him in for questioning?"

"They would if they could find him. He hasn't been back to his apartment in days. They've staked it out but no luck."

"You think he's gone to join Molino?"

He shrugged. "Molino doesn't keep anyone but old, trusted lieutenants close to him. Certainly not a fresh-faced kid who didn't do the job he set him to do. But if we can get our hands on Darnell, we may persuade him to help us trap him."

She asked cautiously, "How?"

He lifted his brow. "Not torture. Though I'd use it if I had to do it. At this point I'd do anything that had to be done. But it would probably be more efficient to pull out the bag of tricks you're so wary about. I'm a Controller and there aren't many people I can't influence. I take it you wouldn't mind if I made Darnell do what we want?"

"No."

"I suppose I should be grateful for small favors." He turned away. "At times I suspect you're just as prejudiced as Molino about so-called freaks."

"That would be irrational considering I'm one of you."

"But a small part of you is still fighting accepting that." He said over his shoulder as he walked down the hall, "Harley's cooking breakfast and it should be ready in thirty minutes. Don't be late. Harley's temperamental if his food gets cold."

"Heaven forbid." She threw the photo on the night-stand and headed down the hall toward the bathroom. She was glad that Grady had the news about Darnell's identification to balance the discouragement she'd felt gazing at the photo. It had lifted her spirits that they weren't operating in a complete fog. It might be frustrating and maddening to have to wait for developments that would let them go after Molino, but at least they were making tiny steps forward.

SEVENTEEN

MEGAN'S CELL PHONE RANG late that afternoon.

Dr. Jason Gardner on the ID. Hope soared through her. He'd said he wouldn't call unless there was something to report.

Oh, God. Let it be good news.

"How is he?" she asked as soon as she picked up. "You said you thought there was a change. Bad or good?"

"Don't get excited," he said cautiously. "I can't promise anything. I told you that your uncle—"

"He's better? Stop being diplomatic and *talk* to me."

"I think he's better. Twice he squeezed my hand when I asked him to answer yes or no to a question."

"You're sure?"

"It was weak, but I don't believe it was an automatic reflex. The machines don't indicate any change, any spiking, but it may be a beginning."

"Thank God."

"But we need a breakthrough. It's as if he's wandering through a maze and can't find his way out. I've seen a few cases where this happened and in a few weeks the response just faded away. I can't let him backslide."

"What can we do?"

"I'm with him as much of my day as I can manage. My head nurse, Madge Holloway, is there the rest of the time. We talk to him. We ask him questions." He paused. "But

I believe we need a more personal contact. We need someone who knows and cares about him, someone he cares enough about to make the effort to come back."

"He needs me?"

"I believe it would be . . . helpful."

"I'll be there tonight. You'll be at the hospital where I can talk to you?"

"I'll make sure I am. What time?"

"Nine or before. We may have to make plans. What room is he in?"

"Suite fourteen B. It's at the end of the corridor."

"I'll be there."

"I'll be waiting for you. Thank you, Dr. Blair."

"No, thank you." She hung up and whirled to face Grady. "Phillip may be coming out of it."

"That's wonderful," he said quietly. "But it's not wonderful that you intend to go flying to his side."

"You're not going to talk me out of it. He needs me."

"I wouldn't think of it. I'm not into futile efforts. I'm just making a statement."

"It's better than sitting here twiddling my thumbs waiting. There's a chance I can do something useful. It may make a difference in whether Phillip comes out of that coma or not."

"Okay." He got to his feet. "Then will you let me set it up so that it's as safe as possible for you? There's a chance that Molino is having the hospital watched."

She nodded. "As long as I can spend some time with Phillip."

"Can you limit it to one visit?" He saw her start to frown. "We'll play it by ear. I'll go with you to his room. Harley and Renata can do reconnaissance around the hospital grounds to make sure that the area's safe. Okay?"

"It will have to be." She started toward the staircase.

"I'm going to get my suitcase and medical bag. I may have to spend the night with Phillip. As Gardner said, what Phillip is going through is like wandering through a maze. There's no telling when he might come to a break in the hedge."

"Let's hope it comes early on the path," Grady said gently.

"I'm crossing my fingers."

"So am I."

She hesitated. "Thanks for not making this difficult for me, Grady."

"For God's sake, he's my friend too," he said harshly. "I could have wished it had happened a few days down the road but that's the breaks. We'll get you there and keep you safe." He headed for the door. "I'll go get Harley and Renata stirring."

GARDNER TURNED BACK TO Nurse Madge Holloway after he'd hung up the phone. "She's coming, Madge."

Madge grinned. "Did you have any doubt? You said she was one of the ones who cared." She looked down at Phillip Blair. "And it's not often that we can give a relative hope. Lord, I hope we can bring him back. There's a chance?"

"There's a chance." He came closer to the bed and took the man's limp hand. "There's always a chance, isn't there, Phillip? You're a good man and God should be on your side. That should weigh in for something."

"And he has you," Madge said. "It should count that you're on his side too."

"Tell that to the five other patients in this annex that aren't doing as well as Phillip here," he said wearily. "But

I've got to hope, Madge." He turned away. "Is that guard of Phillip's still outside the door?"

"Jordan?" Madge nodded.

"Tell him to come in the room for today. I want to make sure that Phillip and Megan Blair are safe."

"Right away." She hurried out of the room.

Gardner gazed down at Phillip for a long time. "Keep fighting, Phillip Blair. You'll be okay if you keep fighting." Damn, he hoped he was telling the truth.

"IT'S NOT SMART," HARLEY SAID. "Molino could have tapped the line and sent a welcoming committee. You shouldn't let her go."

"I know that," Grady said impatiently. "I knew he was a weak link from the time we put him in Bellehaven. That's why I had Megan limit the time of her calls when she was checking on him. There was always the possibility of them being able to trace the call."

"And now they don't have to trace it if Megan goes running to Phillip's side."

"We're not sure that the line's been tapped." He made a motion as Harley started to speak. "Okay, we can't take the chance. That's why we have to be sure to clear the way for her. Call that guard you set up to watch Phillip . . . what's his name?"

"Lee Jordan. A good man."

"Put him on the alert. I'll go with her to Phillip's suite. You and Renata scout the parking lot and surrounding grounds for snipers." He reached in his pocket and handed him a copy of the photo he'd given Megan and a driver's license photo of Darnell. "Pictures of Molino, Sienna, and Darnell. Other than the three of them, you're on your own."

"And Darnell has a Chevy pickup truck?"

"If he's still using it."

"He sounds like a hot dog. Men who beat up women love people to think they're macho. He probably likes the tough image a truck gives him. If not this truck, I'd bet he has another one by this time."

"No bet. Just don't let him slip away if you spot him."

"You can't talk her out of this?"

"No." Grady turned away. "I didn't try. She's operating on a purely emotional level. I can't fight that side of her. Hell, I don't want to fight that side of her. It's pretty damn wonderful."

"If it doesn't get her killed."

"It won't. I won't let it." He strode toward the front door. "Just do your job."

Bellehaven

THE PARKING LOT OF ANNEX 4 contained only a few cars that were parked fairly close to the small building.

"Evidently visiting hours are over," Grady said as he got out of the car. "Or maybe they don't get many visitors in the coma wards. I suppose it's easier to forget them as long as the families know the patients are well cared for."

"And, remember, there are only six patients in this ward. Gardner believes in being able to concentrate fully on individual patients." Megan moved toward the entrance. "But I wouldn't forget."

"I know you wouldn't." He opened the glass entrance door for her. "And that's why we're here."

The corridor of the rectangular building was shadowy and dimly lit and there was only one nurse at the circular desk just inside the door. She looked up from her paperwork as Megan and Grady came toward her. She was plain, a little plump, somewhere in her thirties. Her RN badge identified her as Madge Holloway. She smiled regretfully. "I'm sorry. No visitors are allowed in the wards after nine. I was about to lock up for the night. Would it help if I checked the latest report on your patient's condition for you?"

"We've had a report from Dr. Gardner," Megan said. "I'm supposed to meet him in Suite fourteen B."

"Oh, yes." Nurse Holloway's face suddenly lit with eagerness. "The Phillip Blair case. I was hoping I'd be here when you came. We've been so excited at his progress. Dr. Gardner never gives up. You're so lucky to have him working on the case."

"I realize that," Megan said as she moved down the hall. "The far end of the corridor?"

"That's right. Good luck."

"Thank you."

"Wait for me." Grady took her arm. "You're almost running."

"I feel like running. I'm excited." She glanced at him. "And I know you want to tell me not to get my hopes up, but don't do it. I can't help it."

"I wouldn't think of it." His gaze was wandering from side to side as they passed the hospital rooms. "It would be an exercise in futility. But I'm a realist. I'll reserve my excitement until I see Phillip coming a little closer to consciousness."

He stopped a few yards from the door at the end of the corridor. "Stay here. Let me go in first."

She glanced back at the nurse at the reception desk and frowned. "Everything seems okay here."

"And hopefully Harley and Renata are having an equally good experience outside." Grady moved toward the door. "But let's not rely on what seems to be taking place. I've shaped reality too many times myself to have any faith in it."

"Yes, but Molino is no Controller. And this is—what's wrong?" He was looking beyond her toward the front entrance. "Why are—"

"Shit!" He opened Phillip's door and dove to one side and into the room. "Get down!"

THE NURSE WAS MOVING AT a fast walk, almost at a run, as she came out of the annex building. Her stride was purposeful as she moved toward the SUV parked in front of the door.

Renata didn't like it. The nurse was moving too fast and Megan and Grady had just entered the building. Mark had always told Renata that any irregular behavior was a red flag in a surveillance situation. Of course, this was a nurse and there were always emergencies. She scanned the exterior of the car the nurse was now driving out of the parking lot.

No, dammit, it wasn't right.

Renata reached for her phone as she started her car and followed the nurse's SUV out of the lot.

Warn Megan. And hope Grady was observant enough to keep Megan alive.

GRADY DREW HIS GUN AND rolled over and under the hospital bed a few feet from the door.

No gunfire.

No curses or exclamations.

From where he was under the bed he could see no one in the room.

"Grady, dammit. What's happening?"

"Stay where you are, Megan. No problem that I can see."

In the adjoining bathroom?

He started to slowly ease himself from beneath the bed.

Something warm splattered on his hand.

Blood.

He froze as he watched the blood that had dropped from the bed run off his hand onto the beige tiles.

Oh, God.

Don't look at the man on the bed. Not yet. Not until he was sure there was no one in that bathroom waiting to pounce.

HER PHONE WAS RINGING, Megan realized dimly. Ignore it. Every nerve of her body was tensed and focused on what was going on in Phillip's room.

It was only a few moments since Grady had last told her to stay in the hall, but it seemed a century.

"Grady."

No answer.

"Unless you let me come in there I'm calling the police."

"You don't want to come in here. I'll come out."

Panic jolted through her. "If there's not a problem, why don't you want me to—" She jumped to her feet and moved slowly, cautiously into Phillip's room.

Blood.

The sheet on the bed was soaked with blood from the throat and face of the man in the bed.

"Dear God." She recoiled back against the wall. Her knees gave way and she slid to the floor. "Phillip . . ."

"No." Grady was kneeling beside her. "That's what I thought too. But it's not Phillip. It's hard to tell from that carnage of a face but I think it's Gardner."

"Gardner?" Her gaze flew to his face. "Dead?"

He nodded. "I'd judge it happened within the last few hours." He paused. "And there are two more bodies in the bathroom. According to his ID, one of them is Jordan, the guard Harley hired. He was shot at close range. He must have been taken by surprise. The other one is a woman in a nurse's uniform. It's probably the head nurse, Madge Holloway. Her neck was broken."

Madge Holloway. "The woman at the front desk had an ID badge with that name."

"And I saw her hurrying out the door as we reached Phillip's room. She waited just long enough to put up a normal front for us and then took off."

She rubbed her temple. "But where's Phillip?"

He shook his head.

"He has to be— How could they get him out of the building?"

"How could Molino kill Gardner and the nurse? He wanted it done. If he had Gardner prisoner for any length of time before his death, he could make him pull strings. It appears as if they toyed with him before they cut his throat."

"Sons of bitches." Her voice was shaking with anger. "Gardner was a good man. He cared about Phillip. He cared about all his patients. All he wanted to do was bring them back to—"

Her cell phone rang.

"Answer it," Grady said.

She'd already punched the button.

"Darnell tells me there was a good deal of blood," Molino said. "Isn't it good that you're a doctor and not squeamish?"

"You bastard. What did Gardner ever do to you?"

"Nothing. He was very helpful, but he would have been expensive and he was no longer useful."

Shock jolted through her. "What?"

"I offered him an astonishing amount of money to lure you there. I've had Sienna in negotiations with him for some time."

"He wouldn't sell out a patient to you."

"Everyone has a price. He's an idealist who believed in the sacrifice of one for the many. They were going to withdraw his funding."

"I don't believe you."

"Believe what you like. Of course, I told him what he wanted to believe. Blair was only going to be held as a threat. The only reason we wanted you was to get the Ledger. He bought it because he was desperate for the cash. He made it easy for Darnell. He called the guard into the room so that he could be disposed of in private. Sienna told him Jordan would just be tied up and left in the bathroom. Gardner was supposed to send the nurse away but Darnell came a little early."

An assassin had come early so another precious life had been taken, Megan thought, sick. "Is Phillip still alive?"

"As much alive as a lump of unthinking flesh can be. I was really surprised that you didn't just write him off after my friend Darnell made a vegetable of him."

"He's not a vegetable," she said through her teeth. "And he's getting better."

"So Darnell overheard when he was trying to trace you. I had him monitoring Gardner's phone from the moment you took off for Sweden."

"Was Gardner telling the truth about Phillip getting better?"

"Oh, yes, and Gardner was torn. But not enough to sacrifice his little kingdom. Sienna and I were debating whether you'd take the risk. Though neither of us understands your reasoning we thought you might since your uncle seemed to be improving. Of course, we would never be that foolish."

"Because you're both cold as ice."

"I wasn't cold about my son. And there's nothing cold about my hatred of you, bitch. It's white hot and eats at me every minute of the day. I could have sent in Darnell and a few other men to take you down once I knew you were going to Bellehaven. I thought about it. Then I realized that there was no way I was going to do it. It would have been chancy with Grady and Harley, but that was only one reason. I want to see you die slowly." His voice was thick with malice. "I want to hurt you as I did Edmund Gillem. I want to do it myself. I want to watch your face and know you're in pain."

"It won't happen."

"Yes, it will. Because I have this disgusting zombie you appear to be so fond of. Of course, he won't be as well cared for as Dr. Gardner and his nurses have been doing. No warm bed. I'm putting him in the cellar and it's a little cold and damp down there."

"That could kill him. His immune system isn't functioning as—"

"Then come after him."

"Will you let him go if you have me?"

She heard a curse from Grady.

"It's possible. I've no use for him."

Her hands tightened on the phone. "Where?"

"Redwing, Tennessee. Isn't that a pleasant name for a town?"

"You're staying there?"

"Of course not. Come to the graveyard on the hill and we'll discuss an exchange."

"Discuss? I'm not a fool, Molino."

"But you have a strange mind-set where the helpless are concerned. Come to the graveyard tomorrow night at eleven. If you're lucky, one of the corpses won't be Phillip Blair." He hung up.

"An exchange?" Grady asked.

She nodded jerkily. "Redwing, Tennessee. A graveyard on a hill. He wants to discuss terms. Tomorrow night at eleven."

"It's a trap. He won't give up Phillip. He wants to hurt you and he knows it will hurt you if he kills Phillip."

"I know that." Her gaze went to the blood-soaked bed. "Gardner was a Judas. He killed him to keep from having to pay him. He killed Jordan and the nurse just because they were there."

"We have to leave, Megan," Grady said gently. "If the nurse shift changes anytime soon, we don't want to be caught here. There would be too many explanations and explanations will bog us down."

She didn't want to leave yet. Gardner had betrayed Phillip and she cared nothing about him. She didn't care how idealistic his reasons were for doing it. For once she felt no empathy for another's pain. He could have found another way to get his funding. But Jordan and the head nurse had also died in this room. It seemed callous to just walk away from them.

"Megan."

"Okay, okay." She got to her feet and headed for the

door. "I know what you're saying. I just don't like it." She strode down the hall toward the front entrance. The corridors were as dim and quiet as they had been when they had walked toward Phillip's room.

Dead quiet.

And so were those three people who had been alive and well and full of purpose only hours before.

She took out her phone as they reached the car. "I'm calling 911 and telling them that there's an emergency situation in this annex. I can't leave this place unattended. There are helpless patients that might need urgent care."

"Go ahead." He started the car. "We'll be blocks away before they get anyone over here from the main building." His phone rang and he picked up. "We're leaving the grounds, Harley. You and Renata get out quick." He listened for a moment. "Okay, we'll get back to her." He hung up. "Renata has been following the nurse who ran out of the annex. She didn't like the fact that she was in such a big hurry and that her car had no hospital parking ID. She tried to call you but wasn't getting an answer. So she called Harley and told him to get in touch."

"Did Harley spot Darnell or any other Molino men here?"

He shook his head. "But he found a truck that met the description. Darnell might have had to transport Phillip in an ambulance to avoid suspicion and been forced to leave his truck. Harley's going through the glove box now."

"If Darnell's as smart as you told me, he won't have left any evidence."

He shrugged. "You can never tell. At least, we have two threads to Molino to work on that we didn't have before."

"If Renata doesn't lose that nurse she was following."

"I don't believe Renata has a habit of losing what she's going after," he said dryly. "Call her."

"After 911." She was already dialing. "The patients."

He nodded. "By all means, after the patients."

RENATA'S CELL PHONE WENT immediately to voice mail when Megan called. She tried three other times and got the same result.

"She has her cell phone turned off." She bit her lower lip. "Or someone else turned it off for her."

"The nurse?"

"If she worked for Molino she could be as bad as he is. For God's sake, the least she did was stand by and let three people be butchered."

"I don't believe she could take down Renata. From what Harley said she's remarkable."

She dialed again. "Renata is wounded. And she doesn't know for certain that the nurse was— She's picking up. Thank God. Are you okay, Renata?"

"I'm fine," Renata said. "I was just a little busy. It was a trap?"

"Yes. Dr. Gardner, the head nurse, Madge Holloway, and Jordan the guard were murdered. Phillip is gone. Molino has him. The woman you followed is a phony."

"I'd already gotten that far. Well, a little more, actually. The name of the woman I followed is Hedda Kipler. She does work for Molino and she's pretty good at his brand of ugliness."

"How do you know?"

"I told you I was busy. We're at her motel room at the Fairfield Inn on Highway 40. Come and get her."

"We're on our way."

"Take your time. We're having a nice chat, aren't we, Hedda?"

Megan hung up and turned to Grady. "Fairfield Inn on Highway 40. She said that there's no hurry, but I'm not sure that's true."

"Why?"

"She already knows the woman's real name. I don't know how much Cousin Mark has taught Renata about interrogation methods."

THE FIRST THING MEGAN SAW when Renata opened the door was Hedda Kipler tied to a chair with a drapery cord. She was gagged and her face was bruised and bloody.

Megan glanced at Renata with a frown. "Renata."

"I didn't do that while I had her trussed up like a turkey," she said quickly. "She jumped me when I got out of the car here at the motel. I had to defend myself." She made a face. "She got in a few licks herself. You're going to have to restitch me."

For the first time Megan noticed the bloody patch on Renata's shoulder. "You opened your wound. Sit down and I'll fix it."

"Not now," Grady said. "We need to know about her orders from Molino before he finds out we have her." He glanced at Renata. "How much did you get out of her before we came?"

"I need to tend to that wound," Megan said. "And she said she was only defending herself."

"To start off with. I imagine she's not totally innocent, are you, Renata?"

She met his gaze. "No, I'd already shaken her up. I had to follow through or it might have taken hours or days to pump her. Mark would have thought it 'inefficient.' " She turned to Megan. "I didn't do any permanent damage. Just enough to make her know I was serious. She helped them take your Phillip. Would you rather I let her lie and make up stories until it was too late for him?"

She wearily shook her head. "No, but I don't like it that it was you who did this. There has to be damage to you too."

"What did you find out?" Grady asked again.

"She's worked for Molino in Paris, Athens, and Miami in the past ten years. She's done everything from transporting drug money to be laundered to jobs like this one tonight. She thinks he's got a hideaway in Tennessee, but she's never been there."

"Shit."

"But she has been to an apartment he keeps in Miami. 1230 Ocean View. Last month she delivered a package to him there from Central Africa."

"He's not in Miami now, dammit."

"No, but you can get the CIA to go to his apartment and get me that personal object I need to find him. They don't seem to be able to get anything from anywhere else."

"Are you sure there's something you can use in that apartment?" Megan asked.

Renata's lips twisted. "Oh, yes. Hedda Kipler says he keeps the things she brought him in the second drawer in the chest by the bathroom door. Tell them to bring me any object in that drawer and I'll be able to find Molino."

"You seem certain."

Renata's gaze shifted to meet the malevolent glare of Hedda Kipler. "Absolutely."

"Megan is supposed to meet with Molino at Redwing, Tennessee, tomorrow night. Redwing could be a starting point for you." Grady shrugged. "Or maybe not. He could have chosen a place to meet at the opposite end of the state from his headquarters."

"I'll try Redwing. If you can make the CIA move fast, I'll be out there on the road tomorrow."

"I'll call Venable right away," Grady said. "He can send someone to pick up Hedda Kipler and get a man out to Molino's Miami apartment. Will Molino be expecting a contact from her?"

Renata shook her head. "She phoned Sienna when she left the hospital. Darnell had left over an hour before with Phillip in an ambulance. He'd pretended to be delivering a new patient to the annex and he and another of Molino's men were sent into Phillip's room to see Gardner. After that it was all over." She glanced at Megan. "You did know that Gardner was in Molino's pay?"

Megan nodded. "Molino told me."

"Gardner had it all set up. At that time of evening there are only two nurses on duty at a time. There's not much to do for coma patients after they're tucked in for the night. Gardner said he didn't need them and to save money he sent both of them back to the main nursing home. Hedda's job was to stay until Megan was inside the room and Molino could contact her."

"Cold bitch."

"She's foul. I was almost hoping she'd give me an excuse to put her down," Renata said. "But she has guts. Anyone could have come in and questioned her right to be there. She obeyed orders and stayed."

"And she didn't make any other calls?"

"She would have told me if she had." Renata sat down in the chair. "Now patch me up, will you? My damn shoulder is starting to bleed again."

EIGHTEEN

HARLEY ARRIVED AT THE MOTEL while Megan was still stitching the wound.

"Tsk-tsk." He shook his head. "All my excellent first-aid work going down the drain because you got careless." He grimaced as he saw the gaping wound. "It looks worse than it did before. I hope you're not going to ask me to do your rebandaging again. I hate wasting my time."

"I wouldn't think of it," Renata said. "I always knew you were squeamish."

"True. Where's Grady?"

"He took Hedda Kipler to the Publix parking lot a few blocks from here to turn her over to the CIA agents Venable sent to pick her up," Megan said.

"Good idea. He was telling me on the phone that the Kipler woman was a little worse for wear and he didn't want them to have to enter Renata prominently in their report." He reached in his back pocket and pulled out a brown leather sunglass case. "I brought you a present, Renata. This case was in Darnell's glove box. As long as you're in this Finding business, I thought you might as well try your hand at Darnell."

"Leave her alone," Megan said. "You can talk to her after I finish."

But Renata was already picking up the case. "This

Darnell was the one who killed Gardner, Jordan, and the nurse?"

"Yes."

Her fingers lightly moved over the leather. "He's nowhere near. I'm getting only a vague impression. He's . . . happy. Almost exultant."

"Is he with Molino?"

"I don't know. I told you, it's vague."

"He may be with Molino." Megan finished the stitching and started to bandage. "If he's delivering Phillip to him."

"I don't like this 'vague' business, Renata," Harley said. "You sound like something on one of those psychic TV shows. I thought you were supposed to be the genuine article." He sighed. "I'm losing faith in you. Maybe all this paranormal business is only a bunch of malarkey."

"Which you suspect anyway," Renata said dryly. "I don't have to account to you, Harley." She stood up and pulled on her shirt. "Be as skeptical as you wish. Just don't get in my way."

"I'll stay humbly in the background while you sniff and howl like a bloodhound on the trail. But I hope you won't mind me tagging along. You may need someone to stand in for Megan when it's time to change your bandage."

"You can come." Her gaze slid away from him. "If Venable manages to get what I need. Perhaps he won't. Maybe Molino has moved his stuff somewhere else."

There was a note in Renata's voice that Megan had never heard before. She studied her expression and saw the usual trace of bravado, but there was something else. "What is it? You don't want to do this, do you?"

She didn't answer directly. "I wouldn't have told you where to find the damn thing if I wasn't willing to do it." She headed toward the door. "I'm heading for Redwing.

If there's a chance of locating Molino or Darnell before Megan has to meet him tomorrow night, I'll do it. I'll take the glasses case and see if I can get any vibes close to there. If Venable comes through, call me and I'll meet you." She glanced at Harley. "Coming?"

"Of course, how can I resist such a gracious invitation?" Harley murmured. "I'll follow you in my car."

"You're shutting me out, Renata," Megan said. "I'm not going to let you do that."

"Yes, you are. If you can contribute, you can come along. Otherwise stay here with Grady and let us do the groundwork. Your job is to make sure Venable comes through for me." She didn't wait for an answer but walked out of the motel room.

"I'll keep an eye on her, Megan." Harley made a face. "Though it may be from six feet behind her."

"I don't like this. There's something wrong about how . . ." She drifted off in frustration. "We'll be in Redwing as soon as we can tomorrow. Don't let anything happen to her, Harley."

"I won't. I may not have any voodoo talents, but there's something to say for superb intelligence and experience." He moved toward the door. "And the willingness to duck and run to fight another day is really handy. You should learn to cultivate that philosophy. I've noticed you have a tendency to attack first and worry about repercussions later. See you tomorrow, Megan."

She watched the door close behind him with frustration and a sense of helplessness. She was the one who should be going after Molino. Phillip was her responsibility and the reason he was in this predicament was because Molino had found her Achilles' heel and was using it against her.

She turned, and began to straighten her medical bag. It

was surprising that Renata had managed to subdue Hedda Kipler with that wounded shoulder.

No, not really surprising. Renata had a determination and endurance that Megan had seldom seen before. She would never give up and would ignore all obstacles in her path.

"You're frowning." Grady had opened the door and his gaze was on her face. "What's wrong now?"

"Me," she said unevenly. "It appears I'm not qualified to go after Molino. Renata and Harley have taken off for Tennessee and I've been told to sit here and stay out of their way."

"Which promptly goads you to do the opposite."

"Yes. But I won't do it, because they're right. I'm not a Finder. I'm not a Controller. I'm not some hotshot soldier of fortune like Harley. I have a talent that's not going to help Phillip one bit." She snapped her medical case shut. "So I'll step aside and let everyone do their thing until I can see a way to help."

"That's the smart course to follow."

"Smart, hell." She whirled on him. "It's the only path. I opened my mouth and made Molino come after me frothing with craziness and venom. Do you know what could happen if Molino pulls those feeding tubes?"

"It's not your fault. You did what you thought was right."

"I thought he'd be coming after us, after me. Who the devil could believe that Molino would be able to snatch Phillip out of that place? But people died because I underestimated Molino. I won't let that happen again. I'm not putting anyone else on the line. What did Venable say?"

"He'll have a man in Molino's Miami apartment within a few hours. The personal object Renata needs will be delivered to us by eight A.M. tomorrow morning." He glanced at his watch. "That gives you at least six hours to sleep. Suppose we check in here for tonight?"

"Whatever," she said wearily. "Anywhere will do."

"I'm sleeping with you tonight." He shook his head as she opened her mouth to speak. "Sleeping. You've called me insensitive before, but even I have my limits." He took three steps forward and pulled her into his arms. "You're stretched tense and fragile as a rubber band," he said roughly. "You're full of sadness and worry and guilt and I can feel every single nuance of it. It's driving me crazy. If you'd let me, I could take it away and let you forget. But you won't do that, will you?"

She shook her head. "No." But he was taking away some of that disturbance just by holding her and letting her realize that she wasn't alone. Her arms slid around him and she buried her face in his chest. Her voice was muffled. "Thank you. This feels good. I'm not really . . . fragile. You know that, Grady."

"Yeah." His lips brushed her temple. "But let's pretend you are for tonight. It will make me feel as if I'm doing something worthwhile. Let me hold you, Megan."

Let me hold you. Let me share your burden. Let me be part of you. Sweet thoughts, a sweeter reality.

"Okay," she whispered. "For tonight."

"HERE IT IS." GRADY CAME into the motel room the next morning and tossed a briefcase on the bed. "Venable's agent delivered it fifteen minutes ago." He paused. "He appeared anxious to get rid of it."

She swung her legs to the floor. "I'll call Renata and tell her we're on our way. What time is it?"

"Seven twenty." He turned and headed for the bathroom. "We should be on the road in fifteen minutes."

"Right." She was already dialing Renata's number. "We've got it," she said when she reached her. "We'll be there in a few hours."

Silence. "You've got it?"

"Yes, I told you. Venable came through for us. Were you able to zero in on anything from Darnell's sunglasses?"

"No, the vibes were stronger but still inconclusive. If Molino is in this area, then Darnell isn't with him."

"Well, maybe you'll have better luck with one of Molino's possessions."

"Maybe."

"Where shall we meet you?"

"There's a side road on the other side of Redwing just after you pass a little restaurant called Roadkill."

"Yuck. What a name. That will stick in my memory. You'll be waiting on the side road?"

"I'll be there." She hung up.

Megan slowly pressed the disconnect. There it was again; that odd note of which she'd been aware when Renata had spoken about the objects in Molino's Miami apartment. Tension? Fear?

Megan's gaze shifted to the briefcase on the bed.

He appeared anxious to get rid of it.

Why would Venable's agent want to get this briefcase out of his hands?

She slowly reached out and pulled the briefcase toward her.

RENATA WAS LEANING AGAINST the side of her SUV and straightened as she saw Megan pull up. "Where's Grady? He shouldn't have let you come alone."

"He's right behind me. I told him I wanted to talk to you." She grabbed the briefcase and jumped out of the car.

Renata stiffened, her gaze on the briefcase. "Is that it?"

"Yes. Let's go for a walk."

Renata didn't move. "Why?"

"Stop asking questions." Megan didn't look at her as she strode ahead of her down the road. "I have a few to ask myself."

"Just give me the briefcase."

"Later."

Renata caught up with her a minute later. "You opened it, didn't you?"

"Yes."

"What was in it?"

She stopped and turned to face her. "Don't you know?"

Renata shook her head. "The Kipler woman said the drawer was crammed. It could have been anything."

"But you knew whatever it was that you'd be able to use it."

Renata moistened her lips. "What's in it?"

Megan's hands were shaking as she opened the brief-case. "It's a child's pink dress. It's ragged, faded, and it must have belonged to a little girl, no more than seven or eight." She pulled out the dress and offered it to Renata. "Such a little thing to upset a tough CIA agent. Grady said he couldn't wait to get rid of it."

"It's not such a little thing." Renata didn't take the pink dress. "He must have known what it was."

"And what is it, Renata? What was in that drawer? You've been acting scared to death ever since we talked about it."

She lifted her chin. "I'm not scared."

"Then take the dress."

"I will." She didn't move for a moment and then reached out and her hand closed on the cotton material of the dress. She shuddered. "Oh, God."

She ran over to the side of the road and threw up.

"Renata." Megan was beside her, her comforting hand on the other woman's shoulder. "For heaven's sake, Renata."

"I'm sorry." She gasped. "I didn't mean—I'll be better soon."

"Sit down." Megan gently pushed her to the ground to lean against a tall pine tree. Renata's breathing was harsh, rapid. Megan knelt down beside her. "What's wrong? What's happening?"

"It's pretty obvious, isn't it? I got sick."

"Why?"

Renata looked down at the little dress she was still clutching. "Maybe I don't like pink."

"Then let me have it back." Megan took the dress from her hand. "You don't have to use this. We'll get something else."

"No." But her breathing appeared to be less labored now that she was no longer clutching the dress. "It has to be this one. Or something like it."

"Why? What is it?"

"I think you know."

"I made a guess when I saw it. I almost threw up too." Her hand tightened on the dress. "Did it belong to one of the little girls Molino sold into slavery?"

Renata nodded jerkily. "The Kipler woman told me that Molino was into collecting trophies. He had everything in that drawer from body parts of men who had crossed him to the hair of children he'd raped and killed." The tears were slowly running down her cheeks. "He particularly liked the dresses the little girls had worn the day they were captured. Hedda Kipler made a number of trips from various parts of the world gathering booty from customers and bandits and delivering them to Molino. She said she'd seen him sit at his desk, smiling and fondling them."

The horror that image brought was almost overpowering. "And you still told us to go get . . . this."

"You want Molino, don't you? This will make it certain I can find him for you."

"You can't even touch this dress without throwing up."

"Yes, I can. Give me a little time." She reached out a tentative finger and touched the dress. She shivered, but her finger remained on the material. "I'm not usually this much of a coward. It's just that I can *see* her."

"You can?"

"And Molino too. They're all mixed up together. I was afraid it would be like that. It's happened to me before. I'm not like you. I . . . can't handle that kind of emotion. It's feels as if I'm being beaten." She drew a deep shaky breath. "And it wasn't only the money for him. It gave him a sense of power to destroy those little girls. He liked to stroke these clothes and think about it."

"A monster."

Renata nodded. "And these trophies couldn't be sending out stronger signals. This is the essence of that son of a bitch. I'll be able to find him even if he's a thousand miles away."

"You said it was mixed up with the little girl."

"Once I get used to her, I'll be able to isolate him." She said hoarsely, "She was so frightened, Megan. Her name was Adia and she ran and ran, but the bandits were on horseback and they caught her. She was crying but nobody cared . . ."

"Maybe we can find her, Renata."

"Maybe. If she's still alive." Renata's eyes were glittering with moisture. "But first we have to find Molino." She sat upright and wiped her cheeks with the back of her hand. "Sorry. I'm okay now."

"For heaven's sake. There's nothing wrong with—" She wasn't reaching her. Renata's moment of softness was over and she was pushing her away.

Why accept it? She felt closer to Renata now than ever before. Renata would just have to learn to deal with affection.

Megan deliberately reached out and took her hand. "I think you're nuts to put yourself through this, but I admire and respect you for it." She got to her feet. "If I can help, let me know. What do you do next?"

"I drive around and see where it leads me." Renata smiled unsteadily. "I'll try hard to find Molino for you before tonight, Megan."

"I know you will. But if you don't, stay away from the graveyard. Do you hear?"

Renata didn't answer.

"I mean it. I don't know what to expect, but I don't want Molino to make any phone calls that will hurt Phillip."

"I'll think about it. It wouldn't do any good to try to make a connection with Molino there anyway. It won't be the place he has your Phillip. And it would be broken when he put enough distance between us. What's the plan?"

"Harley is going to scout around the cemetery and make sure Molino doesn't have backup there. Grady will stay in the trees with a rifle trained on Molino."

Renata thought about it. "I suppose that's as safe as Grady can make it for you."

"Then promise me you'll stay away from the cemetery."

"If I can locate Molino before that it will be a moot issue."

"Promise."

She frowned.

"Promise."

"Hell, no." She turned on her heel and walked back toward her car.

10:45 P.M.

"HARLEY SAYS THE IMMEDIATE area's clear," Grady said. "There are four of Molino's men in the forest across the way. I didn't expect him to take a chance and come alone." He gestured to the south. "I'll be in that patch of trees with a rifle trained on Molino. Harley will circle and keep an eye out to make sure Molino's men don't start moving toward you. Understand?"

She nodded her gaze on the top of the hill. "I understand."

The Redwing cemetery had been in existence since the start of the Civil War and it showed its age. Rotting wooden crosses and stone markers with the inscriptions eroded by time, overgrown patches of grass sprouted between the graves.

"Don't get too close to him. I might need a clear shot."

"You can't shoot him. He has Phillip and Renata still hasn't been able to find where Molino's keeping him."

He put the scope on his rifle. "If I have to make a choice, it won't be Phillip," he said grimly.

"Molino doesn't want to kill me. Not yet."

Harley appeared out of the brush. "Molino's here. He and Sienna are starting up the north slope of the hill."

She stiffened. "Then I'd better join him, hadn't I? We wouldn't want him to become impatient."

She heard Grady's low curse behind her as she moved up the path. He was feeling helpless and out of control and he hated to be put in that position, she knew. Well, he would have to deal with it. She was feeling pretty helpless herself at the moment.

The moon was full and shining brightly as she caught sight of Molino and Sienna standing on the crest of the hill. Her pace hesitated for an instant as a thrill of fear went through her. Don't tense. They might be monsters but monsters could be destroyed.

Molino was smiling at her. "Ah, Sienna, here she is. I told you that she'd be scampering to save that human refuse, Phillip. Her mother was just the same. Like mother, like daughter."

Sienna shrugged. "And neither of them is very smart. You're wasting your time. You have her now, kill her."

"What do you say about that, Megan?" Molino asked. "I keep telling Sienna that you're a worthy opponent, but he won't believe me. He thinks that I should concentrate on business."

"If you can call that filth you do business," Megan said as she came level with them. "Tell me how I can get Phillip back."

"Presently."

"Is he still alive?"

"Yes, but I can't dial him and have him talk to you." He chuckled. "His communication skills aren't exactly top-notch at present. I understand Gardner was excited about him squeezing his hand, but we haven't bothered to explore that route." He tilted his head. "I'm more interested in having you squeeze Sienna's hand."

"What?" Sienna jerked his head around to stare at Molino. "What the shit are you up to?"

"Why, Sienna, there's nothing to worry about. You've always doubted that my Steven was victimized by that whore who bred this viper. I could see how contemptuous you were of me and my crazy ideas. If you're right, then you can prove it now. Let her take your hand."

"I don't want to touch him," Megan said. "He's as dirty as you are."

"But you were boasting how you were going to turn me into a vegetable. Such an ugly threat. Were you bluffing?"

"I don't want to touch him," she repeated.

"But I insist. That's why we're here. I had to know what I had to face with you, what I have to face with all those freaks listed in the Ledger. You boasted that you could find me, but that didn't happen. You bragged that you had powers like your mother, but there's no proof of that either." He smiled. "Show me proof, Megan."

"I don't have to show you anything."

"You do unless you want me to make a call and tell my men to disconnect the feeding tube from Phillip Blair."

She shrugged. "All right, I'll admit it. I'm no Pandora. I just wanted to make you angry."

"Show me," he repeated softly.

"Screw you," Sienna said. "I'm not going to put up with this bullshit."

"Scared?" Molino asked. "Why? As you said, it's only bullshit. My Steven went insane for no reason at all."

"Don't be an ass," Sienna said. "It's just that I'm not willing to play your game."

"And you're scared of the pretty lady. My, my."

"Oh, for God's sake." Sienna took one stride forward to stand before Megan. He thrust out his hand. "Get it over with."

She didn't move.

"Take his hand," Molino said. He took out his phone. "I'll give you thirty seconds before I make the call."

She glared at him. "Why don't you let me take your hand, Molino?"

"Because Sienna deserves whatever happens to him for doubting me. And I've always liked the idea of those Egyptian poison tasters. There's something regal about it. Fifteen seconds."

She reached out and took Sienna's hand. It was big, warm, and soft and all she could think about was how he had tortured Edmund Gillem with those hands.

"Press it," Molino said. "Hard."

Her hand tightened. She was *hating* this.

"Harder," Molino said.

She tightened her grip again.

"Crap," Sienna said. "This is taking too long." His hand crushed bruisingly around Megan's.

Pain. Anger. Hatred.

Then Sienna released her and stepped back. "Satisfied?" he asked Molino curtly. "I almost broke her hand. Do you want me to do it again?"

Relief soared through Megan with dizzying force. Nothing had happened. She hadn't realized until this moment how afraid she'd been.

"No." Molino was studying Megan's expression. "I believe I'm disappointed. I admit I hoped to get a little of my own back by having you teach Sienna a lesson. It might not be as entertaining to kill you as I'd hoped. You're obviously not going to be the challenge I thought."

"I told you I wasn't a Pandora."

"But you're Pandora's daughter and that will have to be enough for me." He turned away. "Come along, Sienna. Let's go back to the house and pay a visit to Blair."

Megan tensed. "What are you going to do to him?"

"Make sure he's still alive in that cellar." He paused. "Then tomorrow night I'm going to cut off his feeding tube."

"No!"

"Yes." He stared her in the eye. "If you want him back then you have to give me something in return. I think you know the terms I'll accept. You want Phillip Blair, I get you. Unless you show up here tomorrow alone without Grady or Harley or that other freak, Renata Wilger, any-where in the background, you won't see Blair again alive." He glanced around the cemetery. "My men told me that Grady and Harley came with you. I'm sure they're still somewhere close. I was willing to let you feel safer to-night. Tomorrow is different. I want you to feel vulnera-ble. No, frightened. I want to taste your fear. Steven was frightened that night before he died. He whimpered and cried."

"You promise you'll let Phillip go?"

"I told you I would, under certain circumstances."

"I'm willing to make a trade, but I won't risk my life for nothing." She moistened her lips. "You bring Phillip to that open field just north of the cemetery and I'll arrange for a helicopter to pick him up and take him back to Bellehaven in Atlanta. When the helicopter takes off, you can come and get me."

"That's not satisfactory," Molino said.

"Hell and damnation," Sienna said. "Stop bargain-ing. What do you care about Phillip Blair? You'll have the woman and that's what you want. Let's put an end to this."

"So eager," Molino said. "Sienna, I can't decide whether you're pissed because I made you risk your sanity by holding hands with our little Megan or you're just eager to get her in bed." He smiled at Megan. "I did promise him he could rape you as a fringe benefit. That should give you something to anticipate for the next twenty-four hours."

"Send Phillip to be picked up in that field."

Molino was silent. "Very well. Sienna is right. I don't really care about anyone but you." He turned and started down the hill. "Let's go, Sienna." He added maliciously, "Tell me, are you feeling dizzy or light-headed? Any delusions?"

"Sorry to disappoint you," Sienna said dryly. "I'm normal as I've always been. This whole business is a bunch of baloney and she's a phony."

Molino's smile faded. "But her mother wasn't a phony. Steven was as sane as I am before she poisoned his mind."

"If you say so."

"I say so." Molino looked back at Megan. "I'm glad we came to an agreement. I'm sure if Phillip Blair was anything but a useless carcass he'd appreciate it too."

"Keep him warm and on those tubes," she said. "If he's in a deteriorated condition when I see him, I'll get on that helicopter with him."

"And I'd blow you both out of the air. Don't threaten me, freak."

She watched him walk away. She had never before encountered ugliness like she'd seen tonight. She glanced down at her hand that was still tingling with pain. Sienna's brutality had been the least of the horror of these minutes. She had suspected Molino's instability, but tonight it had been clear. His malice and viciousness had shaken her more than Sienna's cruelty.

But that viciousness might be of help to her. If he was absorbed with all the obscenities he was going to visit on Megan, then he might let Phillip slide away—

"Oh, I just remembered something of interest to you." Molino had turned and stood looking at her. "I got the call just before I arrived at the cemetery tonight."

She stiffened. She had thought it was over. It wasn't over. She could tell by the malice in his expression that this horror of a meeting was not at an end.

He took a piece of paper out of his pocket and dropped it on the ground. "I told you I couldn't understand how you could be drawn into my net by that vegetable." He started back down the hill.

She stared after him in shock. What was he up to?

She ran over to the piece of paper he'd dropped on the ground.

Not a piece of paper. A photo.

She snatched it up and turned on her flashlight.

No!

She flew down the hill after Molino. "Stop, you bastard."

He turned and smiled. "Oh, that did hurt you where you live, didn't it? I thought it would be much better insurance for me than Blair. Such a cute little fellow."

"You're saying you have Davy?" Her voice was shaking. Her whole body was shaking. She felt as if she'd been punched in the stomach by an iron fist. "It's a lie. I received an e-mail from his father yesterday and he would have told me if something was wrong."

"My men took him tonight. They went through the window of his room while he was sleeping. We have a good deal of practice at that kind of thing. His parents don't even know he's gone." He added softly, "Call them. Tell them where their little boy is spending tonight."

"You son of a bitch. Don't you lay a finger on him."

"I believe I'll let you worry about that. Though I do prefer little girls, I might force myself to—"

"I'll *kill* you."

"No, you'll show up in that field tomorrow and if you're lucky I'll give you both the old man and the child."

"It has to be both. I won't bargain for one without the other." She paused. "And if you hurt Davy I won't go through with the deal."

"Damaged goods?" He frowned. "Yes, I understand the loss of value on damaged goods. I'll think about it." He turned and strode down the hill.

"Oh, God," she whispered. Don't let it be true. Let it be a lie.

She dialed Scott's number. It rang seven times before he picked up. "What are you thinking, Megan?" He sounded as if she'd woke him from deep sleep. "It better be important. I've got to be at the hospital at six in the morning."

"I hope it's not important. I'm praying it's not important. Look, Scott, do me a favor and go and check on Davy."

"YOU LOOK AS IF YOU'VE been run over by a bull-dozer." Grady met her as she was coming down the hill. "What the hell did he do to you?"

"It's not me. He has Davy too." The tears were running down her face. "That bastard has Davy."

Grady muttered a curse. "You're sure?"

"I hoped it was a lie. Molino was toying with me. He dropped it on me as he was walking away. But I called Scott and— They didn't even know Davy was gone. Molino let me tell him they'd taken him. Scott and Jana are scared to death. *I'm* scared to death. Do you know what that son of a bitch does to children? Yes, of course you do. You're the one who told me."

"He may not—"

"And he might." Her fists clenched. "He might, Grady. I let him see how scared I was. I shouldn't have done that. My only hope is that he thinks of children as something to buy and sell, and damaged goods aren't as valuable. He didn't understand why I'd want to save Phillip. In his eyes he wasn't a prime specimen any longer. He might think I'd refuse to go with him if he hurts Davy." She said unevenly, "I feel so damn helpless. I've got to find a way to help them."

"We'll work it out." He took a step toward her with his hand outstretched. "There's got to be a—"

"Don't touch me." She knew he only wanted to comfort her but she felt as if she would splinter like broken crystal. She couldn't risk any weakness. "Not now."

His hand dropped to his side. "Okay, I understand. How can I help? What else happened up there?"

"I told Molino he had to bring Phillip to that field to the north and I'd have him airlifted out by helicopter. When he told me about Davy I told him he'd have to bring him too or it was no deal."

"And the deal?"

"After Phillip and Davy are gone Molino can come to the field and pick me up."

"The hell he can." Repressed violence vibrated in Grady's voice. "No way."

"It's the only way I can be sure Phillip and Davy will be safe and not used to hurt me. They have to be totally out of the picture."

"So you're going to walk in and put your head on the block?"

"Yes, and it's your job to make sure it doesn't get chopped off. He's not going to kill me right away. If he'd wanted to do that, he wouldn't have taken Phillip and Davy." Her pace quickened. "But I'm not looking forward to being raped and tortured while you spin your wheels. You won't be able to get near me after he picks me up, so you'll have to know where we're going. Renata said she'd be able to find him."

"She had a chance and she didn't find him today," he said grimly.

"She said she'd have trouble making adjustments."

"And you're going to rely on her overcoming her 'trouble'? I know how hard it is for a Finder to focus. You could be dead by the time Renata comes through with a location."

"Then come up with another solution. I'm making sure that Phillip and Davy stay alive. That's my job. All the rest is in your court."

"And my job is to keep you alive."

"That's not how this started. You wanted the Ledger, you wanted Molino dead."

"My priorities have shifted."

"And I have only two now. Phillip and Davy. The rest is—"

"Why are you rubbing your hand?" he interrupted.

She hadn't realized she had been. It had been a purely automatic reflex. "It's a little bruised. Actually, it feels as if it's been crunched in a vise. Molino wanted Sienna to play guinea pig. I think he likes the idea of Sienna turning into a gibbering idiot. He was very disappointed that I turned out not to be a Pandora."

"And you were relieved."

"I never really thought there was a possibility that— yes, I was relieved." Her lips tightened. "Even though I would have liked to hurt Sienna in any way I could.

What a piece of crap. Molino and he deserve each other. No, Molino's still number one on the horror chart." She headed toward the trees where they'd parked the car. "Arrange with Venable for that helicopter. I'm going to be in that field tomorrow."

NINETEEN

RENATA STEPPED FORWARD OUT of the trees to meet Megan and Grady as they reached the bottom of the hill. "What happened up there with Molino?"

Megan's pace didn't slow. "You're not supposed to be here, Renata."

"I had to make sure that you were—"

"Just find Molino's hideaway." Megan passed her and moved toward the car.

Renata could sense the storm of tension and turbulence that was gripping Megan as she gazed after her. "I've never seen her like this. What did he do to her, Grady? What happened?"

"Molino pulled a surprise ambush on her. It wasn't enough that he had Phillip. He kidnapped little Davy Rogan. It's her worst nightmare."

"A little boy . . ." She had a sudden memory of that little pink dress that she had been living with for the last hours. "I can see how it would be. She told me about Davy that first night I met her. She loves him, Grady."

"Yes. And Molino left it to her to break it to the kid's parents."

"Monster. What is she going to do?"

"She made a deal to go to Molino if he released Phillip and Davy."

It didn't surprise her. "When?"

"Tomorrow afternoon in a field north of here."

"Can't you talk her out of it?"

"What do you think?" Grady asked curtly. "You know her by now. It's her nature. She couldn't do anything else. She doesn't care if the odds are against her. She's not going to let Molino hurt them."

Yes, she knew Megan, Renata thought. She had even used that knowledge to nudge her in the direction she'd needed her to go. From the moment she had met her she had been drawn to the warmth that surrounded Megan. She had tried to fight it because she knew that affection could make you vulnerable. Hadn't she learned that when Edmund had been killed? Yet here she was again, feeling once again all the worry and emotion that interfered with clear thinking and efficient action. Ignore it. Think what's best to do, what Mark would do. "Would you like me to give her a shot of methohexital? That would take her out of the picture and buy us time until we could—" She saw him shaking his head. "No?"

"A very cool and efficient solution. Just what I'd expect of you. But that would still leave Phillip and Davy in jeopardy and when she woke up, she'd be coming after both of us. She doesn't understand cool and efficient."

"Then she's right. I'll just have to find Molino. And I'd better get back to it. I covered the south hill country today and I got a few vibes when I headed toward Murfreesboro. Then they disappeared. I wasn't sure if it was my loss of focus or if I was on a wrong track. But then it was time to get back to Redwing in case she needed me."

"The only thing she needs from you right now is to find Molino's headquarters. She had me. She had Harley. You should have realized that we'd take care of her."

"I didn't know if I could trust you. I do know I can trust me." She moved toward her car. "I'll call you when I zero in on Molino. You and your CIA friends had better be ready to move."

A moment later she was in the driver's seat and staring blindly into the darkness. She had used the word *when*, not *if* she found Molino. Yet she had not been able to focus enough to get a strong lead earlier today.

Because she'd been afraid of the pain.

Whenever she touched the dress, she was swamped with sorrow and pain that tore her apart. She'd told Megan she could overcome it, dammit. She looked down at the briefcase on the seat beside her. Okay, she couldn't fight the memories of that little girl, she would have to absorb herself in them, become one with them.

She drew a deep breath and opened the briefcase. A shudder went through her as she touched the dress.

She couldn't do it.

The hell she couldn't.

Her hand clenched on the material and was immediately bombarded by emotions. Fear, bewilderment, and pain from the little girl. Ugliness, exultation, sick pleasure from Molino. It was too much, too much.

"Such a pretty little girl." Molino was sitting on a camp stool staring at Adia. *"In a pretty pink dress. Take it off her, Kofi. I want to see what the client will see."*

No! Fight them. Hands on her. Shame.

"Now hold her. How they cringe when they're frightened. Isn't it interesting, Kofi?"

Terror.

Dammit, Renata wanted to *kill* that bastard. She had to separate them in her mind. She couldn't deal with Adia's panic and despair and the total ugliness of Molino too.

"Help me, Adia," she whispered. "I'm no good at this. He has another child now and I have to find him right away. I'll come after you later, but I have to let you go now."

But she couldn't leave her while the image of her was this tragic. Think of the little girl before this happened. Happy, loved by her parents, playing in her village. But even that scenario brought anger that a child's happiness could be destroyed by that son of a bitch.

Try again.

She drew the dress close to her chest and held it close.

Oh, dear God. Don't throw up. Get through it.

Help me, Adia.

6:30 A.M.

A CLIFF.

Straight and almost sheer, plunging to the valley below. *Yes.*

Renata's hands clenched on the pink dress. After all these hours she'd managed to make the connection with Molino. Not only the connection, but she was also receiving a picture, a view. Renata's hand tightened on the dress as her foot hit the accelerator.

Northwest.

More, she prayed. Give me more.

A house on a cliff. Two-story brown cedar with lots of glass. She could see Molino walking on a path by the edge of the incline, looking out over the valley several hundred feet below. Toward the back of the property a helicopter pad was occupied by a blue-and-white helicopter. A utility shed several yards from the pad. What was the registration number on the helicopter? Dammit, the image was too blurry. But in the distance Molino was able to see a glimmer of steel, a bridge over a wide expanse of water.

Then the vision was gone.

But the tether was still present. Follow it.

Northwest.

She put down Adia's dress to dial Grady. "Molino has a house on a cliff. It's somewhere in the northwest of the state."

"How certain are you? We don't have much time before Megan meets with Molino."

"I'm sure. Molino can see a bridge from the path by the cliff."

"What bridge?"

"I don't know. It's all blurry. Steel. It's no Golden Gate but it's big enough to see from a distance."

"Anything else?"

"No, I lost the view. But the tether is still strong. I'm heading toward it now."

"Where are you?"

"The last town I passed was Pulaski."

"I'm sending Harley in a helicopter to meet you."

"I don't need Harley."

"If you can narrow down the target area, maybe he can find that bridge from the air and spot the house."

"Maybe."

"At noon Megan is going to be in that damn field with Molino. I can't touch him as long as he's a threat to Phillip and Davy, but I have to know where Molino's taking her."

"I know all that. Harley may get in my way."

"I'll chance it. He'll call you from the helicopter."

Renata hung up. She didn't want Harley here. She didn't want anyone to see her this weak and trembling. She picked up the dress again and clutched it beneath her hand on the wheel where it had been for the past seven hours. Even after all this time, her hand was still shaking and her emotions were raw.

"We'll just have to put up with it, Adia," she whispered. "Maybe he will be able to help."

Then she blocked out all thought of anything but the tether leading her to Molino.

Northwest.

"I'VE JUST HEARD FROM RENATA," Grady said as he came into the sitting room. "She thinks she has an idea where Molino's place is."

Megan straightened on the couch. "Thank God."

"And she's getting a general picture. It's northwest and near a bridge. I'm calling Harley."

"Good. I'll feel better with him there if she's really near Molino. She likes to do things a little too much on her own."

"She does them well."

"You're defending her." She managed to smile faintly. "That's a surprise."

"It shouldn't be. She's proved she's on your side. That's all the qualification I demand these days. If she was a witch incarnate, I'd help her gather eye of newt for her brews if I could be sure she'd be able to find Molino."

"Witch," she repeated. "I suppose in the past she might have been considered a witch. It's so unfair."

"Along with present company." He was dialing the phone. "But I have to get Harley going to help our witch."

She got to her feet and headed for the kitchen. "I'll make some coffee."

"Go to bed, Megan," Grady said quietly when she came back with two cups of coffee fifteen minutes later. "You've been sitting on that couch like a frozen statue since we came back from the cemetery. You won't sleep but you can at least stretch out."

She shook her head. "Scott is going to call me back

after he talks to the police." She swallowed. "I asked him to have the police talk to Venable. I told him it wouldn't do any good to contact the police, that I'd get Davy back, but he wouldn't listen. I probably wouldn't listen either. He sounded as if he hated me."

"He's your friend. He'll get over it once we have the boy safe."

"Will he? What friend would put a little boy in danger? He doesn't care about anything but getting him back."

"Did you tell him about Molino?"

She shook her head. "Not about what a monster he is. I hope the police don't tell him. He and his wife don't need to know that. It would put them through even more hell than they're going through now. It's enough that I know. He's such a sweet little boy, Grady." She looked down at the photo she was still clutching. It was a shot of Davy on his new bicycle. Not the same one Scott had sent her. Davy's expression in this picture was intent, concentrating, and totally adorable. "They must have been watching him for a long time."

"Probably since you took him to the zoo. Darnell was watching you during that period. Since he was no relation, Molino wouldn't have regarded Davy of much importance. He only grabbed him when he wasn't positive Phillip would be enough of a draw."

"A double whammy," she said bitterly. "He found a way to—"

Her cell phone rang. Scott. She quickly punched the button. "Have you talked to the police?"

"The bastards are stalling," Scott said harshly. "After they talked to Venable they're not even trying to find him. They said it wouldn't be safe to muddy the waters. My God, Davy is alone with those sons of bitches and no one is doing anything."

"We're doing something. I won't let him be hurt, Scott."

"You'd better not. You're my friend but this happened because you got yourself involved with scum. Now get my son back."

"I'm so sorry, Scott," she whispered.

"Sorry isn't good enough. Jana's hysterical and had to be sedated. I'm a basket case and my son could be dead tomorrow. Now *fix* it." He hung up.

She looked at Grady. "Venable called the police off the case. Scott doesn't understand." She put the phone down on the table. "Except that I'm to blame and he wants Davy back." She added unsteadily, "And he's right. Maybe we're all wrong about this Pandora business. Perhaps my 'talent' is that I let loose pain and disaster on everyone around me."

"Shut up," he said curtly. "This is Molino, not you. Now stop feeling sorry for yourself."

She lifted her head, startled. "I'm not feeling sorry for myself. I just—"

"Good. Because I can't take any more. Every word you say feels like it's stabbing me."

She smiled faintly. "Then maybe you should be the one to stop feeling sorry for yourself."

"I'll work on it. But it would make me feel better if you'd let me touch you." He pulled her down beside him on the couch. "Okay?"

It would make her feel better too. The first shock had passed, but the raw pain remained. "Okay." She cuddled closer to him. She was silent a moment, letting the warmth and togetherness flow into her. "I hurt them, Grady," she whispered. "I can almost see why Renata won't let anyone come near her. I don't want to ever hurt anyone like this again."

"But you're not Renata. You can't do that." His hand gently stroked her hair. "You have to live with it. This isn't going to last forever. It's all going to straighten out. We'll see that it does."

"I wish I were with Renata. I'm afraid for her, Grady."

"Dammit, stop being afraid for everyone but yourself." He added roughly, "Renata's not the one who's going to let someone whisk her off to maim and mutilate her."

After his previous gentleness the sudden brutal frankness shocked her. She stiffened and tried to pull away but his grasp tightened. "I don't want to hear this, Grady."

"No, but it felt good to let it out." He put his cheek against her temple. "I *hate* it. You have no right to make me feel like this and then go off and risk your damn neck."

"Let me go."

"In a minute." He was holding hard and tight, but it was less than a minute when he released her and got to his feet. "I'm calling Venable and telling him to send some agents into Nashville in case we need them. If Renata is right about the general direction, then that should be a good jumping-off place." He headed for the door. "Nothing is going to happen to you, Megan. If Molino hurts one fingernail, one hair of your head, I'll find a way to send him to hell in the most painful way he could imagine. He thinks he wants to destroy freaks? Wait until he sees what this freak can do to him."

The door slammed behind him.

Megan shivered at the violence that was still electrifying the room. She had always been aware of the underlying violence that lay in Grady but she had still been unprepared for this explosion.

She had a sudden memory of what he had said when he'd said he wanted to have possession of the Ledger because he was afraid of what would happen if one of the family were cornered by Molino.

Well, Grady felt cornered now and there was nothing

she could do about it. She was soon going to have her hands full dealing with Molino.

7:40 A.M.

"I'VE BROUGHT A TOPOGRAPHICAL and navigational map of the area." Harley laid the map on the car seat between him and Renata. "Turn on the top lights."

She switched them on. "We're wasting time. I need to get back on the road." She had met him at a small airport where his helicopter had landed near Lewisburg, Tennessee. It had not been out of her way, but that didn't stop her from feeling the panic rising. Every minute was worth its weight in gold right now. "Can't you do this yourself?"

"Since you described the bridge as being large I'm almost sure that it has to be across the Mississippi River." He'd drawn circles around two bridges on the river. "And both these bridges have hilly terrain on the Tennessee side. You said Molino's house was on a high cliff, right?"

She nodded.

"How far was the house from the river?"

"I don't know." She tried to think. "Fifteen. Twenty miles."

"Was Molino looking north or south at the bridge?"

She closed her eyes for an instant. "South."

"The bridges are about sixty miles apart. We can't make a mistake about the area. It could be a disaster for Megan. Take a look at the map. Does it trigger anything?"

She shook her head in exasperation. "For God's sake, I can't look at a map and expect it to tell me secrets like a Ouija board. It doesn't work that way."

"How was I to know? Megan explained all about your connection and tethers, but it's all Greek to me. You have to admit I'm being outstandingly tolerant and reasonable in trying to work with you on this. I trust my map more than I do your 'tether.' "

"Tolerant?" she repeated. "You're tolerating me?"

"No." He smiled. "But the thought made you angry enough to make you let go of that little dress you were clutching. I thought you needed a diversion."

"You don't know anything about what I need." But he had meant to be kind and maybe it was better if she concentrated on something else for these brief moments. She looked down at the map. "Both the bridges are located in the general area where I'm being led. But which one is the right one?"

"Since I'm not getting any mystical help from you I'll have to fly over both of the bridges and see what I can see." He started folding up his map. "So I'll let you get back on the road. I'll call you when I'm close to either of the bridges and describe the terrain to you. Or do you want to come in the helicopter with me?"

She shook her head. "Flying doesn't work as well for me with the tether as being on the ground."

"Suit yourself." He picked up the dress from the seat and held it for a moment before handing it to her. "You know, the thought of this makes me very, very angry." He closed the car door and strode back toward the helicopter.

10:50 A.M.

"ARE YOU READY?" MOLINO asked when Megan picked up the phone. "I know I am. I can't wait to meet with you."

"And you're bringing both Phillip and Davy?"

"I told you that I would."

"How are they? Did you hurt them?"

"You'll see for yourself." He added, "I know you're going to have Grady and his CIA friends hovering nearby and I'm laying out the ground rules for you. After the helicopter picks up and leaves with Blair and the boy, you're to remain there in the field until my own helicopter picks you up. Don't be impatient; it will only be a few minutes. If there is any attempt to interfere with you coming with me, I'll give the order and your friend Phillip and the child will be blown out of the sky by a ground-to-air missile. If anyone attempts pursuit after you board my helicopter, then they'll see you hurtling to the ground from several thousand feet. Since you haven't displayed any other of your mother's freakish talents, I doubt if you can fly."

"You didn't answer me. Did you hurt them?"

But he had already hung up.

11:35 A.M.

THE TETHER WAS GONE, Renata realized in a panic.

One minute it had been strong and tight and now she couldn't feel it at all.

Please, not now. She had thought she was so close.

Her hand was shaking as she dialed Harley in the helicopter. "It's gone. The tether's gone."

"Calm down," Harley said quietly. "I know that must mean a hell of a lot to you, but I can't grasp it."

"Dammit, I *felt* him. It was getting stronger and stronger and then I lost him. He was gone."

"Then let's think about it." He was silent a moment. "What time is it?" He answered himself. "It's quarter to twelve, Renata. He's supposed to meet Megan at noon. If he suddenly took off and headed south to Redwing, would you lose the tether?"

"Shit." She felt like a dunce. "Yes. I was zeroed in on him at that location. It would have been like having the rug pulled out from under me. Why didn't I think of that?"

"I've heard geniuses sometimes have trouble tying their tennis shoes."

"What's that supposed to mean?"

"Words of comfort?" He added, "See if you can get a handle on this tether and call me back. I'm over the first bridge now and I want to go lower." He hung up.

She closed her eyes, her hand on the dress.

Where are you, bastard?

Nothing.

No, there was a faint pull, gossamer light to the east.

She waited a moment but the tether was getting weaker by the second.

She dialed Harley. "He's heading southeast."

"Redwing," Harley said. "He's gone to pick up Megan."

"How long do we have before he brings her back?"

"I'd say two hours maximum."

Two hours.

Another ripple of panic went through her. Dammit, what was wrong with her? She'd been trained to be cool and always keep her head.

The answer wasn't difficult to find. This meant too much. She could see why Mark had always cautioned her against becoming emotionally involved.

Well, it was too late now. She was involved.

"The tether's not going to do me any good from now on. I'll have to try to identify his place by your description. We'll have to find Molino's place right away, before he comes back. Grady will need an inside man there. Hell, Megan's going to need all the help she can get. Are you above the bridge?"

"A little to the east."

"What do you see? Any cliffs?"

"Not yet. I'll do another pass . . ."

LORD, SHE FELT ALONE, MEGAN thought as she shaded her eyes and lifted her gaze to the sky. The hay field was flat and barren and she could only hear the wind through the surrounding trees.

She wasn't really alone, she told herself. Grady was somewhere in those trees with a few of Venable's men, who had shown up a couple hours ago. That should have lessened the fear but it didn't. She hadn't realized until she'd gotten out of the car to wait for Molino how much of a coward she could be.

It didn't matter what she was feeling as long as she didn't break and run. She'd be better once Phillip and Davy were safe and away. She just wanted it over and both of them on their way to Bellehaven where Jana and Scott would meet them.

Where was Molino? He'd mentioned a helicopter but there was—

A roar of a motor erupted from the trees bordering the road.

She tensed and turned to see an ambulance heading toward her, bumping over the ruts in the field.

The driver pulled up and jumped out of the cab. "Hi, little lady. I have a package for you." He was young, good-looking, dressed in a sweatshirt and blue jeans. "Not that he's much of a prize since I clipped him. I'd think you'd have written him off." He ran around to the back and opened the doors. "With Molino's compliments." He wheeled out the stretcher. "And mine of course."

"You're Darnell," she said slowly. "You're the man who shot Phillip."

"I won't be Darnell for long. Molino's promised me a new identity and a job out of the country if I delivered this old guy to you. It's getting a bit hot for me here. Not that it's my fault." He adjusted the feeding tube and wheeled the stretcher over to her. "I did everything right."

"Killing. Crippling. Oh, yes, you do everything right. Where's Davy?"

"Oh, the kid?"

Her heart was beating so hard that she could scarcely breathe. "Davy is supposed to be here. Where is he?"

"He wasn't as cooperative as the old guy. He fought me."

Panic soared through her. "What did you do to him?"

"He acted like an animal. I treated him like one." He strode back toward the doors of the ambulance. "Come and get him."

She was already beside him as he climbed into the ambulance. "Is he hurt?"

He jerked a white cover off a wire cage in the back of the ambulance. He jumped out of the ambulance. "A little, maybe. I wasn't gentle when I was stuffing him into that dog kennel."

Davy was bent almost double in the small dog carrier, his mouth taped shut.

"You bastard." She jumped into the ambulance and released the latch herself. "It's all right, Davy. You're safe." She helped him out of the cage and carefully removed the tape. His eyes were swollen from crying and his lip was cut. "It's okay." She hugged him close and rocked him. "You're going home to your mama and daddy."

He was holding her tight. "I'm scared, Megan. They're bad people."

"Yes, they are. But you're not going to have to be with

them anymore." Her hand stroked his hair. "Did . . . they hurt you, Davy?"

"Yes."

She tensed. "How?"

Davy looked at Darnell. "I bit him and he slapped me and cut my lip."

"What else?"

"They tied me up and put me in the dark."

"That's very bad. But no one else hurt you?"

He shook his head. "But I was awful scared."

Relief was surging through her. Thank you, God. "I know you were." She took him by the hand. "But it's over now. You're going to go home." She helped him out of the ambulance. "Can you be a good boy and come with me while I take a look at my friend? He's very sick."

"He's asleep," Davy said. "I saw him when they put him in the ambulance. When is he going to wake up?"

"Soon, I hope." But she didn't know how much was truth or fiction in what Gardner had told her. Phillip was so pale. She took his wrist and checked his pulse. Slow but not fluttering. He smelled terrible, but not of infection. She could usually tell the difference when—

"He's alive." Darnell's gaze was on her face. "He's a tough old bird. I didn't think he'd make it."

"Yes, he's tough. He's stronger than you could ever be. You've delivered them. Now why don't you go away?"

"I'm supposed to stay here and be picked up with you by Molino." He smiled. "And shoot them both if I see you trying to get on the helicopter with them."

"I'm not going to try—" She lifted her head as she heard the helicopter. She said fiercely, "You stay away from them."

He leaned back against the ambulance and crossed his arms across his chest. "I'm not putting a hand on either of them as long as you do what you're supposed to do."

Her own hand gripped Phillip's, but she felt no response. She'd had so much hope when Gardner had called her. Had that window passed that would allow Phillip to come back? If he'd been present when that massacre of Gardner and the nurse had taken place, would it have made him want to withdraw permanently? Who knows? She couldn't think about that right now. All she could do was make sure he survived.

"Don't cry, Megan," Davy whispered.

She looked down at him. "I'm not crying." She blinked back the tears. "Or if I am, it's because I'm happy you're with me and everything is going to be fine." She knelt before him. "Now there's going to be a helicopter landing soon and you and my friend are going to get on it. When it lands, your mama and daddy will be waiting for you." She paused. "But I won't be able to go with you. Will you be a big boy and take care of my friend, Phillip?"

Davy looked at Darnell. "I heard what he was saying. He won't let you go?"

She didn't answer him. "But I'll come later. I promise you. Will you take care of Phillip?"

He nodded slowly. "That man won't hurt you?"

"No one is going to hurt me." She hugged him close. The roar of the helicopter was overhead now. She whispered, "I love you, Davy."

It took only five minutes to transfer Phillip and Davy into the helicopter and she stepped back to watch the aircraft lift off.

"What a lot of bother," Darnell said. "It would have been so much harder for Molino to get his hands on you if you hadn't been this stupid."

"Shut up."

"Molino wants to hurt you." Darnell was smiling mali-

ciously. "It's all he could talk about when I went to pick up my cargo."

She ignored the bastard, her gaze fastened on the sky.

The helicopter carrying Phillip and Davy was almost out of sight.

Good-bye, old friend. Please, get well. Good-bye, Davy. Stay safe.

"IT'S THE WRONG BRIDGE," Harley said. "There's nothing like that cliff you described. Gentle hills. It has to be Jefferson Parks Bridge to the north."

"You're absolutely certain?" Renata asked. "If you're wrong, it will be too late to get there and back ahead of Molino. It's going to take me at least forty-five minutes to get from here to Jefferson Parks Bridge."

"Trust me. That house isn't near here."

She never trusted anyone but herself, dammit.

But this time it seemed she would have to trust Harley.

MOLINO'S BLUE-AND-WHITE helicopter landed in the field fifteen minutes after Phillip and Davy had been airlifted out.

She stood straight, back rigid, as the helicopter sat down. Don't let him know how frightened she was feeling. He'd like it too much.

Molino opened the door. "What a delight to see you again. You look a bit paler than last night. The sun isn't kind to you." He smiled. "I won't be kind to you either." He turned to Darnell. "Help her into the helicopter. We have to be off."

Darnell stepped forward, but Megan jerked away from

him. "I don't want him touching me." She got into the helicopter. "He's as bad as you are."

"Oh, no, he doesn't compare to me in any category." He watched Darnell as he took a step toward the aircraft. "He's cocky and conceited and he makes mistakes. You would have been dead if he'd done his job properly."

Darnell's face flushed. "It wasn't my fault. I thought you realized that I wasn't—"

"I don't tolerate excuses, Darnell." Molino pulled a gun from his coat. "You always have to pay for your mistakes."

He shot him in the head.

Megan watched in shock as Darnell crumpled to the ground.

Molino shut the door. "Take off."

"SHIT!"

Grady watched Darnell's body fall to the ground. He didn't give a damn about Darnell's death, but it demonstrated how violent Molino's mind-set was at the moment. He could have hoped that Molino would be in a less volatile state.

Less volatile? The son of a bitch was a sadistic maniac.

His phone rang as he was moving toward his car. Harley.

"It's Jefferson Parks Bridge," Harley said. "I'm flying over the area now. I can see a large cedar two-story house on a cliff facing the river. I can't get too close because I don't want to be spotted but I think there's a helicopter pad to the west of the house. There's no helicopter on the pad."

"There will be in about forty minutes. Molino just picked up Megan. I'm going to meet with Venable now and we'll be on our way. Get the hell out of there. Where's Renata?"

"About fifteen miles from here." He paused. "There's only one road going up to the house and the cliff is almost

a sheer drop. There are a few deep ridges near the top and a few dirt outcroppings, but there's no way anyone could climb it from below. There's lots of trees and brush on the hill, but it's going to be hard as hell to get Venable and his men to that house without being seen unless we wait until dark."

"No way. Do you know how much damage Molino could do to Megan while we're waiting for dark?"

"I know that there's a good chance he might kill her if you attack and he thinks he's going to lose everything."

Grady muttered a curse. He knew Harley was right but he was damned if he did and damned if he didn't move quickly. "Why the hell didn't Renata find him before this? We've run out of options."

"She did her best. It was difficult as hell for her."

"Not as difficult as it's going to be for Megan. Molino just opened the game at the helicopter by shooting Darnell in the head. That should tell you what kind of mood Megan's facing now." The thought of her with Molino scared him to death. He'd known it would be a nightmare and he had been right. "I'll try to give it a little time. I'm not going to blunder up there and get her killed. I'll call you when we're in the area." He hung up.

But how was he going to avoid putting Megan into danger if the house was as hard to access as Harley had said?

It's in your court, Megan had said.

His court, his responsibility, his job. Not much of a responsibility at all. Just keeping Megan alive.

TWENTY

"YOU LOOKED SHOCKED," MOLINO said to Megan as the helicopter took off. "And I thought you'd be happy to see me blow Darnell's head off. After all, he's the one who made a vegetable of Phillip Blair."

"You're the one who did that. You gave the order." She shrugged. "And I don't care if you killed Darnell. It's just one less scumbag to walk the earth. Speaking of scumbags, where is Sienna?"

"He's waiting eagerly for you at the house. I thought you should have a proper welcoming committee."

"I assumed you were joined at the hip."

"We have a mutually beneficial relationship. However, lately I've not been very happy about his attitude. That's why I was comfortable about throwing Sienna to the lions."

"I'm no lion."

"I know. What a disappointment." He chuckled. "You made me look foolish in Sienna's eyes. It wasn't what I had in mind at all. He was still full of ugly thoughts about my Steven when we left you last night." He waved a hand. "But I forgave him before I left to pick you up today. After all, I did promise to let him have you for the first night and I always keep my word."

"I find that hard to believe."

"Well, I keep it when it suits me." He looked out the

window. "We're almost at the house. It's almost time for the game to begin. Are you frightened, Megan?"

"No."

"You're lying. I can see the pulse beating in your throat. If I touched your hand, I'd bet it would be cold and clammy." He smiled. "But I'll wait to touch you until I have you properly tied and ready. Do you know, I learned a great deal from reading the priest's trial accounts of your ancestor, Ricardo Devanez? The tortures used by the inquisitors were both innovative and very satisfying. I used a few of their methods on Edmund Gillem. I can hardly wait to expand my repertoire. There's a particularly exciting one called 'the chair.' "

"What a ghoul you are." She added, "And your son must have been the stupid schizo Sienna thought him. I doubt if my mother did anything to him. He was probably carrying a recessive gene from you that caused him to go off his rocker."

The smile faded from his face. "Liar."

It had been a shot in the dark but she had evidently hit the mark. "Yes, that must be it. Is there insanity in your family? It's clear you don't have all your marbles. You had to have an excuse because you felt guilty that you'd destroyed your Steven. He was as nuts as—" Her head snapped back as he backhanded her with all his strength.

Darkness. The interior of the helicopter was spinning around her.

"Bitch," he hissed. "Whore."

"You did it." The coppery taste of blood was in her mouth. "Sienna proved I was no Pandora. Neither was my mother. You killed your son."

He hit her again. "I'll kill you, bitch. You foul liar. I'll tear you—" He stopped and took a deep breath. "I won't let you do this to me. I'm not going to make it quick." The helicopter was almost on the ground. "You just made the pleasure more intense for me. I can't wait to turn you over to Sienna."

"GRADY'S ON HIS WAY," HARLEY said to Renata. "He said he'll call when he's in the area. I'm landing now." He paused. "We'll be lucky to get her out of there alive."

That's what Renata had been thinking for the last thirty minutes of her drive. "What's Grady going to do?"

"I don't know. I'm not sure he knows. I guess we'll have to brainstorm and come up with the safest way to—"

"There's no safe way," she said fiercely. "And he'll kill her if we keep talking and not acting."

"Grady and Venable won't let the time drag—"

"To hell with Grady. I can't wait around until you all form a damn committee to decide what's to be done."

"And what's your alternative?"

"Stop talking and get her out." She hung up.

She didn't answer when Harley called her back a moment later. He would question and argue and she didn't want to hear either one. She was too tense and scared and she had to clear her mind of both emotions before she could start doing what she did best. Weigh the odds of the different scenarios, estimate cause and effect to predict an outcome that would guarantee Megan would live and Molino would die.

She'd already started the initial process on the drive here when she'd realized that it was going to be too late for any ordinary assault on Molino's stronghold.

She looked down at the pink dress she still had clutched in her hand. "I have to leave you now, Adia." She carefully folded the dress and placed it in the briefcase with gentle hands. "Thanks to you, we know where he is. Now we have to go get the son of a bitch."

"STRAIGHT AHEAD." MOLINO'S hand on Megan's back shoved her forward down the curved steps just inside the door. "You mustn't keep Sienna waiting."

She was shaking. Sienna. She felt sick as she remembered the warm softness of his big hand. Then the softness had turned to brutality.

"You're not talking now," Molino said softly. "You're afraid of him, aren't you? Women are so soft and breakable. Almost as breakable as the children. It's laughable when they try to fight us."

"Is it?" How could she get hold of that gun? If she could catch him off guard there might be a chance. She had been able to push his buttons earlier and she might still be—

"In here." He opened a door at the foot of the stairs. "Sienna always demands his own quarters away from the rest of us. He likes his privacy. I have no problem with it. We're not all that compatible." He stepped aside to let her enter. "Sienna, here's the gift I promised you."

Megan didn't move.

"Don't be shy." Molino shoved her into the room. "He's waiting." He waved his hand to the corner of the room. "Say hello to him."

Oh, God. Don't scream.

Sienna was tied, pinned, to the wall. He was shaved bald, his skull bloody and crushed. His eyes were wide open, his features frozen, twisted, in a death rictus.

"How do you like his new haircut?" Molino asked. "Women sometimes find a bald head sexy, I'm told."

"You murdered him." She said hoarsely, "Why? Because he didn't believe your son—"

"I've lived with his skepticism for years. I could have tolerated it if I'd seen a future use for him." He shook his head. "It's really too bad that I had to dispose of him before I could keep my promise to him about you. Of course, I have other men who would accommodate you but none of them have the talent that Sienna had. Sienna understood pain. He was magnificent with Edmund Gillem."

She couldn't keep her eyes away from Sienna's face. "Did you torture Sienna too?"

"Oh, no. Well, perhaps a little. He kept pulling at his hair so I had his head shaved. He didn't like that at all."

"Pulling at his hair?"

Molino smiled. "Screaming and pulling at his hair and knocking his head against the wall. He was in great pain, so I decided I had to help him. In fact, I became so involved with Sienna that I forgot all my interesting plans for the little boy."

"Pain? What else did you do to Sienna?"

"Not me." He turned to face her. "You. I was so unhappy that Sienna walked away after he took your hand yesterday. I should have known that you wouldn't disappoint me. I just didn't realize that it didn't always happen at once."

She swallowed. "I don't know what you're talking about."

"Your mother grabbed my boy's hand and destroyed his mind within seconds. Maybe you're not as good as she was. Or maybe you didn't want me to know you were like her. Sienna didn't show any signs until almost midnight last night. He was checking the guards along the cliff and they said he kept shaking his head to clear it. Then an hour after he went to his quarters we heard a thumping. When I went down to check on the poor man, he was already gone. Weeping, pulling out his hair in clumps, and hitting his head against the wall as if to drive away the demons."

"It's not true."

"But it is. Why are you denying it? You must have known what to expect. I merely put him out of his misery."

"You're lying. You killed him because he was putting doubts in your mind about the sanity of your precious son and you had to have a scapegoat."

"I have no doubts about Steven." He looked down at her hands that were clenched at her sides. "What I could do with a power to kill like that. It's not right that freaks should be the only ones to be able to—" His cell phone rang. He pressed the button and a smile lit his face. "Good day, Ms. Wilger. What a pleasure to hear from you. This is my lucky day." He glanced at Megan, who had gone rigid. "Yes, our Megan is quite well so far." He turned up the volume on the phone. "And we mustn't leave her out. She can hear you now."

"I don't care if she can hear me or not," Renata said curtly. "She's been trouble for me since the beginning. I've been getting nothing but pressure from Grady and the CIA about trying to make a deal with you to let her go."

"It's too late."

"Good. I don't believe one life is worth giving up the Ledger. Keep her."

"Wait. Don't hang up."

"You said it was too late."

"I might consider a deal. If I was sure that you really have the Ledger."

"I have it."

"Proof?"

"I can show you a few pages of it. You can have it tested for antiquity."

"I want to see the entire Ledger."

"I'm no fool. It's bad enough that I'm being forced to give it up. I won't give it up for nothing. The CIA has promised me compensation and protection from the rest of the family if I get Megan released. The Devanez family doesn't like traitors. I wouldn't last three days."

Molino was silent. "You'll come yourself to show me these pages?"

"Yes," Renata said reluctantly. "I'll come. If you're sure you want to deal. I'm at the Piedmont in Memphis. But I'm going to use my own helicopter. Your men can pick me up and search me and the helicopter for weapons and bugs. I'll let you pick up an expert who can verify the age of the pages and bring him along. Do you know an antiquity expert near here?"

"There's one at the university in Nashville who I use frequently. He was trained at the Louvre in Paris and you won't be able to fool him. I deal in antiquities from the ruins in Egypt and Italy and sometimes I can't trust my sources."

"Imagine that. Okay, I'll bring him. But once we land I'm not moving from that helicopter. You'll have to bring Megan to me so that I can be certain that she's still alive. She'll stay with me until you verify the pages. If you agree to the deal, I'm back in the helicopter and off to get the rest of the Ledger." She hung up.

"Not exactly eager to have you back, is she?" Molino asked.

"She doesn't think my life is worth exposing all those thousands of people in the Ledger to you."

"Thousands. Do you suppose there are thousands of those freaks about?"

"I have no idea. It was just a guess."

"When I first learned about the Ledger, my attention was split because I was obsessed with finding you. But now that I have you, I wonder what my life is going to be like if I don't have purpose to drive me onward. Steven wouldn't like it if I stopped now. No, I really think I have to have that Ledger."

"Then you'll make a deal?"

He looked at her in surprise. "Of course not. Don't get your hopes up. But we'll do a little sleight of hand to make them think I am. I'll arrange to have that Wilger bitch picked up and brought here." He shook his head. "And I can wait a little while to try out those Inquisition toys on you." He turned. "In the meantime, I believe I'll leave you here with Sienna. I did promise him his time with you." He glanced back over his shoulder. "By the way, did I forget to mention that you've done all this for nothing? I won't let either Phillip Blair or the boy live more than a week."

The next moment the door shut behind him and the key turned in the lock.

Alone with that grotesque carcass that had once been Sienna.

Molino had said that she was the one who had really killed him. She wouldn't believe it. Molino was looking for ways to justify his son's madness. She was not a Pandora. It wasn't true.

The shock had been too intense and it had sent her spiraling away from everything else of importance. She had to stop thinking about it.

And that last jab about his intention to kill Phillip and Davy had been meant to hurt and panic her. But Grady would never let anything happen to them now that they were safe.

She tore her gaze away from Sienna and looked around the room. The basement suite was luxuriously furnished in bold colors, but there were no windows, dammit.

Weapons. A man like Sienna would have a gun or knife or . . . something. She started systematically going through drawers.

Nothing. Not even a fingernail file. Molino must have planned to leave her here with Sienna from the moment he'd killed him.

Why not? What could be more chilling or horrible than to make her share quarters with those gory remains?

Don't look at him.

She sat down in a chair by the door. She'd hoped to have a way to defend herself until help came. The call from Renata had been an obvious stall. When Renata had first come into their lives, she might have shown that tough façade, but she had changed. God, they had all changed in these last days. Megan, Renata, Harley, Grady.

Grady.

Whatever Renata was planning, it had to involve Grady. Don't let anything happen to Grady. Don't let anything happen to any of them.

But she couldn't rely on wishful thinking. She had to be ready to find a way to act.

GRADY HUNG UP THE PHONE from talking to Renata and turned to Venable. "She thinks he took the bait." He picked up his rifle. "I'm out of here. I'll let you know what's happening on that hill."

"I have twenty men sitting on their asses in these damn woods," Venable said. "When am I going to be able to tell them to start? Give me a chance to do my job."

"You move one man out of cover before I give the word and I'll shoot him myself," Grady said harshly. "If Molino's men catch a whiff that anything's going on, Megan's dead."

"I'm a professional. I wouldn't let that happen."

Grady shook his head. "Renata's right. When she called me, I didn't want to go along with her. I wanted to be there waiting when they got back and blow the damn place up." His lips twisted. "But she ran that scenario and says that Megan would have an eighty-seven percent chance of dying. That's too high. It scared the hell out of me. So we're going with Renata's plan. First, there has to be a built-in delay to make sure Molino keeps his hands off Megan. Renata and the Ledger. Then we needed a man in the woods on the hill to feed us information. Since Harley was on the spot, he was up there before Molino brought Megan back. Next, we have to have someone go up and take out the sentries." He headed up the path. "That's me."

"And what kind of percentage did your friend, Renata, give Megan on this scenario?" Venable asked.

"Thirty-two percent," Grady answered. "If everything goes right."

Lord, the odds were still too high and the chance of everything going exactly right was laughable, he thought. Nothing ever went exactly as you thought it would.

He called Harley when he was halfway up the hill. "Brief me."

"Megan's in a room in the basement," Harley said. "Molino took her downstairs and came back alone. He's in the main house now."

"Renata made the call five minutes ago," Grady said. "It bought Megan some time, thank God. Where are you?"

"In the pine woods about a thousand yards down the

road from the house. There are three men patrolling the grounds and I've seen four men moving around inside the house. There may be more but that's— Wait a minute. Two men are leaving the house. I think Molino took the bait. They're heading for the helicopter pad. They may be going to pick up Renata." He paused. "It might be a good time for me to try to get closer and see if I can slip Megan a weapon in case something goes wrong."

"Nothing's going to go wrong," Grady said. Maybe saying the words would make it true. "And I'm on my way up to clear the way for Venable's men. I'll take out the perimeter sentries and then move toward the house. Just stay put, dammit. I need to know everything that's happening in that house and you have to be there for Megan. I want to be told the minute Molino goes back to that basement."

"Whatever you say. If you're going to join me, you might want to know that there's one guard with a rifle behind the house. The other two are patrolling the woods bordering the cliff about a quarter of a mile from the house. One rifle. One handgun."

"That's it?"

"That's it. The helicopter is off the ground. You're sure you don't want me to—"

"Keep to the plan. Stay put." Grady hung up.

"COME OUT, MEGAN," MOLINO called as he opened the door of the basement apartment. "I've just had word that our little friend is going to be landing in a few minutes. We're going to meet her so that she'll feel safe and know my intentions are above reproach."

"And what are you going to do to her once you verify the pages?" she asked as she climbed the stairs.

"Why, I'm sure you're aware that there are many ways to get what you want without negotiation. I just have to make sure that she has the real thing." He was nudging her toward the helicopter pad. "And then you can go back and join Sienna. I'm sure he's missing you. Ah, here she comes."

A tan-and-cream helicopter was landing on the pad. Two men jumped out of the helicopter as soon as it landed. "Permit me to introduce you." Molino gestured to the tall, spare, red-haired man. "This is David Condon. He was flying the helicopter that brought you here, Megan. The other gentleman is Ben Stallek. I was a little distracted or I would have been more careful of the amenities. Did you bring Notting?"

A small man in a plaid shirt got out of the plane. "This will cost you. I was practically yanked away from my golf game to come here."

"It will only take a short time. Just a preliminary examination." Molino said to Megan, "This testy gentleman is very knowledgeable or I wouldn't put up with his rudeness."

"He's also very greedy." Renata got out of the helicopter. She handed Molino a large envelope. "Be careful of those pages."

"I always take care of what's mine." He moved toward the house with Notting. "Condon, you stay here. Stallek, you come with us." He glanced back over his shoulder. "Oh, Condon, if either of the ladies decide to be foolish please feel free to shoot them. The stomach, I think. Stomach wounds are so painful."

Condon drew his gun and pointed it at Megan.

Renata ignored him. "Did Molino hurt you, Megan?"

"Not much." She looked at Renata. "You're the one who looks terrible. How did you get those bruises?"

"They did a strip search. I objected." She looked at Condon. "And he enjoyed it. I'm going to remember that." Her glance shifted to Megan. "That test probably won't take over fifteen minutes. Notting has the chemicals he needs to do the job. But Molino won't be in a hurry once he knows that the pages test genuine."

"Will they?"

"Yes. Where's Sienna?"

"Dead. Molino claims he went mad, that I did it, and he had to kill him. I think it's bullshit. Molino was looking for an excuse to kill Sienna."

"I don't care why he's dead. I'm only concerned that he's out of the picture." She looked at the grove of pine trees about a thousand yards down the road, to the left of the cliff. "That broken pine looks dead, doesn't it? These jokers have probably been using it for target practice. But I bet it isn't dead."

Megan frowned in puzzlement. What did pine trees have to do with anything? Dead or not.

"Is it dead, Condon?" Renata called out to the guard. "You've been living here. You should know if that pine tree's—"

The guard frowned and started toward them. "What are you—" Condon arched and opened his mouth in a soundless scream. He stumbled forward and fell.

There was a knife in his back.

"Grady," Renata murmured. "Good job."

Grady appeared out of the utility shed. "Get Megan out of here," he said curtly. "Now!" He disappeared behind the shed.

"Go." Renata pushed Megan toward the trees. "The pines. There's a gun there and I hope to God Harley's there too. He's supposed to be."

"What are you going to do?"

"Help Grady take out the men in the house. Tell Harley to call Venable and tell him to get up here. Hurry. And get that gun." She disappeared after Grady.

Megan wanted to run after her. No, she didn't even have a weapon. The gun! She had to get the gun and get help from Venable.

Megan flew down the cliff road toward the pine trees.

"Bitch!" Molino's enraged howl shrieked behind her.

She glanced over her shoulder to see him running toward her from the house. God, he was close.

He was pointing a gun at her head.

She had to get to the gun hidden in the pines.

No time.

She dove down to the ground even as a bullet whistled past her head.

Another bullet. A different sound . . .

The thunk of a bullet against flesh. She looked back to see Molino stagger, blood blossoming from the wound in his chest, the gun dropped from his hand, but he was still coming.

"Run, Megan," Harley called from the pine trees. "He's too close to you. I can't get a good shot."

"Cheat me. You're trying to cheat me." Molino was on top of her, his hands closing on her throat. "Steven won't let you cheat. Butcher you . . ."

Another shot. Molino flinched as the bullet hit his arm.

Megan pushed desperately and he fell off her and to the side.

But he grabbed her and rolled her over to only a few feet from the edge of the cliff. "Butcher you. Butcher all the . . . freaks."

She fought desperately, panic surging through her. He was going to push her over. He shouldn't have been this strong. But it was as if the bullets had not even touched him. If she'd only been able to reach that gun hidden in the pines.

No gun.

But she had another weapon.

"It won't be in time," she gasped. "Your Steven can't help you. My mother killed him." She freed one hand and reached out to him. "Do you know what it's like to go mad? Talk to Steven. I'm going to touch you, Molino."

He froze and stared at her hand as if it were a cobra arched to strike.

"Are you afraid? You should be. You killed my mother and she wants you dead. Even if I'm not a Pandora, she can act through me. After all, I'm a freak. You know all about freaks, don't you?" She caressingly touched his cheek.

He screamed, his eyes rolled back in his head. "No!" He scrambled backward. "Freak. Monster."

"You're the monster." She crawled closer to him. Only two more feet and he'd be over the edge. "You're going to die, Molino. Do you think madness and suffering follow people into the grave? I hope so."

"Get away from me." He scooted closer to the edge. "Don't get near me."

"But I want to touch you. Let me do it. I want to hold your hand." She lunged forward with her hand outstretched.

He screamed and fell backward over the cliff.

But he grabbed her arm as he fell.

She was sliding, slipping, pulled over the edge after him.

"Steven . . ." Molino gasped. "He won't let me die. We're going to—"

He screamed as his grasp on her arm loosened and he fell.

* * *

SHE WAS SLIPPING!

Megan's nails dug frantically into the narrow crevices in the rough stone.

Don't fall. Don't let Molino win.

Her feet were braced on a slight dirt outjutting on the sheer wall, but the dry dirt beneath her shoes was crumbling, giving way, as she scrambled to get a purchase where there was none.

Her fingers were tearing, bleeding.

"Hold on." Harley's face was peering over the cliff above her. "I'm scooting as far as I can on my belly. I'm going to grab your right wrist and try not to unbalance you."

Hope.

He reached down once. "I can't reach you." He wriggled closer. "Grady's running like hell from the house. We're not going to let you fall, Megan."

If they could get to her in time.

She slipped another inch down the cliff as the dirt continued to crumble. Her arms pulled taut, but she held on.

"God in heaven, just a few inches more . . ." Harley was straining down toward her. He couldn't reach her. He tried once. Twice.

On the third attempt his hand clamped on her right wrist. "Got you."

The earth hillock crumbled entirely away from her feet.

She was falling!

"Help—me." Harley was holding her by one wrist as she dangled over the abyss. "Grab. I can't do it alone."

Her fingers closed blindly on his wrist.

"Megan, give me your other hand." It was Grady kneeling beside Harley and reaching out to her. "Don't you dare fall."

"Shut up," she gasped. She reached out with her left hand. "I'm doing the best I can."

"And it's a good best." He leaned over and grabbed her left hand with both of his. "It's a damn wonderful best. Now hold on a little longer while we pull you up."

Her arms felt as if they were being jerked from the sockets as the two men pulled her slowly up the cliff. It took at least three minutes before they were able to get her entire upper body on solid ground.

"My God." Grady's voice was hoarse. He was suddenly holding her, rocking her. His heart was beating as hard as her own. "My God."

Life. She had been so close to losing it, losing him.

She was holding him with all her strength as she lay there, eyes closed, trying to get her breath.

"Okay?" Grady whispered against her cheek.

She opened her lids to see Grady and Harley kneeling beside her. She pushed Grady away and then pulled him back again. Not yet. She didn't want to let him go. "No, I'm scared and I'm feeling very vulnerable right now."

"You should feel vulnerable." Harley grinned. "Flying isn't most people's strong point." He crawled to the edge of the cliff and looked down to the valley. "It certainly wasn't Molino's. He's lying down there like a broken Chucky doll." He got to his feet. "But in the movies evil Chucky always came back from the dead." He turned and moved toward the road. "I think I'll go down to make sure that there's no way he'll bounce back."

Megan knew what he meant. "I know he's down there." She stood up and moved to the edge of the cliff. "But I want to see for myself."

Grady was beside her, steadying her. "Molino's no Chucky. No one could survive that fall."

"I know that with my mind. But Molino has been the bogeyman for too long. I can't believe he's not going to always be there in the shadows." She stared down at the bottom of the cliff. There he was, lying spread-eagled on the rocks.

A broken Chucky doll, Harley had called him.

Monster.

Someone was coming out of the brush and walking toward Molino. Venable? Harley?

No, Renata. She should have known Renata would have the same instinct as Harley to be sure that Molino was dead.

"Satisfied?" Grady asked.

She nodded. "I think I am. I'm pretty numb right now. I can't sort out how I feel. I'll worry about it later." She didn't want to think of death. She had been too close to it for too long. She needed hope and life. "Get me to Belle-haven. I have to check on Phillip and Davy."

"DEAD?"

Renata looked up from where she was kneeling beside Molino to see Harley walking toward her. She nodded. "Broken neck, one shot in the chest, one in the arm, and his head must have hit the rocks. We don't have to worry about him any longer."

"You didn't have to worry about him at all." He stopped beside her. "I was on my way to confirm his death." He smiled. "Oh, that's right. That would have meant you had to trust someone besides yourself."

"I think I would have—I'm just used to doing as I've been trained." She got to her feet. "And it was Molino. That's why I didn't come running after you and Grady pulled Megan back over the ledge. I had to get down here and make sure. There couldn't be a mistake."

"I don't make many mistakes, Renata," he said quietly.

"No, you don't." She stood looking at him. "Of course, you could have done better shooting the bastard."

"I was almost a thousand yards away. And she was too close to him."

"Well, on the whole, I suppose you did very well today."

He chuckled. "Lord, I feel as if I've been awarded a gold medal." He tilted his head. "Except I've never seen a judge who was as beat up as you are. You look like you've been rolling in dirt, that blasted wound is bleeding again, and you have a bruise on your cheekbone." He reached out and touched her cheek. "Molino?"

"Condon, one of his men." She took a step back so that his hand fell away.

"Cousin Mark should have taught you to take better care of yourself."

She shrugged. "Mark says the first rule of safety is to do the job and not to get involved. I didn't play by the rules."

"For which Megan is no doubt very grateful."

"Why? I should have found Molino before he got his hands on her. I did a lousy job."

"Oh, yes. I can see it was entirely your fault."

"I would have done better if I hadn't let emotion throw me off-kilter." She turned and headed for the path leading up to the cliff. "I've got to go see Megan and then call Mark and tell him about Molino."

"Just look at you. You're even limping."

She glanced over her shoulder to see Harley watching her with a frown. "I'm fine. Mind your own business."

"It is my business." He moved after her. "Megan wouldn't like it if I let you try to make it up the cliff alone.

You know how softhearted she is. She's gone through enough today. Let me clean you up before she sees you." He slid his arm around her waist. "Come on. You've leaned on me before and it wasn't so bad."

Why not? She was hurting and experiencing a hollowness that could be . . . loneliness. It was probably the last time that she would need to take help from Harley or any of them. She'd be on her own again.

"You're right; Megan is much too softhearted." She leaned against him. "But I wouldn't want to make her feel bad . . ."

TWENTY-ONE

"HOW IS HE?"

Megan turned to see Renata standing in the doorway of Phillip's hospital room. "Not good." She shrugged wearily. "Or maybe he's not so bad. They still have all kind of tests to make, but the specialists here don't believe his condition deteriorated irreparably while Molino had him. It's just that I was hoping Gardner was right and I'd be able to see some sign of him coming out of it."

"No luck?"

She shook her head. "But maybe it will come later. Who knows if Phillip understood anything about what was happening to him? Maybe he suffered some kind of shock that caused a setback."

"You're reaching, aren't you?" Renata asked gently.

Megan's hand tightened on Phillip's. Feel me, friend, know I'm here. Let's work through it together. "Yes. But hope can work miracles. I've seen it. It was a miracle that Davy got away from Molino without harm." She changed the subject. "Where are Grady and Harley? Still at Molino's place? Grady dropped me off and told me he was going back to join Venable. They're trying to gather information from Molino's files about the bandits and sleazebags Molino was working with."

Renata nodded. "Harley's there too. I told him to look for any records concerning victims. I need to find Adia."

Megan had a poignant memory of that little pink dress belonging to the child. "Of course, we do." She paused. "I wanted to thank you for risking those pages of the Ledger to buy me time with Molino. I know it was difficult for you to give them up."

"No, it wasn't."

Megan stared at her in disbelief.

Renata smiled. "Well, it would have been difficult if they had been Ledger pages."

Megan's eyes widened. "But you said they'd tested positive for antiquity."

"When I took over guardianship of the Ledger, I had Mark create two counterfeit Ledgers. No genuine names or addresses, but the paper was treated to make it test positive for antiquity. I thought that maybe Edmund might not have died if he'd had something to give those bastards until he could find a way to escape." She shrugged. "I brought one of the copies with me when we left Munich in case I found a way to set a trap for Molino."

Megan had a sudden memory of how reluctant Renata had been to have anyone touch her suitcases. "You didn't tell us."

She grimaced. "We've already established I'm not good at sharing."

"Oh, I don't know. I believe you're getting the knack of it." She had a sudden thought. "I'm surprised the family hasn't put the Ledger on computer disk. Wouldn't it be safer?"

"It depends on how you look at it. Computer records are more readily accessible. If stolen they could be copied in five seconds and we might not know it was done in time to protect the family. Edmund started to try to put the records on a disk to be sealed away with the originals, but it's a nightmare process. The only person who has access to the Ledger is the Keeper."

"That means it's up to you?"

She nodded. "I'll try to do it, but it's not high on my priority list. We can't scan it because it was handwritten by different people and there might be blurring and discrepancies. We have to destroy hard drives every time we make an entry to make sure no fragment of data can be retrieved. We can't trust the software that supposedly wipes them clean. And there isn't only one volume to the Ledger. The family has been growing for centuries." She made a face. "And I assure you that as the Keeper I have other things to do besides sit and enter data. It's enough that I'm able to do the entries into the original Ledger."

"It does sound like a nightmare." Megan studied her face. "What if you'd had the real Ledger in that suitcase? Would you have used it?"

"No." She moistened her lips. "I'd like to tell you I would but I'd be lying. I couldn't do it. I care about you but I wouldn't take a—"

"Stop agonizing. It's okay, Renata," she said gently. "I wasn't backing you into a corner. I always knew that would be your priority."

"I'd have found another way. I wouldn't have let Molino—"

"You did find another way."

"But I always thought any decision connected with the Ledger would be simple, black and white. Nothing's black and white any longer."

"Good."

"Not for me. It's going to be much harder for me." She made a face. "And it's your fault. You've made me question things I've believed all my life." Her glance shifted to Phillip. "Was your life really worth the risk when you may never bring him back?"

"It was to me. I love Phillip."

She shook her head. "No reason. Just emotion."

Megan smiled. "And you're all reason and no emotion. At least you try to be. But you're slipping, aren't you?"

"I'll get back on the right track." She moved across the room to stand beside Megan. "I have to go. Mark called me and said that it would be smart to fade away into the sunset. Too many people know that I'm connected to the Ledger now."

"Only the CIA."

"The CIA is composed of people with opinions, ambitions, and their own agendas."

"You don't trust them."

"I don't have the right to trust them. The Ledger is more exposed to threat now than it has been for hundreds of years."

"And it has to be protected."

"You don't understand that?"

"I understand that you have a right to your life too."

"I'm not going to give up my life. I'll just have to make adjustments." She paused. "Like you're going to have to do. You're a Listener. Every now and then you'll hear your voices and have to choose to ignore or try to help as you did Edmund."

"I don't want to think about that now."

Renata was silent. "Then think about being a Pandora."

Megan shook her head emphatically. "I told you, Molino was nuts. He wanted Sienna dead and constructed a scenario that would agree with his fantasies."

"Harley said Molino was scared shitless when you threatened to touch him at the cliff."

"It was the only weapon I had." She smiled mirthlessly. "And he was out of his head. It was fitting that he killed himself because of his own delusions. It was almost as if my mother was finally able to get her revenge."

"And you're sure you're not building your own scenarios?"

She stiffened. "I'm being practical and reasonable. You of all people should appreciate that."

Renata squatted beside her chair. "Megan," she said gently. "We need to talk."

GRADY MET MEGAN WHEN THE helicopter landed on the landing pad at Molino's place two hours later. "What's wrong? I told you that I'd join you as soon as I—"

"She couldn't wait." Renata got out of the pilot's seat and jumped to the ground. "I tried to tell her that a few more hours wouldn't—"

"Renata, I may have found a lead on Adia." Harley was walking toward them. "Venable is being very close with those records, but there's a big file Molino kept that was cross-referenced with Hedda Kipler's activities. You said that she brought Molino that dress as a trophy?"

"Right."

"Well, if Grady can pry those records away from Venable, I may be able to trace—"

"Later," Megan said curtly. "Come with me. I don't want to be stumbling over any of Venable's men." She turned and headed for the small utility shack a few yards from the helicopter pad. She turned on the bare lightbulb hanging from the ceiling of the shack. "I want this over quickly."

"Phillip?" Grady said gently. "He didn't make it?"

"He's still alive. If you can call that coma being alive. But that's not why I'm here."

Grady's gaze was narrowed on her face. "You're excited. You're tense but I can practically feel the— What's happening?"

"Something good for a change." Her hands were opening and closing at her sides. "Renata, do it."

But Renata already had her shirt unbuttoned. She slipped the bra straps off her shoulders. "It's a good thing I have no false modesty. I'm getting a little tired of—"

"My God," Grady whispered.

Megan took a step closer and touched Renata's shoulder. "No wound. No scarring. The skin is smooth as silk. It's as if she'd never had a bullet tear through her shoulder."

Harley gave a low whistle. "What happened? What on earth did you do, Megan?"

"Nothing." Megan paused. "You did it, Harley."

He stared at her, stunned. He shook his head. "Bullshit."

"That's what I said when Renata showed me her shoulder at Bellehaven. I was looking for any explanation that wouldn't lead to you." She added grimly, "Believe me; I didn't want it to be you, Harley. Because that would mean I had to accept the unacceptable."

He shook his head again.

"Renata," Megan said.

Renata shrugged. "You're the one who bandaged my shoulder this afternoon, Harley."

"Come on. I've done that any number of times in the past few days," Harley said.

Renata nodded. "But this time about an hour after I left the cliff it started to itch. I began to rub the scab around the wound but it felt . . . funny. So I pulled aside a little of the bandage to look at it." She paused. "The scab was flaking off and the wound . . ." She lifted her shoulders. "You saw it. Total healing."

"Then you did it, not me," Harley said defensively. "You're the one who's got all that psychic mojo."

Renata shook her head. "I'm not a healer."

"Neither am I. Don't you try to tell me that I'm—"

Renata chuckled. "You're scared. I was wondering if you would be."

"I'm *not* scared. It's just that this is all crap." He glared at Megan. "What are you trying to do to me?"

"Easy." Grady was frowning thoughtfully. "The cliff, Megan?"

Megan nodded jerkily. "That's what Renata's guessing. I don't know how this Pandora stuff works but it may be triggered by extreme emotion. I was scared out of my mind when Harley grabbed me. It was life or death."

"And you were angry and afraid when Sienna crunched your hand."

"I still won't admit that I did that to Sienna. It could have been Molino."

"And it could have been you," Renata said baldly. "Stop hiding your head."

"It wouldn't do any good when you keep making me face it. Do you mind if I ignore that ugliness for a moment?" Her gaze was fixed eagerly on Harley. "You're darn right I'm excited, Grady. This is the first positive thing that's happened to me since all of this started. Harley, I know that it's hard to accept and we don't know exactly how your gift works, but I'll work with you. We'll all work with you."

"No, you won't. Because it's not true." Harley was scowling. "I know that I'm as normal as I've been all my life. I'm not like you guys who are—"

"Freaks?" Megan supplied. She smiled. "It's like looking in a mirror. I reacted the same way."

"Keep your mirror." Harley started to turn away. "I'm very happy the way I am and I'm not going to let you convince me that—"

"What?" Megan's smile faded. "Why are you behaving this way? This is something *wonderful*. After I thought about it, I realized that your being a healer isn't that foreign to your nature. Whenever I've been with you, I've been aware of a sort of . . . comfort. Just being around you brought a kind of healing when I was upset."

"Imagination." Harley's lips were set and stubborn. "And I'm not seeing any of this as wonderful."

Megan couldn't believe it. She had expected a little resistance but not this total rejection. Why couldn't he see the boundless possibilities? "And do you think I like this? The last thing I want in the world is to be a Pandora. Do you think I'm looking forward to walking on eggs, afraid to reach out to anyone? So far all anyone has told me is that it can drive people mad and kill them. But I touched you and you're not mad and now you have a gift I'd give anything in the world to possess." She added simply, "You're my salvation, Harley. You're proof that my being a Pandora can do some good in this world."

"I don't want to be your salvation," Harley said roughly. "Even if I could, I wouldn't want to be tied down. My God, I've been running away from responsibility all my life. And now you're trying to put a yoke around my neck? Thanks, but no thanks. I'm out of here."

"Then I'll follow you," Megan said. "I don't have time for you to spend six months or a year getting used to the idea that you're a healer. Phillip needs you now."

"Phillip?"

"It was the first thought I had when Renata told me about that healed wound."

"I'm supposed to lay my hand on him and make him come back to the world?"

"You're supposed to try."

For a moment Harley's expression changed, softened. "I'm sorry, Megan. I can't be what you want me to be. Even if I believed all this nonsense I couldn't. . . ." He turned and walked away.

Megan stared after him in frustration and disbelief. "I'm going after him."

"Don't push," Renata murmured. "He'll bolt. This has come as a shock and he has to work his way through it." She glanced at Grady. "Talk to her. She's pretty much in shock too. She could deny that she was a Pandora until I threw this at her, but she had to accept the healing." She turned and started toward the house.

"He just walked away," Megan said. "It's a chance for Phillip. Harley has got to believe me."

"He'll believe you. Give him some time." Grady took her hand. "He'll get over the first shock, then he'll get curious. It's after he actually starts to believe that he's no longer 'normal' that you'll be having trouble. His first reaction was pure Harley. What does a rolling stone do when he's forced to stop and have the world reach out and cling to him?"

"He gets scared and runs away," Megan said grimly. "I won't let him do it."

"It has to come from him, Megan." He pulled her out of the utility shed. "Come on. Let's go to the house and I'll introduce you to Venable and we'll go through those victims' files Harley was working on."

"Are you soothing me, Grady?"

"I'm trying. How am I doing?"

"Not so good. I'll give Harley a little time to adjust but I won't be distracted." She stepped closer. "But thanks for the effort."

"My pleasure." His lips brushed her temple. "Entirely my pleasure."

IT WAS OVER AN HOUR LATER that Megan heard the helicopter rotors.

Her head lifted sharply from the files she was looking through. "What's that? Renata . . ." But she had a feeling it wasn't Renata in that helicopter. She jumped to her feet and ran out of the house.

Renata was standing looking up at the helicopter that had just taken off. "He's flown the coop."

"Harley? Why didn't you stop him?"

"Leave him alone and he'll come home, wagging his tail behind him," Renata quoted. "Though I'm not sure about the wagging tail. But you have a better chance than if you went after him."

"You can't know that," she said in despair.

"No, but I'm very good at estimating cause and effect and projecting a final result." She smiled. "If I'm wrong, then I'll help you track him down and drag him back. I'm good at that too." She took Megan's arm. "Come on. Let's go and see if we can find Adia in that mountain of files."

Bellehaven

"HARLEY'S NOT ANSWERING his phone," Grady said as he met Megan in the hall coming out of Phillip's room. "And I've tried every source I know to contact him. He's dropped off the face of the earth."

"Because that's the way he wants it." Megan shook her head. "Renata says he'll come back on his own but it's hard to be patient. It's been three days, Grady."

"You said they're still running tests on Phillip?"

She nodded. "They don't think any damage has been done because of treatment by Molino but they're not sure." She said unsteadily, "But he's not giving me any sign of a response as he did for Gardner. I examined Gardner's notes and he did document that he thought there was a slight improvement. That part wasn't a lie."

"Did Scott call you?"

"Yes, he was a little stilted, but he wants me to come and see Davy when I get the chance. I think it's going to be okay between us." She turned back toward the door to Phillip's room. "I want to get back to Phillip. I keep hoping that—"

"Miracles?" Grady asked. "I'm hoping with you, Megan." He paused. "But I'm not going to be here to see if you're able to pull a miracle off."

She turned back to face him. "What?"

"Oh, I'll be back. You're not going to get rid of me. But Venable is going to North Africa to try to track down those child victims we found in Molino's files."

"You're going with him?"

He shrugged. "I can do some good working with him." He met her gaze. "And you don't want me here right now. Even when I try to stay in the background, it doesn't happen. I disturb you. You don't want to deal with what we are together." He added roughly, "Hell, you were dodging coming to terms with me before. If I pushed now, you'd bolt and run like Harley did."

"I'm done with running." But she realized she was feeling a rush of relief. Even now she could feel the heat she always experienced when she was looking at him. He did disturb her, both mentally and physically, and she didn't need any more turmoil right now. She was going through enough emotional chaos trying to adjust to the Pandora reality and Phillip's lack of progress.

He was studying her expression. "You see?"

"I hate it when you're right."

"Get used to it. I can't help it." He gave her a quick, hard kiss. "And I'll be understanding and noble for a month, no longer. After that I'm going to come back and disturb the hell out of you."

He was already disturbing her as she watched him walk down the corridor away from her. She might be able to ignore Grady's effect on her on a conscious level but he was always there, beneath the surface, waiting.

Well, she would take what peace and space she could get.

She turned and went back into Phillip's room.

Bellehaven
Two weeks later

"I'VE COME TO SAY GOOD-BYE." Renata stood in the doorway of Phillip's room. "Can you leave him for a few minutes?"

"Why not? Maybe he'll miss me." She stood up and followed Renata from the room. "I'm willing to try anything these days."

"You should get away for a while." Renata walked toward the atrium. "You've been cooped up here for weeks. I've been worried about you." She paused. "And Grady's been worried about you."

Megan stiffened. "You've talked to Grady?"

"Two days ago. He's made progress finding the victims.

He and Venable have located forty-five of them alive so far. He said that he's going to Tanzania to follow up a lead on Adia. He thinks the tribal leader has changed her name."

"But she's alive?"

"That's the report." She returned to the original subject. "You're spending too much time here. You need a break."

"I'm afraid not to be here if Phillip begins to stir again. What if he does and I'm not there? We may have lost an opportunity, but there may be another one. I have to hope." She tried to distract her. "I thought you were going to leave last week."

"Mark wanted me to do it. He says that it's not good to become as close as I am to you. He's probably right." She shrugged. "But I can't do what Mark wants all my life. I have to make my own decisions. I didn't want to leave until I was sure that you— I was the one who made you accept that you were a Pandora. I could have kept the healing of that wound to myself. After Sienna I just didn't want you to believe that you were some kind of Franken-stein." She smiled faintly. "I choose to believe the more positive myth about Pandora; that besides the evils of the world she also set free the virtues."

"You were right to do it. I had to know. I couldn't keep on lying to myself." Megan leaned against the rail and looked out at the peaceful stretch of lawns and trees. "And you only meant to be kind. I just wish Harley— You said he'd come back, but he hasn't. I just don't un-derstand him."

"Because with you, the giving would never stop be-cause it's your nature. Not many people are like you. You gave Harley the gift. It's his choice whether he wants to use it."

She made a face. "I wish this Pandora business would let me pick and choose instead of it being a wild card.

What's the good of a gift that could benefit humanity if it's passed on to someone who ignores it?"

Renata shook her head. "The Ledger contains hundreds of accounts of use and misuse of powers. You should read it sometime."

"As if you'd let it out of your hands."

"You're right. Well, maybe someday." She turned away. "I'll let you know if I hear anything more about Adia. Good-bye, Megan."

"That's not good enough."

Renata stopped, frowning. "What?"

Megan took two steps and took her in her arms. "Take care of yourself. I'll miss you . . . my friend."

Renata didn't move for a moment and then her arms tightened for the briefest moment before she stepped back. "Yeah, me too," she said awkwardly.

Megan watched her walk quickly out of the atrium. The room was suddenly darker without that vibrant presence.

Phillip.

There was nothing vibrant about him right now and he lived in a dark world. She had to get back to him.

SHE STIFFENED IN SHOCK as she opened the door.

Harley was sprawled in the visitor's chair beside Phillip's bed. He glanced up as she came into the room. "Hi, what's new?"

Good God, he was as casual as if he'd just run into her in the neighborhood bar.

"Not a damn thing." She went over to the bed and took Phillip's hand. "Just hanging around with an old friend."

Harley was silent a moment, gazing at Phillip. "It may not work, Megan. It doesn't happen all the time."

Her heart started to pound. "How do you know?"

"I've done a little experimenting." His lips twisted. "At first, I tried to crawl into a hole and forget about this entire mess. Then I decided that I had to prove I was normal to myself. So I volunteered as an aide at St. Jude's in Memphis."

"The children's hospital?"

"Yeah, I like kids. I thought it wouldn't hurt to volunteer as an aide and help out in the wards. Of course, I was wrong. It did hurt. There's nothing that can break your heart like a sick kid." He met her eyes. "My percentage of successes was about eighty-two percent. Of course, I can't verify all of those cases. I wasn't going to ask anyone to take X-rays or anything. God forbid that anyone suspect I was some kind of psychic quack messing with those kids."

"God forbid," she repeated unsteadily.

"Well, most of them appeared remarkably better. I know for certain one little girl did go into remission. She was scheduled for tests two days after I got there and she came out of the MRI clean as a whistle." He frowned. "The healing seems to work better on open wounds rather than disease. I worked in the emergency room one night and the percentage went up to ninety-three percent."

"That's wonderful."

"I don't think so. I hate it. I never wanted this. Do you know how it feels to be able to heal one kid and not another?"

She nodded. "I'm a doctor. It happens all the time to me. And I don't have anything but knowledge and experience to rely on."

He scowled. "That's not what I want out of life. What if someone found out I could do this stuff? They'd smother me; they'd try to make me out as some kind of saint."

"You obviously have a problem. What's your solution?"

"Are you laughing at me?"

"Oh, no, I'm laughing because I'm happy." She smiled luminously. "I'm laughing because for the first time I have hope. I did something right and maybe this Pandora thing is going to turn out okay." She repeated, "What's your solution?"

He shrugged. "I go back to living my life as I did before. But maybe it wouldn't hurt if I spent a few days a week at the hospital. That should be enough to identify and help the critical cases. As I said, I like kids."

She could feel the tears sting her eyes. "No, I don't think that would hurt at all."

Harley looked back at Phillip. "I can't promise anything, Megan. I don't know how this works. Before you came in I put my hand on his temple and there was no response. Of course, it sometimes took days with the kids."

"Just try, Harley."

He nodded. "I'll give it my best shot. But not with you hovering over me. I feel weird enough doing this stuff. It embarrasses me."

"Embarrass? That's hard to believe."

"Just go away for a few days. I'll call you if I have any news."

"I want to stay here."

He shook his head. "I stay, you go." He smiled. "Go to Tanzania. Renata tells me that Grady may need help with some work to be done there."

"Renata?" She paused. "Did Renata bring you here tonight?"

He nodded. "She tracked me down like a bloodhound. She thought I'd be curious enough to explore the possibilities and called every hospital in a three-state area. She said I'd wasted enough of her time and that I had to straighten out things close to home." He made a face. "I got the impression that if I didn't do what she wanted she'd blow my cover at the hospital and set up an interview with Oprah about faith healers of the recent decade."

Megan smiled. "What a wicked woman she is."

"Tanzania," he prompted.

Grady was going to be in Tanzania. She hadn't seen him in over two weeks and he'd made no attempt to contact her. Hell, maybe he'd found himself relieved to put a little distance between them. She wasn't the only one who'd had to make major adjustments since they'd met. Perhaps she should wait for him to make the next move.

Wait? Her whole life seemed to be put on hold lately. Phillip, her medical career, exploring and coming to grips with being a blasted Pandora.

And, dammit, what was between her and Grady had to be clarified before she could move forward in any area.

She nodded slowly. "Definitely. Tanzania."

TWENTY-TWO

Tanzania

MEGAN TENSED AS SHE HEARD Grady's hotel key turn in the lock.

"It's not locked, Grady," she called out.

Grady opened the door and stood there looking at her without speaking. He was dressed in khakis and desert boots, his dark hair looked lighter than the last time she had seen him, his skin tanner, bronzed by the African sun.

"I bribed the desk clerk," she said. "I didn't want to meet you down in the lobby." She moistened her lips. "You should really stay at a classier hotel. That bribe was really cheap. I could have been a thief or a murderer or—"

"This hotel suits me." He closed the door but didn't move toward her. "I'm negotiating with a tribal chief and if I'd stayed at a more expensive place then the price would have gone up."

She frowned. "Negotiating? You're buying those poor girls?"

"I can't walk in and take them away from their owners. They're considered slaves and I'd probably end by getting them killed." He smiled. "And I can usually persuade the owners that they wanted to rid themselves of the girls and that I'm doing them a favor."

"You'll twist their thinking, change their reality." She shook her head. "That's one scary talent, Grady."

"Is that what you flew thousands of miles to come to tell me?" he asked quietly. "Don't you realize that I know that's been the stumbling block? I controlled you for those twelve years and you're subconsciously afraid that I could do it again. It doesn't matter that I swear I wouldn't do it. The possibility is there. I could get stronger. You could get weaker. Who the hell knows how a talent is going to evolve? Or, on the other hand, I might lose whatever power I possess and you might become some kind of psychic superwoman. After all, you're a Pandora. The potential is there."

"Don't say that." She shivered. "I feel like throwing up every time I think about it. I blundered around and managed to do something worthwhile with Harley, but I could be just as much a menace. What if Harley hadn't been able to handle the psychic release? What if I'd destroyed him, too? I've been thinking a lot about it during the last few days. The key seems to be an explosion of intense emotion. But how intense does it have to be? My mother was raped multiple times, but only that last violation caused her to snap. You said she never showed that talent again. Why didn't it manifest itself when she was fighting the man who killed her?"

"Maybe it did. But I killed him so quickly that we wouldn't have been able to tell."

"I've handled patients for years with no sign of facilitation. Even if it's true that the talent doesn't emerge until late twenties, shouldn't I have had some recent indication? Perhaps being under your control kept me from developing but I can't be sure. I was angry and in pain with Sienna, but it was only for a moment. Would that have been enough to cause an explosion of emotion? I was in fear for my life when I was touching Harley and I can see how that would be a trigger. And what made Harley able to accept the talent and Sienna to go mad? Did I unconsciously do something twisted and deadly because I was full of hate for Sienna? Harley was able to heal Renata within an hour after I touched him. Why didn't Sienna show signs and go mad at once like Steven Molino did?"

"In the Tribunal Report, it said one of Rosa Devanez's volunteers was found dead later," Grady said. "So it doesn't appear to happen the same way all the time."

"But what makes the difference? Can it be stopped before the madness occurs? What signs should I look for?"

"That's a lot of questions."

"The tip of the iceberg. I have a thousand more buzzing around in my brain. And every one of them terrifies me."

"So what are you going to do about it?"

"Learn the perimeters and the pitfalls. I can't go back to medicine until I'm sure I can make it safe for my patients. I've decided to go after Renata and make her let me read the Ledger. It won't be easy. She'll probably put me in solitary and chain me to a table while I'm studying it. From what she's mentioned it's not just a giant address book. They documented family history and there have to be records of other Pandoras. One of them must have learned what to do with the talent. It's the only way I can think to control it." She smiled crookedly. "You should understand. You're into control."

"I could help you."

She shook her head. "I learned something from Harley. This Pandora thing is my talent or curse. It's not like being a Listener. It's too dangerous. I'm the one who has to take responsibility for what I do. I don't want to have anyone to blame but myself."

"That sounds lonely," he said softly.

"Oh, God, I hope not." She drew a deep breath. "Because I hate the idea of being alone. You know that. After my mother died, you sent me Phillip so I wouldn't be by myself. You knew me better than anyone in the world."

"And you resented me when you found out how I managed to do that."

"I don't now." She smiled unsteadily. "You're right, I was afraid. I'm not afraid any longer."

"No?"

She shook her head. "I can handle it. I . . . care about you, Grady. I love your body and the things you do to me. I always feel more alive when you're with me. I tried not to miss you when you left me, but I did."

"Good."

"But I don't really know you, do I? You've told me a little about your childhood and how you feel about things, but we haven't had time to go any deeper."

He smiled. "What's to know? I'm a shallow sort anyway."

"Liar."

"Okay, then are you going to plumb my soul's untold depths?" he asked lightly.

"Maybe."

His gaze narrowed on her face. "I warn you. If it means keeping you around, I'll keep you probing for the rest of your life. I'll tell you a tale every night like Scheherazade."

For the rest of your life. She tried to smother the joy that soared through her. "I'm not asking for a commitment like that."

"Too bad. You've got it." He started toward her. "I want one thing from you. You've dissected how you feel about me into sterile little pieces. Now put them all together.

Whether you think you know me or not, do you love what you know?"

"I have to have time to—"

"Commit."

"I wouldn't have come here if I hadn't thought we could have a relationship."

"Commit."

"Dammit, Grady, you're trying to control—"

"Commit."

"Oh, for heaven's sakes. I do . . . love . . . you." She shook her head. "Dammit, I wanted to go slow. It's too important to—"

"Shh." He kissed her, hard, sweet, good. "I know. I'm not dragging you to a justice of the peace. All I'm asking is that for this day, this moment, you love me. We'll take every day one at a time." His hands moved to cup her face. "Okay?"

She turned her head and her lips brushed his palm. "Okay."

"And now that we have that settled, may we please go to bed?"

"You're damn right." She smiled as she backed away from him. "After all, it's one of your very best talents. I like it much more than—"

Grady's cell phone rang.

"Grady, don't you dare take that call," she said with soft emphasis.

"No danger. I'll put it on—" He glanced at the ID. "Shit." He punched the button. "It had better be important." He listened for a moment and then a broad smile lit his face. "She's right here." He handed the phone to Megan. "Someone wants to talk to you."

"Who?" she asked impatiently. "Can't they call back

later?" Someone on the other end of the line was speaking, but she couldn't understand him. "You're talking too low. I can't hear you. Speak up."

Then her hand suddenly tightened on the phone and her voice was only a whisper. "Phillip?"

Read on for an excerpt from
Iris Johansen's next book

QUICKSAND

Available in hardcover from
St. Martin's Press

ONLY TOBY RAN TO MEET Eve Duncan when she drove up to the cottage. The house was dark and Jane's rental car was gone from the driveway. Joe could be working late, but where was Jane?

She patted the dog's head absently as she got out of the car. "Did Jane leave you, boy?" She moved up the steps and opened the screen door. "Have you been fed?"

Toby gave a mournful woof.

"I don't know if I believe you. You like food too much." She turned on the lights. "And you lie a lot." She headed for the kitchen. "But we'll start off with a snack until I call Jane." She filled Toby's bowl half full of dry food and set it down. She dialed Jane's cell but only got voice mail. Well, maybe she was at a movie or something. She had grown up here in Atlanta and had old friends with whom she kept in touch. "Okay, you win, Toby." She poured the rest of the food into his now-empty bowl. "Now be good while I get some work in on Carrie's reconstruction." She moved across the room to the skull on the easel in the studio area. She had been chomping at the bit to get back to Carrie all afternoon. She was nearing the end and she was always intense when she got close to the point when an identity revealed itself beneath her fingers. But she didn't spend enough time with her mother these days and during their last phone conversation she had seemed needy.

She took off the drape covering Carrie's skull and tossed it on the table. Another few days and, hopefully, Carrie would no longer be her name. Eve always gave her reconstructions names because it seemed more respectful and it helped her to draw closer to them. This child had been close to ten years old when she had been murdered and buried near a freeway in southern Kentucky. The local police had no missing children of that age in their files, but if she could put a face to that skull, then she might be able to bring Carrie home.

Might.

So many children victimized by the beasts that prowled the earth remained lost from everyone who had loved them.

Don't think about it. She could only do what God had given her the talent to do. Sometimes identifying the children helped the police to find their murderers; sometimes the killers were never caught. But at least she could give these children a chance for proper burial and their parents the opportunity to come to a final closure. Eve had never had that closure when her own seven-year-old daughter had been kidnapped and presumed murdered several years ago. She knew the pain those parents were feeling.

"Come on, Carrie," she murmured as her fingers began to mold the clay. She had spent days before this carefully measuring the tissue depths and then marking them. Then she'd taken strips of plasticene, applied them between the markers, and then built them up to the tissue depth points. After that it was an excruciatingly fine balance between concentrating on the scientific elements of depth and contouring until she was ready to let instinct take over. She was almost there. "Let's see what we can do before Jane gets back. I'll have to stop then. You're very important to me, but if I've learned anything over the years of working with you and the other children, it's that you have to cherish every single moment of life with the ones you love . . ."

THE KNIFE SANK DEEP in the man's back.

No scream.

Kistle twisted the knife as he drew it out. He hoped the bastard was still alive enough to feel it.

The man wore a sheriff's uniform. He was a cop. That meant that there might be others nearby. He'd have to move quickly. He rolled the body into the bushes and searched his pockets. A notebook, ID that identified him as Sheriff James Jedroth, a cell phone, a couple pictures of a woman and a teenage kid. He grabbed the cell phone and headed for his car. He checked the last number. Not local. So he hadn't been checking in with his wife when Kistle had noticed him on the phone. Who had tipped off the police he was here? Who had forced him to run?

He didn't try the number until he was a few miles from town.

No answer. On the fifth ring the voice mail picked up.

Joe Quinn. Eve Duncan.

He went still as he made the connection.

Eve Duncan.

He drew a deep breath. It had been a long time, but it was all coming back to him. An explosion of pleasure tore through him. He had to talk to her. He had to tell her how glad he was that she had come back into his life.

THE PHONE WAS RINGING AGAIN, Eve realized impatiently. It was the third time in fifteen minutes and she supposed she'd have to answer it. It couldn't be that important. Joe or Jane would have called her on her cell phone when she hadn't answered. They knew how absorbed she became when she was working.

She glanced down at the ID. Bloomburg, Illinois. Sheriff James Jedroth. It had to be another police department asking her to do a reconstruction. Since she'd become so blasted famous, those requests never stopped. But it was nearly ten at night and evidently Sheriff Jedroth didn't understand the concept of business hours. Well, Eve didn't either, so she might as well answer.

"Eve Duncan."

"Do you still miss your little Bonnie?"

Shock jolted through her. "I beg your pardon."

"She had curly red hair and on the last day you saw her, she was wearing a Bugs Bunny T-shirt."

"Is this some kind of sick joke, Sheriff Jedroth? I'm not amused."

"I'm amused. Amused and excited and full of anticipation. I haven't felt like this for years. I didn't realize I was getting stale and that the kill was losing its luster. Then I heard your name on your voice mail and suddenly I felt reborn."

"Kill." Her hand tightened on the phone. "Who is this? You're not a sheriff, are you?"

"I impersonated a sheriff once. It was in Fort Collins, Colorado. Children are taught to trust policemen."

"Who are you?" she repeated. "I don't know you. Why are you calling me?"

"Bonnie knew me. She knew me very well before the end."

Don't show him the wrenching pain his words are causing. "You son of a bitch. What are you trying to tell me?"

"You shouldn't have tried to track me down. Now I'll

have to punish you. I never let myself be victimized without making sure that my pain is reciprocated." He chuckled. "Though this time I'm not feeling nearly so bitter. I've been following your search for Bonnie for years and it's lightened many a dull moment."

"I didn't try to track you down. I don't even know your name."

"Henry Kistle."

Kistle. The name of the man Montalvo had given her as one of the possible murderers of her daughter.

"Yes, you know me. You set that asshole, Jedroth, to watch me."

"Where are you?"

"It would be no use to tell you. I've just left town. I'll be hundreds of miles away from here before you can call and get someone to try to find me. I know about red tape."

"What . . . do you know about Bonnie?"

"That she was seven years old and a beautiful child. Do you know how many pretty little girls I've killed since your Bonnie died? Though I always regard her as my inspiration. She was like a burning arrow lighting the darkness. I remember how—"

"Shut up." She couldn't take any more. "Don't talk about her."

"I'm done for the time being. I just wanted to touch base with you. I needed something to keep me up and zinging."

"Zinging?"

"That's what life's about. You have to keep on top of it, keep excited and moving. I got a little buzz earlier tonight but nothing like the one I'm feeling now. It's not as good as a kill, but maybe you could make the next kill extraordinary."

"What kill?"

But he had hung up the phone.

She was shaking.

She had curly red hair and the last day you saw her, she was wearing a Bugs Bunny T-shirt.

Kistle.

Joe. She had to call Joe.

Her hand was shaking as she dialed his cell number. No answer. The voice mail picked up immediately. His phone had to be turned off.

She hung up. Dammit, she *needed* him. Where the hell was he?

Stop whining. He was a cop. There were all kinds of situations where he'd turn off his cell. Okay, she had to handle it alone. She'd reach Joe as soon as he was available.

She was like a burning arrow lighting the darkness.

Bonnie.

Block out the pain. She had to try to catch that bastard before he was out of reach.

Sheriff James Jedroth. Kistler had used Jedroth's telephone and Jedroth was located in Bloomburg, Illinois. Call information and get the number for the sheriff's department. Move.

Five minutes later she had reached the sheriff's department and been transferred to three different extensions before she reached a Deputy Charles Dodsworth. "I'm sorry, ma'am"—he had a distinctly midwestern twang—"but Sheriff Jedroth isn't on duty. May I help you?"

"I was afraid he wasn't on duty. I only used his name to get through to anyone in authority." Eve continued urgently, "That's why I've been trying to contact someone, anyone. I received a phone call this evening from Sheriff Jedroth's cell phone. Only it wasn't the sheriff. It was Henry Kistle."

There was a silence on the other end. "Kistle. You're positive that was the name?"

"Dammit, I'm positive. You know who he is, don't you? I can tell by your tone."

"I'm familiar with the name," he said cautiously.

"Then go get him. I think he was in a car and on the move. He boasted that you wouldn't be able to catch him. But it's been less than ten minutes. He must have been under investigation by you or he wouldn't have been able to take the sheriff's phone. Can't you call the highway patrol and try to stop him?"

Silence. "He really had Jim's phone?"

"That's what it said on my ID."

"Shit." The deputy's tone was now curt. "I'll get back to you." He hung up.

Good. She was encouraged that he had wanted to get rid of her so that he could take action. At least there was a hope that Kistle could be intercepted. Hurry, she prayed. Don't let him get away.

She called Joe again. His phone was still turned off. She left a message for him to call her as soon as possible.

But there was a car driving up the road to the cottage.

She ran out on the porch to see Jane getting out of the Jeep. "I can't get in touch with Joe. Have you heard from him?"

"Yes." She gave Toby a hug in greeting and pushed him aside. "And you can't get in touch with him because he probably had to turn his phone off on the plane." She grimaced. "Though he might not have answered you anyway. He didn't want to have to deal with you until he was sure."

She stared at her. "Deal with me? Plane?"

"I told him he wasn't handling this right." Jane was climbing the porch steps. "But you know Joe. Stubborn. He had to get on that damn plane to Bloomburg."

Eve stiffened. "Bloomburg?" she whispered. "Kistle."

"Yes." Jane's gaze narrowed on Eve's face. "How did you know?"

"Kistle just called me," she said numbly. "He was telling me what a beautiful child my Bonnie was."

"Damn." Jane's arms slid around her and she held her close. "I wish I'd been here with you. You shouldn't have had to be alone."

She wasn't alone now. She had Jane, and the healing comfort was like a blessing. "I'm okay." She hugged Jane before letting her go. "And we have a chance of getting the bastard. He called from an officer's phone and I was able to notify the sheriff's department pretty quick."

"Come on." Jane took her arm and pulled her into the cottage. "I'll make some coffee and you can tell me about it."

CHARLIE DODSWORTH HESITATED, staring at the phone after he'd hung up from talking to Eve Duncan. She'd sounded scared and desperate, but who knew if she wasn't some kind of nut? He was only a deputy. He had no business calling the highway patrol and setting up roadblocks. That was a sheriff's job. Jim's job.

He dialed Jim's cell number. No answer.

Jim always answered. Unless his cell was no longer in his hands, as Eve Duncan had claimed.

Damn, that scared him.

He punched the number for Torrance with the highway patrol and while he was waiting he called out to Annie Burke in the front office. "Get that report Jim requested on Joe Quinn." After he had read the report, the sheriff had thought Quinn might have valid reasons for suspecting

Kistle and had started the surveillance on him. He needed
to know everything Jim knew.

"Ten minutes," Annie said. "I'm on my lunch break."

"Now!"

Annie would probably give him hell later. He couldn't
worry about it. Torrance had picked up and Dodsworth
was telling him what had to be done.

"By whose authority?" Torrance asked. "I'm not about
to send my guys off on a wild-goose chase at this time of
night."

"Sheriff Jim Jedroth," Dodsworth lied. "I'm just relay-
ing his orders."

"Got you." Torrance hung up.

Annie was standing in the doorway holding a folder.
"You lied to him. What's got into you, Charlie
Dodsworth? Jim's going to have your ass."

"I hope he does." Dodsworth got up from the desk. "I
haven't got time to read that report. Walk me to the patrol
car and fill me in, Annie."

"Where are you going?" She fell into step with him as
she took out the report.

"I can't get in touch with Jim."

"He could still be okay. That doesn't—" She broke off,
her gaze scanning the report. "Joe Quinn is a lieutenant
with ATLPD. Lots of commendations, formerly with the
SEALs and FBI. There's a photo."

He glanced at the picture. Quinn appeared to be in his
late thirties, brown hair, square face, broad mouth, and
wide-set brown eyes.

Annie went on, "He went to Harvard and is supposed
to be very, very smart. He lives in a lake cottage outside
Atlanta with an Eve Duncan."

He punched the elevator button. "Tell me about Eve
Duncan. Is there anything on her?"

Annie nodded. "Yeah, evidently they've worked together on several cases. She's a forensic sculptor, one of the best in the world, and does work for police departments all over the country. Several years ago her daughter, Bonnie, disappeared and was presumed killed by a serial killer who was later executed. Her body was never recovered and later it was suspected that the man who was executed for her death was innocent of that particular killing. Though he was guilty of several more child murders. Eve Duncan went back to school to study forensic sculpting and has been searching for the killer and the remains of her murdered daughter ever since. Joe Quinn has taken several leaves of absences from the department over the years to investigate possible suspects."

"Like Kistle," Dodsworth said grimly. "And this time he may have hit the jackpot." He was going down the steps toward the patrol car parked in front of the building. "Why the hell couldn't he have stayed out of our town?" He jumped into the car. "If Torrance calls back, cover my ass, Annie."

She frowned. "What's happening, Charlie? Where are you going? It must be pretty serious if you're willing to risk your job like this."

He backed out of the parking spot. "Dead serious."

Coming soon...
#1 *New York Times* bestselling author

IRIS JOHANSEN

teams up for the very first time with Edgar
Award–winning author

ROY JOHANSEN

in

SILENT THUNDER

ISBN: 0-312-36799-6

Don't miss this exciting, first-ever
publishing event!

AVAILABLE IN JULY 2008, IN HARDCOVER,
FROM ST. MARTIN'S PRESS